OUR SECRETS WERE SAFE

OUR SECRETS WERE SAFE

A NOVEL

VIRGINIA TRENCH

 CROWN
NEW YORK

Crown
An imprint of the Crown Publishing Group
A division of Penguin Random House LLC
1745 Broadway
New York, NY 10019
crownpublishing.com
penguinrandomhouse.com

Library of Congress Cataloging-in-Publication Data
Names: Trench, Virginia, author.
Title: Our secrets were safe: a novel / Virginia Trench.
Description: First edition. | New York City: Crown, 2025. |
Identifiers: LCCN 2023056613 | ISBN 9780593798522 (hardcover; acid-free
    paper) | ISBN 9780593798539 (ebook)
Subjects: LCGFT: Thrillers (Fiction) | Novels.
Classification: LCC PS3620.R44527 O97 2025 | DDC 813/.6—dc23/
    eng/20231215
LC record available at https://lccn.loc.gov/2023056613

Hardcover ISBN 978-0-593-79852-2
Ebook ISBN 978-0-593-79853-9

Editor: Lori Kusatzky
Production editor: Liana Faughnan
Text designer: Andrea Lau
Production: Dustin Amick and Jessica Heim
Copy editor: Nancy Inglis
Proofreaders: Chris Fortunato, Sibylle Kazeroid, Tess Rossi, and Miriam Taveras
Publicist: Josie McRoberts
Marketer: Kimberly Lew

Manufactured in the United States of America

9 8 7 6 5 4 3 2 1

First Edition

The authorized representative in the EU for product safety and compliance
is Penguin Random House Ireland, Morrison Chambers, 32 Nassau Street,
Dublin D02 YH68, Ireland, https://eu-contact.penguin.ie.

FOR MY SISTER AND THE STORIES WE LOVE

OUR SECRETS WERE SAFE

CHAPTER 1

Sofia

Then

This time, they catch her watching them.

Sofia doesn't look away fast enough. Brooke drops her eyes back to her color-coded sixteenth-century lit notes, and Caroline's glance flicks away from Sofia's in the corner of one of their mirrors. They'd hung the gallery wall together, Caroline and Sofia, before Brooke Winters ruined everything. Afternoon light glares at the three of them through a brass-edged looking glass. It's so much easier to appreciate its eclectic whimsy when a hangover isn't burrowing into your optic nerves.

Brooke and Caroline are out of the room before Sofia's even really there—probably off to jog around campus and love every minute of it. Jenna is volunteering for a blood drive or something else that will look great on her medical school applications. The roommates are busy enjoying a bright Sunday fall morning in Connecticut, crisp and admissions-brochure-ready. What could be better?

More wholesome?

More vomit-triggering?

Sinking onto the just-vacated couch, Sofia is alone in the common space of their suite. A sharp ache encircles her waist. She's still in the clothes from last night in Manhattan with Leo: mercilessly *skinny* skinny jeans (Caroline's) and a silky tank top, her boots splayed at lopsided angles next to the door. Sofia gingerly peels off the jeans.

The inseams have dug shallow, ribbed trenches in the skin that runs from her hips to her bony ankles. She rubs at the marks as she swings her legs onto the floor, dislodging her flip phone. Sofia got it in exchange for writing a few papers for a senior whose trust fund hung in the balance of graduating on time. She flicks open the cracked screen. Leo Archer: three missed calls. Caroline Archer: one text message:

> We need to talk.

A fist clenches, then tightens in her stomach. Sofia can't handle either of the Archer siblings right now. Those conversations will have to wait until she rejoins the land of the functional living. She rakes through her thick strands of hair that gleamed in perfect loose waves last night but have now collapsed into a tangled mess. She considers taking one of Leo's little blue pills. There are probably a few left at the bottom of her purse. She could blow the lint off one and make the pain float away on a pharma-cumulus cloud. Tempting, but no.

Sofia can see into Brooke's room from here: she always leaves her door open like a trusting idiot. Everything changed when Brooke arrived on campus, assigned to Caroline, Sofia, and Jenna's lives through the kind of registration "coincidence" rich Yale donors like Brooke Winters's family seem to arrange all the time. Brooke's arrival coincided with the end of Sofia and Caroline's relationship, another "coincidence" Sofia won't ignore. And the worst part is, Sofia didn't even realize how fragile everything was between the two of them. How wide the chasm between Caroline's world and hers will always be.

Sofia slouches over to the refrigerator in the cramped kitchenette, opens a carton of day-old lo mein, and takes a few gloriously greasy bites, wishing the Imperial Palace sold the stuff by the yard. Some people responsibly burn off empty calories, while others revel in shamelessly piling onto the damage. Without question, Brooke falls into the former category. As much as anything else, that just makes Sofia hate her more.

Brooke doesn't strike an outsider as the sort of person who could ruin people's lives. To the untrained eye, she is all sweetness and pedigree, paper-thin cashmere cardigans and effortlessly understated good taste that says *old money* in a very carrying whisper. The kind that's loud enough to make people like Sofia want to scurry back into their proper places: basement kitchens, damp groundskeepers' sheds, or steaming laundries, a discreet distance away from oaken offices and time-weathered statues of important men.

Like Caroline, Brooke is fluent in the language of boarding schools and the best places to ski, the thousands of unwritten rules that govern a world Sofia can only ever press her nose against and try not to smudge the glass. "Winters," like "Archer," is the gloss that smooths Brooke's path to a life spent flitting from waterfront properties to charity galas and handsome investment banker husbands. Brooke is someone without a chip on her shoulder, without baggage, without a constant ache for something she can never have.

Sofia spools more glistening brown noodles around the plastic fork and into her mouth, and a slimy chunk of chicken falls with a moist splat onto her bare thigh. There's nothing like eating leftover takeout in your underwear to make it clear that yes, you really do need to get your shit together. And as a matter of fact, that's precisely what Sofia intends to do. As long as she doesn't get caught in the more unsavory aspects of her plan.

She leaves the empty container next to the vase of flowers Bryce had delivered to Caroline yesterday. The spray of funeral-scented lilies and roses is intended to make up for his checking out the coxswain on the women's crew team. It's the kind of fight only rich people can have. Guys like Bryce Hostetler don't have to say they're sorry. They buy "sorry," and it arrives, beautifully packaged. Resisting the urge to topple the vase to the floor, Sofia stretches and leaves the kitchen.

Her room is spare and nowhere as stylish as the rest of the suite. She'll probably never know what it's like to have $40 to spend on "designer candles"—which are apparently a thing. But the bittersweet smell of cigarettes, forever steeped into Sofia's sheets and clothes, and Yaya's lavender sachets reminds Sofia of the tiny room she'd shared with Drea in their apartment above Mom's restaurant. Of seagull calls and storm-chilled wind rushing through the salt grass. Of the island. Home. Sofia struggles to remember what happened last night, but the hangover prevents her from uncovering more than fragments. Instead, the familiar, well-worn reel of the summer she met Caroline flickers to life in her mind.

The Archers came to Nantucket for the season every year, along with the tide of dozens of families exactly like them. Caroline's stepfather, the steely, formidable Bill Archer, and her mother, the fragile, glamorous Diana Archer, were carbon copies of most of their little Greek bistro's Chardonnay-mainlining clientele. Leo and Caroline looked so alike that no one would have guessed that Bill wasn't Caroline's biological father. Not unless they noticed the impatience mixed with disapproval on Bill's face whenever his inconvenient, willful stepdaughter was in view.

It didn't matter how much Leo, Bill's son with Diana, loved his half sister. Caroline might be legally allowed to call herself "Archer," but she would always be stray trash stuck to Bill's shoes. Caroline was the most beautiful thing Sofia had ever seen all those summers ago: wild white-blond hair and eyes like the sky in a gathering storm. Sofia had no use for Leo then, the little brother utterly eclipsed by his sister.

Bill and Diana allowed Caroline and Leo free rein through the hot, salt-sticky days between June and August in Nantucket, more out of lack of interest than kindness. Their children's absence made it easier to spend their days playing tennis or hunting poor people or whatever it is the rich do with the stretch between Memorial Day and Labor Day. Whenever Sofia wasn't working shifts at Santorini's, she got to bask in Caroline's world, a world that for one blissful summer after the next, became hers, too.

Nights in the sand dunes under the stars. The crowded downtown and scorching restaurant kitchen melted away to the multimillion-dollar peace behind gated estates. Days spent in the ocean, on the sand, reading and sharing secrets in the attic of the Archers' summer "cottage." It doesn't matter that, on the surface, their relationship doesn't make any sense. The particular loneliness of all outsiders brought them together, and it kept them entwined in a new reality of their own making. One just for the two of them.

Stripping off the remainder of her clothes, Sofia piles them neatly into a plastic hamper. If you've never had a space of your own, taking good care of your first is automatic. Instinctive. Jenna has it, too. Sofia noticed it in her roommate's compulsive cleaning, probably ingrained from the summers Jenna spent sweating in a Merry Maids van and lugging around mops with her mom instead of at a cushy internship or doing "ecological restoration work" between tequila shots in Costa Rica. She wraps herself in a towel, extracts a makeup remover sheet from its crumpled pack on the dresser, and wages a short war against the makeup, oil, and dirt smudged on her face. Gradually, her unvarnished features emerge in the mirror.

Skin like milk. It's stark against eyebrows almost as dark as the eyeliner blackening the makeup remover sheet that swipes across

Yaya's high cheekbones and around the Eliades hazel eyes. She combs her hair into a curtain that hangs past two of her favorite features: sharp, prominent shoulder blades. After the first time Leo and Sofia had sex, Leo said she looked like someone had sawed off angel wings and left the stubs behind. The thought makes her shiver.

In the bathroom, Sofia turns on the water as hot as it will go and steps into the shower. She had underestimated Brooke. But she's not the only one guilty of underestimation these days. She used to think that Caroline knew better than anyone that nothing is as it seems. Until everything changed. Brooke came here. Sofia got desperate.

She rubs shampoo into the roots of her hair and thinks about her mom's last voicemail, the one that arrived within minutes of the latest warning from her academic advisor, Fiona Landers. Kendra Eliades was all rapid Greek and pride for her brilliant daughter, the writer, the scholar, the first in their family to go to college. The most recent email from Fiona was much less glowing:

To: sofia.e.eliades@yale.edu
From: fiona.k.landers@yale.edu
Subject: Scholarship Eligibility

Hi, Sofia, I need to meet with you so we can make a plan for the rest of this semester. It's important to get your GPA back on track to maintain your scholarship eligibility and ensure your on-time graduation. If the university doesn't see you're making an effort to turn things around, I'm concerned for your future here. I want you to be successful . . .

The email loosely translates as "Get back in line, or you might as well book your ticket back to waiting tables for the summer tourists, charity case." Fiona used to only reach out when she wanted to put Sofia on display for deep-pocketed alumni. Those were the days.

Sofia reaches for the dollar-store soap wedged between Kiehl's bottles. A smirk roots at the corners of her lips as she runs through the plan one more time. She has just the thing to avoid death by drowning in student loan debt and the long walk of shame back home to Nantucket. The perfect fiction project—the one she was supposed to be working on all semester. It's weighted heavily enough to get Sofia's GPA back into shape, get her back in the English department's good graces, and—crucially—get her advisor off her case, at least until the next fundraising event.

The solution is simple—she has to write what she knows. Sometimes that's all it takes to blow up someone's world. With a little help from Leo, Brooke will be out of their lives for good. And with that happy thought, Sofia shuts off the shower and squeezes the water from her hair. She reaches for a towel but stops suddenly, blinking in disbelief at her right hand. Blood stains her skin, forming tiny webbed canals of red in her palm and between her fingers.

Her eyes cut to the shower floor, where a long scarlet tendril coils around the drain.

CHAPTER 2

Brooke

Now

My mother is already several sauvignon blancs to the wind when she raises her champagne flute and taps against it with her salad fork.

"Ladies!" she trills, setting down the fork and patting her hair, as if there could possibly be a single mutinous strand out of place. A hush falls over the terrace, and faces turn away from their gossip and hors d'oeuvres.

"Before we open gifts, I'd like to say just a few words about our mommy-to-be, my beautiful daughter, Melissa." High-pitched *aww*s chorus right on cue. I keep my eyes trained on Mel: her nervous smile has frozen in place. I rearrange my features into an encouraging expression, hopefully one that will get my sister through whatever passive-aggressive poison our mother has up her hand-painted silk sleeve.

"Melissa, when I look at you, I'm so reminded of myself at your age. You're a wonderful wife, you've got a great career, and I mean, just look how you've kept your figure. Are we jealous or what, girls?"

My mother's gaggle of tennis friends laughs. Mel folds her hands self-consciously over her belly. It's literally the only part of her body that looks pregnant, a fact my mother is quick to gloatingly point out.

"You have so much ahead of you, sweetie, and since you can get a *little* overwhelmed sometimes, I just want you to know that I'll never be far away!" She rests a manicured hand on Mel's shoulder.

"Melissa's little girl will be my *third* grandchild, if you can believe it. My wonderful son Landon blessed us with twins last year." She pauses and lays her other hand over her heart. Across the terrace, Emma, my brother's wife, freezes mid-chew. Evidently, the physical act of pushing two human beings out of her body doesn't count for much when Daphne Winters's perfection parade is in motion. Across the table, I catch Jenna raising an eyebrow almost imperceptibly, and I stifle a snort of laughter. I was surprised Jenna made the time to come today, but I guess she felt obligated to because she and Mel work so closely together in oncology at St. Luke's Hospital: Mel as a nurse, Jenna as a surgeon. Jenna's been dodging my calls for weeks now, but I'm grateful she's here. On my mother's turf, I need all the allies I can get.

"And my oldest, Brooke, is also here today." She extends her glass in my direction, the pale gold liquid nearly sloshing over the rim. Wonderful son. Beautiful daughter. I get *oldest*. In her world, that's more than fair for a woman who dared to pass thirty without collecting a boring, successful husband and an SUV full of kids.

"We recently celebrated Brooke's engagement to an amazing man—a *gorgeous*, very promising attorney. We all know it'll be your turn soon, sweetheart!" She bestows a knowing smile on me and gestures around her. I can't tell if she's indicating the baby shower, the collection of *Real Housewives* franchise–worthy friends, or the Greenwich country house. She probably means all three, a sunny promise that manages to sound more like a threat.

I twist my new engagement ring, and it pinches against the circular groove the size-too-small heirloom has cut into my skin. It was Josh's mother's, 2.5 brilliant cushion-cut carats nestled between exquisite sapphire accents. I can still see his face when he'd asked me, and my stomach flips at the memory: the sunset framing his face, so handsome, so sure of the future we'd build together. Him, the intrepid attorney destined for a brilliant political career with me, the dedicated high school English teacher, by his side.

"But I digress," my mother continues, as if all this humblebragging isn't choreographed. "This is *your* day, Melissa, dear. Please raise your glasses to my baby girl and her baby girl!"

The clink of crystal and squeals of *Cheers!* are enough cover for my sigh of relief. Quiche churns in my stomach along with champagne, macaroons, and all the raw insecurities only Daphne Winters could expose like live wires.

"That was brutal, even by her standards," Jenna mutters in my ear as she appears behind me, the better not to be overheard by the group of Mel's friends seated near us. I give Jenna a smile that's part rueful, part pure gratitude that she's here, perhaps the only person besides my sister who won't judge me for sport.

"I'm used to it," I lie.

Jenna's gaze sweeps the gathering, cataloguing every detail, most likely making mental notes for when she and Bryce have their next baby. It's perfect, the ambience my mother arranged for today. Pastels and peonies and strings of lanterns transform the terrace into a masterpiece that would bring a single tear to Martha Stewart's eye. Jenna didn't come from this world, but through years of careful observation, plus a marriage into a prominent family, she fits right in. Still, I catch her self-consciously adjusting the backs of her tasteful diamond earrings, as if double-checking she looks like she belongs here.

I glance at my sister. She's surrounded by a hive of middle-aged day-drunk women, and her stamped-on smile doesn't reach her eyes.

"How are things at the hospital?" I ask.

Jenna doesn't respond immediately. Her eyes are glued to her phone.

"Everything okay?" I ask, noting the tiny indentation between her eyebrows that manages to emerge despite the Botox. I can see the phone in her hand and make out the text on the screen. The contact isn't identified, just a phone number.

> Last night was amazing. xx

Jenna gives a sudden start and tucks the phone into the Chanel bag dangling from the back of her chair. "Yeah, sorry. It's just Bryce." I nod and let her lie slide. It's a truth universally acknowledged that husbands are saved contacts, and if they're texting to say how "amazing" last night was, it's probably not meant for their wives.

"And Hayden? How's he doing these days?" I ask, thinking of her adorable three-year-old son. Instantly the clouds in Jenna's eyes clear.

"He's great, never stops asking us for a puppy, but great," Jenna says, a radiant smile blooming on her face. But the smile flickers and fades almost as quickly as it appeared. "I think Mel could use a friendly face," she adds hurriedly, casting her eyes to where my sister is sitting.

I want to find out what's bothering Jenna. But Mel is in immediate need of rescue, so I make a mental note to follow up with her later. Unsticking my dress from the backs of my thighs, I make my way toward my sister, and Jenna follows me across the terrace. I pause to ask a waiter to bring Mel a sparkling water. For all the alcohol being guzzled this afternoon, no one seems to notice the very sober, very pregnant woman in their midst. I weave through clusters of my mother's friends, plus a few of Mel's, and approach the table where my sister is cornered.

"So I said, 'Sweetheart, learning to roast a chicken is so much

easier than getting back on all those tragic little dating apps *again*.'"
Catty laughter punctuates the dig. My mother is, of course, talking
about me.

"Mom, it's not 1950, and Josh loves to cook for her," Mel says,
her voice firmly cutting through the giggles. I clear my throat to
announce my presence. "And you deserve it, Brooke. You work so
hard taking care of your students—Josh's baking is just his way of
taking care of *you*. Have you all met my sister, Brooke? And this is
her friend Jenna," she says. Jenna gives a polite little wave.

"Hi there," I say as a dozen eyes clock my weight, age, and the
carats of my engagement ring. It takes these women seconds to
complete their assessment. I think I passed.

Mel beams at me. "Brooke starts teaching English at Woodlands Academy this year." She places just the right amount of emphasis on the name: she knows it's elite enough to immediately
register with this crowd. In this corner of the world, prestigious
learning institutions are traded like their own form of currency.
Name-dropping Woodlands Academy was Mel's clever way of
driving my stock values up.

"Oh, Woodlands is *fantastic*!" a blond woman in a fluorescent
pink Lilly Pulitzer dress proclaims. "We sent our kids there for
high school, and Hunter graduates from Georgetown this year.
Frances is starting as a freshman. Maybe she'll be in your class?" A
southern drawl sugars her voice. I'm not sure if the impact is actually sweet.

"I'm teaching junior-level classes this year," I say. "But I'd still
love to meet your daughter."

"The students will *adore* her. Brooke was teacher of the year at
her last school," Mel gushes, and I feel a rush of gratitude for her.

"Well, that *inner-city* school was a nightmare," my mother interjects. She's never forgiven me for actually staying in the classroom after my Teach for America fellowship ended, instead of
using it as a springboard to get into law school like all her friends'
kids. "I'm sure they have different standards than we do."

"What do you mean, *we*, Mom?" I ask before I can stop myself. My tone is light, but there's no mistaking the challenge. An awkward silence snags the atmosphere like fabric caught on something sharp. Around us, the women are all suddenly fascinated by their wineglasses and shoes. Mel shoots me a look that says *Don't start*.

"Brooke," my mother says, her voice low and icy with warning, "let's not—"

"Actually, can I steal Mel for a sec? Some of her friends would love a quick picture," I say. My mother's expression puckers for a split second. She can't stand anyone shortening "Melissa" into something that, to use her words, "sounds like an obese truck driver from Long Island."

"Now isn't a good time for that, dear. But would you be an angel and get the rest of the gifts from the foyer?" The command is clear behind her tight smile. I steal a glance at Mel, and she gives me an *I'll be fine—really* nod.

Stepping through the open French doors, I wave aside the sheer curtains that billow outward from the living room. My eyes linger on the framed photographs that cover the liquid black surface of the grand piano, and my gaze falls on the picture that still sends a shiver skittering across my skin. Caroline, Jenna, and I, arm in arm at graduation. Sofia had been dead for over a year when it was taken, but I still find myself half expecting to see her smirking face in the photo every time I glance at it. As I trace its silver frame with my index finger, a hushed conversation drifts in from the foyer.

"I'm just glad to see Brooke doing so well after, you know, what happened all those years ago. Such a nasty business," someone stage-whispers, and I recognize the drawl of the Woodlands mom.

"Well, that family certainly knows how to cover their tracks," comes the reply, a voice that's unknown to me. "I mean, she got kicked out of Brown her sophomore year—all very hush-hush as to why, by the way—then sent to Silver Hill for a month. You know, where Cynthia went after her breakdown?"

"I heard that place costs an arm and a leg, but at least it's discreet. *Poor* Cynthia." Insincerity and schadenfreude drip from every word. "Daphne must have been *very* generous for Brooke to end up at *Yale* after all that. And then she gets mixed up in that awful car accident!"

A second's pause freezes my blood.

"If it even *was* an accident."

"Someone . . . died—didn't they? A friend of theirs, I think."

"And another woman—the other driver, with her child left behind in the car, apparently. I don't know how they managed to hush it all up, but it's amazing what you can get away with if you tell the right story. I mean—Daphne Winters and those Archers should know that better than anyone." Their voices grow fainter.

"Oh, Anna Leigh, you're *so* bad."

Hot tears flood my eyes fast. I blink, swiping away the overflow as quickly as I can, and I realize I'm shaking with shame. I can't be seen like this. I rush up the stairs and down the hall, not realizing where I am until I'm already there, with the door slammed behind me and the lock twisted in place.

CHAPTER 3

Caroline

Now

"Let's talk about the elephant in the room we can all see."

I arch an eyebrow and sweep my arms wide before the audience of the Women Who Tech Startup Accelerator. Hitching a conspiratorial half-smile on my lips, I click the Bluetooth remote, and a statistic as tall as I am appears on the screen behind me:

This year, women earned 79 cents for every dollar earned by men.

"Yep, even today. Even in 2019," I add, allowing the reaction to travel through the room of its own free will. Sighs, nods—I can even see a few eye rolls in the front row.

"Ah yes, *that* elephant." That gets a few rueful laughs, just as Eric predicted. I make a mental note to thank him for that one on our way back to the office. I adjust my glasses in a pointed gesture and tuck a strand of dark hair behind my ear. I dyed it from its natural blond years ago, sick of hearing how much I looked like Elizabeth Holmes. The comparison usually came from male executives who accepted the Theranos scandal as definitive proof that female CEOs are not to be trusted.

"I don't need to tell you about that. Or this." I click again.

Women make up just 32 percent of C-suite executives.

Click.

In 2019, Black women were paid just 63 percent of what white men were paid.

"Or that."

The Equilibrium logo blooms, graceful and minimalist, on-screen.

"I'm not here to tell you that the twenty-first-century workplace is out of balance. Most—if not all—of you have experienced it firsthand: the imbalance of power." I take a step across the stage.

"Of opportunity." Another step.

"Of the expectations women face at work." I stand my ground.

"I'm here to do something about that. I'm here to change the narrative and balance the equation." Our mission statement appears below our logo: **Together, we can build a future of gender equity in the workplace and beyond.**

"Equilibrium technology instantly tips the scales and cracks the glass ceiling in ways even we sometimes forget about or don't notice are still there today. Let me show you what I mean." My heart steadies as I slip into the pitch I've given more times than I can count. I need this to work. Everything I have, everything I've built, hangs on the next four minutes.

"Like everyone in this room, I want to see more women in tech. So do companies looking to diversify their workforce. At least that's what they *claim* they want. Here's what that actually looks like most of the time." A LinkedIn job page for software engineering positions appears and scrolls on-screen.

"Let's say I'm a female computer science grad looking for my first job. Or maybe I'm a mom who's excited to return to the workforce. This is one of the first places I'd go, right? Let's see what I'd find there." I zoom in on one job posting and read it aloud.

We are a fast-paced industry leader seeking a driven individual to join our product and engineering team. We're looking for superior problem-solving skills and a proven track record of meeting aggressive targets.

"If you're like me, you're thinking: Who actually talks like that?" Another murmur of laughter. A touch of relatability goes a long way. Right again, Eric.

"The short answer is: it happens more often than you think. I pulled this word for word from a job posting for a company that most of you have interacted with already today on your smartphones. Don't believe me?" The text blurs on the screen. "Let's take a closer look at what you already know is a little *off* about this post. Tell me, do these words generally apply to men or women?"

The post fades from the screen. One by one, words reappear, smoothly changing color to a bold red font. **Leader, fast-paced, competition, aggressive, proven track record, individual, superior.**

"Leader. Competition. Aggressive. These sound like descriptors for men, right? These traits describe virtues and behavior that align with masculine stereotypes and gender norms. Language is a powerful means of reinforcing these norms. Take it from a woman who's been called 'bossy' her entire life." I grin along with the audience.

"Studies show that the language we use is gendered. I don't mean in terms of gender identity, I mean in terms of the value we place on what and *how* men and women should be at work and in our society as a whole. Psychologically, it's a self-fulfilling prophecy when we use language that says loud and clear: this is a boy's club." I wipe the screen dark and empty.

"How many millions of women get that message every single day?" I know my passion is showing, and now is the moment to show it. But will it be enough to win over investors? A broke company can't save the world, after all. "And that's just the tip of the iceberg, isn't it?" I give those words time to summon memories of claps on the back, of locker-room talk, of interruptions in meetings, and of the last time someone mansplained their areas of expertise.

"Further studies show that women will apply for a job only if they have 100 percent of the qualifications and experience asked. Men don't need that certainty. Sixty percent is good enough to throw their hats in the ring—not that there's anything wrong with that." Likable Feminist 101: never let anyone dismiss you as a man-hater, or it's death by Twitter quicker than you can say *patriarchy*.

"What can we do to ensure women get their fair shot at that dream job alongside their male colleagues? If we actually want to see a representation change in our industry, we need to start from the ground up. That means attracting diverse talent through intentional hiring practices and inclusive storytelling." They watch my elegant AI work its magic on-screen, scrolling the job board and highlighting key words in on-brand turquoise.

"Equilibrium AI analyzes corporate websites and job postings for gender neutrality and instantly eliminates unconscious gendered bias. Our technology checks for blind spots for you, so you can hire the best candidate on a more level playing field."

The scrolling stops, and the job posting reappears. The text brightens, then transforms. **We are looking for solution-oriented team members with excellent problem-solving skills and high standards of project management.**

"Here are just a few organizations that have experienced the Equilibrium difference." Our clients' company logos populate the screen. The cloud of text looks impressive, a convincing facade. "Since adding Equilibrium to their hiring equations, 64 percent of our partners experienced an increase in female applicants within a year, 81 percent within two, and 100 percent can say they're putting their money where their mission statements are in advocating for gender equity. Join us, and together, we can ensure your organization lives its values and cultivates an inclusive, thriving culture."

I step forward, allowing the screen projection to skim across my body.

"My name is Caroline Archer, and I invite you to join Equilibrium in equalizing the balance of power in the workplace. Thank you." Enthusiastic applause ripples through the auditorium, but only time will tell if that translates to what we desperately need to survive: investors, clients, and an influx of cash.

I beam my most winning smile and wave with confidence I don't have as I walk offstage. Eric waits for me behind the curtain, eyes glued to his iPhone. I carefully detach my mic and hand it off to one of the event staff before taking a shaky breath.

"Well? How'd I do?" I ask.

Eric's fingers whir across the surface of his phone. "You crushed it," he says. He doesn't look up right away, and his well-groomed eyebrows are uncharacteristically furrowed.

"What's up?" I press.

Even by the internet's standards, it's a little early to take the temperature of how this went over on social media, especially at the tail end of the weekend as the conference wraps up. Eric finally meets my eye. "I think we have a troll." He hands me his phone. I stare at the screen. My heart quickens, then hammers hard in my chest. What I see on the screen makes no sense. It's not possible.

"Who the hell is Sofia Eliades?" Eric asks.

CHAPTER 4

Sofia

Then

Sofia rinses the blood from the shower and wipes the steam from the bathroom mirror, and it's a long moment before she can bring herself to look at the back of her neck. At this angle, she can barely see the edge of a bruise the color of a rotting plum. Her fingers have to do the rest. They find a small gash congealed overnight with hair and dried blood. She touches it gingerly. It stings, freshly sore.

She racks her brain for some clue as to what happened last night. Dread creeps into the space where answers should be. Lately, scrapes and bruises have had a way of following her home, especially in the dark.

Okay, retrace your steps. Caroline's voice echoes in her mind as Sofia gets dressed. She doesn't want the memory to linger, but she can't help herself. Caroline's face, the impish smile that accompanied these words, the rush of the waves behind them. Sofia can't remember what exactly she lost that day. It might have been a bracelet Drea made her. Or a paperback with water-swollen pages. She just remembers laughing with Caroline as they literally tiptoed back through the sand: Caroline in Sofia's footprints, Sofia in Caroline's.

Willing herself to focus, she brings herself back to the unanswered question of last night. She remembers Leo's arm around her shoulders, pulling her closer against the chill that sent litter and dead leaves swirling across the Lower East Side. The smell of him. Cigarette smoke, in his hair, on his tongue. Expensive cologne that seems permanently seeped into his skin. It was their latest in a frayed string of reckless weekends.

Sofia had taken the now-practiced train ride into the city, gleefully free of Yale's tether. Leo, an NYU dropout, doesn't play by the rules, because for him, there aren't any. She remembers his fingers, blackened with oil paint and charcoal, curled around her shoulder in a gesture that said *mine*. She digs a Band-Aid out of the pack she thought she'd never need but finds herself reaching for more and more these days.

They had started at his studio, Sofia on her usual perch as she watched him work. She loves the way his brush moves across a canvas as if with a life force of its own. Leo was brimming with frenetic energy, his eyes alight. He got like that when he was painting. Or high. More so when he was both. She can remember that at least, and their drunken laughter as they stumbled down the stairs and out to a bar to meet Brooke and Caroline, who'd taken a later train from Yale.

They were planning on telling Caroline about their relationship that night—finally. Leo thought Caroline would be happy for them, that she would roll her eyes and say that she always suspected something. He never knew the truth about Sofia's history with his sister, and Sofia ached for the moment shock and jealousy would register on Caroline's face.

The sound of keys turning the front door dead bolt rips Sofia back to the present. She rushes out of the bathroom, shuts her door, and yanks on jeans and the faded Yale sweatshirt Caroline had bought her when they'd gotten their acceptance letters. Jenna's voice and Caroline's throaty laugh come from behind the door, and Sofia can distinctly make out the male voice that muffles them both.

Taking a deep breath, Sofia steps out into the living room. Bryce has a massive proprietary hand on Caroline's shoulder. He stands somewhere north of six feet, and his rower's physique dominates the space by virtue of his size alone. They both make Jenna look tiny: she's the sort of petite person who always seems intent on making themselves even smaller to fit into that double zero dress. Sofia has never understood the appeal of being less than nothing. They're taking off their coats and tossing them carelessly on the couch. Caroline's back is to them, so she doesn't catch how Jenna's watchful eyes linger on Bryce's broad shoulders.

"Hey, Sofia," Bryce says, clearly unsure if he is allowed to speak to her or not. "Uh—how are you?" Like he cares.

"I feel like I got hit by a Jameson truck," she says as lightly as she can. He smiles weakly back at her, as far as weakness is possible with that Captain America jawline. Caroline is facing away from Sofia, unwinding an ivory scarf from around her throat. Sofia can hear the familiar *crick-crack* Caroline's graceful neck makes as she rolls it—perpetually tight, ever since that time Bill slammed her against the kitchen wall.

A fleck of lint clings to Caroline's blouse. Sofia wants nothing more than to reach out and pluck it off the thin fabric. No one in the room can see her forefinger twitch at the thought. Caroline's eyes meet Sofia's in one of their mirrors. They both look away.

"Hey, babe, can you give us a sec?" Caroline says.

"Sure," Bryce says, unable to hide the relief from his voice, and he lumbers into Caroline's room. Jenna takes this as her cue, and with just a glance in Sofia's direction, disappears behind her door.

Caroline exhales and turns around. For once, Sofia can't read her expression. "Are you going to tell me what the fuck you were thinking?" Caroline asks coolly.

"I don't remember anything from last night," Sofia pleads as if she's on trial, which in a way she is. Caroline lets out a short, impatient laugh and shakes her head.

"How convenient." Caroline's tone is harsh and disbelieving. "Were you ever going to tell me about Leo? That's low, even for you." Sofia turns her back before Caroline can see the tears, and she swipes at them so fast, her nails scrape the delicate skin at the corners of her eyes. It takes an effort to face Caroline again.

"It's not going to work, you know." Caroline crosses her arms tight as she says this, as if she's trying to put up every possible barrier between them.

"If we could just—" Sofia starts, and the desperation that cracks her voice makes her want to dissolve into the floorboards.

"And you called Brooke *pathetic*." Caroline cuts off her words.

"What are you talking about?" Sofia asks in a small voice that gets even smaller as she takes in the sheer indifference on Caroline's face. This was not how this was supposed to go.

"Are you serious?" Her gray eyes flash protectiveness over her new best friend. "That's what you called her when she was just trying to talk to some guy. You humiliated her in front of, like, the entire bar. It was so fucked up, Sofia. You have *no* idea what she's going through right now." Now it sounds like she cares. That, more than anything else, shatters Sofia.

"I'm sorry." Sofia says this because she has to. "I love—"

"I know," Caroline interrupts and looks down at the scarf in her hands. Sofia wonders if she's thinking about their past, or the fact that she would never tell her brother the truth, or anyone else for that matter, about their history. Caroline always said their secrets make what they have special. Sofia believes her.

Caroline closes her eyes, then meets Sofia's gaze with an effort.

"I care about you, too. Our friendship is important to me. But you have got to let the past go." Caroline throws out the word *friendship* so casually that it creates a crater at the bottom of Sofia's stomach. Caroline stands up. "I can never give you what you want." She looks at Sofia with pity in her eyes. It's worse than anger, worse even than indifference.

Sofia thinks of the last day they were together, the summer after their sophomore year at Yale, barely a year ago, as they laughed, naked except for a hazy blanket of smoke hovering over Caroline's bed. Outside the window, the sound of waves created a lulling hush in that enchanted hour, casting a spell that froze time in place. That spell was abruptly broken by Leo's father, Caroline's stepfather, crashing through her bedroom door just as Sofia embraced her, barely coherent as he demanded they both get out of his house. Caroline doesn't understand Sofia's vision, how her dating Leo makes it so much easier to pretend they're just friends. But she will.

"You have to stop making things more than they were," Caroline says evenly, and Sofia wants to scream.

"And be nice to Brooke. If you just let her in a little, you'll see she's not out to *replace* you or anything. I don't understand why we can't just all be cool." Caroline releases an exhausted sigh. "What we had was fun, but I want us to stay friends. I'm not interested in you or Brooke or anyone except Bryce, okay?" Her voice is lowered to a crouching murmur, the register of all shameful secrets spoken aloud. Sofia thinks of their sunlit mornings in bed. She knows it isn't over.

"This is all in your head," Caroline says so gently that for a split second, Sofia wants to believe her.

"I—"

Caroline holds up a hand to stop her. "I can't do this anymore," she says heavily. "Please just think about what I said." She turns, crosses the room, and snaps her door shut. A tear clings to Sofia's lower lashes, and her fingers tighten around the secondhand Nokia cell phone. All of this is in her head, is it? We'll see about that. She texts Leo.

> Hey you :) Are you still in touch with that guy who knew Brooke from a few years back?

He responds immediately. Unusual for Leo, but she'll take it.

> Hello gorgeous. Yeah—he's actually in the city right now for a film thing.

Perfect.

> You up for creating a little chaos?

Sofia smirks as she heads back toward her room to select something Leo will like. A quick inventory of the closet confirms that just about anything that cost more than $40 was either his gift to her or a hand-me-down from Caroline. Leo loves dressing Sofia, his muse. Caroline never realized when she was throwing a good thing away. As Sofia reaches for a butter-soft leather jacket and a gunmetal Alaïa slip dress printed with twisting vines, her phone buzzes with Leo's response.

> Always. Come to my place tomorrow and we can plot our next move ;)

It's not a request. Leo doesn't make requests. Sofia slides the dress and jacket to the center of the rack where they dangle, ready for tomorrow. For now, she buttons up her catering uniform, a crisp white shirt and black pants that will make her invisible to the Winterses' guests at tonight's event, no more than a sentient table or a roving bottle of wine. People like Brooke can't see people like Sofia.

But she can see them.

CHAPTER 5

Brooke

Now

My instinct to hide from the baby shower must have kicked in—flight over fight. Typical. The windows in here don't overlook the backyard, so at least I can panic in private. Resisting the vivid nightmarish flashback of a smoking, overturned car, a crying child, and two lifeless bodies, I lean against the closed door of my parents' bedroom. I shut my eyes for a moment, as if doing that has ever made the memories stop. Opening them again, I take a deep breath and straighten up.

Growing up, this was my favorite room in the house, as long as it was empty. When my parents were away for the weekend or at some charity gala, Geneviève, our au pair, would sneak Mel and me up here. I can still see the two little girls we once were taking turns sitting at our mother's beautiful vanity: glass over an embroidered drape that covered legs too short to reach the ground from the tufted stool.

Geneviève would give us makeovers: first brushing our hair with the silver filigree hairbrush, then dabbing our lips with a cheap lipstick from her pocket—she wouldn't dare touch my mother's lacquered cosmetics case. "*Très belle, ma petite princesse,*" Geneviève would say to me. The ritual continued until my parents got home early one night. I can still see my mother's look of horror when her eyes fastened on my made-up face, and I can still hear the words that spewed from her mouth: "You can put a fat little pig in lipstick, but it's still a fat little pig." As she spoke, her piercing gaze swept up and down my flabby arms, my thick little calves, my nonexistent chin that threatened to tremble into two—wobbling, unpretty, and weak.

I snatch a few tissues from the vanity and cross into the palatial en suite bathroom. Geneviève was gone the day after my mother caught us at her dressing table, which became the same day my first diet started—and has extended into years of skipping lunch, telling Josh "I'm just not that hungry," and inventing the meals I've "already eaten." I straighten the straps of my size four sundress. Noticing my smudged mascara, I open the medicine cabinet in search of a Q-tip.

There they are: the battalion of orange bottles arranged in a neat line, all prescribed by a family friend who didn't ask too many questions about my mother's sudden and completely fictional "fear of flying" or "trouble sleeping" or whatever else rich women say to get their hands on their little chemical helpers. Xanax. Klonopin. Ambien.

My phone buzzes. It's Jenna.

> I have to head out a little early—Bryce forgot to pick up Hayden again. Couldn't find you to say goodbye, so sorry!

Wondering if her husband would ever deserve Jenna or their son, I extract a Q-tip and reach to close the medicine cabinet. My hand hesitates. I consider opening the pill bottles and spilling their contents into the toilet. Medically speaking, my mother shouldn't be mixing these with alcohol, so I'd be doing her a favor, really. I imagine the little happiness substitutes spiraling out of her reach. But as usual, I chicken out. I pull myself together, because this is who I have trained myself to be. Sweet Brooke. Thoughtful Brooke. She doesn't lose control. She has her life on track. It's who I have to be after everything I've done.

I tap out a response to Jenna.

> No problem—thanks for coming today!!
> See you at Leo's art show next week?

I text Josh next.

> Heading home—want me to pick up
> anything for dinner?

Gray dots flicker his response.

> You survived!

I smile and tap back.

> By the skin of my teeth, yes.

> Went into the office today, and we'll
> probably need to keep working through
> the weekend. Cool if some of the

> associates come over to prep for tomorrow?

My face falls at the prospect of an apartment full of lawyers when all I want right now is Josh, but I remind myself how hard he works and how much this case means to him—he's been working late for weeks. And to be fair, working on weekends isn't unusual for either of us, and that's part of why we both love and "get" each other.

> So, takeout for hungry justice warriors?

He responds with five heart emojis. I sigh, set my shoulders back, and make my covert escape.

———

The greasy pizza boxes are hot enough to scald the palms of my hands as I awkwardly maneuver out of my car and toward our apartment building. But the prospect of warm carbs to be enjoyed away from Daphne's critical eye is more than enough to propel me up three narrow flights of stairs. Fumbling for my keys, I can hear voices in rapid conversation on the other side of the wall. Josh, another male voice, and a female voice I recognize instantly. Chloe. I let out a sigh of annoyance as I balance the stack of boxes with one hand and unlock our front door with the other.

"I come bearing sustenance," I say, tossing my keys into the bowl by the door and depositing the boxes on the hall table. Our apartment is small but cozy: a light-filled open kitchen and living area lined with mismatched bookshelves. There's a warm nudge against my leg, accompanied by a chirping mew. Piper rubs her face against my ankles and stretches upward on her back paws, peering at me with her good eye. She was the last of her litter left at the shelter long after her brothers and sisters were adopted, probably because of the patch of fur that covered where her right eye should be, and she stole my heart immediately.

"How's my girl?" I murmur, bending to scratch beneath her tabby chin. Josh, Chloe, and another colleague are gathered around the kitchen table, which is covered in papers and three open laptops. The binders and neat files of lesson plans I had spread out there are carelessly piled on the floor, some of the papers lolling out like brightly colored tongues. Josh is hunched over his keyboard, typing with one hand, reaching for a thick folder with the other. He looks every inch the determined environmental attorney, so much so that he could have answered a casting call to play one in a movie: dark tousled hair, five-o'clock shadow, Warby Parker glasses, a slightly rumpled blue Oxford shirt.

"Hey, babe." He gives me a tired smile. "You're a lifesaver. I think it's time we took a break anyway, right, guys?" He stretches. "You've met Chloe, right?" I nod and give her a tight-lipped smile. "And this is—"

"Josh, we really need to review the water rights amendment," Chloe says, her eyes skating across the text on her computer screen. "I think the easement they're asking for is a clear exception under—"

"I know, but come on, it can wait ten minutes, Chlo," he says, nudging her shoulder. She looks up at him and smiles, using her index fingers to brush aside the long, beachy waves that frame her heart-shaped face. Josh stands and, remembering what he was about to say, adds, "And this is Ganesh. He's new to the team." Ganesh raises a hand in greeting.

"Thanks for the food rescue. Can I give you a hand with those?" Ganesh gestures to the pizza boxes as he rises from his seat. Piper trots after him, sniffing the air hopefully.

"Thanks," I say, and I head to the kitchen for plates, napkins, and a bottle of wine. "How's the case going?"

"It's a beast," Josh replies. He joins Ganesh on the couch and opens one of the pizza boxes. "We're trying to stop a pipeline from cutting through wetlands, but IWWA isn't exactly on our side here." I set the plates and napkins down and set to work uncorking the red.

"What's IWWA again?" I ask. It's impossible to keep up with all the acronyms in Josh's work.

"The Inland Wetlands and Watercourses Act," Chloe rattles off impatiently, settling herself in an armchair. She repeats the gesture with her index fingers and hair, though I suspect she knows it looks exactly how she wants it to look.

"Gotcha. Wine, anyone?" I hold up the bottle.

"Sure, I'll have a little bit," Josh says. Ganesh shakes his head, yawning.

"At least one of us needs to stay sharp, so I'll take a coffee," Chloe says. Thankfully, Josh steps in.

"I'll make some in a bit, Chlo," he says. Again with the "*Chlo*." I wish, not for the first time, that I am above letting this annoy me.

"So," Ganesh says, turning toward me from his spot on the couch, "Josh tells us you're a teacher—what do you teach?"

"High school English," I say, grateful for a conversation topic in which I can actually participate.

"That's awesome," Ganesh says. "My sister teaches history, and she loves it—most of the time." He gives a commiserating grin. "When does school start for you?"

My mouth is inconveniently full of pizza. "In a week, but we start meetings and prep tomorrow," I say.

"I'd *kill* for summers off." Chloe sighs. "Can you even imagine? Or do we not remember free time?" Her words have a serrated edge of sarcasm that's barely masked by a playful tone. She flicks her eyes from Josh to Ganesh. Josh grins wryly.

"Vaguely," Josh replies, tilting his chin and placing a fingertip to his temple as if lost in thought. I feel the back of my neck flush.

"I don't know," Ganesh interjects. "Mina says that it's really not all it's cracked up to be. She has a lot to do over the summer, and her school district piles on a crazy amount of workshops and stuff."

"Where does she teach?" I ask.

"DC public schools."

"Wow," Chloe says. "Good for her. That's tough—public school teachers are *so* underappreciated," she adds knowledgeably before nibbling at a slice of pizza. Piper rolls over at Chloe's feet. Traitor. "But I guess I don't have to tell you that, Brooke."

"Actually, I—"

"She works at a private school now," Josh cuts in. There's something flat in his tone. Was it disappointment?

"Oh," Chloe replies shortly. "Well, we can't all be super-Minas, right, Ganesh?"

Ganesh raises his hands in a gesture of neutrality. "I'm in awe of anyone willing to go toe to toe with a bunch of hormonal teenagers."

"Especially the entitled offspring of the 1 percent. It's not for the faint of heart," Josh adds, raising his wineglass in my direction. I let out a nervous laugh, but there's a darkness in his expression that unsettles me. Before I can read too much into this, my phone pings twice. Something from school, probably. I tap on my mail icon and open the new message. The air in my lungs instantly hardens to lead.

As if scorched by the screen, I nearly drop my phone onto the floor.

"Sorry—gotta answer this," I mumble to the blank stares of everyone in my living room as I fumble to pick up my phone. I try to look as normal as possible as I walk out of the room. The sound of Josh, Ganesh, and Chloe's conversation fades as my pulse accelerates to a pounding, panicked staccato. Our bedroom door rattles shut, and it hits me that this is my second time hiding in twenty-four hours. I reach for my phone, but my hands are shaking so badly, I have to stop and grip our bed frame. From behind the fleeting safety of my eyelids, I tell myself this isn't what I think it is.

To: bwinters@woodlandsacademy.org
From: sofia.m.eliades@gmail.com
Subject: Miss you, B

Brooke, I've always loved this picture of us, but I think I like the second one of you even better (and so will everyone else). xx
Sofia

Dead people can't send emails. Dead people can't do anything but stay dead. Sofia Eliades is nothing but a ghostly presence in the ether of my nightmares. And yet here she is in my hand. Or at least someone pretending to be her. But that someone knows where I work. The email was sent to my Woodlands email address.

The message has two attachments. My index finger wavers as I find the first one, and as the top third fills the screen, I recognize it instantly. It's a picture of a Polaroid, glossy and starkly framed in chalk white. Four girls smile back at me through the years and the horror of that night. Caroline, looking like she stepped off the page of a J.Crew ad, tanned and lanky. Jenna in a fitted minidress, clutching a glass of rosé. Sofia, that mysterious, mocking grin curled lazily on red lips, cigarette in one hand, the other tightly wound around Caroline's waist. Me, mid-laugh, blissfully unaware of what was waiting for us.

There was only one way anyone could have gotten their hands on this picture: by taking it out of its frame on top of the dresser to my right. I keep Sofia in plain sight. Partly to convince myself that I'm not afraid of her ghost, partly to prove what a normal, grieving friend I am. My eyes feel heavy as I lift them from the floor to the space the picture frame should be.

But it's gone.

This psycho was in my apartment. Feet away from where Josh

and I sleep. I try to swallow, but my throat is dry and corset-tight with fear. Whoever this is knows where I live. Do they know everything else?

I'll call the police, report a break-in, change the locks, make up some excuse to tell Josh. I'll order one of those door cameras tonight. Josh doesn't have to know this happened. Josh can't know the truth—how could he want to marry someone who's done what I've done? Call the police, change the locks, get a security camera. It's just a picture. Everything is going to be okay. Repeating this in my head almost makes me feel better.

And then I remember the second attachment.

CHAPTER 6

Caroline

Now

I don't answer Eric right away, but I take his phone as he hands it to me. It shows Equilibrium's Instagram page: Eric's most recent post, a photo of me shaking hands with a LinkedIn executive at the start of this weekend, already has over two hundred likes. Not bad for twenty-four hours. Extending my thumb and index finger, I magnify the comments section.

A few fire emojis. One "Yass queen." But there's one more, "What's dead and buried doesn't stay dead and buried forever, does it, C? @seliades2009." I can almost feel the color drain from my face as my eyes slacken. Sofia died in 2009, while we were at Yale. The comment contains a link. I click. Sofia's obituary from a Nantucket newspaper appears in black and white. A shiver crackles through me, signaling disaster along the ridges of my spine. It's time for damage control, and I'll need Eric in the loop in order to make that happen.

"Okay . . . ," I start, lowering my voice. Even with the mic off,

I'm paranoid so close to the stage. "The short version: I was in a car accident in college. My friend Sofia was driving, and the crash killed the driver of the other car and almost killed my other friend and me. It was awful. I don't like to talk about it." I let it out in a rush. The short, edited version, the only version I can live with, has become so ingrained in my mind that I feel almost nothing when I rattle it off. Everything gets easier with time, especially living with the lies you tell to protect the ones you love.

Eric's expression softens. "Caroline, I'm so sorry. I had no idea," he says. He reaches out to touch my shoulder, but I gently wave away the gesture and resume my businesslike tone.

"Obviously, she can't just come back from the dead. But someone clearly wants to dig this up to make us look bad, even though it was just an accident. Someone must have something against me, against Equilibrium. Or both, I don't know." I lie convincingly to Eric. I can't drag him into this. It's been hard enough keeping Equilibrium's current financial crisis from him, and if he knows about what really happened that night, he would probably jump ship before I could explain the truth about Sofia. About what she was. About what she did.

Her face surfaces in my memory. I can still see the glow of obsession like hot coals in her eyes that sparked a few weeks after we started sleeping together. The warning signs were always there. Those little red flags didn't go anywhere when she and Leo started dating, and now we're all paying the price. Eric needs to believe that this is just a personal tragedy I don't like to think about. I roll my neck once, and the familiar, ensuing crack steadies me.

"But now really isn't the time to get into all that. Can you block the user and send me a screenshot of the comment? I'll look into this as soon as we wrap up here." Eric runs our social media and PR: he and two programmer contractors are all the employees I can afford. For another few weeks, anyway.

"Don't worry. We can bury this—you'd be surprised what

people can forget if you play it right. Especially on the internet," Eric says confidently. "I'll also keep an eye out for any similar usernames—trolls can have a lot of time on their hands."

"You read my mind," I say.

"A key part of my job description." Eric throws me a sideways smile and a slight bow as he opens the door that leads back to the main conference center.

"And you do it so well." I smile back and cross into the fluorescently lit hallway. To the rest of the world, we look completely ordinary, an unstoppable executive and her right-hand man. No crisis to see here.

"Okay, game time," Eric says in the sly but efficient tone that's another one of our defaults, the one that we use to remind each other that we play to win. I need to hear it all the more, now that we're actually playing to survive. "You have about half an hour and then—"

"They announce the funding decision. Right." I nod and bite the inside corner of my lower lip. I survey the room we've just stepped into. It's brimming with overachievers and idealists, all busily exchanging contact information, pitching their startups and apps, or snatching a second to fire off a quick email.

"Incoming," Eric murmurs, inclining his head toward two people walking in our direction, a petite Indian woman accompanied by one of the few men in the room. A few heads turn in his wake, which, by the looks of him, is not unusual.

"We really enjoyed your presentation," the woman says with genuine warmth and enthusiasm as they approach us. "And we'd love to learn more about Equilibrium. We think your software might be a great fit for Quantum." I'd heard of Quantum, of course. As a rising star in customer relationship management, they are exactly the sort of fish we're here to reel in.

"Thank you," I say. "I don't think we've met," I say, turning toward the man on my right. I know perfectly well we haven't met.

I would certainly have remembered the blue eyes that meet mine as he leans forward, extending a hand.

"Milo Armstrong," he says, his voice silkened by a British accent, one that sounded Cambridge polished and might even be swoon-inducing if his audience happened to be the swooning type. "And this is my colleague, Sara Patel." A hint of a much lower-brow London accent escapes on Milo's last syllable: a slight *w* instead of an *l* consonant. His tone is professional, but I catch a glint in his gaze that tells me he knows exactly what I'm thinking. He knows that landing Quantum as a client would be a huge win for us, a whole new level of exposure.

"It's been quite a year for you guys, congratulations," I say. I'd read about their latest successes. They have the luxury to attend events like this that cost upwards of $1,000 a head, not to mention the need for a diversity-conscious profile now more than ever. I'm about to launch into my standard spiel for prospective clients when my phone starts to buzz. I silence it. But almost immediately, the pulse begins again.

"I'm so sorry—would you excuse me?" I ask, a steady adrenaline drip beginning in my veins. No matter how hard I try to push the thought away, these back-to-back calls might have something to do with the "Sofia" trolling our Instagram. "This is my right-hand man, Eric. He'll be happy to answer any of your questions. I'd love to follow up with you personally ASAP, though. Eric, can you find time on my calendar?"

In the split second before he nods, Eric shoots me the *What the fuck are you doing?* look that I fully deserve. I keep my smile locked in place, and I quickly touch his arm as I step away.

"Sure thing." Eric relaxes and turns his beam of professional charm toward Sara. Eric is gay, and he knows how to work women better than any straight man I've ever met. But I'd wager Milo could give him a run for his money. I turn and take a few steps before my phone resumes its doomed heartbeat, and I feel a tap on my shoulder. I catch an intoxicating suggestion of sandalwood and sage as I glance at the tasteful watch—rich mahogany leather, not titanium—and look up at its owner.

"Forgive me, Caroline," Milo says. That damn accent is the last thing I need right now. "My card. You can reach my office or my mobile—that's the second number there—anytime." He hands me a rectangle of thick card stock before turning away.

I pocket Milo's card. As soon as he's out of sight, I answer the phone on its last ring before the call would have gone to voicemail, expecting the worst. But it's not a call from a sketchy number. It's Leo. He's calling from Oak Grove, the rehab facility I checked him into ninety days ago. His time's up.

CHAPTER 7

Brooke

Now

The second image doesn't open right away, and my eyes cling to every speck of the excruciatingly slow download. Finally an envelope materializes, next to what looks like a manila folder. I tap the picture to zoom closer. In neat letters, the label on the folder reads: *Winters/Adams Incident, 4/23/2008.* I recognize the Brown University watermark on the front of the folder.

How the actual fuck did "Sofia" get their hands on this? Before I pan to the rest of the image, I'm consumed by an irrepressible feeling that I know exactly what's coming. Josh's parents' address is typed on the envelope. My breath staggers to a complete stop. A Post-it note dangles from the bottom right corner. I stretch my index and middle fingers apart another inch to zoom in and read what's written on it.

Thinking of telling our little secret? That is to say, your little secret? You know better, B. We do things my way this time. xx, Sofia

And just like that, my pathetic little plan full of locks and places to hide shrivels up and dies. Memories sharpen in my mind and form a reel that unspools at double time. Music vibrating the floorboards. A dark hallway kaleidoscoping in and out of focus. The slam of car doors. Then screams, sirens, cold rain stinging the cuts on my face. Sofia's body splayed at impossible angles, half on the road, half on the damp grass. Not far from her, a crying child kneeling next to a mangled heap of metal.

Blood is still thudding hot and fast in my ears when I hear a soft knock on the bedroom door. Wiping my eyes and sliding my phone back into my dress pocket, I get shakily to my feet. Josh steps into our bedroom, followed by Piper.

"Hey, they're gone," he says shortly before taking in my swollen eyes and paper-white face. "Jesus, Brooke. Were you crying because of what Chloe said?" he asks. His arms are crossed, and he sounds annoyed.

"What?" I mumble, my mind still heaving with waves of fear and regret.

"That stupid comment she made about teachers. You're being overly sensitive," Josh says, taking a step closer to me. "You can't let her get to you. She's just under a lot of pressure right now." He runs his hands up and down my arms before pulling me in for a hug. His muscular embrace is so comforting I almost start to cry again.

"I love you," I say, my voice muffled by his shirt. I breathe in the scent of the fresh linen dryer sheets he loves. Josh kisses the top of my head, and Piper winds herself between our feet, mewing happily up at us. It's almost enough to feel normal, to forget that someone knows what we did to Sofia. And that it might be only a matter of time until Josh does, too.

"I love you," Josh says, releasing me. He keeps his warm hands on my shoulders. "It's just—I'm worried about you." His eyes tell me he's serious. He takes my hand, and we sit on the bed.

"I'm fine," I say, thinking of the words I'd just read. Whoever is pretending to be Sofia doesn't want me getting ahead of this, controlling the narrative, or getting away unscathed—which is exactly what I've tried to do for the past ten years.

They want me to suffer, to be afraid, to wonder what is going to happen when they're ready to blow up my life. No one can know about this, especially not Josh. He thinks that night was just a tragic accident, and Sofia's death is just a sad shadow cast over my past. Just like he thinks I transferred to Yale for the better English department. When people look at me, they think they're looking at someone who isn't a good liar. They're sure of it. I work hard to keep it that way.

"No, you're not fine. I can tell," Josh says, firmly but kindly. He rubs the bridge of his nose where his glasses always leave symmetrical indentations like tiny footprints of worry. It's little things like this that made me fall in love with Josh, the world-weary lawyer who's always looking out for the underdog. Right now, that happens to be his basket-case fiancée. "You've been obsessing over this new job for weeks now."

This is not what I was expecting. "What do you mean?"

"Seriously?" He gives me an exasperated look. "You're up until midnight going over and over your lesson plans, rereading books you could pretty much recite by heart. This Dr. Lutz guy seems to expect you to have everything planned out through January." He stops, takes a breath. "And school hasn't even started yet." He makes this eventuality sound like a minor apocalypse. "I just thought the whole point of you working at Woodlands was to have *less* on your plate. You know, that was the trade-off for the bigger impact you were making at Inspire."

"Bigger impact?" I ask, comprehension unfurling like a poisonous weed. The Inspire Charter School is the last place I worked, and it's located in a community where poverty and everything that goes with it was the norm for most of my students. "Would this have anything to do with your '1 percent' comment?" I slide away from Josh.

"Oh, come on," Josh says, rolling his eyes. "That was a *joke*."

"Yeah, one you made at my expense in front of your colleagues. Who all seem to think my job is some sort of *joke*," I fire back.

"You've gotten *so* crazy sensitive about this stuff," he says, and every word is like a rubber band snapping against the inside of my wrist. Josh lets out a deeply aggrieved sigh. My sensitivity has been coming up a lot recently.

"It's not Chloe's fault you have a chip on your shoulder," Josh continues, and I'm fighting not to take the bait. "I *thought* the trade-off here was you'd spend less time obsessing over work because this job would be less demanding," he says carefully, and I can tell he's realizing how harsh he just sounded.

"Let me get this straight. Because my new students will come from privilege, my work doesn't matter?" I suddenly realize I'm on my feet.

"That's n—" he starts, but now it's my turn to interrupt.

"I didn't exactly hear you rushing to my defense when *Chlo . . .* "— I spit out her name—"basically said I'm less of a teacher slash human being because I work at a private school now. No." I shrug my shoulders and hold up my hands in a sarcastic gesture. "You were more than happy to join right in." I hear my voice rising, but I'm too angry and scared and exhausted to care. Piper sensibly dashes into the other room.

"I just think you're happier when you're working for a really important cause," Josh says, his tone smooth.

"A *cause*?" I ask, my anger rising. "They're human beings, not *trees*, Josh." Faces from the last school year flash through my memory. Jasmine giving a speech that got a standing ovation from the class. Daniel getting one of his poems published in a national liter-

ary magazine. But my students' progress came at a high price, usually it was my sanity or any semblance of a life outside of school. Or
making time for Josh.

Josh looks at me blankly. "This place already seems like it's
going to run you into the ground," he says. "And then what will you
be left with? More stress for *what*? To make sure some kid can go
to Colgate instead of—god forbid—a state school?"

His words hang in the air as if suspended from invisible
strings, each tied to an unpleasant truth. He's hit the nucleus of
my guilt, the thing that hurt the most when I packed up my classroom. The kids I'd abandoned, all for that elusive work-life balance.

I go back on the offensive. "You went to private school just like
I did," I say, firing out a fact that Josh hates to admit. His wealthy
family background clashes with his current ideals. "Are you honestly saying that there was never a teacher or a coach or someone
who was there for you when your mom left?" I glare at him. "I care
about being the best teacher I can be. What, since my hours aren't
billable, they're not worth doing?"

But Josh's shoulders slump, and he looks at the floor. "You know
I can't talk to you when you're like this." The coldness in his voice
brings me back to earth. Josh always shuts down when I push him
too hard. What was I thinking? Now is not the time to push my
fiancé away. I think again of the day Josh proposed to me: the love
in his eyes, the promise of never being alone again. And if the message I just read tells me anything, it's that I'll need him now more
than ever.

"I'm sorry," I say, stepping closer to him. "I care about this,
okay? I want this to work. Things will calm down once I get into
a rhythm—they always do." I reach for his hand and give it a
squeeze.

"Okay," he says. "Just promise me you won't put too much pressure on yourself. And chill out a little bit—maybe learn to take a

joke?" There's something indulgent in his smile I don't like, but anything is better than detached resignation. "That way we can get back to *us*?" He looks at me with so much kindness in his eyes that I just want to hold him until all of this just goes away.

"I promise," I say, and I seal the lie with a kiss.

CHAPTER 8

Sofia

Then

When Sofia passes the painting Brooke's uncle donated to the Yale Art Gallery, she honestly can't see what all the fuss is about. But then it's hard to get a good look when balancing a tray of stain-ready glasses of red wine and trying not to trip over the well-heeled guests. They're not paying her to have an opinion, anyway. It's just her job to keep everyone from crossing the fault line between tastefully toasted and sloppily drunk. Once her shift at this event is done, her real work can begin with Leo.

Tonight's soiree is hosted in a smoky alumni club that still manages to be cluttered despite the size of the place. Rooms like this always make Sofia think of Caroline's stepfather's study, the shadowy lion's den she always avoided for Caroline's sake but secretly found fascinating. Sofia discreetly offers the tray to a cluster of sport-jacketed men, and her eyes slide to the dim portrait enshrined by a hulking gold-leaf frame.

"Remarkable, isn't it?" It takes Sofia a second to realize one of the men is talking to her. He has a drinker's swollen nose, and the edges of his words blur together as his leer hovers somewhere near the third button of her blouse.

"Richard, don't bother the poor girl." A second man drops her a wobbly wink. "She's not exactly being paid to be an art expert, are you, my dear?" They chortle at the joke, at her. Sofia gives the practiced close-lipped smile she always uses to respond to remarks like this. The last thing they want is to hear her talk.

"Now, this one you can quiz," the man continues, and he plucks a slender honey-blond woman out of the crowd milling around the painting. It's Brooke. Sofia wishes she could stop the angry red blotch of shame before it spreads from the back of her neck to her face.

"Gentlemen, this is my niece, Brooke, a promising young Yalie," he says with pride, and Brooke gives an obedient smile that falters when her eyes meet Sofia's. Sofia's spine stiffens, and her feet are suddenly glued to the plush Turkish rug. Brooke opens her mouth to acknowledge Sofia, but she's interrupted immediately.

"We saw this two summers ago at the Prado, didn't we?" Her uncle gestures at the painting. Brooke nods, and the tiny gesture exudes sophistication you can't buy. It's the first time Sofia has ever observed Brooke in her natural habitat: the effortlessly elegant cocktail dress, the pearl drop earrings that are probably an heirloom, the self-assured way her eyes appraise the painting as she demurely sips her wine. "You should have heard her going on about Velázquez—definitely gave our tour guide a run for their money!" The group chuckles again. Sofia tries to back away, but Brooke's uncle snaps his fingers in her direction.

"Your glass is *perilously* close to low tide there, Brooke," he says as if this is some sort of emergency. He reaches for one of the wine-glasses on Sofia's tray and hands it to Brooke, discarding the near-empty glass in its place in a smooth act of dismissal. Unable to stand this encounter any longer, Sofia cuts off Brooke's sheepish "thanks" by walking away as fast as the crowded room will allow.

Tightening her jaw, she grips the tray hard to stop the glasses from shaking.

Jenna is stationed behind the bar on the other side of the room, and Sofia can't help but admire the flirtatious smile she gives an expensively dressed man as she shakes his cocktail. Jenna asked Brooke to put in a good word, to hire the catering company she and Sofia work for to staff the event. Brooke would be doing them a favor—the tips would be amazing, blah, blah, blah. It never bothered Jenna—the subtle and not-so-subtle reminders of their different backgrounds or the regular dosage of evidence that Caroline and Brooke have had so much handed to them.

Jenna strains clear liquid into a frosted glass and balances an olive-skewered toothpick on its rim. The man doesn't take his eyes off her, drinking in her pretty face just as much as the first sip of his martini. As he tucks a folded twenty into the tip jar on the gleaming bar before turning away, Jenna wins the game she plays with people like him. Sofia and Jenna are alike in that way: they share an innate understanding of how to manipulate those who look down on them. The kind of people who say their housekeepers are "like family." Or think that calling their driver "sir" once or twice is the same as treating him as an equal.

These people start with the upper hand. And there's nothing sweeter in this world than taking it back. Jenna's just better at hiding the raw, scrappy desire to get it than Sofia ever will be. Jenna takes particular pleasure in taking it from people who feel entitled to what she wants most: the wealth, the man, the life she wasn't born into. Catching Sofia's eye from across the room, Jenna allows her good-girl mask to slip for one blink of her long eyelashes and flashes a lupine smile. But as she turns to serve the next septuagenarian guest, Jenna's eager-to-please expression is firmly back in place. Brooke is too gullible to see Jenna for who she really is; Caroline too busy to notice or care. But Jenna is banking on them underestimating her, and that's why she'll win every time.

Sofia smiles to herself and resumes her circuit around the stuffy rooms of the Yale Club.

＝＝＝＝

The look of triumph on Jenna's face lingers in Sofia's mind's eye the next morning as the train rumbles toward New York City. Sofia needs to be on Jenna's level of ruthlessness if she's going to get Caroline back. She gazes through the milky filth clouding the train window and watches how green and brick smoothly turn to steel and glass. A secondhand copy of *Paradise Lost* lies face down and half-finished on the seat next to her. The train shudders to a halt, and a monotone recording announces their arrival at Penn Station.

Around Sofia, the other passengers hurry up the aisle, pulled into the irresistible current of Manhattan. She gathers her things and joins the throng pushing into the bustling atrium. The deafening cacophony of heeled shoes and voices and the grind and screech of metal surrounds her and scales the vaulted ceiling. She stops and wonders if she should turn back, if all of this is worth it. Start over. Leave it all behind. Let Leo choose another conduit for his genius and Caroline find another love to abandon. The Archers are nothing if not takers.

But as Sofia thinks of Caroline, her feet propel her forward into the city. She considers hailing a cab she can't afford, but the pavement is steadying under her feet. Light is starting to seep out from behind the clouds, and she savors the warmth as she passes storefronts and piles of garbage. She shifts her bag so that the strap digs a fresh track into her shoulder. Days with Leo easily stretch into nights, so she'd stashed some essentials for the inevitable. He enjoys the sort of freedom that only comes with burning through a substantial trust fund. Being *bohemian* is fun when you're rich.

They both have a love-hate relationship with New York City, Sofia realizes as a breeze stirs up half a dozen smells in the air, few of them pleasant. A drill thuds to her left, loud enough to drown out her thoughts if she could only let it. Leo loves talking about building an idyllic retreat upstate, one that lies in wait for when he decides it's the quiet, not the noise, that his art needs most. Sofia thinks of him reigning over dark woods and filling secluded places with people like him, and a chill traces along her spine.

As she crosses 28th Street, Leo's building comes into view. A fire escape zigzags across the front of the weathered brick walk-up with a barbershop at street level. Sofia steps over the jagged cracks in the sidewalk and reaches for the grime-ringed buzzer next to the front door.

"Is that you, gorgeous?" asks a muffled voice from the floors above her head.

"In the flesh," she says coyly. "Let me up?"

A buzz rattles the dented metal door, and she climbs four flights of stairs. Paint peels off the walls in strips yellowing to the color of nicotine. With every step, the narrow stairwell gives the sense that it's closing in on itself. Leo could afford a nicer place, but this building better suits his artist persona. His door is cracked open when she reaches the landing.

"Hello?" she says to the empty room. She shuts the door and steps into the dimly lit space. Like Caroline, Leo was never expected to clean up after himself. Half-empty liquor bottles, packs of cigarettes, painting supplies, and other junk are scattered over the kitchen counter and coffee table.

"We're out here! Join us." Leo's voice floats in through an open window. We? She shrugs off her bag and clambers through the door that leads to the balcony. It's so narrow, the balcony is hardly more than an outcropping from the wall. There isn't much space to stand, so she leans against the doorframe and smiles at the two men seated in front of her.

"I see you've somewhat recovered from the other night," Leo says, his Cheshire cat smile spreading across full lips. He balances a joint between two fingers and sips from a can of beer.

"Somewhat." She bends to kiss him, careful to drape her hair over one shoulder to hide her bruise from this stranger next to Leo. "Hey, I'm Sofia."

"Avi," he says, and he adjusts his sunglasses. The circular lenses are like two black holes perched on his delicate, almost elfin features. He's bare-chested with several gold chains glittering around his neck, and he wears an open, silky kimono embroidered with poppies. With the look of a vampire or a half-starved couture model, Avi radiates cool indifference.

"So." Avi stubs out a cigarette and incrementally lowers and raises his head as he unapologetically looks Sofia up and down. "*You're* the girl Leo won't shut up about," he says flatly. "His childhood love."

Sofia wonders how much of the truth Leo has told Avi. Did he tell him that she was the tragic working-class girl who has tagged along with the Archer family for years? Or did Leo describe her as the manic pixie dream girl she wants him to see? She'll need to tread carefully with Avi; something tells her that he's sharper than his exterior lets on.

"That's me," she says, turning on her charm. She takes the joint Leo proffers and inhales, her eyes on the gray horizon.

"That's sweet," Avi says this with the tone of someone who rarely finds sweetness in anything. "This guy is a genius, you know. I'd be his muse in a heartbeat." It's true. Leo's work was already gathering both buzz and extra zeros on discreetly placed price tags. He is undeniably talented: it's part of what draws Sofia to him, despite everything.

"Sorry, the position of muse is filled," Leo says, and reaches out to pull Sofia onto his lap. She curls into him and drapes her legs over the arm of the narrow metal chair. Leo's magnetic pull is already starting to work, to make her feel wanted, a part of the untouchable Archer world.

"This is the friend I was telling you about, Sofia," he continues after exhaling a stream of smoke. "Av, you knew Brooke Winters at Brown, didn't you?" Leo's blue eyes sparkle with curiosity.

"Oh god, yes," Avi says as he pushes his sunglasses back on his head, revealing purple half-moon shadows under hazy eyes. Sofia can tell he's trying very hard to sound as if he's bored with this conversation already, but he's not entirely successful. "That little psycho." Sofia's heart trips, like it missed a step going down the staircase in Leo's building. "We thought for sure she'd dropped out of school for good after sophomore year—just like you, Leo." Avi smirks.

"That was different," Leo says defensively. He'd lasted a few semesters at NYU before realizing there were more pleasurable uses for his inheritance than tuition. "Pursuing art isn't the same as fucking one of your married professors, now, is it? Most of the time, anyway." He lets out a laugh.

"What?" Sofia asks, and she can hear the hunger in her own voice. She inches to the edge of the seat, the arm of the chair digging into her legs, but Leo pulls her back.

"Or something like that. It got weird. I heard Brooke was arrested or something and had to transfer out. But honestly, we all saw it coming," Avi says, stretching his arms behind his head. "My roommate's girlfriend was a friend of hers—she said Brooke's that preppy 'Goody-Two-Shoes with daddy issues' type who turns into a complete freak when an authority figure in a tweed jacket walks in the room. Hot but crazy, you know?" He pauses to light another cigarette.

"I heard she was *obsessed* with that professor," Avi goes on, relishing the juicy details. "Full pathetic stalker level. Like, the guy was *married with kids* and everything."

Sofia thinks of Brooke: the kind of girl who seems incapable of an overdue library book, let alone a full-blown home-wrecking scandal. But then, that's how so many girls like her seem, isn't it?

"But is it true, this whole affair thing?" she asks.

"Who knows," Avi says. "She literally disappeared like a thief in the night, so it must have been bad, but not bad enough to stop her from getting into Yale, clearly." He shrugs. "If you really want to know, I have a friend with, let's say . . ."—he smiles wryly—"a *flexible* approach to his job in the office of student conduct."

"Tyler?" Leo asks. He rubs her thigh absent-mindedly.

"Yeah." Avi stands and stretches, lazy as a house cat in a patch of sun.

Leo laughs. "So his parents finally made him get a real job?"

"It happens to the best of us," Avi says. "I'm getting another drink." He clambers back into the apartment. Sofia runs her fingers through Leo's hair and angles her body even closer to his.

"That was interesting," she says, gazing at him and seeing only *her.*

"*Mmm,*" Leo replies, exhaling the earthy smell of the weed. He closes his eyes and tips his head back. Statuesque and effortlessly handsome, even more so in a relaxed pose, he is every inch an Archer. Sofia remembers glimpsing their family through the Santorini's kitchen door as it swung back and forth, the image shrinking with every swing. They were the very picture of the sort of people who ruled over Nantucket—and over Sofia's family. So close, and yet so indescribably far away. Sofia traces Leo's jawline, savoring the feel of Archer skin on hers.

"Remind me why you care so much about this Brooke situation?" he asks, opening his eyes and staring at the sky.

"Isn't it obvious after the other night?" she asks, hoping for some clue about Caroline's cutting, cryptic words the morning before.

"What are you talking about?" There's genuine confusion in Leo's question.

"It's just—" She hesitates, wondering if it's worth digging for answers. "Caroline mentioned I might have gone a little overboard, maybe said some things to Brooke. I was mean, apparently, but I didn't say anything untrue."

"Oh, that. She'll get over it," Leo says. "She's just jealous I'm with her best friend." His fingers knead into her skin.

"I know." She sighs, refocusing on the task at hand. "Anyway, I think Brooke has some serious issues and is, like, *latching* onto your sister ever since she moved into our suite. It's weird, especially now considering her history. I just had this gut feeling something's off with her. Would *you* want someone like that around Caroline all the time?" she asks, carefully calculating the impact these words will have on Leo. He doesn't answer right away, but his eyebrows furrow.

"Of course not," he says finally. Each of these words sags under a heavy weight. Having lost their mother as teenagers, Caroline and Leo were left to more or less fend for themselves as Bill Archer, the only father figure Caroline had ever known and Leo's actual father, had a very public affair with his married secretary and started to drink his way toward an early grave. They fiercely protect each other unlike any brother and sister Sofia has ever known, both determined to shield the other from more emotional blows.

"Neither do I," she says as she softly kisses his cheek. "Besides, I know you love getting to the bottom of a mystery as much as I do."

"That *is* true. I'm not one to let a little risk get in the way of a good story," Leo says with a conniving smile.

"Words to live by, indeed," Avi says archly as he steps back onto the balcony with a tall glass filled with ice, clear liquid, and lime slices. He swipes compulsively at his nose. "Remember Paris?"

"Barely, but that's the point. Can you text your friend, Avi? I think I sense a reconnaissance mission brewing," Leo says.

"Sure. The guy owes me a favor anyway." Avi pulls out his phone. "And I wouldn't mind knowing what happened there. My mom loves getting dirt on her friends or, like, her friends' kids or whatever. I'm heading back up to Providence today if you're up for a little fun."

"That's perfect, actually," Leo says. "A buddy of mine is working on a light installation I've been wanting to check out. What do you say, gorgeous?" he says, his breath hot in Sofia's ear. "Come with me? I want to finish our session from the other night anyway." His nonchalance unnerves her.

"You know I'm game," Sofia says. "I just need to be back in New Haven by Tuesday, or they might actually kick me out this time." She tries to keep her tone light, but fear swoops low in the back of her mind. But then she looks at Leo's face, and she can almost feel the manic energy surging through his body. She loves this about him. The two of them are never more restless than when they've been standing still too long, and for Leo, that usually means not standing still at all. Unlike at Yale, Sofia actually belongs in Leo's tumultuous art world. Women like Sofia always do. As long as they're sexy enough, game enough, tireless enough, women like her can always find a perch in the gilded cages men like Leo create for them.

"Excellent," Avi says, downing his drink so fast, it's as if he's unhinged his jaw to ease the passage of alcohol into his bloodstream. "I'm too fucked up. You can drive."

He tosses Sofia his car keys in a motion perfected by a life of valet.

CHAPTER 9

Caroline

Now

Eric is standing in a far corner when I walk back into the room, his eyes locked on his phone. Sara Patel has vanished into the swelling crowd of the Women Who Tech conference: the aspiring #boss-babes, power-suited women, and tech nerds like me gathered to launch their brands out of garages and coffee shops and into the real world. I wave at a few of the people I recognize from the week's workshops: a mother of four launching an organic kids' meal sub-scription service, a woman who founded a microloan company for veterans, the CEO of a new dating app. Throughout the weekend, the organizers encouraged us to network and "share our stories," but we all know only one of us is walking out of here with a $200,000 investment. Play nice. Pretend it isn't a competition. Pre-tend we don't care about winning as long as everyone had fun and felt *seen*. Embrace "sisterhood," even if we have to manufacture it out of thin air. Isn't that what women are supposed to do?

"Thanks for covering for me. It's my brother," I say when I get back to Eric, and he looks up from his phone immediately, eyes wide with concern.

"Oh my god, is he okay?"

"Yeah, he'll be out tomorrow and is already planning an art show in a few days. Let's hope rehab sticks this time." A mixture of hope and dread cinches its familiar knot in my stomach. It comes with the territory of loving an addict. With loving Leo.

"It will," Eric says, his tone reassuring. "Should we get back to it?"

"Please," I say, desperate for the distraction. The room is filling as the final conference sessions empty around the vacant podium facing us.

"I went ahead and did some damage control with our little troll situation," Eric continues. "I don't think the comment was posted long enough for that many people to see it."

"Good," I say. I'm about to ask Eric how it went with the Quantum execs, but the words evaporate along with the rest of my thoughts as Issa Blake, chairwoman of the conference, takes the microphone, and a hush falls hard and fast around us. An electric current of tension circulates through the crowd, intensifying in the faces looking hungrily at the podium.

"Thank you all for a remarkable Women Who Tech Startup Accelerator," Issa says before stepping back to join in the applause. My palms swap sheens of sweat as I bring them together, and I replay the past two days in my head. Meetings with impressive female executives, a panel dedicated to reviewing my meticulous business plan—hell, Sheryl Sandberg herself said Equilibrium has promise. I leaned the fuck *in*. Would it be enough?

"The talent, vision, and drive each of you have demonstrated this week is truly an inspiration. When I look around this room, I *know* the future is female!" Issa's eyes shine, and she pauses for more applause, a torturous delay that I remind myself to smile through. "And now it is my pleasure to announce the recipient of our Accelerator Investment Fund. Please join me in congratulating . . . Sergeant Camila López, founder of Phoenix Rising Capital!"

I vaguely register Eric's arm around my shoulders as Sergeant López takes the stage in her army fatigues and shakes Issa's hand. Even as wave after wave of panic crashes over me, I think about how much she deserves this. Camila and her wife had built the fund from the ground up, and they are going to impact so many women and their families. A real smile finds me in the midst of my downward spiral.

"I'll check in with you tomorrow, okay?" I say to Eric, who pulls me in for a quick one-armed hug just before I turn to get out of here.

"Hey," he says, resolutely upbeat, "this wasn't for nothing. Quantum wants to meet with you next week." I nod. That's something, I guess.

But as I take the subway to the bus home, darkness cloaking the city around me, all I can think about is the last resort that's glaring me in the face. And as I unlock the bottom, top, and double dead bolt of my Queens studio, I can almost feel my pride scraping at the sides of my throat as I force it down.

Loud, rhythmic thuds from the floor above announce that Rick and Letizia have—enthusiastically—reconciled. I pry off my vintage Jimmy Choo's, Mom's favorite pair, and inspect the black leather. Another scuff. Fifteen years will do that to a pair of shoes, but I know I'll wear them until they fall apart. She's been gone for so long, but I still cling to every piece of her I have left. I take the six steps necessary to cross my tiny, spartan apartment and ink in the scratch with a Sharpie from my desk. I sink onto my bed, rub at my throbbing temples, and close my eyes, trying not to replay the past few hours in my head. When I open my eyes, I see that the stain on the ceiling has gained an inch or two around its splotched brown-gray perimeter.

I have to ask Leo for more money. There's no other way out of this now, not unless I walk away from five years of growing my company from a speck of code. Rolling onto my side, I face my favorite photo of the three of us: Mom, Leo, and me at the beach, snapped on one of the rare weekends Bill let her out of his grasp. The thought of my stepfather stokes rage in the pit of my stomach. It didn't take Bill long to drink himself to death after Mom died, or to ensure that the entirety of their estate went to Leo, his heir and golden boy. *Bill takes care of us, sweetie:* Mom's words, spoken in a half-hopeful, half-terrified whisper, echo in my memory. It had been her mantra since the wealthy, powerful Bill Archer deigned to marry her, a fragile single mother with a two-year-old in tow. You grow up fast when you learn to recognize your mother's lies, especially the ones she tells herself. She said it after he locked her in their bedroom for two days. She said it even after he'd made her lip bleed, breaking his rule of keeping her face pretty. It was a rule he mostly followed when he moved on to me.

I sit up, and I do some mental math that does nothing to ease my mind. Tomorrow I'll be picking up Leo from his most expensive attempt at sobriety yet, The Oak Grove Center. His inheritance from Bill had been dwindling even before this rehab stint, his third, and I know how much just a week at Oak Grove costs. Hating myself, but knowing I have to get a grip on the situation somehow, I do what I've been doing everything in my power to avoid. I pull up the Chase banking app on my phone, type Leo's email address into the log-in screen, and put in the password I remember from the last time I had to stoop this low. Rejected. Biting my lip, I rack my brain for what the new password might be.

Leo was always lazy with technology, so I start with the obvious, his favorite pet: Bella, the sweet-natured golden retriever puppy Mom got us when I turned ten. Her name and Leo's birthday in a variety of combinations doesn't work. Bella made the mistake of chewing through Bill's Gucci loafers on Christmas Eve. I try her name with the year Leo sold his first painting. Nothing. I can still hear the gunshot that cut through the crystallized icy stillness of that night, still feel the tears that froze on my face after Bill screamed at me to *take care of it,* still see Bella's little body disappearing as I buried her in the snow. I remember thinking about how little she was. How cold she must be.

I direct a sigh at the stain on my ceiling. It wasn't until Sofia that I had anyone but Leo to hide with, anywhere to run. Bill made being nowhere safer than home, and with Sofia, that was easy. All those summers, she knew better than anyone how to disappear: hidden coves, lonely crests on the dunes where we could stare at the stars until someone noticed I hadn't come home. More often than not, no one did. Leo had driven off three nannies before Bill gave up. *Nowhere.* That's what Sofia and I called our secret world.

It occurs to me that I probably have just one more attempt before Leo's account gets automatically locked and a warning email sent. My fingers hover over the smudged screen. Bella's name with our mom's birthday makes a spinning wheel appear as the app loads Leo's account. I hold my breath, but the number, the impossibly, dangerously low number, that stares back at me knocks all the air from my lungs.

CHAPTER 10

Brooke

Now

Josh's side of the bed is cold when I wake up. Glancing at the alarm clock, I see it's just after six A.M. An hour's sleep, maybe two, snatched between replaying the worst of my past over and over again as the hours crawled sluggishly toward morning. I roll toward where Josh should be and run a hand over the rumpled empty sheets.

My movement displaces Piper, who had been nestled cozily in the nook between my shoulder and neck. She starts to meow in protest as I sit up, but it gets lost in a yawn. Clearly I'm not the only one who would rather avoid the world waiting outside this room. I reach for my phone, dread stirring from where it had barely settled in my mind. Nothing. Just texts from Mel and Caroline—the only two people I know who are regularly up at this hour, Mel because of her third-trimester insomnia, Caroline because she has never needed more than four or five hours of sleep—both wishing me luck on my first day at Woodlands.

I consider the plan I'd come up with as I watched the ceiling fan spin in endless circles past one and two A.M. There's something I have to do, but first I need to make sure Josh really is gone. I step out of bed and open our bedroom door, sure that the apartment will be empty. An unexpected, delicious smell of apples, cinnamon, and toasting walnuts drifts through the hallway.

"Morning, sunshine," Josh says as I walk into the kitchen. He's in running gear that emphasizes his tall, lean physique, and there's a dish towel draped over his shoulder.

"Morning," I say hesitantly. It comes out like a question.

"I call these my I-was-an-asshole-to-you-and-I'm-sorry muffins." He bends to extract a fragrant tin from the oven. Josh sets it on the counter, crosses over to me, and pulls me in for a hug. "I'm so sorry, Brooke," he says into my hair. "I don't know what got into me last night. We should have just stayed at the office so you could rest up before your first day of orientation." Josh's words spill out in a rush like they always do when he's stressed, sorry, or desperate to explain himself. "Of course this job is important to you, and kids everywhere need good teachers." I gently push him away so I can look into his eyes and start to believe what he's saying.

"And Miss Winters is the best there is, *but* . . ."—he holds up his index finger and turns back toward the oven—"she simply cannot be expected to dazzle on an empty stomach." He says this in the tone of a prim schoolmarm as he extracts a fresh muffin and places it on a plate next to a steaming thermos of Lady Grey tea, my favorite.

"Absolutely no chance of dazzling. Not without baked goods," I say with a smile that makes me want to burst into tears. "It's okay, babe. I love you." I lean over to plant a quick kiss on his cheek before tearing off a piece of muffin so it can cool faster. "But don't think I can always be bought with carbs after we're married," I say, blowing on the golden-brown bite. "That'll work only 50 percent of the time."

"I'll take it," Josh says. He whips off the dish towel and reaches for his right ankle for a quad stretch. "Seriously, though, good luck today." He wobbles slightly as he switches legs.

"Thank you," I say. After I feed Piper, I walk back across the apartment toward the bathroom. "Have a good run," I call over my shoulder. I surprise myself at how normal it all sounds, like a script I'm writing live for my new *Twilight Zone* life, with me both on-screen and in the audience.

The medicine cabinet mirror, however, brings me crashing back to reality. My face looks drawn, my skin so pale it's almost gray. As expected, the dark circles under my eyes will require industrial-strength cover-up. For a second, I wonder why Josh didn't say anything about my appearance, but then, *Wow, you look like shit* doesn't have a conciliatory ring to it. This is not the face of a great first impression, not even a decent one. If my whole life is about to explode, I'll be damned if I look like a Tim Burton character when it happens. After a top-speed shower and meticulous layers of makeup, the kind designed to make it look like I'm not wearing any, I think I'm beginning to resemble my old self. A swipe of mascara and deep berry lip gloss, and I at least look the part of a functional person.

Outside, the sky is brightening from pewter to brilliant blue. I pad across the hall to our bedroom and open the closet: suits in black, navy, and charcoal on one side, bright sweaters, cute but practical dresses, and other standard teacher wear on the other. The outfit I'd selected for the first day of school is eager at the front of the rack, a habit I've had since I was eight.

I lay the herringbone sheath dress and black cardigan on our bed next to a snoozing Piper. Glancing back at the closet, I remember the less pleasant task I have to do. Disposing of evidence is never pleasant. The shoebox at the back of my closet will have to be dealt with, and fast, now that Josh is out of the apartment. That is, assuming "Sofia" didn't take it when she snapped the photo.

Kneeling on the floor of the closet, I extract my most comfortable pair of pumps before reaching for the box I kept hidden behind some old winter boots. The cardboard blends in perfectly with the dark corner of the closet. Years ago in that horrible facility, my therapist looked at me through the rectangular glasses at the end of his nose and said that I needed to compartmentalize my trauma and own my role in the disaster that followed. In this box, I took his advice literally. My fingertips graze the lid and instinctively retract, as if high voltage runs through the contents, warning me not to disturb their secrets or their pain. But I have no choice, not if I want to stop "Sofia" from getting their hands on it. I slowly lift the lid.

I breathe a sigh of relief as I see that the handful of photographs, the fragments and tiny artifacts of Patrick and me, and everything else I'd buried, are still stashed away. But this is far from the only proof of what happened, it's just my part in it, and I can't know for certain if this box is as untouched as it looks. My knees crack as I stand, holding the box away from me, careful not to let flecks of dust scatter onto my skin. Placing it carefully in a plastic bag, I resolve to dump it at a random gas station on my way to Woodlands: if my stalker knows where I live, they know where my trash goes. I should have disposed of this years ago for my own sake. Now I have no choice.

The clock reads 6:55. Time to get moving. Each carefully selected garment slides snugly on my frame, and as I step into my heels and fasten a delicate pearl drop in each ear, a flutter of excitement flickers in my chest, as unlikely as the beat of hummingbird wings in a hurricane. Josh was right about one thing: I love what I do.

As I shove the trash bag into the depths of my massive leather tote bag, I remind myself that Caroline will know what to do about this Sofia situation. Caroline always knows what to do. I type the Woodlands address into Google Maps to make sure I take the quickest way there, and the app populates with a route highlighted with red. *Shit.* It's going to take me twice as long to get there as I thought. The disposal of the shoebox will have to wait until the end of the day. Snatching my keys from the dish on the hall table, I rush down the stairs and into my car. Bluetooth activates as soon as the keys are in the ignition, and Florence and the Machine surges on the stereo. I turn the volume up and peel out of our apartment complex parking lot as fast as I dare.

For months after the accident that killed Sofia, I couldn't be in a car, let alone drive one, for longer than ten minutes without panicking. Even now, the memory of Caroline's sheet-white face at my hospital bedside sends a trickle of fear straight through me.

All I know is what she told me over the sound of the machines in the hospital that confirmed I was still alive with each low beep. Caroline filled the black void of my memory with the story it couldn't supply on its own: Sofia was driving Caroline and me home, wasted on booze and whatever pills Leo had given her. We all looked the other way with anything to do with Leo back then.

Sofia lost control on a tight turn and spiraled into an incoming car, sending Caroline, Sofia, and me crashing into the two shadowy passengers in the other car, a collision that sent us all careening into the woods on the side of the highway.

I can still see Caroline's haunted face as she told me this, how, just for a split second, every muscle in her face stilled, and her eyes fixed on mine. Her face formed the very picture of truth. It's what she always does when she lies. And in that moment, I recognized exactly what she was doing to protect both of us, and I knew I had to play along, no matter how twisted the game.

The driver's window was completely shattered, and they found Sofia's body crumpled on the ground a few feet from where we'd smashed to a halt. Sofia was driving, that's what we told the police. Sofia took the blame. The extent of her injuries made our story believable, and our pretty faces made the narrative easy to swallow.

The dead don't have anything left to lose. That's what I told myself every time the guilt threatened to consume me: what we did was better for the living, better for everyone. But even at Sofia's funeral, something lurked in Caroline's eyes and the set of her jaw that told me it was never that simple. I knew Caroline wasn't telling the whole truth about what really happened.

But as usual, I was too much of a coward to ask questions.

I shake myself out of this rabbit hole and back to the present. I half reach into my bag to text Caroline and set a time to meet. But I stop. This person can access my home: what are the odds they're monitoring my email, phone calls, text messages, everything? If I'm going to get out of this unscathed, I have to be smart. The light turns red, and traffic slows to an impatient stop. There's a gas station on the left, one I wish I had time to stop at now and be rid of the black hole at the bottom of my purse. A neon-green sign in a grimy window behind the gas pumps reads: "Cell phones here."

Yes. This is exactly the sort of situation that requires a burner phone. Another little errand to do, and the sooner the better. Google Maps instructs me to take the next left, onto a quiet, tree-lined drive. Shining granite plaques mounted on twin pillars mark the entrance to Woodlands Academy. One plaque tells visitors the school was founded in 1904. The other is engraved with the motto *Cum conatus et scientia, erit lux.* No English translation. No pity for the peasants who can't read Latin, apparently.

Morning light glances off the glossy ivy that covers Woodlands' brick walls. Surrounded by precisely trimmed hedges and pruned rosebushes, colonial-style east and west wings flank either side of the main school. I can glimpse sprawling fields and outbuildings as I turn down the music in my car and pull into a full staff parking lot. Everywhere, the campus is buzzing with action. I hear the low growl of lawn mowers perfecting the already immaculate grounds, and there are a few purposeful-looking people, no doubt other teachers preparing for the start of the school year, walking in and out of the building.

I switch off the engine and reach for the compact in my bag. Checking my face in the mirror one last time, I add a swipe of powder to my forehead and nose and arrange an approachable expression. As I open my car door, the smell of freshly cut grass and August sun warming asphalt floods inside. After a deep, steadying breath, I take confident, brisk strides across the parking lot and up the stairs to the main entrance. Past the heavy oak doors, a woman in her mid-fifties at the reception desk smiles broadly at me as I step into the atrium.

"Hey there! New teacher?" she chirps, leaning forward with a clipboard in hand.

"Hi, yes. Brooke Winters, English," I say.

"Welcome to Woodlands, Brooke. I'm Wendy Campbell, reception." A row of silver charm bracelets rattles as she shakes my hand. Wendy has a kind face, close-cropped iron-gray hair, and a warm smile sure to set kids and parents instantly at ease. "This is my first day, too." Wendy puts on the turquoise glasses attached to the beaded chain around her neck. "Now let's see here." She consults the list on her clipboard. "Winters . . . Winters. Here you are." She makes a tick on the clipboard and reaches into a desk drawer.

"Here's your classroom key and a building fob that will unlock the external doors. But don't worry, maintenance said they won't activate those until the students get here. Makes it easier for teachers to set up." She slides the keys and a folder embossed with the Woodlands crest across the desk to me. "You'll want to swing by IT to pick up your computer and such. Oh, but look at the time," she says, glancing at her desktop screen. "The teaching staff is meeting in the library in a few minutes." I nod. "Yours is classroom 135, just down that hallway to your left."

"Thank you so much," I say, and I set off down the corridor. The window-lined classrooms I pass are spacious, each containing no

more than a dozen or so chairs arranged in seminar-style semicir-
cles. My heels echo against the polished floor, and I follow the neat
brass numbers beside each door until I see 135 at the end of the
hall. I twist my key in the lock and step inside.

It's a beautiful room, the sort I used to fantasize about while
scrubbing crusted gum and graffiti off the undersides of desks
bolted to my old classroom's floor. Bright sunlight streams through
arched windows along the right-hand wall, and four well-stocked
bookshelves stand along the exposed brick at the back of the room.
Pristine carpet muffles my steps as I walk past two short rows of
student desks toward the brand-new Smart Board facing them. To
the left of the screen is a massive teacher's desk made of solid, shining wood.

I reach into my bag to take out a notebook and the folder Wendy
gave me and stash my bag under the desk. After checking the campus map, I walk as fast as I can without running back down the hall
and up a flight of stairs. Voices grow louder as I approach the open
double doors that lead to the library.

"Glad I'm not the only one who's running late," a deep voice
says behind me. Startled, I turn abruptly, and I bump into a tall
man holding a Starbucks cup and a stack of papers.

"Oh gosh, I'm so sorry," I say, looking up into a pair of smiling
dark eyes.

"Hey, as long as you don't spill my coffee, we're good," he says,
and he leans in conspiratorially. "Lutz's meetings are hard to get
through without it." His grin broadens to show a row of bright
white teeth that contrast strikingly with his tawny skin. He looks
to be in his late thirties, early forties maybe, with thick salt-and-
pepper hair, and I imagine he is rather popular with the moms of
Woodlands Academy. "I'm Antony, by the way. And you must be
new here."

"Actually, I'm Brooke, not 'new here.'" I say it before I realize
that I have made quite possibly the worst joke of all time. He laughs
anyway, and it even sounds genuine.

"Nice," he says, raising his eyebrows as we step into the crowded library. Groups of teachers are already seated at long tables arranged at the center of the room.

"Sorry," I say as my cheeks flush, and I resist the urge to resign and start over at a new school, ideally in another state. "English-teacher humor really is as bad as the kids say it is."

"I think *cringe* is the preferred term now," he quips. "And that's perfect, actually, makes my first order of business easy. Akira asked me to find you and bring you over to meet the rest of our department." We wind our way between tables of teachers and stop at one at the back of the room. Five people in deep conversation are seated around it.

Antony raises his voice slightly over theirs. "New blood, everyone. Best behavior, please." The English teachers turn toward us.

"It's wonderful to have you at Woodlands, Brooke," Akira says, rising from her chair. I remember Akira Go from my job interview: a blunt black bob almost as formidable as her PhD, cheekbones that could cut glass, and disruption-quelling *Don't mess with me* eyes. It's jarring to see a friendly smile replace the inscrutable poker face she wore when we met.

"Let me introduce the rest of the team," she says. "I see you've met Antony Ramirez, first-year English. He'll be your induction mentor." Antony raises his Starbucks in my direction as he sits and opens a notebook. "This is Kelly Fitzgerald, sophomore World Lit." A petite blond woman about my age waves. "She's—" Akira is interrupted by a raised voice coming from the front of the room.

"Welcome back, faculty." A man I recognize as Dr. Lutz, the principal, or rather *headmaster,* of Woodlands, is speaking. "Please take a seat so we can get started." He adjusts his crimson tie and surveys the room.

"Mrs. Quinn, if you please." A tiny woman wearing librarian glasses, who is probably in fact a librarian, scurries over to change the PowerPoint slide for him. "*Cum conatus et scientia, erit lux,*" Dr.

Lutz intones with gravitas and, I assume, perfect pronunciation as the words appear on-screen. "I find revisiting our Woodlands motto so invigorating, especially at the start of term, as I'm sure do all of you." He pauses to check for nods around the room.

I do my best to look like I know exactly what he's talking about, and I feel a nudge at my elbow. Antony slides a paper toward me. Neat handwriting in green pen: **With endeavor and knowledge, there will be light (had to google it).** I mouth *thank you.* He gives me a smile that crinkles the corners of his eyes and reveals symmetrical dimples.

"Just a few start of term business items to get us all on the same page before we break into departments for this morning's curriculum alignment session. Last year was a banner year for our school." Dr. Lutz nods to Mrs. Quinn. "Not only did we send a record number of students to the Ivy League and other top universities, but our return to traditional methodologies and classical education produced the highest test scores in the state." Numbers much too small to read appear on the Smart Board behind him. Kelly shifts uncomfortably in her seat.

"Our community of parents has never expressed higher approval ratings," he continues, perhaps unaware of how much he sounds like a gloating politician. "And I know I can rely on each and every one of you to continue this trajectory of excellence into this year and beyond." Dr. Lutz gives a pompous little bow. "Especially our department chairs." His gaze lingers on Akira for a moment. "Who will be leading us all into the breach, as it were." Dr. Lutz chuckles at his own wit. His Latin might be good, but his Shakespeare references need work. I glimpse a tiny eye roll from Antony, and I suppress a grin. "Get cracking, then, and I look forward to reviewing this year's academic plans from each of you."

"Did he just say he hasn't reviewed the lesson plans he asked for over a month ago?" Kelly asks Antony in an undertone. I was wondering the same thing and am relieved someone else brought it up.

"Yes, Kelly. Yes, he did," Antony replies. The two exchange a significant look. Most people know what hotbeds schools are for rivalries, gossip, and power struggles: they just don't realize that the staff can be just as bad as the students, if not worse. Akira clears her throat.

"Let's meet in my classroom in five minutes," she says, keeping her tone upbeat. "It's right across the hall from you, Brooke." I nod and smile at her. Our group gets up and starts making our way back toward the stairs.

"Like Akira said . . ."—Antony catches my eye—"I'll be your first-year mentor. God, that sounds pretentious," he adds with a dose of self-deprecation. "Basically, I'll show you the ropes."

"Great," I say, hoping I effectively masked my disappointment. I'd been looking forward to learning from Akira herself.

"Don't worry," Antony continues as we head toward the English wing. "I won't be breathing down your neck or anything, just making a few observations here and there, and I'll generally give you some pointers: which parents are a nightmare, what Lutz looks for in evals, all that good stuff."

"That'll be very good to know," I say.

"This is me." Antony pauses at the classroom door next to mine. "See you in a few."

I step back into my classroom and let my shoulders untense. The morning's whirlwind makes it impossible to linger in my own head, and right now, that's a very good thing. Crossing over to my desk, I'm about to reach for my laptop when something catches my eye. I roll my chair backward a few inches. And with a sharp intake of breath, I realize what it is. My bag is knocked to one side. The shoebox that had been safely tucked inside it is gone.

Seizing at the bag's handles, I rifle through the contents desperately as if my fingers could somehow force the box to materialize. Nothing. All the proof of my shame, my affair, my darkest hours is in someone else's hands. I stare in disbelief at the ink-stained lining at the bottom of my bag as my throat goes dry, hating myself for delusionally thinking that life could be normal again. That mundane things like faculty meetings or attractive colleagues mean anything when all my secrets, my job, my relationship, the life I had built hangs by spider silk thread, and someone with a very sharp knife is waiting for their moment to slice it in half.

Just then, there is a knock at my door. Antony sticks his head into my classroom, and I try to extinguish the shock from my face as fast as I can, praying it wasn't a split second too late.

"Ready?" he asks with a grin.

"Yep." I add this to the growing list of the day's lies as high-octane dread roils in my gut.

CHAPTER 11

Caroline

Now

I take a few of the deep breaths Brooke is always telling me to take as swaths of green whoosh past my rental car's windows. I've forgotten what it's like to look at growing, living things. I pull off the highway and up a sloping drive that winds through groves of oak trees. A rambling white farmhouse appears ahead, the picture of tranquility and healing. I think I remember those exact words appearing on the website. There's nothing like the rolling green hills of Connecticut to incubate fragile recovering addicts.

I climb out of the car and walk through double doors into an open-concept space bathed in natural light. The walls are painted a soothing sage green and decorated with black-and-white nature shots: a mountaintop, a waterfall, a canyon. A fountain in one corner sends trickling water over smooth black stones. None of it is enough to set my mind at ease.

"Welcome to Oak Grove," says a woman clad in a uniform the same color as the walls. "Are you here to visit a patient?"

"Yes, Leo Archer. He's actually checking out today. I'm his sister," I say, handing over my driver's license. I know the drill by now.

"Wonderful. We are so glad to have been a part of Leo's recovery," she replies placidly, tapping away at the keyboard in front of her. I think back to how Leo looked the night I'd checked him in here. Emaciated, frantic, out of options, and—as I know now—burning through cash. I almost hadn't recognized my brother when he showed up at my office, veins popping out of his neck and red blotching the whites of his eyes, insisting we visit our mom's grave in the middle of the day. Leo calmed down only after I got him out of the building, promising to drive him to her memorial. Instead, I brought him here.

"You're all signed in." She slides a visitor's badge across the desk, and I pin it obediently to my shirt.

"Is he in his room right now?" I ask.

"Actually, I think he's in the pavilion finishing up some work. It's just through these doors across the lawn and past the therapeutic garden." She indicates the direction, then leans forward. "Leo is so talented. Your family must be so proud," she says. I immediately recognize the dreamy look on her face. I've seen it plenty of times when women talk about my brother.

"We're really proud of him for being here," I say as steadily as I can. *We* is easier than the truth.

I make my way across the manicured grounds, past a pristine swimming pool, a group doing yoga, and people taking leisurely walks. For the cost of this place, you'd think even the birds chirping in the distance were well paid for adding to the tranquility, peace, and healing. A breeze lifts my hair and shoots a spray of goose bumps down my arms. I feel exposed here. But then, I'm vulnerable everywhere now. Whoever is impersonating Sofia saw to that. I glance at my watch and remind myself that Eric can keep things under control for another few hours before I can get back to the city and salvage my workday.

The pavilion is a whitewashed building mostly made of tall, graceful windows. Despite everything, I smile slightly, thinking about the fantastic light Leo must be getting in there. The only movement comes from a figure in a far corner. Leo faces away from me. He's seated before a canvas covered in blues and shades of gray, his left hand working on what looks like a face at the center of the painting. I open the door and cross into the sun-dappled room. In the stillness, bright light captures every particle of dust, suspended as if frozen in the air.

"Hey, Leo," I say, stepping closer to the artist and his work. He ignores me, his brush still in motion. I can make out more details now: a sheet of dark hair, skin like ivory, those eyes. I freeze. For a long silence that stretches, then tautens, the only thing I can feel is a tentacle of unease coiling around my insides. For the second time in a few days, Sofia seems to hover somewhere between my peripheral vision and my subconscious.

"You can't show this," I say, my voice breaking. "Not to anyone."

"Why not?" Leo asks without missing a beat. "This is the best thing I've done in months. Years, maybe. It'll anchor my show next week." Leo turns to me, and his signature grin, mischief that emanates from the shine of his perfect teeth and a glint in his eyes, unfurls across his features. Words turn to ash in my mouth. He's captured her perfectly.

The shadowing renders the exact scythe's curve of her cheekbone. The sharp angles of her hip and elbow complement the fluid twist of the bedsheets in the background of the canvas. Sofia had a haunting face, even when she was alive. Even as she slept. With her dark features on alabaster skin, she always reminded me of a princess plucked from a Gothic fairy tale with a morbid medieval ending.

"Please." It scares me how much desperation and panic creep into that one syllable. She needs to stay in the past, not on public display for questions to lead down the twisted rabbit hole that is Sofia Eliades's death.

"Afraid people will ask questions?" His brush continues its delicate detailing of her eyelashes. A flash of white-hot anger cauterizes my fear. I used to think trouble followed Leo. The pills started after Mom died, her cancer too sudden and too consuming for him to handle. And after Bill's heart attack, everything just got worse. Leo retreated into his art, his rotating door of sycophantic friends, into what he could control, indifferent to any consequences outside his orbit.

"Yes. I *am* afraid people will ask questions," I say far too loudly as I step nearer the canvas and face him. We're lucky the pavilion is empty. "And if you had any idea what we *both* could lose, you'd be scared, too." I lower my voice to a whisper. "Something weird is happening, Leo. I don't know what's going on or why, but just trust me, okay? The very last thing we need right now is people asking questions about Sofia. My company can't survive if there's a *smudge* on my record, let alone something like this." My chest is heaving, but still, he paints. "No Equilibrium, no way for me to pay you back. Ever."

I'm referencing our unspoken agreement that, with enough profit or a private equity sale, a portion of that money would be Leo's safety net. We like to pretend his art sales won't stall, that Leo would deign to get a real job and lose his appetite for the finer things, but we both know he'll need my help. It's a fact as inevitable as the relapse I'm trying not to dread, to mentally prepare for. But he can't know that I know his inheritance is almost gone.

Leo spent the bulk of the Archer estate on a twenty-acre parcel of land in upstate New York. His vision was to establish a creatives' retreat and gallery away from the city, an oasis for writers, filmmakers, and artists. And he'd realized it with no expense spared: he had studio cabins built in the thick woods, and he transformed a massive barn into a multilevel gallery space. It was even featured in *New York* magazine when a few big names cycled through the Oasis. With those names came a juice bar. Then a yoga studio and a Zen garden that just had to be crafted by a world-renowned feng shui expert flown in from Shanghai. But there was never any money coming in, not that it mattered to Leo, as long as creativity was thriving and his name was in the press. Everything was going well until it wasn't, until he started using again. Even though he's facing away from me, I keep my face set in a neutral expression.

"Is that why you're really here, dear sister? To ask for more of *my* money?" Leo says blithely. My cheeks flare, but not before I register his complete lack of reaction to what I just told him about Sofia. "You *were* going to ask for money, weren't you?" Leo accurately reads my silence, maybe even my mind. He sighs and presses his paintbrush into the palette. "How many more times do I need to bail you out, Caroline?" he accuses. Part of me cowers in shame at this. Another part thinks of that fucking juice bar.

I decide it's best to be honest. "I was going to ask. But I want to make sure you're okay first, you know that, right?" It's Leo's turn to stay silent. "You have to understand, Leo. At the rate you're going, with the way you've structured the upstate property, there's money going out but nothing coming in. Equilibrium can save both of us, but not if *this* . . ."—I gesture at the painting—"gets out there."

Maddeningly, Leo hasn't missed a stroke. He's still as intent on painting as if I weren't there. As Leo reaches his brush toward the nearly finished image of Sofia, I snatch it, pulling it away from him. I want to snap him back to the ice-cold reality ahead of us. But his grip is too strong, and our hands push and pull the brush until a slash of paint rips across Sofia's body in one long jagged stroke.

"Caroline!" Leo growls, his voice low and feral. The stool he was sitting on knocks to the ground with a crash that seems to echo in this empty, beautiful room. His face, so serene seconds ago, is contorted with rage, eyes fiery, fists clenched. I wince. He won't forgive me for this easily, or at all.

"I'm sorry," I say, a mixture of fear and anger writhing inside me. He turns his back to me and runs paint-stained fingers through thick curls of dark gold hair that have regained their shine since he stopped using.

"I'm sorry, Leo." My voice breaks as I swipe my tears away. Leo still won't face me.

"I can fix it," he says, more to Sofia's disfigured likeness than to me. "And I thought you said Equilibrium is doing well." His voice stays calm, but not as calm as he thinks it is. For the first time in this conversation, fear shadows his words.

"It is. But there's something I have to tell you while I drive you back to the Oasis," I say, resigned to what has to happen now: he has to know everything. He finally looks me in the eye.

It's almost a relief, telling Leo the truth. "There's something you should know about what happened that night." I take a deep breath. "And we need to talk about Jenna."

CHAPTER 12

Sofia

Then

"And you're sure he's got a class this afternoon? Brooke's professor?" Sofia asks Avi as she downshifts with difficulty. Sleek though it looks, his vintage Porsche is a pain in the ass to drive.

"Positive," Avi says from where he lounges in the back seat. "The girl I'm seeing is in his British literature seminar, which ends at three. She always comes out of it horny as fuck."

"I thought you and Zara were still together," Leo says curiously.

"Yeah, well we decided that being exclusive is for our parents' generation," Avi says with a sigh. "Polyamory is just so much less oppressive. She'd never want me not to be *me*. Zara's not like other girls." He says this as if it's the highest praise he could bestow upon anyone with ovaries. Sofia bites her tongue and presses down on the gas pedal.

Their surroundings take on an increasingly hipster-friendly character as they approach Brown's campus. Students sit hunched over laptop screens at coffee shops, Bose headphones shutting out the world around them. Bikes tick alongside the car, their riders' jean cuffs rolled up past their ankles, expensive-looking backpacks slung over their shoulders.

"My place is just up here on the right," Avi says lazily. "You can park anywhere on the street." Sofia pulls up to a neat brick building just outside of the campus. She and Leo get out of the front seat and follow Avi through a set of polished doors to an elevator caged in an elaborate brass grate.

"If you're going to blend in, you might want to change," Leo says to her as the metal doors creak open.

"True," Sofia agrees, looking down at the dress no college student would ever wear to class. The contents of her bag will come in handy. On the top floor, they walk along a paneled hallway covered in green carpet that looks and feels like moss under Sofia's feet. The wallpaper is intricate, vines throttling plump rosebuds. It's narrow, claustrophobic even, and a faint smell of mothballs and a sickly floral perfume follows them through the building.

Avi's is the second door on the right. This stifling place, with its grandma aesthetic and dim lighting behind scalloped light fixtures, is the last place Sofia would expect someone like him to live.

"My parents bought the apartment my freshman year, after taking one look at those god-awful dorm rooms," Avi says, as if reading her mind. He pats down the pockets of his black jeans and artfully acid-washed jacket in search of his keys. As Sofia steps closer, she notices a brown envelope sticking out from underneath the doorframe.

"What's that?" she asks, indicating the envelope.

"*That* is Tyler making good on that favor he owes me," Avi says, snapping up the envelope and turning his keys in the lock. The room they enter was clearly furnished by a middle-aged woman who equates youthful masculinity with a nautical theme. Sofia suppresses a snort. For all his free-spirited bullshit, Avi knows that keeping his trust fund means remaining in mommy and daddy's good graces.

"Carol sure has a—um—aesthetic," Leo observes sardonically, taking in the sailboat-shaped lamp on the hall table and a distressed wood sign that asserts "Life's a Beach."

"Yeah, yeah," Avi says, throwing himself down onto a navy and white plaid sofa with red accent pillows. Sofia settles herself on the matching armchair opposite him and sinks at least two inches into the upholstery.

"You want to do the honors?" Avi hands over the slim envelope with exaggerated ceremony. Her pulse quickens. She slides one finger under the gluey lip of the sturdy paper, and the edge leaves her fingertip bright with a slice of red. But her hand is steady as it extracts the sheets of paper inside and catches a thumb drive.

"Okay, on a scale of one to straitjacket, what level of crazy are we looking at?" Leo joins Avi on the couch clutching three beers in his hands. Sofia takes one and savors the feel of the cool, dewy glass against her cut finger as her eyes skim gleefully through the deliciously detailed text.

"Um," Sofia says, taking a swig from the bottle, "an eleven?" A victorious smile spreads across her face.

"Well, we'll leave you to it. We're gonna go check out my friend's show. Be back later." Leo kisses her cheek.

Avi turns to Sofia on his way out the door. "Spare key is in the dish by the door. Just don't burn the place down or fuck with those figurines." He jerks his head at the porcelain whale and seamen frolicking on the mantelpiece.

"Got it," Sofia says. They shut the door behind them, rattling the seashells that dangle from the chandelier in the hallway. Her eyes resume their voracious tear through the documents.

Student Disciplinary Incident Report

Student Name: Brooke Winters

Complainant Name: Dr. Patrick J. Adams, Department of English

Student Conduct Liaison: Ann Jeffries

Date Submitted to Office of Student Conduct: 4/23/2008

Date of Incident: Multiple incidents have taken place in the past several weeks. Most recently on the 2nd, 5th, and 14th of April, 2008.

Incident Description: Brooke Winters, a sophomore at this university, was enrolled in two of Dr. Adams's literature classes in the past academic year. While she produced excellent work, she gradually developed an unhealthy attachment to Dr. Adams, one that has recently escalated. Dr. Adams noted that she attended biweekly office hours, often lingered after class to ask questions, and frequently sent emails late at night, some of which were of a personal, rather than academic, nature. Dr. Adams dismissed these actions as those of an overeager undergraduate student.

But when Dr. Adams was unable to recommend Miss Winters to his upper-level literature cohort, a distinction reserved primarily for graduate students, her behavior and attempts to contact him became increasingly troubling. Miss Winters began regularly waiting outside Dr. Adams's office, demanding that she speak with him and causing multiple scenes within the English department building. On more than one occasion, Miss Winters appeared in classes for which she was not registered and refused to leave.

Dr. Adams encouraged Miss Winters to seek psychological counseling through the Student Wellness Center, ascribing her behavior to high stress, which is not uncommon among students at this university. Not wishing to damage Miss Winters's academic standing or mental health, Dr. Adams hoped that soon the situation would resolve on its own.

However, on the dates recorded above, Dr. Adams was deeply disturbed to hear from his wife that a young woman matching Miss Winters's description had been seen outside their home and the nearby day care their son attends. On the most recent occurrence, Mrs. Adams was able to photograph Miss Winters (see attached). Dr. Adams feels he now has no choice but to pursue disciplinary action against Miss Winters in the interest of his family's safety.

Complainant Signature: Patrick J. Adams

Director of Student Conduct Signature: Ann Jeffries, PhD

———

So Brooke was stalking one of her professors. Was she in love with him? Or, more accurately, obsessed with him? Regardless, the little miss perfect facade was cracking fast. Sofia flips to the next page. It's a black-and-white photocopy of an image. Either the original or the copy is blurry, but she can clearly make out a slim blond woman across the street from where the photo taker stands. Brooke's face, illuminated by bright sunlight in the photo, wears an expression of shock and horror. Caught by the wife, the little psycho. The next page is a neatly typed letter with an official-looking watermark.

———————

May 1, 2008

Dear Miss Winters,

It is our duty to inform you that, pursuant to the investigation following the formal complaint filed by Dr. Patrick Adams, no further disciplinary action will be taken against you.

Dr. Adams has withdrawn his complaint, and the university considers the matter closed. This incident shall have no current or future bearing on your good standing as a student at Brown University. Notice of the conclusion of the disciplinary inquiry has been communicated with the relevant offices and academic departments.

We thank you for your cooperation and wish you a successful conclusion to the academic year.

Sincerely,

Elaine Webster
Associate Dean of Student Affairs
Brown University

———————

Sofia's brow creases, and she feels her elation dissipating like air out of a pinprick puncture in a life raft. Everything she had heard about Brooke indicated that she was expelled. What happened in the two weeks between the professor's complaint and this letter, which essentially said all was well? That would explain how Brooke was able to transfer to another elite school, but Sofia had always assumed a fat check from her parents could make that happen with or without such a nasty stain on their daughter's record.

It doesn't add up. There has to be a reason that explains why the school's official stance flipped so quickly. Not to mention how she ended up at Yale without a fuss, and it must be the same reason Brooke had no choice but to leave.

Sofia sits back and is temporarily discombobulated by her surroundings. She'd forgotten she's sitting amidst the tackiest waste of money she has ever seen in her life. And that includes a lifetime of watching WASPs buy everything from crustacean-emblazoned shorts to spa treatments that left circular burn marks on their perfectly tanned skin. Averting her eyes from a framed watercolor of a blank coastline, she casts her gaze down to the thumb drive.

This must contain a missing piece. Hope resurging through her, Sofia searches the apartment for a computer to unlock its contents. A glance at her phone tells her that she'd better get a move on if she wants to catch Dr. Adams alone. She paces from the living room to the spotless kitchen and bathroom, doubtlessly the handiwork of hired help, then through to Avi's bedroom. The desk facing the window presents nothing but a blank surface. As she rifles through drawers, taking care to keep everything in place, she finds nothing but Avi's trove of sex toys. At least he's imaginative.

Sofia hurries to pull on jeans and a nondescript sweatshirt, much more convincing as an undergrad who was simply curious about taking Dr. Adams's class next semester. Pocketing the spare key and the thumb drive, Sofia slings her bag over her shoulder and heads toward the campus at the exact moment when, across Brown's campus, Dr. Adams's class should be filtering out.

CHAPTER 13

Caroline

Now

Fresh mountain air mixes with the thin trail of smoke from my cigarette as I scroll through Friday's unanswered emails. The cell reception in Leo's compound is spotty at best, but he must have forgotten to turn off the Wi-Fi. Technically, cell phones are not allowed inside the Oasis—all the better to "unplug with intention" and "authentically connect" with the art, so I consult my contraband outside the gallery.

The response from the conference was good, and a few leads trickled in throughout the week, a start to the bolstered client list we need to survive. I don't see anything from Quantum yet, no matter how many times I refresh my inbox. Ambient electronic music emulates from the three-story barn behind me, if you can really still call it a "barn" after Leo's renovations. The sleek structure, complete with surround sound, a museum-quality gallery, and a performance art space, is disguised well enough to blend into its surroundings. If only we could all be so lucky.

"I thought you quit." A familiar voice cuts through the dusk. The years have not been kind to Bryce Hostetler, who has suddenly materialized under a strand of string lights. I should have assumed he'd be here. Bryce and Jenna Hostetler have been entwined in my social circle since Yale. In the decade since we dated, Bryce embraced a "dad bod" and a few large scotches to conclude each of his days in suburbia. It's sad seeing him go to seed. But then I guess that means I was right about him, and right to hand him off to Jenna. Let some other woman overshadow him for the rest of his life. As I shrug, he takes my cigarette and inhales. The sounds of cicadas and the rush of the river that runs through Leo's property seem louder in the awkward pause that follows.

"I could say the same to you," I say. "Tough day?" As it was preordained, Bryce is a low-level executive at his family's pharmaceutical company. Not important enough to shoulder real responsibility, not junior enough to embarrass the Hostetlers.

He closes his eyes as he exhales. I can tell that he's relishing the bad habit as much as I had been until a few seconds ago. "Tough day as Mr. Jenna Hostetler-Lee." Bryce says this with the uneasy familiarity of two exes who have become "friends." He and Jenna got together almost immediately after I broke up with him, a few weeks before Sofia died. Wandering eyes, zero drive, both daddy *and* mommy issues—cutting Bryce loose was an easy decision for me. But Jenna saw in him everything she always wanted: the prestigious Hostetler name; heavyweight social clout; the complete package of money, power, and pedigree, none of which she had.

"Wouldn't you technically be Mr. *Dr.* Jenna Hostetler-Lee?"

"That's right." Bryce lets out a short, mirthless laugh. "My amazing wife is literally curing cancer, and I sit behind a desk all day and hope we don't get sued. The family certainly never hesitates to remind me of that." I fight to keep my expression impassive. If Bryce knew half of what his wife is capable of, he would trade that self-pity for very real fear in a heartbeat.

"Well, this shit won't do either of us any favors." I snatch the cigarette back from him and crush it under my heel. "But it was good of you to come support Leo," I say, meaning it. Bryce might be clueless, but he was never heartless. "Is Jenna here, too?"

"Yeah, I think I saw her talking to Brooke earlier," he says.

"I'd better go say hello," I say, as if I just wanted a chat, even though his words had sent a rush of nervous adrenaline through me. "It was good to see you." I give him my emotion-proof CEO smile.

"You too, Cee," he says, making my skin crawl at the sound of the old nickname. "And listen, I'd love to talk to you about investing in Equilibrium," he adds. "I know you're doing big things."

"Yeah, let's do that sometime," I say lightly before turning away. Poor Bryce. He actually thinks they have the money to invest. Jenna must be even better at keeping secrets than I thought.

I walk around the broad side of the barn, catching glimpses of the party in full swing inside. I spot Leo and pause. I can tell he's in his element. Dressed head to toe in black, he looks every inch the brilliant artist and is talking animatedly to a woman, probably a reporter, who holds out a slim device to catch his every word. Natalia, Leo's latest girlfriend, must have invited her to this event, since I know Leo never calls press himself. For the entirety of Leo's adult life, there's been a pretty woman waiting at his elbow to support him, inspire him. Whatever he needs.

As I approach the front doors, the sound of raised voices from somewhere on the grounds stops me. I can just make out a woman's figure in the distance, standing in the shadow of one of the willow trees that droops over the river. She's reaching for something I can't see.

As I take another step toward the gallery entrance, my gut tells me to get behind a tall wrought-iron statue. Suddenly a lanky man emerges from the woods, striding rapidly around the building, away from the woman following him. The two figures grow clearer as they make their way across the damp grass. He steps into a pool of light that catches his expression: it's Josh, with a look of extreme anxiety on his face. Moments later, the other figure emerges from the thickening darkness.

The woman is a few inches shorter than Brooke. What the hell was Josh doing in the woods with a woman who is not his fiancée? Unsteady on her feet, the woman sways as she draws closer. I can hear twigs snapping under her wobbling steps. It's Jenna. Her sheet of dark hair catches the light as she makes a wavering beeline for exactly where I'm standing. As quickly as I can without being seen, I wrench open the door and step inside.

Noise spills out from the gallery, amplified by the soaring ceiling crossed with the teak beams Leo had imported from Laos. I should be surprised, shocked. I think of the day I introduced Jenna to Brooke: how Jenna's eyes drank in Brooke's effortless patrician beauty, that "it" factor ingrained from a lifetime of the right schools, the right friends, the right clothes, the right everything. Bryce bought Jenna status and the right name, but he would never be Jenna's equal. That must be where Josh came in, and the fact that he was Brooke's made what I just saw seem not just likely but inevitable. Wanting something you can't have opens a wound in your soul that won't close until you get it. Sofia taught me that.

I scan the crowd for Brooke. I find her at the far end of the room clutching a vodka soda, which is what she always drinks when she's watching her weight. If I just saw what I think I saw, the truth would crush her. She's standing in front of the last painting in the exhibit and looks as if she's just seen a ghost. Winding my way through the people clustered around Leo's work, I make my way over to her, dreading what I feel certain I'm about to see. And sure enough, there Sofia is, her portrait in full view, my last-ditch begging ignored, as usual, by Leo.

Brooke turns in my direction, and I can see tears glistening in her eyes. She pulls me into a hug. "I have to talk to you," she whis-

pers. She sounds terrified. As I stare over Brooke's shoulder at Sofia's portrait, I dread what she's about to say.

"I got this email from someone claiming to be Sofia. They sent
me a picture of that Polaroid of us, taken from my bedroom. They
were *in my apartment*. And they were in my school earlier this
week," she murmurs.

I take Brooke's hand and pull her away from the painting and
the clusters of people gathered around each installation. Her cold
fingers are trembling.

"*What?*" I hiss. "How do you know?" I eye our surroundings to
double-check no one is standing within earshot.

She closes her eyes and takes a shuddering breath. "I'll show
you. But I have to warn you, there's some stuff in here about Brown,
things I haven't told you, because . . ." Brooke trails off, and I can
see a sheen starting to coat her eyes again. She's never given me the
details about why she transferred to Yale, except to say that a
breakup got messy, and she wanted a fresh start. Apparently, it was
even messier than I thought, and this "Sofia" person knows all
about it.

"You don't have to explain, but I think they're after me, too," I
say quickly, taking Brooke's arm and inclining my head toward the
closet at the gallery entrance. We walk over to the coat check,
which at this time of year is really just a holding area for purses
and the banned cell phones. After a word with the bored-looking
twenty-something posted there, Brooke reaches into her bag. We
step farther away from the crowd for privacy.

"This is the message I got a couple days ago."

I scan the email and attachments. "It's scary how much this
person sounds like her," I say. "They're trolling the Equilibrium Instagram, too." Brooke stares at me. "I have someone looking into
it." I hand back her cell phone.

"That reminds me," she says in something close to the signature
English-teacher tone I love. "You might want to get one of these."

Brooke reaches back into her bag and pulls out a cheap flip phone. She doesn't say why. She doesn't have to.

"Good idea." I make a mental note to get a burner of my own as Brooke hands me a sticky note with her burner's number on it.

"I also changed the locks to our apartment." She hands me a new key. We always keep a copy of each other's apartment keys for emergencies. "I just told Josh the neighbors had a break-in. He didn't question it, thank god." She sighs. I suppress a wince at the mention of Josh's name.

"Yeah, that makes sense," I say reassuringly. "I'll do the same. We're just monitoring all our channels for any more comments or DMs."

"I knew something like this would happen one day. Those poor people in the other car—" Brooke's voice breaks as she wipes a tear from her eye. "I *knew* someone would find out we lied and come for us."

I take her by her shoulders. Now is not the time to fall apart. For both our sakes, I shove my unease to the back of my mind. "We did what we had to do," I say firmly. "There was no point ruining *all* our lives." She nods, but her expression is anything but certain.

"I just wish—" Brooke's voice breaks.

"I know," I say. "Me too." I've tried to protect Brooke for so long—I can't let things spin out of control now. "We can figure this out, B," I say, keeping my tone gentle but determined. "I run a tech company, for fuck's sake—we can track down whoever is doing this." Brooke doesn't look heartened, but at least her tears have stopped. "If it has anything to do with Sofia, it's going to be per-sonal, and it's going to be on their terms—whoever they are," I say.

"Yeah, and—" Brooke is interrupted by the woman I saw Leo talking to earlier.

"Hi, sorry to interrupt, ladies," she says crisply. "Jacqueline Moore." She gives me a very firm handshake. Jacqueline is willowy and Black with tight coils of braids piled elegantly on top of her head. She has the poise of a pageant queen but a piercing gaze that perfectly suits a journalist. Turning to me, she says, "I'd love to talk with you for a minute about Leo. As his sister, you undoubtedly know his story as an artist better than anyone."

"I'm going to go check in with Josh," Brooke says.

"I'll catch up with you later," I say with a meaningful look at Brooke before switching gears and giving Jacqueline my full attention.

"Mind if I record this, just on background?" she asks, whipping out her cell phone so smoothly it appears as an extension of her hand.

"Go ahead," I say. Anything to raise Leo's profile and lock in great reviews, to keep him on track, and potentially bring some money into this place.

"Great. What would you say inspires Leo's work?" Jacqueline gestures to the paintings around us as we make our way back into the gallery. "These pieces seem to hit close to home."

"Honestly, it changes with Leo—different things, different days. As an artist, he is very focused, and everything he sees is interconnected through a lens of what he can create," I say. Jacqueline inclines her head encouragingly.

"And how would you say this piece, for instance, fits into that lens?" she asks, gesturing toward Sofia's portrait behind us. "There is so much intimacy here. Can you tell me more about the woman in this painting, whom I am assuming was painted from life?" She's pressing, never a good sign from a journalist.

"She was a good friend of Leo's, of both of ours, before she died," I say, keeping my answer as minimal as possible.

"Just a friend?" Her tone is approachable, but there's a barbed curiosity in her voice that tells me her question isn't quite as innocent as it sounds.

"They were together for a while," I dodge. Vague is better. Vague is safer.

"And how would you describe their romantic relationship?" She's getting at something. I wonder how much she already knows.

"What do you mean?" I try to read her expression, but she's clearly had a lot of practice keeping a straight face.

"Oh, you know—*artists*," Jacqueline says, raising her eyebrows. "Sometimes their art is their whole world, no matter what the consequences might be." My eyes narrow.

"What publication did you say you represent again?"

"I didn't," Jacqueline replies evenly. "I freelance art and culture stories. As I was saying, were you ever worried about Sofia while she was dating your brother?"

"I don't know what you're implying," I say, noting that at no point in this conversation did I mention Sofia's name.

"I think you know exactly what—" she starts.

"I'm going to have to ask you to leave," I say. Her eyes are fixed on mine, searching for the emotional reaction I'm determined not to give her. Unfazed, Jacqueline slips her phone back into her bag and extracts a business card.

"I understand this might be a difficult topic to discuss. Especially given your family's history. The circumstances surrounding your stepfather's death, for instance." She places deadly delicacy on all the right words, each one like a slick marking of warning on a poisonous reptile's back. "In case you want to tell your side of the story." Jacqueline hands me her card before turning gracefully and walking away. She's good at this. She's done this before.

I take the card and grit my teeth to stop myself from saying anything in response. I watch as her updo weaves through groups of people just here for the art and open bar. The bones in my fingers crack as they crush the rectangle of paper in my fist. Its edges are sharp enough to pierce my skin.

CHAPTER 14

Brooke

Now

Jenna looks exhausted, a far cry from the shiny version who presented herself at Mel's baby shower. Her typically glowing skin is dull, and her mane of dark hair hangs lankly down her back, looking in need of a wash. Even as she juggles her work with parenting a toddler, Jenna usually takes excellent care of herself. In undergrad, that meant daily workout videos in our apartment and plates consisting solely of chicken breasts and steamed vegetables.

Now married to a Hostetler and finished with medical school, Jenna has upgraded her self-care accordingly. Rigorous Pilates sessions on Reformer machines that look like modern torture devices. Weekly facials, plus subtle filler injections here and there to smooth out the toll of a ruthless on-call schedule. An almost comically restricted diet centered on greens, seeds, and turmeric that would get a gold star from Goop. It's ironic how much Jenna's "self-care" actually sounds more like self-deprivation when you think about it. I'm worried about her.

"Sorry, I didn't catch that," I say over the noise of the people commenting on Leo's latest exhibition.

"I was just asking how Woodlands is working out so far. Bryce and I have our eye on it for Hayden when he's older." She sips her glass of red wine. Leave it to couples like Jenna and Bryce to be thinking about prep schools for their three-year-old. Jenna might be my friend, but I have a feeling she'd be a nightmare as a parent of one of my students.

"It's just been orientation and professional development this week, but so far, so good," I say as I nervously swirl the ice in my glass. By "so far, so good" I really mean there's a tyrannical head-master, my mentor is problematically hot, and a stalker has access to my classroom, which will soon be full of children.

Jenna nods absently, and I get the sense that she isn't taking in a word I'm saying. Her eyes scan the gallery in long sweeps as if she's looking for someone. She's always had that tic, always won-dering if there's someone more important to talk to across the room. Her research had been featured in a prestigious medical journal, and not for the first time, so like Josh, I'm sure my work doesn't even register on her radar.

I'm spared the need to fill the silence by Leo, his arm slung over a stunning young woman's shoulders as he approaches us. He looks good, dramatically better than the last time I saw him a few months ago. His features are fuller, no longer stretched taut and skull-like over his face, and there's a light in his eyes that was once extin-guished by the various substances injected and snorted into his system.

"Thank you guys so much for coming," he says.

"The show is amazing, Leo," I say, trying to sound encouraging and sincere. Jenna says nothing, but she smiles with purple-stained lips.

"That's what I keep telling him," the woman says, and I detect a trace of a Russian accent. "But he never listens to me." She grins and kisses his cheek coquettishly.

"Jenna, Brooke, this is Natalia," Leo says. "She's a dancer with the New York City Ballet." That certainly fits. Her perfect poise and posture make everyone around her look like slouching riffraff. The pale skin exposed by her jade satin dress reveals the jutting outline of her clavicle and a complex network of sinewy muscles running down her arms. I can count the bones in her upper rib cage.

"Very nice to meet you, Natalia. I've never met a real ballerina," I say, hearing the superficial pleasantries in my voice and hating myself for it. "That's a beautiful dress."

"Thank you. Leo picked it out for tonight." Natalia looks at Leo adoringly, but her expression is layered with something else that unsettles me. Her constant, almost magnetic nearness to Leo. Her inability to take her eyes off him; something's not right there. Natalia shifts her curtain of raven hair from one shoulder to the other and winces.

"Are you all right?" I ask.

"Just an old injury flaring up. Right, Talia?" Leo asks, rubbing her shoulder. Natalia nods and reaches to clasp Leo's hand. It's easy to imagine those long fingers poised in dance, gliding through the air as if through water. As she opens her mouth to speak, Bryce joins us, and Jenna shifts out of his reach.

"Congrats, man," Bryce says and claps Leo on the back.

"Bryce! Great to see you." Leo pulls him in for one of those brief man hugs. Ever since they crossed paths when Bryce and Caroline dated, he and Leo have shared a sort of fascination with each other. Two sons from wealthy, powerful families, two diametrically opposed life paths.

"Wouldn't miss it," Bryce says with a cheerfulness that doesn't quite make it to his eyes. "Gotta make the most of Hayden being with his grandparents for the weekend." He laughs. Everyone but Jenna joins in. "After this, I'm heading into Manhattan to meet up with some old friends. A few of them are collectors. Leo, I'll be sure to tell them about you." Bryce lifts his glass in Leo's direction as his wife looks at the floor. Bryce got an apartment in the city a few years ago, presumably to keep up with work. Who knows if that's true.

I make a mental note to text Jenna in the morning and ask to meet for coffee while Bryce is away. For all her high-achieving type A moments, there is a Jenna somewhere in there that I absolutely love when her guard is down. The Jenna who would still—even at our age—sing "Mr. Brightside" in the car with me at the top of her lungs and talk for hours over a bottle of wine can't be completely gone.

"Thanks, Bryce," Leo says, inclining his head in gratitude. Over Bryce's shoulder, a man wearing the thick black glasses of an intellectual, or at least an aspiring one, hovers, clearly waiting to speak with the man of the hour.

"I'm going to get a drink, if that's okay with you, baby," Natalia says, curling toward Leo in his embrace.

"Go ahead. I want to have a word with this guy about doing a poetry residency here," Leo says, gesturing toward the bespectacled man. "Great to see you guys." Leo and Natalia disappear among the people circulating the room, and Bryce excuses himself to, in his words, "hit the head." Gross.

Now that we're alone again, I reach for Jenna's shoulder. She jumps slightly at my touch.

"Hey," I say softly, my concern rising. "Is everything okay?" Jenna shakes her head at the question, and to my surprise, I notice her eyes are shining with tears. Before she can stop me, I pull her into a hug. Jenna is limp in my arms, and without her signature perfume, she smells sour, no doubt from a long shift at the hospital. "What's going on?" I ask in a low voice. Maybe I needed to worry about Jenna getting messages from "Sofia," too. "You can talk to me, you know."

"I'm sorry," she manages as I let go. "It's just some stuff with Bryce. It's nothing." She says this in the universal tone of women who say *it's nothing* but really mean that everything is falling apart.

Jenna takes a deep breath. "But there's something else I want to talk to you about, Brooke. Not here, though." She looks uneasily around her. "It's important."

"Of course," I say. The darkness in her eyes gives me pause. "You haven't gotten any strange messages in the past few days, have you?" I ask.

"No. Why?" Jenna answers immediately and sounds genuinely confused. I search her expression. I believe her.

"Never mind," I say, wondering perhaps too late if I'd put her in danger just by asking that question.

"Okay," Jenna says seriously, lowering her voice. "Will you do me a favor?" She casts a searching eye across the room. Her gaze rests on Caroline. "Don't mention our conversation to Caroline. I have to go, but I'll text you tomorrow."

"No problem," I say, sounding much more assured than I feel. Jenna tries to smile at me, but her mouth, thin and tight as wire, twists into a grimace as I leave.

Josh looks so handsome tonight, polished but relaxed in a blazer, crisp white shirt, and dark jeans. I slip my hand into his as I reach the group gathered in front of a series of intricate charcoal drawings. For the second time that evening, I make someone jump just by touching them. Josh looks at me, bewildered for a moment, but then he smiles, and the familiar sensation of champagne bubbles bursts in my stomach.

"Hey, babe," he says, giving my hand a squeeze. "This is my fiancée, Brooke." I smile at the people Josh is talking to. "We were just saying how cool these drawings are. Want to take a look?" The drawings are set under a layer of glass. Josh hands me the magnifying glass that's attached to the exhibit. I take it and lean in close to the backlit display.

Each scrap of paper bursts with exquisite detail: an entire city block covering a few inches, complete with a little old lady walking her dogs and a couple climbing out of a cab. But then my eye stops. Everything stops. Barely visible in one of the windows of an apartment building, but unmistakably there, is a wall covered with antique mirrors. And standing before them with her back facing the window is a tall woman with hair shaded black. Sofia, or someone like her, is in every single drawing. I almost drop the magnifying glass as I step away. I feel sick. Sofia is everywhere in this room.

"Ready to go?" I ask Josh, desperate to get to the car and out of this haunted place.

"That's probably a good idea," he says, putting his arm around me. Leo and Caroline are nowhere to be seen for a goodbye, so we head directly out the gallery doors and down the curving path to the parking lot, which sits a good distance away. Josh lights his phone flashlight to navigate the uneven paving stones slickened by damp weeds. All around us, the air is deliciously heavy with the earthy scent of the dense woods and mossy riverbank.

"Thank you for coming to this," I say, and Josh places a tender kiss on the crown of my head. Ahead, the taillights of Jenna's SUV glow red as she slows her exit down the long, winding dirt road. Josh stops stock-still.

"What is it?" I ask, wondering if somehow he'd overheard my conversation with Jenna. He hesitates.

"Nothing," Josh says, but a slight frown betrays him. I let it go. For what feels like the first time I can remember, my muscles relax and my mind goes blank as radio silence as we drive home.

CHAPTER 15

Caroline

Now

Across the conference room table, everything about Rob Peterson, the founder and CEO of Velocity, tells me I have as much chance of selling his recruiting firm on Equilibrium as his wife has of having an orgasm that night. His pallid face is creased in a scowl, and his arms are firmly crossed over a gut that strains against beige slacks. On either side of him, however, the two other executives show polite interest as I wrap up the presentation customized for their company in the hopes that this week could start with a sale—hopes that are dwindling by the second.

"As our market research shows, corporate investment in diversity and inclusion is on the rise, and today's tech firms are looking to keep up," I say confidently over the merciless blast of the air-conditioning that sends a chill up my arms, even under my suit jacket. Though still fairly prominent in the tech recruiting space, Velocity is swiftly becoming a dinosaur in their methods. They would be wise to partner with us, but with every impatient exhale from Rob, that prospect shrinks.

"We would love to partner with Velocity and combine its decades of excellent recruiting with the conscientious practices today's workplace demands," I add. "Thank you so much for your time today." I smile and take a seat at the table. "Do you have any questions for me?"

I've barely finished my sentence when Kate, Rob's colleague, starts to speak, but he interrupts her. "Yes," he says, shifting forward in his chair. "This is all very impressive, but as you said, we know what we're doing. I built this company from the ground up. No one gave me any handouts or special advantages," he says proudly. I surmise from his colleagues' subtle changes in facial expression, the slight glazing over of their eyes, and their almost imperceptible shift away from him that Rob is launching into familiar territory.

"Our clients expect us to bring them *the best*. And that means whoever is most qualified for the job, right?" He looks for a reaction. "Why should we lower that standard just so a bunch of millennials don't cry into their avocado toast?" Rob sneers at me. I start to respond, but he holds up a finger, the universal male signal for *I'm not done, sweetheart.*

"What if, say, the best candidate just happens to be a white guy? Are we just supposed to look the other way?" He holds his hands up in a gesture of confusion. I get this reaction a lot from men like him, but as I ready my counterargument, I'm spared the need to answer when Kate muscles into the conversation.

"I think what Caroline just pointed out is that many of our clients may be willing to pay for a wider range of options. The data indicates that's where the wind is blowing," she says reasonably. "It doesn't cut it to just *say* you value diversity and inclusion anymore. To the extent that it ever did." She shoots me a small smile. "The numbers show that right here." Kate flips to the relevant page in the folder I'd given them at the start of the presentation.

Rob's eyes follow Kate's finger to the data Eric had helped compile. "Corporate culture is changing," I say, picking up Kate's thread. "Companies want to make an impact, and that helps their bottom line in a literal sense and improves talent retention." I flip to the relevant data. "We would love to bring these impacts to Velocity," I say, and I watch as Rob skims the page.

"Exactly," Kate says. She looks up at me with a combination of shrewdness and optimism.

"That may be the case," Rob says as if he doubts that very much. "But we need to look at the *bigger* picture, Kate." I'm not sure what "bigger" picture he could possibly mean, but then, it doesn't really matter. This is just his way of telling me the partnership isn't going to happen. "Let's discuss this further with the team," Rob says, standing up to indicate I'm dismissed. "Thank you for coming in, Carol Ann," he adds.

"Thank you," I say. We exchange meaningless handshakes, and they exit the conference room at almost the exact moment that an assistant materializes to remove me from Velocity's offices. None of them take a sleek Equilibrium folder with them as they go. Aware of the glass walls that surround the conference room, I maintain my body language carefully as I pack up my things and stride through the open door. My stilettos are silenced by slate-colored corporate carpeting, and I move almost soundlessly down the hallway and past the reception desk. Elevator doors close in front of me and shut out the sounds of dully ringing phones.

I can finally relax my face. Rejection isn't new. The *no* to *yes* ratio for Equilibrium must be five to one, but every single client counts more than ever now. As the elevator glides downward with halting stops on a few floors, I pull out my phone and skim my texts and emails.

Still nothing from "Sofia." The silence is almost a relief. But then I remember the time Leo and I watched a shark fin circle my stepfather's sailboat off the Nantucket coast. When it disappeared beneath the foam-peaked waves, we didn't feel any safer. A monster is most dangerous when it's out of sight.

When I step out onto 46th Street, the sounds of New York City engulf me instantly and completely. Hot, stinking air presses at my skin like a heavy, unwashed blanket. The traffic, the rush of people on the street, the millions of lives stacked stories high on top of one another: it's an instant injection of purpose. I square my shoulders, descend the concrete steps, and stick out my right hand for a cab.

Equilibrium's "office" is really just a cluster of desks rented in Thrive, a warehouse turned coworking space. Eric is seated at his desk when I walk in, headphones on and laser focused on what he's doing. He looks up as I throw myself into my chair across from him.

"No luck with Velocity?" he asks, pulling off his headphones and draping them around his neck.

"Nope," I say briskly as I open my laptop and start clicking through my inbox. "At least, it's not looking good. They have a standard-issue 'pull yourself up by your bootstraps' founder calling the shots."

Eric rolls his eyes. "At least the Rob Petersons of this world are a dying breed." He effortlessly recalls the name from my calendar. Eric has an almost photographic memory, one of many assets that make him indispensable to me.

I let out a snort of laughter. "True," I say. My eyes land triumphantly on the email from Quantum I've been hoping for. It's from Milo Armstrong's executive assistant: an invitation to meet and talk more about a partnership.

"How are you doing today, by the way?" Eric asks.

"Hmm?" I say, my eyes still scanning my calendar for the soonest possible time to meet with Quantum.

"With the anniversary?" He hesitates and leans forward. "I know those can be tough." I look up and meet Eric's concerned eyes.

"Oh." I take my fingers off my keyboard and run a hand through my hair. "Yeah, I'm actually okay, thanks." And to my surprise, I realize I mean it. Recent events have been more than enough to make me forget about it completely until Eric mentioned it. Today is the anniversary of my mom's death.

"That's good," Eric says comfortingly. "I can never function, like, at all, on the twenty-sixth," he adds in the preemptively self-deprecating tone he always uses when he's vulnerable. Losing our mothers is something we have in common, something that brought us together within minutes of his first interview with me. Both died of cancer: Eric lost his mother to lung cancer; I lost mine to a stage three lump that appeared out of nowhere. We know you're never really whole again.

When he walked into my office three years ago, I instantly recognized something else we have in common: relentless, hungry drive. A determined pursuit of whatever we need to get to where we want to go. I wasn't sure he'd found the right office at first. He wore such an impeccable suit set off by that classic crew cut, confidence, and charisma—he would have looked right at home at a hedge fund. Or at a Brooks Brothers photo shoot for models paid to pretend they work at one.

"Anyway," he says, eager to change the subject, "looking at the rest of your calendar today, I see there's just a follow-up call with Bespoke later this afternoon and then an engineering update." He consults his screen as he speaks. By *engineering*, he means the freelance programmers I hire to update Equilibrium's code when I don't have time to do it personally. Freelancers who, I remember, need to get paid somehow next week.

"Great," I say with relief. Bespoke, a platform for hiring web developers, is one of our biggest clients. Renewing for another year might be enough to tip the scales toward another few months of survival.

"What are you up to?" I ask, my attention already half turned toward the notifications that just buzzed on my cell phone.

"I was just taking a look at how the conference video is doing," he says, returning his eyes to his screen. "Looks like it's doing well on social, and the YouTube content from the conference is picking up traffic. We need to get you more exposure like this."

"Nice," I say absently. I see a reply from Velocity's office, sent less than 15 minutes after I left. They were pleased to meet me but don't think the partnership is a good fit. No surprises there. A thought occurs to me before I open my other messages.

"Any updates on that troll, by the way?" I throw the question out casually.

"Yes, actually," Eric says. He clicks through a few tabs on his computer. "I went ahead and blocked a few more people with similar usernames and deleted their comments."

"Any chance you screenshotted them first?" My phone starts to ring. I send the call to voicemail without a glance, eager to hear his response.

"Yep. I'll email you a copy now." He taps a few keys on his laptop. Before I can click on the attachment that pings into my inbox, my phone starts ringing again. Thinking it must be Leo, I'm surprised to see Bryce's name lighting up the screen.

"Hi," I say, and I realize a millisecond too late it sounds more like a question than a greeting.

"Hey, Cee," Bryce says in a rush. His voice is tight with anxiety, and I can hear his strained breathing through the phone.

"Is everything okay?" I ask.

"It's Jenna," he says, and his voice breaks. My muscles still and my jaw clenches as I brace myself, rising from my desk and stepping into the hallway out of Eric's earshot.

"She didn't come home from the Catskills this weekend."

"What?" I interject and feel a surge of disbelief.

"She said she just needed to clear her head, but then my mom called to say Jenna never picked Hayden up. That's not like her *at all*. You haven't heard from her, have you?" Words catch in my tightening throat. This is the beginning of something terrible. Or, maybe it's the dark, inevitable end of what we started with Sofia all those years ago.

CHAPTER 16

Brooke

Now

No matter how many times I adjust it, the *Leaves of Grass* poster I'm trying to hang between bookshelves looks crooked. I take a few steps backward and collide with the row of desks I'd arranged that morning, tipping my mug of tea so that it spills onto the stack of papers next to it.

"Shit," I mutter under my breath as my classroom door opens and I scramble to move my lesson plans out of harm's way.

"Did I catch you at a bad time?" Antony wears a wry grin and a well-fitted burgundy sweater over jeans.

"Hi, no," I stammer. I tear off a paper towel for damage control on the puddle of tea. Antony walks over to the desks and lifts the top sheet of paper.

"Starting with poetry?" he asks, his eyes skimming the page.

"Yeah," I say, stepping closer to point out some of the key elements of the first week of school.

"Smart," Antony says thoughtfully. "Ease them back into the routine, no crazy reading assignments yet."

"Exactly. And we can start practicing—"

"Close reading techniques, nice." He finishes for me with an approving nod. "On to official mentor business." He places air quotes around *mentor*. "Let's schedule a check-in for some time after the first week of school. And can you send me a copy of this unit plan? Technically, I have to give you formal feedback."

"Will do," I say.

"Carry on, Miss Winters," he says in a spot-on impression of Dr. Lutz's pompous manner. "Oh, I think your poster is lopsided," he adds, and reaches out to straighten it before leaving the classroom. Finally it looks perfect on the wall.

I sigh, return to my desk, and scan what's next on my long list of things that need doing. Clicking through the electronic gradebook and attendance system, I find my class lists and send them to the printer in the copy room down the hall. I get up, stretch, and as I'm about to leave, I hear a muffled vibration coming from inside my desk. For a moment, I freeze. I had made sure to silence my other phone, so I could know exactly when I needed to react. The vibration repeats, insistent, impossible to ignore.

The bottom drawer of the handsome wood desk is locked. No repeating that disastrous mistake of my first day. My fingers trace the edges of the desk key, safely attached to the ID badge on a lanyard around my neck. Hesitantly, I slide the key into the tiny lock and lift out the burner phone. This could be nothing. It could be Caroline. I think of the evidence "Sofia" has in their possession now; they are in full control of my story. On the screen, a tower of text messages appears. They're all from a number I don't recognize.

It's me—I got a burner like you suggested.

Jenna is missing.

She didn't come home last night or show up to work this morning—Bryce has been calling me. He's panicking.

Apparently she was last seen driving to their house upstate. Have you heard from her?

Call me ASAP.

I close the phone and drop it on my desk. My last conversation with Jenna replays in my memory—she wanted to tell me something. Something important. Half-formed questions and a decade of memories overwhelm my thoughts, muddling together and confusing one another. There's just one thing I know for sure. Jenna loves her son, and she would never, ever leave him. Not by choice. I close my eyes and will my brain to slow down and process what Caroline had just texted me.

Maybe Jenna just needed a night away from Bryce. Maybe pressure from work was too much for her. I pull out my iPhone and text Jenna as my brain races to find an innocent explanation for this.

Hey, is everything all right? Worried about you.

Just as my mind begins to clear, the burner buzzes with an incoming call, and I scramble to flip it open.

"Hey," I say, my eyes flicking to double-check my classroom door is shut. "I don't have much time, but—"

"I know. I just wanted to make sure you're okay," Caroline says in a hoarse undertone.

"Do you think . . . ?" I ask, and the rest of the terrible question collapses in my mouth.

"Honestly? I don't know," Caroline says, her words echoing my train of thought, all with the ugly truth left unsaid.

"She'd never just up and leave her job and her kid, right?" I say, thinking aloud. "And she wasn't in the car with us. I don't think 'Sofia' could have anything concrete against her, but—"

"What?" Caroline's question is urgent and sharp.

"I don't know," I start. "Jenna was definitely *at* the party that night before we left. Maybe she saw something? Or maybe there was a history between her and Sofia that we don't know about?"

"That's a good point," Caroline says, and there's another long pause. I can almost hear the gears of her brain turning as mine keeps spinning in circles.

Did Jenna know who was behind the threats, and was she silenced? Or, I think, drumming my fingers against the desk, was there something Jenna wanted to confess just to me without Caroline knowing? And then there's the fact that Caroline and Jenna were never exactly open in their mutual dislike, but I know that deep down, Jenna worried that her husband never really got over Caroline.

"Do you think Bryce could have had something to do with this?" I ask, the thought all the more terrifying spoken aloud. All at once, a few pieces snap into place in my mind. Bryce was at Yale with us. Bryce *knew* Sofia—but well enough to impersonate her all these years later?

"It's possible," Caroline says quickly. "I gotta run, just wanted to make sure you knew what's going on. Be careful, Brooke."

"You too," I say and hang up.

Remembering where I am, I grip my desk and force myself to calm down. If I stay busy enough, I can hold it together until the end of the day. I just have to make it to the end of the day; then I can fall apart.

But then my iPhone lights up.

> B—so sorry to hear our roomie is MIA. Do you miss her as much as you miss me?

My vision blurs as if through a haze of heat scorching the ground. They know. "Sofia" is watching. Maybe even now, somehow, they're behind all of this. Getting uneasily to my feet, I will myself to keep going. There's no point losing my grip now. And besides, I can't forget the explicit threat of the picture they sent me. One misstep, and they tell Josh everything.

In the sunlit hallway, the gleaming floors echo with the footsteps of teachers busily preparing for the students who will soon arrive. Half-open doors reveal classrooms coming to life with all the color, order, and optimism that mark the start of a school year. The copy room is just ahead on my right, and I can hear whirs of printers and voices from the other side of the door.

"How's it going?" Akira asks as I step inside. She stands at a counter next to Kelly and is slicing laminated documents with a paper cutter.

"Great." I lie easily as I step toward the behemoth of a printer, which is laboriously ejecting a stack of papers. "How about you?"

"You know, it's funny," she says, meticulously arranging the next sheet of paper under the blade. "Even after ten years, the start of a new term never gets old. You'll see what I mean one day." Akira

looks up at me and smiles. "I think those are yours," she says, gesturing toward the printer.

"You'll have your work cut out for you with the juniors," Kelly
observes archly as she scans the top roster. "Stop by my room if you
need advice, okay?"

"Will do," I say, shocked at how normal I sound. Kelly hands
me the stack of papers. "Have a good one, everybody." I turn and
walk from the room, my mind already on the next few items on my
list. As I pass the atrium on my way back to my classroom, I hear
voices clustered around Wendy's desk. Parents—well-dressed
mothers plus a token dad—are gathered there, accompanied by
their nervous-looking kids intent on not seeming nervous. I had
forgotten that there is an orientation for new students this afternoon. One of the women facing me is vaguely familiar. Ballet-
barre-skinny, blond, and speaking animatedly in a lilting southern
accent to the pair across from her, she catches my eye as I pass the
group.

"Brooke." She waggles bejeweled fingers in my direction. "I was
so hoping I might bump into you," she trills. "We met at your sister's baby shower. Anna Leigh Richardson." She places a hand on
her chest. "And this is my daughter, Frances."

"It's *Frankie*," the sullen girl half hidden by a black hoodie
mumbles. Anna Leigh purses her lips before twisting them upward
with an effort.

"Hi, yes, of course," I say, remembering how she had spewed vicious gossip in saccharine tones at my mother's house. "Nice to
meet you, Frankie." Frankie's attention has already reattached to
her cell phone.

"I was just chatting with another Woodlands mom, and I think
her son will be in your class." Anna Leigh casts her eyes around the
atrium and calls, "Yoo-hoo! Rebecca!" I didn't know anyone actually
says *yoo-hoo* anymore. In response, an auburn-haired figure with
her back to us turns, and as our eyes meet, my heart plummets.

Rebecca Adams has aged gracefully in the decade since our last encounter. The creamy skin around her bright green eyes has barely started to crease, and just as she had when she calmly informed me that I'd never come near her husband again, she wears an effortlessly imperious expression. For a fleeting moment, recognition flashes on her face. But just as suddenly as the expression appeared, the woman whose marriage I destroyed when I was nineteen smoothly replaces it with neutral politeness.

"Hello," she says in a husky voice that no doubt enticed Patrick right away all those years ago.

"This is Miss Winters. She teaches English," Anna Leigh says, oblivious to the disaster unraveling invisibly between us. Words fail me completely, and there's an awkward pause that Anna Leigh is happy to fill.

"It's *so* good to have you on the PTA, Rebecca. Of course your family has been so generous to Woodlands over the years. Brooke, Rebecca is a professor, you know. Literature, wasn't it?"

"Retired professor. I taught psychology," Rebecca answers tightly. "Now I'm just focused on my family and my next book. Let me introduce you to my son. Ezra!" She calls his name over her shoulder without taking her eyes off mine.

As the boy materializes from the crowd, I feel as if the wind has been knocked out of me. The boy crossing the atrium is the mirror image of his father: the same strong jaw, the same thick dark hair and dark eyes. Sickening déjà vu twists my stomach.

But as the teenager looks our way, there's a certain cruelty in his expression, an upward tilt to his chin, and a swagger to his walk. At a glance, I can see that he has none of Patrick's humor. None of the thoughtfulness that kept the two of us up discussing Homer and Chaucer late into the night, entangled in bed.

"Ezra is very gifted," Rebecca says as he appears at her left shoulder.

"Welcome to Woodlands," I say, forcing myself to look the boy in the eye. He is impassive, bordering on bored, but he still hitches half a smile onto his face in response. That face. That profile: Patrick in miniature. His son's face sends me reeling down a mine shaft of memories.

It started innocently enough. These things always do. I was in his sixteenth-century lit class, and it was just coffee at first. Then the notes on my papers got longer and longer. More provocative. More personal. He thought I was brilliant, special. Two words too bold to ever materialize in my nonexistent sense of self-worth, which my mother had plucked at like unwanted weeds in her garden. I'd stay up late into the night rereading his notes over and over, learning the rhythm of his writing, what his shorthand meant.

I would recite them in my head as I walked across campus, and I'd get lost in his seminars as I relived every word. I'd flip over every page and trace the tiny ridges his pen left on the paper with my fingers—the deeper the marks, the more I knew my work made him think. The first time felt inevitable, and that was the sexiest thing about Patrick. Knowing it was wrong, knowing it was going to happen anyway, ensured that the first time he said, "We shouldn't," on a rainy day in his office, we did.

"So we transferred to Woodlands this year because his last school wasn't . . ." Rebecca pauses, perhaps sensing that I hadn't been listening to her, and selects her next words with care: "*challenging* enough for him. I'm sure he'll do very well in your class, Miss Winters." There's no mistaking the meaning she stitched into this sentence: half decree, half threat.

"I have no doubt," a confident male voice chimes in. Dr. Lutz has joined our conversation. Between Rebecca and the mysterious "Sofia," the six-foot-thick layer of concrete sealing my fate just dried.

CHAPTER 17

Brooke

Three Days Later

"Too cupcake," Caroline says decisively, glancing up from her phone. She's perched on a salmon-colored chaise longue opposite the giant three-way mirror that reflects racks bursting with the tulle, silk, and crepe skirts of wedding gowns. I run a hand over the embroidered folds of the A-line strapless dress clipped to fit my body. We'd agreed to act as normal as possible in order not to draw attention to ourselves and go about our lives. That includes things like trying on wedding dresses, but as I eye myself in the mirror, I feel as disconnected from my body as if I were watching someone else go through the motions of a happily engaged woman.

The bridal, non-panicked version of me blinks at my reflection from atop a mass of white fabric. Well, not white, the stylist said, *shell*: the exact shade that describes how I feel as I turn and glance at the back of the dress. Jenna's been missing for seventy-two hours, and the unanswered texts I sent her are burning a hole in my mind.

"Sofia" has kept quiet, but it's hardly silent, more like a harsh, constant static layering anxiety onto my every waking hour.

"You're right," I say, and I carefully step off the velvet-carpeted platform. Caroline's eyes snap back to her inbox. It's a small miracle she made it to this appointment during the workweek, even at six P.M. With Mel on bed rest, Caroline is the only one whose opinion I trust.

"What's up?" I ask. The anxiety I'd barely suppressed these past few days flares at the sight of Caroline staring at her phone. My plaster-like facade of calm cracks every time I remember my last conversation with Jenna and Rebecca's appearance at Woodlands. Caroline's expression tells me she's struggling, too.

"Yes, sorry. Turning this off now." She gives me a tight but determined smile and stashes her phone back in her purse. "Honestly, I think the simpler the better. You don't want to look back on shoulder pads."

Alice, the eager saleswoman who overhears Caroline's comment, bobs back into view. "I'll just pull a few more dresses for you," she chirps. She disappears into a maze of white, ivory, and champagne.

"Did my mother forget? It's not like her to miss an opportunity to criticize my life choices." I hoist the voluminous skirts over my bare feet and pick my way back to the dressing room.

"Not exactly." There's a familiar dry undercurrent to Caroline's tone. "But I did forget to mention that we're at *this* Bella Bridal location, not the one in Ridgefield. Which is about an hour away from here. So I think she'll be a little late." I stick my head out from behind the door.

"I don't think *bridesmaid* does you justice," I say, in something close to awe. "That was above and beyond the call of duty." Caroline has gifted me an hour without my mother's relentless disapproval. And I'm doing something with my best friend that doesn't involve fear or secrets or lies, a break from the dumpster fire I've been living in. I could even pretend I was a normal bride-to-be, just like the serene women plastered all over the magazines covering the fussy little table in the dressing room.

"Try that one next." Caroline eyes a simple dress that hangs to my right. I pluck it off the rack and run a finger over the satin-covered buttons that descend the length of the back. Taking it with me into the dressing room, I'm careful not to step on the train.

"Need a hand?" Alice's feet appear under the door, accompanied by the swish of fabric and the rattle of hangers.

"I've got it, thanks," I say as I find a mercifully straightforward zipper tucked into the left seam. It's amazing how few wedding dresses are designed to be put on without assistance, punishing shapewear, or both. The material oozes over my frame as I step into it, the cool silk delicious on my skin. It grazes my curves with ease, neither denying their existence nor clinging to them too tightly. A delicate clasp completes the fit, and I step back out into the bridal salon.

Caroline's face lights up as I approach her.

"Oh my god," she starts, but trails off with a smile. I turn toward the mirror. Looking back at me is a confident bride smoothed into chic unembellished material that forms a fluid hourglass on my body. Elegant off-the-shoulder sleeves wrap around my arms, and as I turn, I admire the dipped back that flows into a subtle train. A smile dawns across my lips, and I look back at Caroline. In the split second my attention was fixed on the dress, something in her expression darkens, but maybe it's just my imagination.

"Seriously, Brooke, I think this is it," she says. My smile widens as I imagine Josh in a tux at the other end of the aisle. He'd love the simplicity of this dress, and the thought of his arms encircling me in it sends a flutter through my chest.

"Think Josh will like it?" I ask, adjusting the sleeves to a different angle on my arms. There's that look on Caroline's face again, one that flickers out of her eyes so fast I can barely catch it. She opens her mouth to respond, but Alice interrupts her.

"That was made for you," Alice says, bending down to fan out the skirt behind me.

"Can we take some pictures?" I ask.

"I'll grab your phone!" Alice darts into the dressing room to retrieve it. As I turn back toward the glass and tilt my hips to one side, a sharp voice jerks me back to reality.

"Oh, honey, you're not thinking *that* one, are you?" My mother tips her sunglasses back into freshly blown-out hair as she strides into the room. Her expression sours with distaste at the sight of me in a formfitting dress. "Sorry I'm late, girls." She pecks Caroline on both cheeks and settles herself on the chaise. Her eyes take their standard sweep of my figure, and she shakes her head.

"I love it," Caroline says clearly, almost defiantly. She's one of few people alive willing to go toe to toe with Daphne Winters.

"Honey, it's just not *flattering* on you. With your body type, you'll want something more forgiving. And nothing as revealing as that fabric."

"I think Brooke looks amazing," Caroline says, shifting in her seat to look my mother square in the eyes.

"I'm just trying to help!" She actually manages to sound wounded. "Look at how it bunches in the waist and under the arms. No one wants a lumpy bride." My mother says this as if droves of lumpy women are to blame for the general decline of American family values. Now I notice how the dress exposes my less-than-perfectly-flat stomach and creates twin rolls of fat between my upper arms and shoulders. Suddenly the fabric is starting to itch, and I'm aware of how the sleeves restrict my movement. My mother snaps her fingers, and Alice reappears with an anxious expression on her face.

"This dress is all wrong. We'll need—"

"So sorry," Alice interrupts, a decision it looks like she instantly regrets when my mother raises her eyebrows to the extent this is still possible after her facelift. Alice turns to me, hands me my phone, and lowers her voice. "I couldn't help but notice. I think it's urgent." I sway slightly on the platform as I see the screen alight with missed calls and text messages. Without a word or a glance at Caroline that would give me away, I nearly trip as I retreat to the dressing room.

I see Bryce's contact, but the rest of the messages come from numbers I don't recognize. And after I read the topmost text message on the screen, my knees give way and I collapse to the floor in a puddle of silk.

My vision doubles, then re-forms shakily around the words: *They found Jenna's body. She overdosed.*

"Brooke," my mother calls in a singsong voice. "We have more dresses for you to try. I think this Elie Saab would be lovely on you." It's as if she's speaking from the top of a well into the hopeless black depths below. Images of Jenna flood my memory. She wanted to tell me something urgent. That's not the behavior of a woman about to kill herself. The idea of Jenna taking any kind of drug doesn't add up with the obsessively clean diet and lifestyle I'd always known her to have. And Hayden. She would never do this to her son. Nothing is making sense.

I lift my phone closer to my face and try to force myself to focus on the other messages. There's something from Josh and something else about answering police questions and a link to an article about Leo. Dizziness blurs everything again. I need to get home, get back to Josh. Caroline and I need to make a plan. If "Sofia" was behind this, we're next. Reaching for my phone, expecting it, I read the text on the screen, a hard knot lodging in my throat.

> Have you heard the news, B? Time to get your story straight. But of course, that's a real strength of yours ;) xx

"Everything okay in there?" Alice asks with a soft knock. I feel as if I watch myself stand up, hear myself say, "I . . . um . . . have to go. Caroline—" I raise my strangled voice to be loud enough for her to hear me. "Can you check your phone?" I hastily change back into my clothes and carefully drape the dress over the chair in the corner of the dressing room. It hangs there, limp and lifeless.

Wrenching the door open, I startle Alice, who jumps back. "Sorry," I mumble before turning to meet Caroline's horrified gaze. Her face is sheet white, and with one pointed glance at the phone in her hand, she confirms my fears. "Sofia" got to her, too. My mother's eyes flick between our expressions.

"What's the matter, girls? You look like you've seen a ghost."

"Jenna's dead." My voice is hollow.

"What?" My mother's eyes are wide, and her hand reflexively reaches for her throat.

"Jenna's—" I say, and my shoulders start to shake. Jenna, the force to be reckoned with, the girl singing with me in the car, is gone. Caroline is frozen, maybe for the first time in her life at an utter loss for what to do.

"Oh, that poor family," my mother says. She knew the Hostetlers long before Jenna and I roomed together at Yale. "That's the last thing they need right now, what with that article in the *Times* and everything." My cheeks flush, and I take a step toward her.

"What did you just say?" I ask as I register the hot tears streaking down my cheeks. I glare at my mother. And as I meet her cool, unaffected gaze, something inside me snaps.

"I know you're upset, dear, but don't take it out on me." My mother sniffs. "I'm just saying that another scandal will be *so* hard for Penny, what with all the bad press about Hostetler Pharma and—" I cut her off.

"Our friend . . ."—I advance toward the chaise—"is dead. She was a good person." My voice rises. "She was a wonderful mother. She helped people. And all you can think about is the *scandal*?"

"There's no need to—" The look on my face stops my mother's words in their tracks.

"Not that you would know the first thing about Jenna." I'm yelling. I don't care. This has been coming, building, for years, and it feels too good to release it, like a modicum of the power I've lost is creeping back into my bloodstream. I snatch my bag up and sling it over my shoulder. My mother stares back at me, her mouth half-open.

"Do Penny a favor and skip your bullshit condolences. They're not super *flattering* if you don't have a human heart to pull them off."

I can see my mother's face coming back to life, but just as her mouth sets, ready with a retort, I wheel around and spot Alice half hiding behind a rack of dresses. "Thank you very much for your help today," I say briskly. Alice jumps slightly, letting out a barely audible squeak. I am both aware of and completely indifferent to how deranged I must appear.

"I'll take the dress I just tried on in a size six. Caroline, let's get out of here." I dig into my wallet and slap a credit card into Alice's hand. Without looking at my mother or pausing to wait for Caroline, I stalk out of the salon. The sound of the tinkling bell and Caroline calling my name follows me out into the street.

Humid air blasts in my face as I leave the air-conditioned room, and the handle of my car door is scalding hot from baking in the sun. Seething, terrified, and still thinking of the last time I'd heard Jenna laugh, I get into the car and grip the wheel hard with both hands. I'm tired of being scared. Tired of being a punching bag. Tired of being punished for a past I've fought so hard to shake. Fumbling for my keys, I jam them into the ignition. For the first time in days, I resolve to take control. I just know Jenna didn't kill herself, and this stalker is just a person, a person who is vulnerable, a person who can be found. Caroline slides into the passenger seat and places my credit card into the center console cup holder. For a moment, we sit in a tense, horrible silence.

"'Sofia' did this," I say, and my chest heaves and falls with a tide of all-consuming rage and fear. Caroline nods.

"Let's find this maniac before they find us," I say. Again, my voice doesn't sound like mine. But then nothing about this nightmare feels real. And yet it's exactly what I deserve.

I drop off Caroline at the train station, and when I arrive home, I can hear Josh moving around our bedroom. It's too early for him to be here under normal circumstances, but the prospect of literally falling into his arms has never been more welcome.

"Josh," I call into the hallway. There's a scuffle, a heavy thud.

"Hey." He emerges from the bedroom, his face set in a dark expression I rarely see there. I reach out to give him a hug, but he steps back from me. Over his shoulder, I can see two packed bags in the hallway.

"What's going on?" I ask. My eyes flick uncomprehendingly from the suitcases back to my fiancé.

"There's ... uh ... something I need to tell you. Maybe we should sit down?" His voice fractures.

"Did you hear about Jenna?" Desperation expels my words in a gasp. My fleeting illusion of control is slipping from my fingers and being replaced by a pulsing seed of dread.

I sit across from Josh on our couch. I think of how many couches we tried out at the store before choosing this one: a thrifted green velvet with the accent pillows Josh had rolled his eyes at but I knew he secretly loved. I think of the day we moved in: we'd had sex right here, with our life scattered in boxes around us. Piper jumps up to sit next to Josh and starts daintily licking her paws, as if nothing whatsoever is amiss in our little home. He rubs the tops of his thighs with his hands—he always does that when he's nervous.

"What is it?" I ask. The dread is starting to grow, lengthening and darkening like a shadow on the wall.

"You're going to find out some things about me, and I just want you to know that I'm sorry. I'm so sorry, Brooke." Josh won't look at me.

"I don't understand." My brain is short-circuiting. "Sorry for what?" He takes a deep breath and opens his mouth, but before he can speak, there's a loud knock at our door. Piper skitters out of the room to her safe place under our bed. As I get up to answer it, I wish more than anything that I could join her. I open the door to a man who flashes a police badge.

"Can I help you?" I ask.

"Brooke Winters?"

"Yes," I say, and as I say it, I know that my life will be divided into two now: everything before and everything after this moment.

"Is Joshua Green here?"

"Yes," I say hesitantly. "What is this about?"

"I'm Detective Bullock. I have some questions regarding the death of Jenna Hostetler-Lee. Can I come in?"

CHAPTER 18

Caroline

Now

Later that afternoon, I brace myself for the conversation I have to have with Leo. I avoid Sofia's portrait as I enter his Chelsea gallery, my footsteps echoing in the spare, self-consciously styled space. I almost expect her sleeping eyes to snap open, to track me from across the room, but the rational part of my brain silences that absurd thought. The gallery, a normally crowded, trendy hub of the New York art scene, is practically deserted, a fact that intensifies the unease in my gut.

"Leo?" I call past the only other people in the room, a hipster couple holding hands and eyeing one of his landscapes with distaste.

"So derivative," the man mutters, taking a step back from the painting and shaking his head. As if I could shut out his words, I take out my phone and stare for what feels like the thousandth time at the last text message Jenna had sent me.

> We need to make new arrangements. I
> think Bryce suspects something.

Two sentences. Is that all it will take to unravel everything? Brooke knew Jenna and I would never be friends because of Bryce, that we maintained a fragile truce because we both wanted Brooke in our lives. But how long would it take Brooke to wonder if there was something deeper going on? She had never questioned Jenna's friendship, never wondered why Jenna eyed Josh for just a little too long, looked a little too appraisingly at a potential upgrade from Bryce. I delete Jenna's message to stop these questions from running more circles in my mind.

The couple throws Leo's work one last look of disdain before moving on to the enormous abstract sculpture at the center of the room. It partially obscures the slender figure moving toward me, but I can still recognize Natalia's graceful movements and the swing of her long dark hair.

"Caroline, so nice to see you," she purrs. Her Russian accent, maybe like all Russian accents, is both seductive and somehow threatening. She pulls me in for a hug with a warmth that I only half-heartedly reciprocate. I've learned never to get too attached to Leo's girlfriends. They typically last no longer than the period it takes to generate a few pieces before he gets bored: both of the art medium of the moment and of the woman inspiring his work. I notice a tightness in her face as I release her, but it relaxes into a misty, far-away smile as her eyes trace the landscape hanging in front of us. We stand in silence for a beat, and when it becomes clear Leo won't immediately materialize, I force myself to make obligatory small talk.

"Remind me, where in Russia are you from?"

A shadow darts across Natalia's face. "Nowhere you will have heard of or would want to visit." She hazards an attempt at offhand humor, but her tone leaves a distinct aftertaste of bitterness and pain. Inclining her head at the canvas, she changes the subject. "This is one of my favorites. Leo thinks it will sell fast."

"Any buyers yet?" I say, trying to keep my tone casual, as if my future doesn't hang in the balance of Leo's art, Equilibrium's weak profits, and the dregs of the inheritance.

"Your brother has manifested abundance for our plans," Natalia says opaquely, that dreamy smile blossoming again on the face that is so eerily like Sofia's. I'll take that as a *no*, then.

"Plans?" I ask, surprised that Leo had given thought to anything more than a week in the future.

"Leo and I, together we will grow the Oasis to be a true community for artists," Natalia says expansively, and her eyes drift away from mine, back to Leo's landscape. Maybe she sees something more in the waves and the windswept scenery, a representation of the future he's promised her. "What he always intended for the space, I think. But it's too much for one person to do alone, so we will build it together." Where the money for this will come from, I have no idea, and I wonder if Natalia knows something she's not telling me.

"Hey, sis," Leo says, just as I'm about to ask Natalia more questions. He appears from around a corner and looks, I'm relieved to see, as if his sobriety has stuck so far. "I'm so sorry about Jenna," he adds, running a hand uncomfortably through his hair. "I know things were—are—complicated between you two and Bryce, but this still sucks."

"Thanks, Leo," I say stiffly, biting back thoughts of Jenna. "Can we talk in private?" I avoid Natalia's eye.

"Sure, just give us a sec, Talia." Leo motions me toward the opposite end of the gallery, where a small office is tucked into a corner. I mentally rehearse what I need to ask him, what he needs to know if we're going to keep our secrets hidden. But before we're across the room, Leo stops in his tracks. His eyes are glued to his phone. "Actually . . ." I watch as a dark cloud passes over his face. "Can we have a rain check?"

"This is important," I say in a low hiss. Leo is frozen for a beat, then tucks his phone into his pocket.

"What—" I start.

"Something's come up." He looks at me, and in the split second it takes him to smooth over his features, I know he's hiding something important. "I have to deal with it now," he says, physically steering me out of the gallery, past Natalia and toward the street. I start to protest, but under Natalia's watchful eyes, I shut my mouth.

It's not until I'm back in the thick of the foot traffic outside that my phone pings once, twice, three times before I look down at the screen and understand with crashing, awful clarity what Leo had just seen.

⸻

I get back to my apartment in a panicked blur and return the half dozen missed calls from Eric.

"Did you—" Eric starts the second he picks up the phone.

"How bad is it?" I ask, sinking onto my desk chair and staring at the rumpled white sheets covering the bed I barely sleep in anymore. Upstairs, a stereo bass thuds away at the floorboards, piling on to a headache that is starting to gnaw at my temples.

"Um . . ." Uncertainty from Eric is never a good sign. "It's bad. Like, not virally bad, because no one actually reads Gawker anymore, but yeah." His voice climbs a half octave on his last two words, another bad sign. I reach into my bag and open my laptop. Sure enough, emails from clients populate my inbox with subject lines that make me want to crawl out of my skin. My eyes focus on a message that hovers near the top of the screen. I open it and prepare for the worst.

> Caroline, I used to be the only one who knew about Leo's hidden talent. But the nicest journalist convinced me to share my story with the world—turns out, I'm not alone. Are you?
> xx—Sofia

"Shit," I say into my cell phone. "Did you turn off comments on Instagram?"

"Already done."

"Good. Well, it's not good. We have to get ahead of this while we can." I let out a tiny exhale.

"But the tags—" he continues. I can hear the sounds of his getting to his feet, and I can easily imagine him starting to pace. He's probably still at Thrive: its usual hive of striving twenty- and thirty-somethings must have started to thin by now, or at least cluster around the beer taps that were supposed to justify the overpriced rent, so I doubt this conversation can be overheard.

"I know," I say, imagining the tidal wave of mentions and hashtags that must be flooding our social media, erasing every positive online impression we've ever made.

I skim the article as fast as I can, and I can take in only the bits and pieces that might spell out the ruin of Equilibrium, of anything to do with the name Archer, of everything.

> Prominent artist Leo Archer accused of sexual assault . . . Contributes to toxic masculine culture across the New York art scene . . . Accusations of sexual harassment . . . Private compound site of drugging . . . Women report blacking out during Oasis artists' retreat . . . Survivors fear backlash from coming forward, choosing to remain anonymous . . . Linked with rising tech startup Equilibrium, run by none other than Archer's sister, a self-proclaimed feminist.

A nauseating spike of heat shoots from my fingertips through the rest of my body. I run through what I've always told myself: Leo went to the Women's March with Brooke and me. Leo has never had problems attracting women. And yet I can't pretend that there have never been rumors. I shake off the thought. There must be some mistake—just "Sofia's" next stab at revenge.

"Okay, so we put out a statement," Eric says, jerking me back to the issue at hand. "We control the narrative. Your being related to someone who was accused of something doesn't mean anything." He's reactivating. This is the Eric I need.

"Yes," I say, closing my laptop and crossing the room to make coffee with the fancy machine Leo got me for my twenty-fifth birthday. "And that means—"

"What?" Eric prompts, but I hesitate. I have no choice but to tell Leo about the statement we're about to release. Make him understand why I have to do this.

"Any statement that doesn't unequivocally distance Equilibrium from Leo won't be enough. We can't be seen as complicit in this," I say, dreading what that distance might cost. My hands are surprisingly steady as I measure out tablespoons of the coffee, the only food item I consistently keep in my apartment.

"Right," Eric says. I can tell he's gaining confidence as a plan formulates in his mind. "You want to call him while I draft something?"

"Yeah, let's do that. Thanks, Eric."

"We can handle this," Eric says, and he hangs up.

I allow myself the time it takes to brew and pour the coffee before I take out my phone and press Leo's number at its usual spot at the top of my outgoing call log. Straight to voicemail. I try again. Nothing. I text him.

> Hey—I just read the Gawker article, and I'm worried about you. I love you. We're going to get through this. I don't believe a word of it, but Equilibrium has to survive. I'll be giving a statement in favor of investigating further. I hope you can understand.

I press send and start to type And forgive me, but I delete the words.

Though Equilibrium's Instagram comments are turned off, users have clearly found my lesser-known Twitter account and are using it to drag Equilibrium's name through the mud. The situation worsens with every scroll of my finger.

@CArcher89. Is this how women empower women? #metoo #Equilibrium

---

@CArcher89. Hypocrites work at #Equilibrium

@CArcher89. There's a special place in hell for women who enable violent men all while making $$ off the backs of #feminism #progress #MeToo #Equilibriumsucks

---

My shoulders are heavy as I sit at my desk, steaming cup in hand, ready for another long night. A draft of a statement is already in my inbox, courtesy of Eric.

This is not an easy post to write, but then, doing the right thing never is. We at Equilibrium were deeply troubled and saddened by the accounts of the brave women detailed in today's Gawker article.

I cut the first sentence before I finish reading. No one is going to feel sorry for us or think we're doing the right thing.

> At Equilibrium, we believe women. At Equilibrium,
> we believe in justice. We believe that a better future
> is built on truth, especially when that truth is difficult
> to face. We want to thank our community for their
> support and to reassure the Equilibrium family that
> we unequivocally support a full investigation into the
> allegations that came to light today.

That's more like it. I reread this a few times, tweaking a word here and there, and type a reply to Eric.

> This is good to post, maybe with a "Believe Women" graphic? Let's get this out ASAP.

I take a sip of coffee. My inbox tells me we haven't lost any accounts, not yet, but a disturbing number have reached out to "discuss concerns raised by recent events." My response to this kind of email, and there are bound to be more, will need carefully crafted messaging, too. I draft replies, reread each one twice, and fire them off.

If we're very, very lucky, this will blow over. If not, if there's any truth to this, we're dead in the water. And that would also mean things too terrible to contemplate about Leo. Looking at my phone, I see that my message to Leo hasn't been delivered. He must be at the Oasis, where cell phone service doesn't reach.

Tapping a few keys on my laptop, I reopen the cryptic email from "Sofia." I skim the email header and find the IP address. Let's see how tech savvy this person is. I open a command window and dig a little deeper to trace where this message came from. Bingo. Whoever sent this message is somewhere off the coast of Nantucket.

Of course.

It's so obvious I can't believe it hadn't occurred to me sooner.
I whip out my burner phone to text Brooke.

> "Sofia" is off the coast of MA . . . Her
> sister still lives there.

If I'm right, there's a chance at least *this* can be over within the
week. My phone buzzes almost immediately with Brooke's reply.

> Is she still working as a caretaker at the
> Archer house?

It buzzes again.

> The police are here, asking about Jenna.
> Can I come over? We need to get on the
> same page.

My stomach plummets as I text back.

> Yes. Drea's been on the property for 5-ish
> years now. 9?

Brooke responds.

> See you then.

Drea Eliades, Sofia's older sister, has worked as a caretaker on
Bill's parents', my surrogate grandparents', Nantucket estate for al-

most a decade now. After they died, the property passed to their oldest son, Todd, who insisted I call him uncle, too, even though we aren't related, and even though Todd has stared at me a little too long ever since I hit puberty.

Drea, who has Sofia's wild streak but none of her focus or determination, drifted back for Sofia's funeral with a broken heart, no job, and nowhere to go. At the time, we thought it was an act of kindness to Sofia to hire Drea, but maybe all I'd done was leave the door to all our secrets wide open. I check my phone again. Leo still hasn't received or read my text message.

I rub my temples, unable to get the memory of Leo's rock bottom out of my mind. And as I open my eyes, I half expect to see him leaning against the doorframe, gaunt, incoherent, and terrifying. If I said nothing about the article, I'd lose Equilibrium, but Leo wouldn't hate me. But without Equilibrium, I can't protect him anymore, and whether he hates me or not soon won't matter. For the "right" decision, this feels like shit.

CHAPTER 19

Brooke

Now

I lead the officer through the hallway and into the living room, my heart pounding so loudly in my ears I can hear it over the sound of my heels on the hardwood floors.

"Thank you for speaking with me," Detective Bullock says. He's a tall, thin man with watery blue eyes set uncomfortably close together.

"Of course," I say, uncertain if I should offer him coffee or ask if we're under arrest. "Would you like a cup of coffee?" I stammer, more out of fear than politeness.

"No, thank you," the detective answers. His tone is brisk, and he checks his watch as he continues. "I don't want to take up too much of your time."

"Please." I gesture lamely at the couch and living room chairs, and the three of us sit.

"I understand you were both close to the deceased, and I'm very sorry for your loss." Detective Bullock sounds as if he's rattling off boilerplate. "But it's standard procedure in the state of New York to investigate all deaths that appear not to be of natural causes."

I interrupt as he's picking up steam. "New York? Jenna lived in Connecticut."

"Yes, but Mrs. Hostetler's body was found two days after her death at a family home in upstate New York, which is what brings me here." I cringe at the thought of Jenna's reaction to the "Lee" being eliminated from her name.

"I know this is going to be hard to hear, but Mrs. Hostetler—"

"Hostetler-Lee. They hyphenated their last names," I interject.

"My apologies. Mrs. Hostetler-Lee was found with a lethal amount of OxyContin in her system. Unfortunately . . ."—he sighs heavily—"we're seeing more and more cases like hers nowadays. It's not just junkies who abuse this stuff. Do either of you know of any reason she might have been depressed or under pressure lately?"

Josh looks at me, then opens his mouth to speak, but I cut across him.

"Jenna didn't kill herself," I say. The detective is trying to put Jenna in a box, because apparently, her being crammed into a casket or splayed out on a cold slab in a morgue isn't enough. I should tell the detective the whole truth about what's been happening. About "Sofia" and the blackmail. But I can't do that without unraveling my life and Caroline's. What little conscience I have is screaming for me to give the police a nudge in what might be the right direction.

"And what makes you say that?" The detective sounds as if this possibility had never occurred to him.

"I've been going over it and over it in my mind, and for one thing, she loved her son more than anything in the world. She would *never* abandon him, no matter what. And the last time we spoke, she said she had something really important to tell me," I say, remembering the borderline desperation in her face. "That doesn't seem like something a suicidal woman would do." I cross my arms and look the detective directly in the eye.

"I'm sure this is painful." Detective Bullock shifts to the edge of the chair. "But the friends and family of suicide victims are often blindsided by things they never knew about, even if they were close to the deceased."

"Then why ask the question?" I say sharply, anger rising in me. Josh closes his eyes, opens them, and looks first at me and then at the detective.

"I want to be transparent with you, Detective, about my relationship with Jenna," Josh says. I turn to my fiancé, brows knitted automatically in confusion. *Relationship?* They were acquaintances at best. But the look Josh gives me before continuing tells a different story.

"Brooke, I never wanted you to find out this way." He says this as if these words cost him everything he has. "Jenna and I slept together. It happened once, about a month ago. We'd been talking for a while. That's all it was at first—just dinner and talking." Josh drops his eyes to the floor. "It was a mistake, it was stupid, and I am so, so sorry. I was going to tell you." His voice breaks. "And I have to be honest, now that she's—because of what happened to her." Josh covers his face with his hands.

I think of the two packed suitcases in the bedroom. Of the late nights he said he was working on a case. Of how, like an idiot, I believed him, blinded by a sparkly engagement ring.

"Why?" It's all I can say. Maybe it's what every person who is ever stupid enough to think they were happy can say when reality sets in. I look at Josh, but his face is blank, his eyes on the floor. His silence expands to fill the suddenly airless room.

"*Why*, Josh?" I press, and he finally looks up at me and shifts a nervous glance at the detective.

"I . . . I don't know. We kind of just saw ourselves in each other, how we both want to really change the world." He looks like he'd dissolve into the floor if he could, but when he opens his mouth again, his voice is determined. Like he practiced in the fucking mirror. "But I ended it. That night at the Oasis." Josh makes eye contact with the detective, who looks so painfully uncomfortable it would have been funny under different circumstances. "I told Jenna we couldn't see each other anymore, and she took it really hard."

Every time Josh mentions Jenna, my anger flares along with shame for the rage I feel toward a dead woman. Jenna, who I thought was my friend, slept with my fiancé behind my back. All because they each have disappointing partners who just aren't as visionary as the two of them. *Had* partners—I correct myself.

I realize that Josh is still talking. "I think she and Bryce have been having problems for a while. He wanted her to spend more time at home with their son. She wanted him to leave the family company because of their role in the opioid crisis. And I think that could be why . . ." He trails off. At this, the detective starts taking rapid notes. He's getting exactly what he came for: reasons to rule Jenna's sudden death a suicide so he can go back to his desk. Case closed.

"That's—uh—very helpful in understanding Mrs. Hostetler-Lee's state of mind," Detective Bullock says, looking up from his notepad. "I think I have everything I need. I'll leave my card if you think of anything else."

Suddenly I feel an overwhelming urge to scream at Jenna, hating that she's gone somewhere that I can't demand an explanation of her, then hating myself for feeling that way. There's a high-pitched ringing in my ears, and as Josh and the detective stand to shake hands, I twist my engagement ring, watching as light glances off the surface of the stones.

As if from miles away, I hear our front door close. I wait for tears to come, but my eyes are dry, out of focus, and vaguely fixed on my left ring finger. Josh is saying my name, then pleading, but I can't bear to look at that face I love and find betrayal there. I think of the first time I saw Josh, boyish and disheveled with a group of law school buddies across the bar. How the butterflies I hated hearing about in corny love songs filled my chest when he looked at me, and the glass of wine I was drinking missed my mouth because we made eye contact. I think about how we'd both laughed about that, and how many times we'd told that story in the years since. I want to lock myself inside the memory and never come out.

I barely register the sound of footsteps walking away from me and back toward our bedroom. Is that where it happened? Neither of them seem like the seedy motel type, but what do I know. Or did they have their affair in her pristine suburban dream home, where photographs of her son smiled toothily down from the walls? I squeeze my eyes shut at the thought.

"Brooke?" Josh is standing directly in front of me. "Did you hear what I said?" I can't move. He kneels at my feet. "I love you. I will never, ever hurt you like this again. And if you'll still have me, I still want to get married and spend the rest of my life trying to deserve you." He reaches for my cold hands.

"I wasn't enough?" The question escapes my lips in a whisper. It contains a universe, a lifetime, the root of every insecurity I've ever had. His eyes swell with tears, and I can see my face reflected in them.

"Of course you are," he says. But what he said to the detective echoes in the emptiness of these words.

"How long were you meeting with her, talking about changing the world, or whatever it is you couldn't do with your fiancée? You know, before you finally fucked her."

"Just a few months, I promise. It didn't mean anything." Of course, that's why Josh fell for Jenna: the ambitious high-powered doctor could meet him at a level that a mere schoolteacher never would. I feel like an idiot for trying.

"Is that supposed to make me feel better?" My voice sounds dead.

"No." Josh grimaces. "Please just don't blame Jenna."

"If it meant nothing, why do you care if I blame her or not?"

Josh runs a hand through his hair. "Because she's dead, and she doesn't deserve to be remembered like this. She was your friend," Josh says. And as if my body was waiting for those words like a physical trigger, I'm seized by an urge to slap him across the face. Hard.

But I find I still can't move. I don't watch him get up from the couch. I'll never know if he looked over his shoulder as he picked up his keys from the bowl we bought together at a garage sale. Or if his glasses make their familiar crackle as he polishes them before getting in his car. I don't look up until I hear the door close behind the man breaking my heart.

CHAPTER 20

Caroline

Now

I desperately need to talk to Brooke tonight, and she should be here any minute. I increase the narration speed on *Planet Money*, and NPR accelerates in my ears as I try to make my apartment presentable. My eyes linger on my phone screen. Jenna's death, the text messages, now the Gawker article—they all upped the ante. I got in touch with Richard Wallace, a private investigator who has worked with our family before through years of discreetly exchanged contacts, to deal with inconvenient problems and people. He knows that the Archers always cough up the cash. Eventually.

Richard still hasn't called me back with anything on Sofia's sister Drea, but I still need him watching her. I can't be everywhere at once. And even though Jenna's death will probably be ruled a suicide, I agree with Brooke that we can't eliminate the possibility that "Sofia" was behind it. We just have to find out why.

The cord of my headphones catches on the corner of a chair, sending it to the floor. Cursing small spaces, I bend to pick it up

and roll my neck, trying to release some of the tension crammed
into my shoulders. The previous night's marathon prep session for
next week's Quantum pitch plus today's news have taken their toll
on my body. I avoid looking in the mirror on the opposite wall.
Sometimes it's better not to know. Skeptically, I envision light and
air spreading through my lungs on every inhale and sooty exhaust
spewing out with every exhale. It's what the yoga teacher with the
unsettlingly calm monotone told us to do at the first and only Bi-
kram yoga class Eric managed to drag me to.

Thankfully, the buzzer sounds in time to rescue me from that
hippie bullshit. Brooke has spare keys to the apartment, but something instilled from her cotillion upbringing stops her from using
them. When she opens the door a minute later, her eyes are bloodshot, and her face is a drawn, expressionless mask.

"Hey," I say, stepping aside to let her in.

"Josh slept with Jenna," she says, walking past me and setting a
bottle of wine heavily on the counter.

"Oh my god," I say, trying to sound as if this isn't something I
already suspected. I want to hug her, but she's already collapsed
onto one of the kitchen stools. Hearing it from Brooke makes it
real, and her words confirm the suspicions I've had since seeing
Jenna and Josh in the woods outside the Oasis. "How did you find
out?" Needing something to do with my hands, I pull a corkscrew
out of a drawer and glasses from the cupboard. I've never seen the
point of wineglasses, so two short water glasses will have to do.

"A police officer came to our apartment tonight, asking questions about Jenna, trying to find a reason why she might have killed
herself. And Josh decided it was the perfect time to come clean,
since he thought it was relevant to Jenna's death. He thinks that
ending their affair could have—" Brooke says, and I'm glad she
doesn't finish that sentence. I've never seen her like this, so detached, so defeated.

"I'm so sorry, Brooke." I pour two generous measures of wine. "I just can't believe they would do this. What do you want to do now?" Her engagement ring catches the fluorescent lighting above my stove.

"Oh, yeah." She says this as if in a dream. "I guess I'm still engaged. Technically. I bought my wedding dress *today*." Her chest heaves in uncontrolled bursts at first, and then her breathing slows and darkens into sobs. They are raw and helpless: she's crying how a child cries. I take a step closer and hug her.

"This is awful," I say, still holding her tight. For several long moments, her body is slack against mine, and finally she pulls away from me, smudging the black rivulets of mascara that trickled under her eyes.

"We have to be careful. Jenna—" Brooke pauses as if the very shape of her name puts a sour taste in her mouth. "This can't be a coincidence. I think 'Sofia' might have killed her. Do you still think Drea is behind all this?"

"I don't know, but we have to find out. I bet she's at least behind these insane texts," I say, and I take a deep breath as I reach for my laptop. I explain how I used the IP address to trace the source of the latest message to Drea.

"But why would Drea want to kill Jenna? Clearly plenty has been going on without my noticing." This afterthought is infused with bitterness.

There's another horrible pause in which I have no idea what to say. "I can go up there this weekend and confront her," Brooke says in a new tone of voice, resolved. Clearly taking action on *something* is helping her cling to a semblance of control.

"I think it's better that *I* go. I need to check on Leo first, though," I say, wondering exactly what I'd find in the wake of the Gawker article. "I have to make sure he isn't spiraling. Did you see this?" I hand her my phone, and her eyes skate across the text, her eyebrows rising as she scrolls past the accusations against my brother.

"Is any of it true?" she asks, her voice low and her eyes slightly narrowed. A shadow crosses her face, and the back of my neck prickles. I know that look. It's what escapes when you can't shove a terrible thought to the back of your mind in time to totally ignore it. Did she know or suspect something about Leo?

"I don't know," I say. "But I do know this 'Sofia' character is behind it."

Brooke rubs her creased forehead. "I keep having to remind myself that Sofia, the real one, is dead."

"I know—I do, too. My money is on Drea being behind this. She must be out to punish us for what happened to her sister."

"Drea," Brooke agrees grimly. I nod. "Okay, are you sure you don't want me to take a look around this weekend and see what I can get out of her? Your uncle is still up there, right?" I haven't been to that house since Bill's funeral.

"Yes, I think Todd is still in there somewhere. Literally and figuratively." I can picture Todd's unsettling leer, hear his comments about how I was "growing up so fast." The memory sends a ripple of revulsion across my skin. "But I'll handle it. I can go next weekend." I hesitate, and I consider telling Brooke about the private investigator. But something in her devastated face stops my words. She's so broken. She doesn't need this on top of everything else, or an excuse to stop being careful.

What's more, broken people can't be trusted.

"You have enough to deal with already," I add hurriedly. "I don't know what I'll find up there, but Todd will talk to me," I say with more conviction than I can afford. My memories of the Nantucket house are full of sinister trapdoors, like the time Bill locked me overnight in the caretaker's cottage's spider-strewn basement for chewing with my mouth open during dinner. I was eleven. Mom was away at a spa. Sofia picked the lock and got me out. I can still see the mischief spark in her eyes as the door swung open, still hear the click and scrape of hairpins against rusted metal. Sofia just knew how to do things like that. How to use arnica on my bruises, how to find the most secluded places to skinny-dip, how to hide.

Brooke nods, then gets up from her seat and starts to pace. She quickly realizes my apartment's square footage doesn't really accommodate pacing, and she sits back down.

"We're going to find Drea," I say. "We're going to find her and make her stop." Brooke nods again, but more vaguely this time. I can tell her mind has wandered back to Josh and Jenna.

"Hey," I say as gently as I can, "what do you want to do about Josh? Do you want to stay here for a while? You're welcome to the—uh—floor?" A spurt of laughter escapes Brooke's mouth as she swipes away a stray tear.

"Honestly . . ."—she takes another gulp of wine—"I have no idea, but the thought of life without him . . ." Brooke trails off, but I know exactly the sort of self-talk that's filling her mind in the heavy silence that falls. She's terrified of being alone.

"You're thinking of forgiving him?" I ask tentatively. I need to assess the speed of Brooke's downward spiral.

"That would be so pathetic, wouldn't it?" Brooke asks in the tone of someone getting a confession off her chest. And even as she speaks these words, I can see hope fill the blank void that was in her eyes until seconds ago.

"Not if it's what you really want," I say, hoping I actually manage to sound encouraging, even though this is the last thing I think she should do. Unless of course getting back together with Josh is the one thing keeping Brooke from falling apart—and doing something stupid.

"This happens to people all the time, right?" Brooke continues. I can't tell if she's trying to convince herself or me. "Josh feels terrible, and I don't think he'd ever do anything like this again. I can tell."

"Just know," I say, taking Brooke's hand and giving it a squeeze, "if you still want to be with Josh, I'll support you. If you decide to kick his lying, cheating ass to the curb, I'll support you. If you have no idea what the hell you want to do and need time, I'm right here." Brooke manages a real smile at that and gives me a quick hug.

"Okay," she says, squaring her shoulders. "We have a plan. You changed your locks, passwords, everything, right?" She shoots me her signature teacher stare.

"Yes." I'd been changing passwords almost daily, in fact. "If we're careful, and I catch Drea off guard, we can end this," I say.

"And then what?" Brooke's resolve has already started to deflate. She crosses her legs tight and cracks her knuckles reflexively. "If it actually *is* Drea, what's to stop her from revealing *everything*?" Aside from Leo's situation, I'd thought of little else in the past few days. But if Drea knows the truth about Sofia's death, she has a stronger motive than anyone to be behind all of this.

"We've saved every communication from her. She's texted, emailed, and trolled us—using multiple methods of communication just to scare us. That picture you sent is evidence of breaking and entering, and we can prove she's been following us, too. We threaten to take all of that to the police unless she backs off," I say, and I can feel a momentum building behind my words. "The Drea I know is reckless, and if she had anything with teeth to tie us to Sofia's death, she would have used it already."

I stop myself before I finish the thought that shocks me, not because of its content but because I could hear something approaching sentimentality in my voice. Thankfully, Brooke is too lost in thought to notice this.

"Is this really someone we want to play a game of chicken with?" Brooke asks, and her voice is steeped with worry, with fear.

"Yes, and if it's Drea, it's one we can win." I mentally run a finger over the trump card I can play. "The law was on our side after Sofia died, and there's nothing to suggest there's a reason to dig all of that up again."

"And if she had a shred of evidence, she would have gone straight to the police years ago," Brooke says, her voice cautious. "It has to be a bluff," she says, knitting her fingers together and closing her eyes. "Okay, that's good. That's good. That's one less mess. The rest of my life, however—"

We're both out of words, and that heavy silence shrouds us again.

Brooke stands, stretches, and glances at the time glowing green from my never-used oven. "I should get back."

"If there's anything you need—" I start.

"I know," Brooke finishes for me before giving my shoulder a quick squeeze and walking out the door. As soon as I've locked the door behind her, I open my laptop and pull out my phone. There are just a few loose ends that need attending to before I confront Drea. I text Bryce.

Drinks sometime soon? I'll come to you.

CHAPTER 21

Sofia

Then

The October air is brisk and cool on Sofia's face as she passes through the wrought-iron gates that mark the south edge of campus. As she weaves through a thoroughfare of people living their ordinary lives and minding their ordinary business, she relishes a thrill of anticipation.

The English department is housed in a stately brick building. Sofia blends in easily as she climbs the front steps. Inside, voices murmur softly from behind closed doors, and she recognizes the rhythm of polite academic conversations. Glancing at the faculty directory plaque on the wall, Sofia finds Patrick Adams's name and heads to the third floor. The voices die down as she ascends to the quieter inner sanctum of professors' offices. By the time she reaches the uppermost landing, it's completely silent, as if the concentration of academic minds and great books casts a hush over their surroundings.

Doors are closer together on this floor, and most are slightly ajar, revealing a woman intently scribbling notes across what looks like a doomed student essay, then a bald man reading a thick volume in an armchair by his office window. A shadow flickers in the inch of floor exposed at the bottom of Professor Adams's closed door. Sofia reaches for the doorknob, but an unexpected noise makes her jump and retract her hand. Laughter. A young woman's laughter, equal parts girlish and sexy. Without another moment's hesitation, Sofia gives two perfunctory raps on the door before pushing it open.

The first thing she sees is a pair of crossed slender legs in sheer black tights. The legs shift to an angle that no longer faces the gorgeous man seated opposite her. Sofia swings the door wider, and a pretty pair of brown eyes peer up at her quizzically from beneath an artfully tousled fringe of honey-colored hair.

"Professor Adams?" Sofia keeps her tone innocent and inquisitive, and her voice comes out higher than usual.

"Yes?" is the deep voice's response. Looking at him, the object of Brooke's obsession, Sofia is reminded of the old Hollywood leading men she and Caroline loved to watch late into the night. Patrick Adams has the classic tall, dark, and handsome look of Gregory Peck or Clark Gable.

"I just wanted to chat with you about a course you're offering next semester?" Sofia hates when women end sentences like questions even if they aren't questions. But it's necessary now. A tentative, harmless, overeager sophomore: that's who just walked into Dr. Adams's office. Nothing more.

"Oh," he says, hesitating and looking at the girl. "We were just in the middle of—"

"That's okay, Dr. Adams," she says, smoothing her tight skirt unnecessarily as she stands. "I think I have what I need for the assignment. Thank you for the *amazing* notes. And I can't wait to read this." She holds up a slim volume of poetry. It's dog-eared and has the unmistakable look of a well-read book, fresh from its slot in this man's personal library.

"Call me Patrick," he says with a lopsided grin.

"Patrick," she says, resting one hand on the doorknob and using the other to tuck a strand of hair behind her ear before leaving the office.

"What can I do for you?" He tents his fingers and indicates the seat that was just vacated. A gold wedding band glints from his left hand. "And I'm sorry, I didn't catch your name? Are you a first-year student?"

"Sophomore," Sofia lies easily. "I'm Amanda Roberts." It was the generic name she made up earlier that day.

"Ah—and are you thinking of majoring in English, Amanda?" Sofia can feel it, the palpable magnetism this man has. The easy way in which he could bring someone into his confidence with a book of poetry or the right personal question.

"Yeah, I'm between English and political science at the moment." An online message board that rates professors told her that Dr. Adams likes to make historical and political connections in his classes.

"I love hearing that from students. We need more fresh young minds shaking things up," he says. As he continues talking, Sofia's attention wanders to the objects on his desk: an abstract glass shape engraved with writing too small to read, probably an award; a green leather ink blotter; untidy stacks of books and papers. There are the standard trappings of a college professor. But conspicuously missing from his desk and from the walls are any photographs, not a single snapshot of his wife.

"Amanda?"

"Sorry," Sofia says. "I was just noticing your bookshelf. I love . . ."—her eyes scan the titles—"Chaucer."

"'Experience, though noon auctoritee / Were in this world, is right ynough for me,'" Patrick recites, leaning back in his chair as if relaxing into the words.

"The Wife of Bath," she says because she can't help herself.

"Very good." He leans forward and arches an eyebrow. "Maybe you don't need my medieval literature class after all."

"I do have one question," Sofia says, preparing to take the plunge.

"Fire away." He's in his comfort zone now: the cool, brainy professor showing off for a new student.

"What was your relationship with Brooke Winters like?" As Sofia holds Dr. Adams's gaze, his eyes harden and his jovial charm vanishes alarmingly fast.

"I don't know who you're talking about," he says. The sexy professorial voice is gone, replaced by a "no comment" monotone.

"Listen," Sofia says, aware that at any second he will probably kick her out of his office, "Brooke is no friend of mine. It's just that I'm worried that she might be latching onto someone I care about. Just like she tried to do to you and your family." It's obvious Dr. Adams is trying hard to stay calm, to keep his face impassive, but his knuckles are white on the arm of his chair.

"Again, whoever this Brooke Winters is, she has nothing to do with me." Dr. Adams says all of this through a grate of gritted teeth.

"So she was never your student, never in your advisory cohort?"

"I teach a lot of undergraduates, I advise PhD candidates, and I'm writing a book. As you might imagine, I'm extremely busy, so I'm going to have to ask you to—"

"You never filed a formal complaint with the university against her? You never claimed that she was stalking you, your wife, and possibly your son?" Sofia interrupts.

He's halfway onto his feet, but at these words, he sinks back into his chair. He regains his professional manner, and before Sofia can blink, the power in their conversation. As suddenly as the barely restrained version of Dr. Adams appeared, he was erased. "I don't know where you're getting that information, but any record like that would be strictly confidential. You should know that a breach of that confidentiality can be grounds for suspension." He says this lightly, but there's no mistaking the threatening subtext. "I'm sure this was just a simple misunderstanding. Now please leave."

Sofia is out of his office as fast as her legs will carry her, and she could swear she hears a lock grind into place after the door snaps shut. She races through the hushed hallway and down the stairwell, back toward the noise of the campus. Nearly colliding with students funneling out of a seminar room, she's through the doors and finally able to breathe again. Back on the path that curves picturesquely through green lawns, she pulls out her phone and sees a text from Leo.

> I want to draw you, gorgeous. Come back to Avi's soon. x

Her eyes linger on his message for just a second, and then Sofia slides the phone back into her pocket and extracts the thumb drive. Even if Professor Adams refuses to tell anything, this might. She pauses to consult the map pinned to a bulletin board before continuing. Bikes whiz past. Chatter from a cluster of sorority girls bubbles ahead.

It's a quick walk to the Rockefeller Library, and its narrow windows remind Sofia of the slits in medieval castle walls. She and Caroline used to spend hours poring over the Archers' vast collection of old encyclopedias, copies of *National Geographic*, and coffee-table travel books, wondering what secrets lurked in the remote castles and dense jungles and inventing elaborate stories about them, vowing to visit one day.

Inside, the linoleum floor magnifies even the slightest noise: the rustle of paper, books thumping into the return slot. She makes a beeline for a bank of desktop computers to her right. A quick scan of their screens shows that they require student sign-in, no doubt to prevent outsiders like her from coming in and using them.

As inconspicuously as she can, Sofia circles the rows of computers and scrambles for a lie she could tell a library employee to get access. But then a hunched student in a hoodie gathers his things and leaves his computer without signing out, and she takes his seat.

Sofia unhooks the flimsy headset attached to the computer and puts it on before she slides in the thumb drive. Excitement pushes her pulse to a rapid drumbeat as she clicks to open it. No password. And as she opens the pop-up that registers the USB, she sees it contains just one file, an audio recording.

A few more clicks, and she presses play.

CHAPTER 22

Brooke

Now

My classroom is bathed in the idyllic light unique to the first day of a new school year. For all the order contained within these four walls—a well-stocked, alphabetized classroom library; a carefully selected array of artwork featuring inspirational literary figures; an inviting area for writing conferences; every nook and corner optimized for a welcoming, productive learning environment—you'd never guess at the storm raging within this smiling teacher's life. I start sorting a stack of papers by class period, and there's a knock on the classroom doorframe.

"It looks great in here," Akira says, entering the room. "Ready for battle?" She certainly looks like she is. She is stylishly authoritative and cool in sleek black pants and a tailored blazer, the outfit completed by a geometric statement necklace and a pair of glasses framed in opaque acetate. If I'd been Akira's student, I probably would have secretly worshiped her and found out where she bought those glasses.

"Thank you. And yes! I'm looking forward to finally meeting the kids," I say.

"Good," Akira says as her eyes sweep over a print of the cover of *The Bluest Eye*. "I just wanted to let you know . . ."—she takes a step toward me and lowers her voice—"Dr. Lutz asked that I pop in sometime in the next week or two to see how things are going. Just an informal observation."

"Sounds good," I say, trying not to sound nervous.

"He wanted my visit to be unannounced, but I don't want you to think of me as Big Brother. Not yet, anyway." She grins good-naturedly. I laugh.

"I appreciate the heads-up, and you're welcome to stop by any-time."

"Great. I'll let you get to it. Good luck today." Akira raps her knuckles on one of the desks.

First period begins in five minutes. Everything is ready: the PowerPoint I created to guide the lesson is projected on the Smart Board and after years of teaching, I have more than a little practice leaving my feelings at the door. The sound of feet, laughter, and teenage voices grows louder outside, and I walk toward the hallway to smile and wave at the flurry of passing faces, tan from summer and flushed with energy.

I've never taught at a school that requires uniforms before, so my first reaction is surprise at just how *tidy* these kids are. They look like they're headed off to little jobs or to the set of a new TV show on the CW. A girl with bright red hair and a shy smile makes her way toward my classroom.

"Good morning," I say brightly.

"Hi, are you Miss Winters?" she asks.

"That's me. What's your name?"

"Hannah," she says, her eyes darting around the room behind me, looking for clues about what to expect from me, an unknown entity. Kids are much more perceptive than most people realize. Before I can welcome her, two boys taller than both of us approach, and my words falter. One of them is Ezra. Patrick's son. I square my shoulders and remind myself that I mentally prepared for this.

"Come on in, everyone. Sit wherever you like," I say, ripping the Band-Aid off. The room fills with the thirteen students on my first period roster, almost all of whom take out a notebook expectantly and settle quietly into their seats. Patrick's son does not. He's eyeing Hannah as he talks in a low voice to the boy next to him. They snigger before looking away from her. When the first bell rings, I close the door and am taken aback by the instant silence that falls as I walk to the front of the room.

"Welcome, everyone. My name is Miss Winters, and I look forward to getting to know you all and exploring American literature together this year." Thirteen pairs of eyes settle on me. "Let's begin by breaking the ice a little bit. I'd like you to discuss these questions . . ."—I tap my wireless keyboard—"with the person to your right. Prepare to introduce your partner to the rest of our class. Yes, I know, one of you will get stuck with me." Obedient titters of laughter mixed with a few tentative smiles. "Let's take five minutes on this. Begin."

The class runs like a dream. Almost all the students participate as we discuss what American identity means and read short excerpts of texts from various time periods, authors, and regions. The bell rings, a deep, old-fashioned sound, long before it feels like the sixty minutes have passed. I hurriedly explain the homework assignment before the chairs push back and the students filter out of the room.

Ezra lingers. He had barely spoken during the class, maintaining instead the haughty, guarded air that's typical of privileged teenage boys.

"Uh—Miss Winters?"

"Hey, Ezra, what's up?" I try to sound as much like my normal, authoritative teacher self as possible.

"My mom said she talked to you?" He's half turned toward the door already, ready to move on with his day. My heart skips a beat, then starts hammering double time. Was there a fresh threat lurking in my inbox, this time from Rebecca?

"About how football will affect when I can turn in homework and take tests and stuff?" Ezra takes my silence for confusion, not panic. Then realization creeps in, its thorny tendrils curling around my thoughts.

"Y-Yes," I stammer. "She did. Thanks for reminding me." Ezra departs for his next class without a backward glance. It's hitting me as I turn to the back of the room, hiding my face from the next class that will arrive any second. Rebecca clearly has no intention of exposing my past. Why would she? Exposing me is one thing: owning me is quite another.

Dangling my secrets over my head is much more beneficial to her son. I'm not sure if Ezra is aware of the free pass he's got tucked in his pocket for the rest of the school year. Perhaps like his father, he's accustomed to special treatment for little or no reason. My way forward is clear: Rebecca made sure of that. As far as I'm concerned, Ezra just became my star student. How long I can keep this a secret without raising suspicion, however, is a lot less certain.

A small voice from behind me makes me jump.

"Can we come in?" A boy hovers in the doorway.

"Please do," I say, pulling myself together.

The rest of the day swirls by in a blur of faces, the noise of teenagers, and frequent interruptions from dark thoughts. I spent years trying to outrun Patrick and the wife whose life we'd destroyed. But now everything is catching up with me. And in the silence that settles after students have left for the day, I watch as the right hand on the clock inches closer and closer to four P.M., the earliest I dare leave without drawing attention to myself. I'm on my way out when Antony calls to me from next door.

"You were a hit today," he says. I turn and I'm met with a broad smile as he leans against the doorframe.

"Oh?" I'm caught off guard. I can't see how word from my older students could have traveled to his ears.

"I have my sources, and they're not easily impressed," he says. "How about I buy you a survived-my-first-Woodlands-day drink?" Compulsively, I twist my engagement ring. This is collegiality, not flirting, I tell myself even as I catch his eyes lingering on the skin exposed by my sleeveless blouse.

"Thanks, but I've got to see a friend." It happens to be the truth. I promised I'd drop off some dinner for Bryce and Hayden.

"Another time, then," Antony says and retreats to his classroom.

I say a forced cheerful goodbye to a few more colleagues before stepping into the hot afternoon. Checking my phone, I see that the Italian food I'd ordered for Bryce and Hayden is almost ready for pickup. It seemed like a good idea to take them dinner, but that was before I knew the truth. Now the prospect of what had been *her* house sends a current of nausea to the pit of my stomach. I should have just canceled. But sheer curiosity drowned out my hesitation. What would I find at Bryce's house? A grieving widower, or something else?

Once in the car, I check my phone. Nothing but desperate messages from Josh and wedding venue suggestions from my mother. I haven't spoken to her since the catastrophe at the bridal salon, but it's deeply ingrained in the woman who raised me that no conflict is ever too great to gloss over for appearances' sake. She and Mel still don't know about Josh's affair. With a few swipes of my finger, I delete every message before I start the car.

Four highway exits later, the Hostetler-Lees' neighborhood unfolds in orderly suburban squares complete with impeccable lawns, cherry-red front doors, and the occasional dog sniffing at the borders of invisible electric fences. I accelerate as I turn onto their street, eager to be free of the pungent smell of garlic that seems to have already soaked into the interior of my car. When I roll down the front windows, I feel a twinge of sadness as I take in what Jenna must have seen here in Ridgefield. It's picture-perfect peace, an idyllic setting that she saw only from a distance during her childhood.

The Hostetler-Lee residence appears on my left: white clapboard with green shutters, darkened windows, and flower boxes stuffed with dead and dying pansies. Mottled and forgotten, they droop forlornly in their beds. I pull into their driveway and swing my legs out of the car, my arms laden with plastic takeout bags. I approach the doorstep and ring the bell. Eight tones echo in the empty house. Every light is off. Bryce's car isn't in the driveway. In his grief, he might have forgotten I was coming, which is probably for the best. Reaching into my bag, I pull out a scrap of paper and consider scribbling a quick note to Bryce, but I think better of it and just set the bags down in front of the door.

My job done, I turn back toward the driveway just in time to nearly collide with the mailman.

"Here you go!" he says brightly, handing me a thick stack of letters. Before I can say so much as *wait,* he's already halfway back down the path that cuts through their front lawn. I move to slide the mail into the slot marked "Post" on their front door, but something in my gut stops me. The same gut instinct that tells me Jenna didn't commit suicide is tugging at me now, urging me to look closer. Shielded by the portico that covers their doorstep, I scan my surroundings for onlookers: housewives power walking with hand weights, neighborhood kids out on their bikes, perhaps a car backing out of a garage. No one is watching the unassuming white lady just checking what's probably her own mail. Casting my eye around the perimeter of the front door, I expect to see a Ring camera peering at me, but I can't find one, so I turn my attention back to the envelopes in my hands.

The first few are made of heavy paper, square rather than rectangular, and addressed in handwritten script. Sympathy cards. I flick through junk mail and a catalogue, and then my fingers pause on what seems like a bill at first, one stuffed with several pages, by the feel of it. The return address reads *Family First Life Insurance.* It's addressed to Bryce and postmarked about a week before Jenna's body was found. I slide it, along with what looks like a bank statement, into my bag before I can let little things like guilt or federal law change my mind.

Shoving the rest of the mail through the "Post" slot, I put my sunglasses back on before walking to my car, the sound of my movements drowned out by the landscapers working somewhere down the street. I shut the car door and drive off at what I can only hope is an inconspicuous speed.

CHAPTER 23

Caroline

Now

On Thursday, I take the train to Connecticut. The face that answers the Hostetler-Lees' doorbell is unshaven, sallow, and bloated. Bryce's breath is already soured by booze and cigarettes. I proffer the bottle of eighteen-year-old Glenlivet I brought with me.

"This sucks. I'm so sorry," I say.

"You remembered," Bryce says, eyeing the scotch. "Come in." His voice is ragged and gravelly, like it's been dragged for miles behind a runaway train. Blearily, he looks me in the eye and our past ricochets against the present. This is the problem with hanging on to relationships for too long. Who we are never really escapes who we were. I break eye contact first.

"Neat?" He calls back at me from down a half-dark hallway. To my surprise, the house, or what I can see of it in the shadows, is pristine: there's not a fleck of dust or a single throw pillow unplumped.

"You remembered," I say as my eyes sweep across the faint pattern of vacuum lines left on the living room carpet. Not Bryce's handiwork, of course. Jenna was always the one to clean up their messes.

I walk into the spotless kitchen, where the smell of burned popcorn is the only sign of human inhabitants, including the hollow man pouring three finger measures of scotch into Waterford tumblers. I recognize the same glasses as those my stepfather kept in his frequently restocked sideboard. Leo and I had once knocked over a tray of them during a game of hide-and-seek, shattering all but one of the glasses. With the only intact tumbler in his hand, Bill told me to bring my favorite books into his study and sipped as he made me place them one at a time into the blazing fireplace.

Bryce plunks a large ice cube into one tumbler and hands me the other. The engraved crystal is heavy in my hand.

"Is Hayden not here?" I ask.

"He's staying with my parents for now."

"That's good," I say. I have no idea if that's actually good for Hayden or not. I can only base this assessment on my last memories of Anderson and Penelope Hostetler, in which the two of them shrewdly appraised me as an ideal match for their son. They come from a particular class of people who show more warmth and affection for their dogs and horses than their human children. Maybe grandchildren are a different story. Maybe Bryce is too broken to care. Regardless, letting Jenna have him was one of the best decisions I've ever made.

Bryce takes a practiced swig as he opens the screen door that leads to a back patio and a darkly luminous swimming pool. I follow him outside, and we stretch out on two of the lounge chairs facing the glimmering water. The submerged lights dance beneath its surface and cast pale flickers across Bryce's face, making him appear even more like a hollowed-out shell of a man. For several long moments, the only sound is the crack of the ice in his glass. He swirls the amber liquid, which is already starting to sweat in the claustrophobic night air.

"This is a stupid question, but I'm going to ask it anyway. How are you holding up?" I ask, turning to face him, but his eyes remain fixed on the surface of the pool. Around us, the pine trees are completely still, almost as if they're holding their breath.

"I—" he starts, and he rubs a hand over his mouth. "I don't know, Cee." I wait and watch the pitch of his shoulders slump.

"I loved her, but you know how miserable I was. It's not like I wished her *dead*." His eyes, unmoving, reflect the restless underwater light. "The police questioned me, you know. I'm pretty sure that if I hadn't been with a bunch of people who can vouch for me, I'd be in jail."

"That's awful," I say. So he has an alibi. I'm thinking through the implications of this when I realize I've let the pause go on too long. "How's Hayden?"

"That's the worst thing about this whole fucking mess. I honestly have no idea how my son is. Father of the year, right here." Bryce toasts himself sardonically and swallows hard. "And now I'm the guy who said that losing his wife *isn't* the worst thing about her death."

"You're not that guy." I say this even though Bryce absolutely is that guy. The guy who would gather an audience to watch him drown in self-pity and forget all about his living, breathing child.

"You're not," I repeat, forcefully this time.

"If you say so." He attempts a small smile, but it collapses into a grimace. The expression barely had time to settle onto his face when Bryce sits bolt upright, his eyes scanning the tree line that borders the backyard.

"What was *that*?" he asks, and I can hear the scotch starting to do its work. I follow his gaze to the trees, but I can't see anything but branches and shadows. Bryce has never been the paranoid type, but he has good reason to be now, just like the rest of us. He sits back uneasily onto the lounge chair.

"What do I *do* now, Cee? I'm already the useless idiot Hostetler, and now I'm also the sad widower with a mortgage I can't afford and a kid who doesn't even like me."

I reach out to grasp his hand, but my fingers find his thigh instead. He doesn't move them, and neither do I. But then another rustling sound comes from the trees, and he gets up abruptly from the chair. He squints at the backyard for a long moment, but with a shake of his head, dismisses the noise.

"I'm going to get some more ice," he mumbles, ruffling the back of his hair in a gesture I've seen hundreds of times.

"No need," I say, and I reach for his glass. "I was going to run to the restroom anyway." He hands me the empty tumbler, and I walk toward the barely lit house. In the reflection of the sliding glass door, I watch Bryce resume his position on the deck chair, staring at nothing.

I close the door behind me, set our glasses down on the kitchen counter, carefully slide my phone out of my pocket, and tap on the flashlight. Bryce might notice the lights turning on in the wrong room, and I can't be seen doing what I'm about to do. Jenna's office is down the hall past the bathroom. The door is firmly shut, and as I push it open, I think about the futility of what I'm about to try: Jenna was a smart woman with the Ivy League credentials and brilliant medical career to prove it. She would know to keep her secrets well away from prying eyes.

The pinprick of light from my phone picks up the glass enshrining Jenna's degrees, a stylish modern print, and photos of Hayden on the walls. Papers are scattered across the desk as if she'd just set them down and there's a notebook splayed open, with a pen still wedged between its pages. Unlike the rest of the house, this room has remained untouched. Why is that?

The grieving widower wouldn't be able to bear being surrounded by his late wife's things. A heartbroken father wouldn't want his son to see them, either. But everything I've heard tonight tells me Bryce is playing the part more than living it. Still, would he notice if something was moved? It seems unlikely, but I still take extra care as I start opening the desk drawers.

Medical journals, notebooks, a rubber stress ball: nothing out of the ordinary for a doctor. A row of files, all with Jenna's barely legible scrawl on their labels, lines the bottom drawer, and I slip my hand into each one, running my fingers along the crease at the bottom of the folders just in case. There's a rustle somewhere outside. My pulse quickens, and I push aside a few of the files, searching for an opened catch or a false bottom to the drawer. But stuffed full as they are, I'm able to expose only a few inches at a time, and after I've worked my way through them twice, I turn my attention to the rest of the desk.

Easing back onto my knees, I tilt my phone, letting the beam of light slide slowly across the surface. Nothing. I examine the row of small cubbyholes and pull out the shallow drawers in the hutch of the desk. Nothing. I exhale in frustration and think of Bryce, who must be wondering what I'm doing by now. Then, just as I shift aside a sheet of paper, a small indentation appears on the desk surface. I press it, and the square of wood lifts, exposing a hidden compartment barely wide enough for a key. Reaching inside with my pointer and middle fingers, I scrape my fingernails against the empty space.

"Cee?" Bryce's voice calls from outside.

Confusion collides hard against fear. This has to be where she hid it. Had she moved it before she died? Did Bryce move it? Does he know? As fast as I can, I check that all the drawers are shut and quickly survey the impact of my search. It's undetectable: the desk looks exactly as it did when I entered the room.

The door gives just a low creak of protest as I pull it closed behind me, empty-handed, worse than back to square one. I wonder if "Sofia" got here first. And if they did, I'll have to take extra steps to make sure Bryce is on my side. I shut off my phone's flashlight as I shake my hair out of its bun and undo one button of my shirt.

Back in the kitchen, I snap a giant ice cube out of its mold and let it clatter into Bryce's empty tumbler. After I refill our glasses, I step back out into the thick summer night air.

CHAPTER 24

Brooke

Now

It's always the husband. That's what they say, isn't it? All those docuseries and true-crime podcasts and Netflix shows Josh likes to binge-watch. That thought races through my head as I climb out of bed and head for the kitchen, my legs half asleep. Blinking back the sting of insomnia, I glance at the clock on the microwave, which reads two A.M. I reach for the kettle but, reconsidering, find the half-empty bottle of wine instead.

The envelopes I'd stolen from Jenna's house are buried underneath a layer of junk in a drawer, like I'm trying to hide what I did from myself. I extract them gingerly to read through them again, and they feel dirty even without a speck of dust on them. Spread across the kitchen table, they look slightly absurd next to a stack of papers I need to grade. The act seems as intrusive to Bryce and Jenna as if I were staring through their bedroom window. But Jenna slept with my fiancé, so I consider all bets completely and totally off. I take a fortifying gulp of wine and reopen the first envelope, which contains their most recent financial records.

For what feels like the hundredth time, I run my index finger down a towering list of recurring checking account withdrawals: Jenna's student loan payments from undergrad and medical school are high enough to make my jaw drop. I feel a prickle of guilt when I think about the times Caroline and I invited Jenna out for pricey cocktails and weekend trips, not giving a second thought to how different our financial situations were.

A creak makes me startle, and I half expect to see Josh emerging from the shower, throwing me a wink as he towels off his hair and pads down the hall. I release my sharp intake of breath and remember he's gone to stay with an old college friend. Brian, I think. Brian with his seal's bark laugh and stupid frat-boy jokes. I never liked that guy.

Refusing to fall down that particular well of misery, I cut my eyes back to Bryce's latest savings account statement. It shows how little safety net was left.

And then there are the credit card bills. Country club fees, day care tuition for Hayden, two leased BMWs, trips to Vail and St. Bart's. It goes on and on down a long list of expensive charges. The third envelope is the most damning: confirmation that Bryce took out a multimillion-dollar life insurance policy for Jenna shortly before her death. Even with their high salaries and regular payments from an anonymous bank account—bailouts from his parents, probably—they were pretty much broke. Worse than broke, they were rapidly digging themselves into a hole. Another pulse of guilt spikes through me. I should give this to the police. Send it in anonymously. But surely there's nothing here they can't easily discover, that they wouldn't already suspect. It's always the husband, and *this* husband looks guilty as hell.

I trace the string of numbers that accompany the odd transfers into their bank account. The sender is the same, but the amounts are irregular, usually between $15,000 and $30,000. There's anonymity in these numbers: clearly, this is from someone either too busy to track their wealth or too unwilling to be identified—or both. The day I stole these documents, I typed the twelve digits into Google and discovered the pattern is consistent with a Swiss bank account. Was this a trust Bryce and Jenna set up for their son that they needed to dip into? A shady business deal Bryce would rather keep under wraps? Caroline might think Drea is behind all of this, but we still can't connect her to Jenna. And I can't ignore Bryce's clear motive.

The thought of him and those incriminating numbers worms its way into every quiet moment throughout the next day. Then come the reminders that my ex-fiancé slept with one of my friends: the empty apartment and the too-tight engagement ring I have yet to take off out of some horrible mixture of denial and pride.

———

All throughout the next morning, I struggle to stay in the present, even in the middle of class discussion.

"Miss Winters?"

"So sorry—where were we?" I'm facing a room of expectant-looking high school juniors. Scrambling to collect my thoughts, I almost don't notice my classroom door opening. "Right, given what we now know about Maya Angelou's life, what is it you think she's rising *against* here?"

"Yes, Evan." I point at the boy with his hand in the air.

"Racism?"

"Absolutely, that's one of many obstacles she faced in her life. Let's expand on that," I prompt. "Where in the text can we point to this experience?" I search the semicircle for someone who has yet to participate. "What do you think, Hannah?" The girl jumps slightly in her seat.

"Um . . ." She pores over the painstaking notes she had been taking in lieu of speaking up. "Where she talks about the past? About history and pain?" I nod at Hannah encouragingly. "It's beautiful. She's saying that she's rising not just against these things, but in spite of them. She's defiant. It's like she's won." Her classmates turn toward her. From their raised eyebrows, I can tell that these were a lot of words spoken in a row for Hannah.

"Excellent. I think you're absolutely right." Out of the corner of my eye, I see we have about ninety seconds until the bell rings.

"For homework, I want you to focus on Angelou's use of imagery in this poem to capture her emotions and experiences. Select one or two lines to discuss in detail on Monday, and start brainstorming how you would illustrate your life and your story with imagery. Have . . ."—the bell interrupts me—"a great day, everybody!"

After the class shuffles out, I open my laptop and answer a few emails and enter a few grades into the online system. Woodlands parents could not be more different from the families I'm used to. This week alone, my inbox had already seen three questions about grades, all from helicopter parents who, as it happens, could probably afford actual helicopters.

Ezra's name catches my eye as I scan the online roster. An A is smug in his column, though he has yet to turn in any work. How long can our little arrangement last? Surely it is only a matter of time before other students and then their parents notice his preferential treatment. That can play out in an uproar about unfairness, or more likely, an influx of demands for the same sort of exceptions, extensions, and "flexibility." I try to crumple these thoughts like loose pieces of paper and toss them away, because other, more dangerous thoughts are impatiently waiting to take their place.

Who am I to judge Josh and Jenna after what I did to Rebecca? I had been the other woman. I could say I was young, which is true, that Patrick had manipulated me, but deep down, I knew what I was doing. Images of us flicker to life in my mind: of me reading his latest manuscript pages aloud, curled against him in the room I knew that he shared with his wife, a fact Patrick made so easy to forget. So easy to believe his wife was jealous of his success, that he had never wanted to have children and felt trapped. So easy to ignore the towels monogrammed with her initials as I showered in her bathroom.

He said he was going to leave her. He made excuses to go away with me: conferences that never happened, literary events that didn't exist. The lies got bigger and bigger until they eclipsed my life completely, casting my reality in his shadow.

My phone pings a distraction. It's Josh. Again.

> Can we please just talk?

Gray dots flicker across the screen, but then they vanish, a vital sign gone dead. But something in my chest stirs when I think of his embrace, how comforting it would be to sink back into his arms. To have some semblance of a safe place whenever my stalker plays their next card. To not be alone with nothing but my mistakes for company.

I type Okay. Then delete it, type it again, and pause as the cursor blinks blankly back at me as if waiting for my next move. I press send. I slept in one of his old T-shirts last night, and tears came when I breathed in his familiar smell and turned over to where an empty space lay where he should be. It was pathetic, but so is being alone. I wonder if it would be simpler, better for everyone, just to forgive him. The phone buzzes Josh's response, but I can't bring myself to look at it.

―――――

By the time I toss my keys into the tray in what was our apartment, I still haven't looked at my phone.

"Pipes?" I slide out of my flats and walk into the kitchen to retrieve her bowl. The sounds of my keys in the door and then the clink on the counter as I open a can of her food are usually enough to send Piper running to greet me, her tail in the air.

"Piper?" I say again, setting down her food and unhooking my bra as I head toward the bedroom and the bliss of after-work yoga pants and an oversize T-shirt. I reach for the bottom drawer, but something in the corner of the room catches my eye. Piper's bed is wedged between a bookshelf and the wall, and a white slip of paper covers it. My breath catches in my throat as if garroted by an invisible wire. I take the four steps toward the harmless little square of fluffy gray fabric, where my sweet girl normally curls up while I'm away, and, my hands shaking, lift the crimson-stained paper to eye level.

> Time to tell the truth, don't you think, B?
> Or has the cat got your tongue?

I'm vaguely aware of screaming Piper's name as thoughts of the kind of monster who harms innocent animals whirl through my seething, panic-stricken mind. Thoughts of sociopaths catching and killing squirrels before they moved on to human prey and flashes of Piper safe and snuggled between Josh and me chase one another in sickening circles. I tear through the apartment, looking under every piece of furniture, opening every closet, and then a terrible realization crashes over me like an inescapable fifty-foot wave.

"Sofia" has a copy of my new key.

I scramble to the front door and slide the chain into place. I crumple on the floor, my back hunched against my delusion of safety, which was really just a stupid slab of wood. Bile rises in my throat, and I have to choke back vomit as tears slick my face. I reach for my burner phone and dial Caroline's number. We're going to need a new plan if we're going to beat "Sofia" in this sick, twisted game.

CHAPTER 25

Sofia

Then

Sofia presses the headphones attached to the library computer to her ears and leans forward in the stiff chair. The first sound is a rustle, followed by a clunk. Whatever was used to record this must have smacked against something heavy. There's a grainy silence. She clicks on the desktop screen to turn up the volume.

"It's on? Okay. Remember, these are people we really, really don't want to piss off. Big donors." The voice is female, authoritative, and cold.

"So we just allow students to act like this girl did?" Another voice, also female, clipped and matter-of-fact. "Borderline deranged and disruptive, that is, depending on who her parents are." Sofia hears what sounds like papers being tapped in a stack against wood, then set down.

"No," the first voice says with strained patience. "It's just we need to get a result tactfully, so I need you not to come into this with guns blazing."

"Consider them holstered. But honestly, Ann, any other student would have been expelled or on probation already." Sofia hunches closer to the computer screen.

"Elaine," says the second voice. It's a warning.

"I promise to be professional. It's just this isn't the first time a student has—uh—*latched* onto Patrick. He doesn't deserve this. Just look at what's happening across the country with stuff like this—guilty until proven innocent."

"And can you *honestly* say that your friendship with Patrick and his wife has nothing to do with this? That you can be neutral during this meeting?" Ann is treading carefully, but Sofia suspects not carefully enough.

"I'm not going to pretend that I don't *know* Patrick is a good guy," Elaine says.

"We can—" Ann stops talking abruptly, and what sounds like a group of people enters the room.

"Good morning," Elaine says after clearing her throat, and she's clearly kept her promise. The tension and anxiety have been polished out of her voice. "Thank you for making the time to meet with us. You must be Mrs. Winters." Sofia's eyes widen as she pictures Brooke's formidable mother entering the room. She had met Daphne only once, when she stopped by their dorm at the start of the fall semester. Daphne had given her daughter a peck on the cheek before leaving to let the housekeeper move in Brooke's things.

"Yes," says Daphne. "Of course, you know my daughter, Brooke, and this is our attorney, Alex Shaw." Sofia imagines hands being shaken across a conference table or office desk.

"I'm Ann Jeffries, and this is my colleague, Elaine Webster. Please sit down." The recording rustles again, and it occurs to Sofia that the device is probably concealed in a pocket, briefcase, or purse. "Thank you for agreeing to this meeting," Ann continues. "I hope you can understand why Dr. Adams will not be joining us today."

"Of course," Daphne says.

"We'll make this quick," a male voice that must be Alex Shaw says. "My client, her mother, and I would like this resolved ASAP. We don't want to take up too much of your valuable time."

"We're all hoping for a positive outcome, but unfortunately, Brooke here is in serious violation of several key points of Brown's code of student conduct," Elaine says.

"And my client would appreciate the opportunity to address that." There's a creaking of chairs, and Sofia can almost see Brooke sitting there, cornered, all eyes on her.

"I would, if that's okay," Brooke says in a small voice.

"Go ahead," Elaine says, sounding anything but encouraging.

"I understand that my actions were inappropriate, and I sincerely apologize for negatively impacting Dr. Adams, his students, and the broader academic community." Brooke pauses for breath in what sounds like a thoroughly well-rehearsed statement. No doubt she was coached by her attorney and her mother. "I am committed to remaining in good standing as a student for the remainder of the semester, and I deeply value the time I spent here. However, out of respect for this university and for my own personal growth, I feel it is necessary to start fresh as a student elsewhere. I plan to transfer to another college at the end of this semester, and I will do everything in my power to conclude my time here on a positive note."

It's good. Sofia will give her that. But she's not fooled, and she doubts this will work on Brooke's audience.

"Thank you, Brooke," Alex says smoothly. "What my client is saying is that she would like the chance to, as she puts it, make a fresh start at another university as soon as she can. I'm sure we can agree that a student with her credentials would find ample opportunities at many excellent campuses around the country." Brooke's lawyer pauses. "In order to do that, she will need to have a clean record and a recommendation from this university."

So that's what this is really about, making sure Brooke comes out of this smelling like a rose, no matter what she's done. A dull soreness in Sofia's back makes her realize she's been perched on the edge of her seat in front of the computer. She sits back and adjusts the headset.

"I appreciate your apology, Brooke. And I hear where you're coming from. Frankly, we agree that perhaps, given recent events, remaining a student here might not be the best fit for you." Elaine speaks in a clear, even voice. "However . . ."—she lets the word dangle in the air a moment—"we cannot simply look the other way in light of the seriousness of her actions both on this campus and off. Brooke is lucky Dr. Adams is not currently pursuing legal action." There's a rustle of paper, and it sounds like something is being slid across the table. "Students in one of Dr. Adams's other classes reported some extremely disturbing behavior from Brooke, as did several of his graduate student advisees. In the first incident—"

"Elaine, we are all aware of what happened." Ann interrupts her.

"I'm not sure we are, actually." Elaine sounds like she's preparing to take back control of the conversation. "While what you shared was very nice, Brooke, and I don't doubt your sincerity, I'm not sure you appreciate the impact of the disruption you caused. Mrs. Winters . . ."—Sofia assumes Elaine has turned her attention to Brooke's mother—"are you aware that your daughter stormed into one of Dr. Adams's literature seminars, clearly inebriated, and verbally abused him for not responding to an email she'd sent, along with making a string of incoherent accusations?" Elaine's voice doesn't rise, her tone doesn't even change, but there's no denying she's going in for the kill. "Thirteen undergraduate students witnessed this behavior. Surely you can understand—"

"I wasn't aware that the purpose of this meeting is to humiliate my daughter." Daphne Winters's stony response sends a shiver down Sofia's spine. "She's been through quite an ordeal as it is. And I'm glad you brought up university policy. Let's talk about when this university does and does not choose to enforce its own rules." Daphne's tone is delicate, similar to the delicacy of a surgeon's work with a scalpel.

"In determining the best next steps for my client, we were surprised to learn more about this university's practices regarding professor-student relationships." Alex chimes in right on cue. "Some troubling information has come to our attention regarding repeated allegations of sexual misconduct against Patrick Adams. Several female students have come forward, in fact, but over the years, these complaints have been ignored."

"I'm not sure where you're getting this information," Elaine cuts in. "But you should know that staffing matters are confidential. All we can tell you is that Dr. Adams remains one of the most popular professors in his department."

"Not to mention a faculty member who's also published two bestselling books. That's quite a feather in the university's cap," Daphne says. "Especially when enrollment and funding in the humanities are at an all-time low. Now would be a rather inconvenient time for a well-publicized scandal, wouldn't you agree?" Daphne Winters's gloves are off, but her tone is honeyed and deadly calm.

"How do you . . . That's not—" Ann blusters, not realizing she's already given herself away. "Of course no one wants this blown out of proportion." She's making a feeble attempt to regain control of the rapidly derailing conversation.

"Especially in light of the other allegations against Dr. Adams and that football coach's racist remarks—which I'm not sure how you managed to keep quiet, by the way." Daphne continues as if Ann had not spoken. "Kids these days care about these sorts of things when they're applying to elite schools, you know, and tuition-paying parents want their children to be happy. If something like this were to get out, I imagine alternatives like Middlebury or Dartmouth would siphon off your top applicants."

"Student enrollment is completely irrelevant to why we are here today." Elaine tries to muscle in, but Sofia can hear the cracks that are starting to show in her calm tone of voice.

"As I was saying to my good friend Dean Wyatt the other day, legacy is everything. So let me ask you this, how much of this fine institution's legacy are you willing to risk by punishing a victim of harassment?" Daphne's words have grown claws.

"Excuse me? *Harassment?* That is clearly not the case in this situation. If anything Brooke is lucky Dr. Adams isn't pressing charges against her for harassing *him*." Elaine's cool has evaporated completely.

"I think you'll find that's not the case," Alex says firmly. "When you look at these." A rustle, sheets of paper being extracted from a folder and slid across a surface, probably toward Elaine and Ann. "Emails, text messages, and phone calls between my client and Dr. Adams. I'm afraid some of these are quite explicit." He pauses. "Some of the—um—more intimate images have been blacked out for Brooke's privacy, but I'm sure you can get the gist of what was going on between Dr. Adams, an employee of this university and, incidentally, a married man and father, and one of his teenage undergraduate students."

So these were their trump cards. Sofia imagines them fanned out across the table, damning and black-and-white. This was the magic that transformed certain expulsion to a smooth, spotless transfer of Brooke Winters and her issues into Sofia's and Caroline's lives. The grainy silence has resumed, peppered only by the sound of pages shifting in and out of hands.

"This email isn't Patrick's Brown address, so I have no way of knowing this is *actually* him. And how do we know these text messages aren't fabrications?" Despite her best efforts, there's something new coloring Elaine's tone. Fear.

"Dr. Adams was careful to ensure these communications do not reveal his personal details or connection to the university," Alex says. "Though, as you can see here, he frequently solicited those details from Brooke, often late at night, often making demands to share her activities and whereabouts." Sofia thinks about how little Brooke has spoken during this meeting and pictures her staring at the floor, terrified about what might happen next.

"I'm sorry," Elaine says, some of the force returning to her

words. "This office does not respond to blackmail. Brooke under-
stands that her behavior was completely unacceptable, and that's
what we are here to discuss. We are *not* here to entertain baseless
accusations."

"That's where I think we disagree," Daphne says, unfazed as
ever. "If my daughter is not permitted to move on with her life with
glowing recommendations from this university, we will have no
choice but to pursue legal action against both Professor Adams and
this institution. All of this . . ."—Sofia pictures her gesturing to the
copies of exchanges between Brooke and Dr. Adams—"goes public. Time, legal fees, and public exposure are of little concern to us,
as the victimized party. Can you say the same?"

"Is that a threat?" Elaine's voice is low.

"Far from it," Alex says tactfully. "We are simply pointing out
that it is in our mutual interest to let this go."

"We understand." For the first time, it's Ann's voice that's
weighted with authority. There's a sound of someone getting to
their feet. "We will discuss the matter and get back to you within
the week."

"We look forward to a swift resolution. Let's go, Brooke."
Daphne's last word, her daughter's name, is harsh and razor-sharp
before a jumble of sounds of feet and chairs moving fills the recording. There's a rustle, a click, and then complete silence. No
doubt the college administrators recorded this to try to get the
upper hand, but Daphne Winters was a step ahead of them.

But unlike Elaine and Ann, Sofia doesn't have anything to lose
by letting the truth get out. Her eyes glint as she starts the recording over to listen again. Brooke has no idea what's coming for her.

CHAPTER 26

Caroline

Now

Bryce is still deep asleep under a thick fog of alcohol and bad memories when I step into the upstairs hallway, shoes in hand. There's just enough time to make it back to the city, shower off the shame of what I'd just done, and get to the Quantum offices, game face firmly in place. But I realize, as I pad down the stairs and out into the gray morning light, I actually don't regret sleeping with him.

I climb into the Uber waiting at the bottom of my dead friend and ex-boyfriend's sloping front lawn. Being with Bryce was like pressing my thumb into an old bruise, aching and irresistible and deep in my skin. But more than anything else, it was necessary for our survival, especially without the one thing I wanted to find in Jenna's house. I can't have her husband asking too many questions, and he won't if he thinks there's a chance of getting laid. That much hasn't changed in ten years.

I remind myself of one more somewhat comforting fact: if "Sofia" actually had what I was searching Jenna's house for, surely they would have done something with it by now. There are a million reasons why Jenna would have covered her tracks. It was worth a shot to look. The secret of that final loose end must have died with her. And with the police ruling her death a suicide after only a cursory investigation, we're safe. For now.

When I reach the quaint small-town station, I blend in with the people waiting for their trains to the city. I buy a black coffee, gum, and a pack of Newport Lights at the stand beside the tracks. The coffee is strong and welcome as I pull a pair of sunglasses out of my bag to ward off the rising sun. I perch the cigarette between my lips and check my phone for any signs of life from Leo. Still nothing. I send him yet another text, which might as well be a slip of paper heading out to sea.

On the train, I confirm the details of the Quantum executives with whom I would be meeting in a matter of hours. In a chaotic situation, you focus on what you can control, and that's Equilibrium right now.

I get to work. I scour LinkedIn, interviews, articles that featured the trajectory of the company, and every other scrap of information I can find on Sara Patel and Milo Armstrong. Their profiles begin to form in my head, ways I can customize my pitch to hit all the right notes and pull on the right strings that would resonate with each of them. This approach failed miserably with Velocity, but then, I doubt anything I could have said would have changed that man's mind.

We've been lucky so far with the response to the Gawker article about Leo. The public and our clients seemed satisfied with the statement we put out on social, and the brief flurry of concerned emails and nasty Instagram comments fizzled out as it became clear that no, this was not going to become a viral moment, and no, our clients didn't feel the need to spring into action and distance themselves from Equilibrium as quickly as possible.

Eric had handled all of that with a few masterstrokes of PR. Equilibrium's Instagram started featuring our social impact initiative workshops and profiles of women who had launched successful careers with our help. I scroll through the most recent updates on our Instagram and LinkedIn pages. There's a good picture of me presenting to the Society of Women Engineers, a quote from a chief technology officer at a company that used our software. It still makes me smile, reading it perhaps for the thirtieth time: "**Résumés we would have missed came straight to me thanks to Equilibrium, and every day the talent we've found makes an impact.**" Tapping through a few more pages, I take in more of Eric's damage control.

He's posted a *Forbes* article about how women find their *why* to succeed in tech. It's gathering likes and comments as I scroll past it. Working women are often told to "return to their *why*," their inner motivation, Zen, purpose, or whatever, when faced with the challenges of "having it all." But that's never the end of it for us, is it? Our *why*'s aren't just there to motivate us: they pull a double shift as our excuse. Our *why* is a necessary crutch that's supposed to make us feel better about hiring nannies, having no social lives outside dating apps or sad weekly "date nights" with our partners, and buying "preventative" anti-aging products in our twenties. Simply loving our jobs, succeeding just for the thrill of it, isn't enough: we've got to have a reason to explain why we aren't better girlfriends, wives, or mothers. They are the reason some women work themselves to the bone, only to add "self-care" as a to-do list item, complete with an empty checkbox, on their already crammed schedules. I refuse to be one of them.

The irony isn't lost on me as I consider the *why* of my company: empowering women in the workforce. I realize that viscerally, at my very core, I do want to change the world. But even more than that, I want Equilibrium to succeed because I am very, *very* good at my job. That should be enough.

I knit my knees closer together so I take up less of the space between the men sitting to my left and to my right. Their suited legs, both pairs a good seven inches apart, keep knocking into mine. But then I change my mind and unwind my legs, planting them in a firm stance to match the two men on either side of me. One of them shoots me a fleeting dirty look from behind his phone before retracting his knee a fraction. I give him my sweetest smile. I almost don't notice the buzz in my purse that comes as I relish their discomfort. But the text on the screen snaps me out of it immediately.

> I thought *we* were soulmates, C? But it looks like old habits die hard. I know I did.

I press the image below the text, and sweat smears the screen. It's a bit blurry, but it could not be clearer in terms of what it reveals from last night. Bryce and I sitting by the pool, his hands in my hair, our faces pressed together, me on top of him, him pulling me into the house. *That* was what Bryce had thought he'd seen in the trees. And like an idiot, I ignored him, chalking it up to grief and paranoia. It was "Sofia," snapping pictures of something they were definitely not supposed to see.

I feel fear dilate and contract from the pit of my stomach to the tips of my fingers as the phone almost slips from my hand. My fingertips hover over the screen for a moment, and before I can think better of it, before I can consider the consequences of actually responding to this monster, I start to type a reply.

> Why are you doing this?

But even as I finish typing, I realize I already know the answer to that. I've always known. I delete the sentence and replace it with what I don't know.

> What do you want?

The response is almost immediate. I grip the phone tighter, as if I could squeeze answers out of it.

> Isn't it obvious?

> I want to watch you lose everything.

My teeth clench and anger pounds hard against my temples.

> And then you and Brooke are going to confess. xx

The man next to me clears his throat and turns a page of his newspaper, jarring me back to my surroundings. And with that, I resolutely return my phone to my bag, making sure it's at the very bottom, under last night's clothes. A single thought is powerful enough to return my pulse to its normal rhythm: if Bryce is all "Sofia" has on me, they're grasping at straws. Jenna never made a backup plan for what I'd hoped to find in her desk. Hooking up with an ex isn't a crime. That thought doesn't comfort me as it should, but I shake off the last two messages and resume my cyber-stalking of Quantum's leadership team.

Three hours later, I'm being offered coffee by the perky executive assistant wearing a Quantum-logoed Bluetooth earpiece. She ushers me into a corner office, where Sara and Milo are already seated. I'm dressed in my go-to professional armor: a sleek black suit and silk blouse, complete with Mom's Jimmy Choo's.

"Thanks, Megan," Sara says warmly from behind a neatly ordered desk complete with a small plaque that reads: *Chief Human Resources Officer.* "Welcome." She turns to me and shakes my hand before gesturing to one of the empty chairs in front of her desk. "Great to see you again, Caroline. Thank you for making time for us." Milo gives me a smile, the full force of his charm behind it.

"I've been looking forward to speaking further," I say, crossing my legs. "I think Equilibrium could bring a lot of value to your platform."

"We agree," Milo says. I hadn't expected it to be *this* easy, so I brace myself for a catch. "Sara and I have already looked over the information your office was kind enough to send along, and we think we'd like to add your software to our global recruiting platforms and listings on our website. It would be right in line with our new diversity and inclusion initiatives." I nod and meet Milo's level gaze. I remind myself that if something sounds too good to be true, it probably is.

"That's great to hear," I say, and I work to keep apprehension out of my voice.

"But before we move forward, we just have a few questions," Milo says. Here we go.

"Yes," Sara says, folding her hands and leaning forward. "I'm sure you can appreciate some of the concerns raised by Equilibrium's recent media exposure."

"Absolutely," I say. I'm ready for this: my talking points are at my fingertips. "The allegations made against my brother are extremely troubling. Our official stance is that the claims should be thoroughly investigated." As I say this, I ignore that familiar gnawing suspicion about Leo, and the truth I know deep down about my brother. I've gotten good at this over the years.

"I'm glad to hear that's Equilibrium's position, but what is your personal stance?" Sara fixes me with a piercing look. "I'm asking because if the situation were to escalate, we would need your reassurance that the integrity of our partnership would remain your first priority." I have to hand it to her. I didn't think it was humanly possible to tactfully say: *We need your word that you're willing to shove your only family under the bus if we're going to touch your company with a ten-foot pole.* But Sara just proved me wrong.

"You have it. I love my brother, but he has had his fair share of ups and downs. He's struggled with addiction. We often don't see eye to eye. Of course, nothing is certain until an investigation is completed, but the issue at hand is both a personal and a professional line in the sand for me."

"Good," Sara says, not quite resuming her collegial manner. There's more. "I'm glad to hear that we're on the same page. We agree that while the facts are being ascertained, it's best to be cautious. And with that in mind, our agreement would need to be a provisional one that reflects Quantum's contributions to our partnership." She opens a folder on her desk and hands me a slim packet of paper.

I open it and am instantly glad I'd braced myself. The terms are a fraction of our usual rates, especially for an account of Quantum's size. And with the amount of technical support they will need, support from engineers I can't afford, we would break even at best.

"Take your time," Sara says. "We know it's a lot to review." I have to admit they played their hand well. If I had been in Sara's chair, I might have done the exact same thing.

"I'd like to handle your consultations personally, and in order to do that, I'll need to adjust some of our programming resources to ensure I can be available to you." Taking a pen from my purse, I circle a number on the sheet. "Would you be able to increase this by, say, 7 percent?" Milo examines the paper, then hands it to Sara, who pauses for a long moment.

"With our current budget, we could do 5 percent," she says.

"Great. In that case, I look forward to working with you both," I say with a smile.

"Actually, Milo is running point on this, and he'll take things from here. But I'll be available in an advisory capacity if you need me. You two will want to work out specifics." Sara stands, and I take this as the cue that we're done here, at least for now.

"Yes, let's step into my office, and I can give you an overview of our recruiting targets this quarter," Milo says in that intoxicating accent. I thank Sara and follow Milo out into the open-concept Quantum workspace. We pass well-dressed people typing away on laptops or deep in conversation. I recognize the assistant who showed me in earlier, and something about her body language makes me slow my pace.

She's inside one of the corner offices. Like Sara's office, the wall facing us is made of glass, but tall bookshelves obscure the back half of the room. She's backing away and looks like she's trying to end a conversation she very much does not want to be a part of, and she takes swift steps out of the office and back to her desk, avoiding eye contact with anyone.

"Caroline?"

"Sorry," I say, taking a last look at the obvious discomfort on the girl's face. "What were you saying?"

"I was asking if you have any plans tonight. Why don't we talk through the next steps over a drink?"

"That sounds great," I say gamely. "Let me check my calendar." On the pretext of doing this, I fire off a text to Eric.

> See if Quantum has any skeletons in their closet, will you?

CHAPTER 27

Caroline

Now

I'm still waiting for Eric's response to my Quantum question when I borrow Brooke's car the next morning. It's Saturday, and with luck, Drea will be at the caretaker's cottage, and I can confront her alone. I don't want memories of what happened the last time Brooke was here to send her over the edge, especially after she called to tell me what happened to Piper between sobs. She also told me about the Hostetler-Lees' bank statements and life insurance policy. It's working to my advantage that she's torn between suspecting Bryce and Drea of being "Sofia." She knows about Bryce's alibi, but I can't fault her for maintaining her suspicions that he was up to something shady. She's probably right, but I have more urgent priorities right now.

A gruff voicemail from the PI confirmed that he hasn't caught Drea doing anything out of the ordinary yet, but I know in my bones that she's behind all of this. It has to end now. I can't deal with this looming over our heads *and* the allegations against Leo, both like blades waiting to fall.

Past the wind-battered gate, the grass is overgrown and Brooke's car maneuvers uneasily through the acres that have passed through four generations of Archers. Borderline sociopathic snobs though most of them were, you can't fault their taste in real estate. Windows down, I can hear the familiar sound of waves and the rush of salty air whisper like ghosts, none of them particularly peaceful or rested.

Even though I've braced myself, the first building that emerges from the tall grass still sends a jolt through my nerves. The last time I'd set foot there was with Sofia. Mostly in shadow, the caretaker's cabin is tucked right where it can be easily accessed but is still well out of sight of where the Archers and their guests would spend their time. It's where Bill liked to send me as a reminder of my place. This is where I'll find Drea. Navigating gingerly around bumps in the uneven road, I make my way closer to the main house.

The scenery opens from shady trees to pristine coastline. Bill's older brother Todd inherited this place, and he should be around here somewhere. I need to get to him first. That way, I can get a sense of where Drea has been and what she's been doing and make up an excuse to talk to her alone. Ahead, a faded shell of the mansion I remember looms on the horizon. The closer I get, the easier it is to make out the cracked paint and the unruly hedges. Sand and salt and rain have faded blue trim to an anemic gray on crooked shutters and chipped siding. It's a weary sight, like an aging society hostess who's fallen on hard times. And as I pull stop at the end of the drive, I see that the front door hangs ajar.

"Hello?" I say as I step under the arched entryway. Termites have left the underside of the wood ridged and pockmarked. My voice soars up a grand staircase that curves toward my feet in a graceful descent from the second floor twenty feet above my head. It echoes through the vast sitting room to my right.

The dust settled on the brass light fixtures in the dining room looks undisturbed. Maybe I was wrong, and no one lives here after all. Then there's movement to my left. But as I wheel around, I'm faced with my own reflection in the mirror above a sideboard. I tentatively proceed down the hallway, past doorways to other wings of the house. The last time I set foot here, the spaces had been richly decorated. But the rugs and the vases are gone. Faded rectangles mark where art used to hang on the walls.

"Todd?" I try again.

"We're back here." The distant male voice makes me jump. I enter what used to be the sunroom and stop dead, taken aback by what the space has become. Plants cover and climb every surface. I recognize some of them—aloe, a snake plant, a fiddle-leaf fig—but most are exotic and unfamiliar. A gong the size of a truck tire is in one corner, a statue of Buddha in another. Faded tapestries that wouldn't be out of place in a college dorm room hang from the walls. The glass doors open onto a patio with a spectacular ocean view, marred only by an empty swimming pool, drained except for a foot of murky, dark green water. By its edge, two figures sit on yoga mats facing the ocean.

"Todd?" I say uncertainly.

"We'll be right with you," a serene woman's voice responds. Light from the glittering ocean and spotless sky glares onto my face and bare shoulders. I hover awkwardly a few feet from where they sit, unsure if it's wise to get any closer. Both people sweep their arms in unison over their heads, bring their hands together as if in prayer, bow forward, and stand.

"That was such a beautiful practice, Thomas. *Namaste.*" It's the calm female monotone again. She rests a hand on the small of the man's back and rubs slowly along his spine before turning to me. I barely save myself from doing a double take as I recognize the woman.

"How can we help you, Caroline?" Drea asks, utterly unfazed by my presence. The only other image I have of her swims vividly on the surface of my memory, and it's at complete odds with the lithe, glowingly healthy person in front of me. At her sister's funeral, she had been too drunk to stand up straight, her figure bulging at the seams of a two-sizes-too-small black dress and ripped tights. I remember how Drea's staring eyes were half-hidden behind stringy, badly bleached hair that reeked of weed. While her mother and the rest of Sofia's family sobbed in the front row, Drea lurked like a second corpse at the back of the stuffy funeral home. Now she would fit right in at Lululemon or as a spokesperson for a juice cleanse.

"I'm here to get some of my mother's things," I say, ready with the story I'd rehearsed on the way here. Drea flicks a thick braid of hair, back to its natural brown, from over one shoulder to down her back. She's so like her sister, only rougher, sharp where Sofia was delicate, and wearing something you couldn't have paid Sofia to put on her back. Drea and Todd—or Thomas now, apparently—are dressed in almost identical outfits: fitted yoga pants with loose linen tunics and tasseled strands of brightly colored beads around their necks.

"So good to see you, Caroline," Todd says with almost unsettling calm. For a moment, I'm at a loss for words and forget about my cover story. He's nothing like the failed investment banker I remember: no paunch, no haughty expression. If anything, he looks barely aware of his surroundings, his face relaxed into a vague smile. "I haven't seen you since my renewal," Todd says, perhaps reading my expression.

"Your renewal?" I ask before I can stop the question.

"Oh yes," Drea answers.

"Drea is nothing short of a miracle worker." Todd says this as he rests a hand on her shoulder, and Drea covers it with her own. Heavy silver and turquoise rings glint from her fingers. "With daily yoga, clean eating, meditation, and her coaching, I'm a new man."

"That's great," I say, trying to sound sincere.

"What are you looking for in particular?" Drea asks, and though her tone does not change, I notice her sage expression harden for a fraction of a second.

"There's a vase she kept here that I'd love to have," I say, inventing both the vase and my desire to use decorative objects.

"I'm afraid that won't be possible," Drea says sweetly.

"Oh?" I say, trying to keep things light.

"I wish you would have come by sooner," Drea says with unconvincing regret in her voice. "Right, Thomas?" She gives his hand a squeeze.

"As part of my renewal, I released all of the baggage from this house that was of monetary, rather than sentimental, value," Todd says with palpable relief. "I can't tell you how healing it was to purge all of that negative energy."

"I can understand that," I say, struggling to maintain a patient tone. "Are my mom's things in storage, then?"

"No," Drea says simply, stepping away from Todd and bending to roll up her yoga mat.

"We were able to use the proceeds from all of that excess to fund Drea's foundation. It's the *least* I could do after everything she has done for me. The rest we've set aside for a renovation we're hoping to do of this place. Don't you think it would make the most amazing yoga retreat?" His eyes are on Drea's limber figure as she bends over, her perfectly toned stomach briefly revealed as the breeze lifts her loose-fitting top. "I'm sorry you came all this way. Can I offer you an iced tea or something? Drea makes a wonderful hibiscus infusion."

Despite the heat, a shiver chills me. Clearly she has grand plans for the besotted Todd, and it would be unwise to confront her now.

"No, that's okay, I can't stay. But before I leave, Drea, I think there's a problem with the gate?" It's another lie I came up with on the way here.

"I'll walk you out," Drea offers, stepping toward me.

"Always nice to see you, Caroline." Todd says this and raises his hand to me before walking toward the stretch of private shoreline. Drea's smile slips from her face like oil from water as we walk back through the house.

"Drea—" I hiss.

"Why are you *really* here?" she interrupts as soon as Todd is out of earshot. All the spiritual yogi pretense has vanished from her tone.

"I think you know the answer to that question." I'm hyperaware of the distance between my car and where we're standing. As we cross into the living room turned greenhouse, I notice the faded patch of blank wall over a fireplace. A landscape, probably a valuable one, had hung there once. I remember staring at it the night Bill died in this room.

"Do I?" A dangerous expression appears on Drea's face.

"I know what you've been doing, and it won't work. And I know what you did to Jenna," I say. My plan has backfired; I have to get out of here. Drea's face remains stony, and she opens her mouth to retort, but I turn on my heel before she can say anything more.

"Who's Jenna?" The question is sharp and urgent, but I don't look back. I'm not going to get anywhere with Drea, not today. The second I saw her with Todd, I knew I wouldn't be able to search the caretaker's cabin for evidence that she's impersonating Sofia or try to find a connection between her and Jenna. Having made the fatal mistake of underestimating my opponent, I have no choice now but to let the PI do his job.

The look on her face remains scorched in my mind's eye as I race toward Brooke's car and gun it back down the winding drive, sand and dirt spraying in my wake. I dare a glance in the rearview mirror. Drea is still there at the threshold, a figure silhouetted in dust, staking out what she's ready to take for her own.

CHAPTER 28

Sofia

Then

Foot traffic has thinned, and dusk has just started to dim the edges of campus by the time Sofia leaves the library. She runs a finger over the thumb drive in her pocket thoughtfully, her mind replaying the loop of what she has just heard, what she knows now about Brooke Winters.

Brooke and Daphne didn't care about what happened to Patrick Adams as long as they could escape unscathed. If what Sofia witnessed in his office was any indication of what happens when his door closes, he's probably preyed on other young women. Not that Brooke gives a shit.

He has probably already moved on to the next perky undergrad, but that doesn't matter as long as Brooke's future is secure. Daphne and Brooke played their roles well: the mother, ice-cold and commanding; the daughter, meek and submissive. They are the worst kind of women, the kind who let men do terrible things as long as they can use their power and money to buy their escape from harassment and abuse. They shed scandal off their backs like a snake's skin, discarding it without a second glance.

Stuffing her hands in her sweatshirt pockets, Sofia finds solace in turning the flash drive between her fingers. She thinks of her plan. She will write this story and submit it as her junior fiction project to resuscitate her GPA, then—in another twist of the knife—give the audio to local news outlets and let them do their worst. She'll enjoy watching as everyone Brooke knows puts two and two together. Everyone loves an Ivy League scandal, and it'll be only a matter of days, maybe hours, before the upper-crust hive of Brooke's world knows the truth. Caroline would see the lies, the deceit, the sheer inadequacy of Sofia's replacement in her life, and she'd finally see things clearly. They'll be together again, just like before.

Sofia reaches Avi's building, and with every step she takes out of the elevator, electronic music throbs louder and louder against the papered walls. As she opens the door to Avi's place, she takes him in, along with Leo and two people she vaguely recognizes, all arranged over the expensively upholstered furniture. A pixieish young woman perches on the arm of the overstuffed armchair where Leo sits, her belly button piercing glittering under a sailboat-shaped lamp. Next to her is a man who looks eerily like Leo, and he has his arm around Avi's bony shoulders. Their smiles wilt as they look at Sofia, and after a beat, the years melt away. She remembers where she's seen these two before, and she does her best not to physically recoil.

"My muse!" Leo exclaims after a two-beats-too-long pause. "This is Sofia, everyone. Sofia, these are some of Avi's friends from Choate." He takes in Sofia's blank expression and adds, "That's a boarding school."

His words stumble into each other, and when he gets to his feet, he does so with the swagger he adopts because he thinks it dis-guises how drunk he is. It doesn't. Sofia waves at the group, and they stare back at her indifferently, except for the girl closest to Leo, who eyes her with disappointment she doesn't hide very well.

"Isn't she *gorgeous*?" Leo continues, encircling her with his arms and planting a clammy kiss on Sofia's cheek. "My little diamond in the rough. You know, I met her for the first time when I was, what—?" He looks at Sofia blearily, and she notices the intricate network of red veins webbing the whites of his eyes. "Eight years old? My family and I were out to dinner one night, and I see this pair of *enormous* hazel eyes bobbing behind the door to the kitchen." Nervous about where this is going, she tries to smile as his grip tightens and her face flushes. "Santana's. No, that's not it. Santo's? What was the name of your mom's restaurant again?"

"Santorini's," Sofia says.

"That's the one! Best seafood in Nantucket. *Such* a shame it had to close." His inflection is so dramatic, it sounds almost mocking. Her cheeks are burning now. She thinks of how she and Drea had tried unsuccessfully to console their mom after they had to shutter the cheery restaurant with its blue-and-white-striped awning and sun-bleached wraparound deck facing the ocean.

Leo lowers his voice to a loud whisper. "My dad said everyone stopped going after one of the staff tried to hit on a few of his friends' wives. *Very* raunchy accusations." He laughs, and Sofia clenches her fingers into a fist as she remembers Gino, the waiter who always had a butterscotch candy or a smile or a funny story for his boss's daughters. Drea told Sofia that Gino had in fact enjoyed a handful of perfectly consensual affairs with more than one bored trophy wife. The women got seven-figure divorce settlements. Gino got his life destroyed.

Leo is losing his captive audience, and he knows it. He claps his hands and pushes Sofia into the oversize armchair, more roughly than he realizes. Her elbow knocks into the rail-thin thigh of the blonde, who relocates to the couch with the others, as if she's afraid she'll catch scandal, poverty, or something from making physical contact. "Drinks!" Leo says before disappearing into the kitchen.

"I think I went to that restaurant as a kid. Only place with half-decent Greek food near our summer house," the girl says, dismissing their livelihood with the same ease with which she must have forgotten Sofia. Her name surfaces sourly in Sofia's mind—*Lennox Davenport.*

Spoiled, bored, and manipulative, Lennox relished in reminding Drea and Sofia of their proper place. With that particular cruelty of teenagers, she knew implicitly that she belonged to the ruling class of their little beach town, and the Eliades girls worked for her just like their mom worked for her parents. But all of them were temporarily united by sneaking out past their curfews to go to a beach bonfire one night. Sofia can still see Lennox's eyes flint vicious steel as she dangled a crisp $100 bill in front of them and dared Drea to swim to a rock off the coast and back. The look on Drea's face broke Sofia's heart: it was the instant mental math of how long it would take to work for something people like Lennox had handed to them. Sofia has seen it all her life.

Caroline and Sofia begged her not to take the bait. It was at least a hundred yards, but Drea was never one to back down from a challenge. Drea gave Sofia the money for safekeeping, and Caroline held Sofia's hand while Drea's figure slipped into the black waves. And when she returned, gasping for breath, soaked and shivering, Lennox and her friends just laughed, saying they couldn't believe Drea actually took her seriously. But Caroline was too quick for her, and Sofia smirks to herself as she remembers how Caroline snatched Lennox's cotton-candy-colored Louis Vuitton wallet and tossed it nonchalantly into the bonfire flames before stalking off toward the dunes.

Sofia glares into those haughty pale eyes, unchanged since they flared in the firelight, set ablaze with anger and humiliation at being outmaneuvered by Caroline. Sofia opens her mouth to say something, but Lennox is already turning her attention back to Avi. "Av," she says playfully, "when does this stuff kick in?"

"Any minute now," Avi says, a mischievous smile playing on his lips. "We'll want to be on the roof when it does, though. I think it's time to dance." Lennox giggles, and he casts an eye to a rooftop terrace lit with string lights. Leo reappears, balancing a tray of shot glasses filled with clear liquid on one hand and clutching a frosty bottle of Grey Goose in the other.

"Why, thank you, Jeeves," Lennox says in an affected British accent, reaching for the shot glass that's closest to her. Leo swats her hand away, and her glossed bottom lip protrudes in an exaggerated pout.

"Do allow me, madam." Leo plays along with his own accent, dropping a bow. He hands Sofia the glass that Lennox had reached for.

"A toast!" Avi says, and he springs to his feet, his leisurely manner evaporating under the chemical influence of what must have just hit his bloodstream.

"Yes." The Leo doppelgänger joins Avi.

"To art, to life, to beauty! To having nothing better to do in this pisshole!" The others stand, and Sofia joins them in pushing their glasses together with a tinkling rattle. The vodka burns a trail from the tip of her tongue to the base of her throat.

"I love this song," Lennox says, closing her eyes and swaying to the beat of the music pulsing from Avi's speakers. She pulls Avi outside under the glow of the lights strung against the blackening sky. Sofia takes a step toward the table for more vodka, smirking at how ridiculous they look. Leo reaches for her right hand and places his at the small of her back, swaying with her to the music as he nuzzles a flushed cheek against her neck. His fingers reach under her sweatshirt and press into the symmetrical indents on either side of her tailbone, hard enough to hurt.

"I want to draw you. Now," he murmurs in her ear. She manages to grin, though a shiver almost gives her away. Leo doesn't seem to notice.

"Like one of your French girls?" Sofia asks, and she starts to relax into him. Her limbs are suddenly heavy.

Leo gives Sofia his most dazzling smile. "Exactly, but first let's get you a real drink. Meet me in there," he says. Moving her arms feels like swimming through mud. He points to the second bedroom before disappearing into the kitchen again. She takes a step toward the door, and her shin slams against the sharp corner of an end table. Cursing under her breath, Sofia picks her way across the cluttered room. The themed knickknacks start to blur eerily before her eyes, and it's with relief that she sinks onto the soft bed. The vibrations of Leo's voice seem distant, though she registers his cold hands peeling off her jeans and his lips on her thighs.

CHAPTER 29

Caroline

Now

"Well?" I almost shout into my phone against the city noise that meets me as I approach my apartment building. Car horns blare at each other in the congested street, and ahead of me a group of drunk men weaves across the sidewalk. I squeeze my way between them, ignoring their wolf whistles. It has been several days since I escaped the Nantucket house, and I'd had cocktails with Milo after discussing the Quantum deal. If I'm going to be on time for meeting him tonight, I need to make this quick.

"How much do you love me?" Eric's reply practically gleams with triumph.

"I thought it was impossible to love you more," I say. Eric laughs. I unlock the heavy door, lean against it, and clamber into the dim stairwell. I'm greeted by the familiar smell of mold and the sounds of another one of Rick and Letizia's screaming matches.

"Quantum has done a very good job of covering up *why* they're investing so heavily in diversity and inclusion initiatives. Very good, but not perfect." He emphasizes all the right words to lift my hopes.

"Go on," I say over the echo of my shoes.

"My little birds tell me a lawsuit, a very *public* lawsuit, is brewing. Really, it's just a matter of time before it's all out there."

"Harassment? Unequal pay? What are we looking at here?"

"Sounds like your typical boys' club kind of stuff. Toxic corporate culture. History of passing over women and people of color for promotions. That sort of thing. Several whistleblowers came forward." I think back to the trapped-looking Quantum assistant. My imagination doesn't need to work hard to think of the kind of things that might have made her look so uncomfortable.

"Do I want to know *how* you know all this?"

"No," he says lightly, and I can clearly picture the sly smile that accompanies all his best work. "Not unless you want to hear the details of my age range on Grindr and preference for silver fox lawyers." I smirk and open the door to my hallway.

"You're a star. I'm meeting M—" My words falter as my eyes snag on the figure sitting in front of my apartment door. Leather jacket. Tousled dark gold hair. A lit cigarette. Leo. At the sound of my footsteps, he gets to his feet, and without thinking, I start to scan for the warning signs. His hands are steady. His eyes are clear. It looks like he's showered recently. A visceral part of me relaxes— Leo hasn't relapsed.

"I'll have to call you back," I say to Eric and hang up the phone.

"Hey," he says, raising a hand in greeting.

"Are you fucking serious?" I spit. "I have been trying to reach you *all week*. How many times did I call you, text you, do everything short of sending carrier pigeons and raising smoke signals?" Leo blinks rapidly.

"I'm sorry. It's been crazy."

"Come in. We need to talk." I sigh and maneuver my keys through their series of locks. I'd never admit it to Leo, but I'm so relieved to see him that my anger quickly runs out of steam.

"I know," I say. He follows me inside and shoves his hands in his pockets, a guilty gesture that reminds me of the ten-year-old who took the blame for spilling orange juice on one of Bill's prized Audubon prints. I send a quick text to Milo.

> Something's come up—can we push drinks back an hour or two?

"How are you doing with that whole Gawker thing?" I ask, hesitation slowing the tail end of my sentence.

"I mean—" He runs a hand through his hair as he takes a seat on my couch. "It's all bullshit. You know that, right?"

"Is it?" The question is out before I can trap it, where it's waited, half-formed, for so long.

"Are you really asking me that? You think I'm some sort of monster?" Leo's eyes widen, and all at once we're kids, and he's just helped me dodge Bill's latest rage. I look at my brother hard, and then I shake my head, wanting to believe what his expression is telling me and what I'm telling myself.

"Who even reads Gawker, anyway?" Leo asks, more to break the silence than to get an answer. I shrug.

"Do you know who might have made these accusations?" I ask.

"You mean, do I know anyone who would make up lies about me? Yes. And you know why?" His calm is cracking. "Because I'm talented. And a man. A straight white one at that. That's basically *illegal* now." He rolls his eyes. "Throw in the fact that our family has money, and I'm a dead man walking." I fight the urge to outwardly cringe at these pronouncements.

"Leo—"

"Spare me the lecture, Caroline. I'm only saying that because it's *you*, and I assume this is a 'safe space,' or whatever." He uses air quotes and leans against the cracked kitchen counter with a heavy sigh.

"Of course it is," I say, and I reach out to grasp his shoulder. "I'm just sorry this is happening on top of everything else. It'll blow over."

"This isn't impacting Equilibrium, is it? I saw your statement on Instagram." I knew this was coming, but I still feel my heart sink.

"You're not mad?"

"Why would I be? You did what you had to do for both of us—my badass sister." He even manages a small smile. I'm so relieved, I throw my arms around him.

"Anyway, we should talk about Jenna," Leo says, gently pulling away from me. "At the end of the day, doesn't this, you know, sort of help things?"

"Don't." I scowl, narrowing my eyes in warning and hating that he has a point. Jenna's death makes quite a few of my problems go away, but I can't think about that now. As long as Bryce doesn't start asking questions, I'll never have to think about it again.

"Sorry," Leo says, and he drops his eyes from mine.

"Yeah. Me too," I say. "Are you going to tell me where you've been?"

"Natalia and I were at Avi's retreat for a few days after the show. We needed to work through some things, and his workshops really helped us, I think." Avi, trustafarian drug addict turned sober therapist and relationship guru. It's still hard to picture him with a real job and a thriving practice that legitimately helps people. "We didn't even hear about Jenna's overdose until a few days after she was found. I'm sorry for disappearing on you like that. After that article, I had to get out of the city, so I went back up to Avi's for a while," Leo says.

I sigh. Disappearing for days at a time is nothing new for Leo. "Just let me know the next time you plan on going off the grid for a while?"

"Deal," Leo says with a grin.

My phone buzzes before I can say anything else.

Want to come over to my place? I have a beautiful bottle of red.

It'll be a pricey cab ride to get to the address Milo texts me next, but it sure as hell beats showing him where I live. I respond that I'll be there and refocus on Leo.

"I have to tell you something about Todd," I say. As I recount everything that happened during my visit to the Nantucket house, Leo leans forward in his chair and his expression darkens with every bizarre detail. When I finish, he sits completely still for a moment as it all sinks in. Then, he's on his feet.

"So you're saying that Drea has turned Uncle Todd—like, golf-playing, twenty-five-year-old-escort-banging Uncle Todd—into some brainwashed yoga puppet?"

"Exactly. As in a 'probably voted for *Bernie*' level transformation," I say.

Leo takes a beat. "We have to do something," he says with a note of desperation.

"And we will," I say. "I've been in touch with Richard."

"*Richard?*" Leo says the private investigator's name as if I'd just told him Justin Bieber has the situation under control. "Richard is drunk like half the time, you know that, right?"

"Oh, come on, he's good and you know it. Besides, he's all we've got," I say, holding up a hand defensively. I don't mention the full extent of the PI's assignment: follow Drea, ascertain if she's stalking Brooke and me, find out if and why she killed Jenna, and get Drea arrested.

"Fine," Leo says.

"Have you sold anything from your show?" I ask this question lightly to disguise how eager I am to steer the subject away from Drea and my plans for her. The less Leo knows, the better.

"A few things here and there, yeah." Leo runs his right hand through his hair again. It's been his tell since he was a child. I don't need to check the Chase app to know he's lying.

"We'll get through this," I say. If everything goes to plan with Milo, we just might have a shot. I glance down at my phone and feel a rush of adrenaline. Eric just came through with exactly the ammunition I need.

"Sorry, Leo, but I do need to kick you out now," I say, and Leo straightens.

"Hot date?" he asks, raising an eyebrow.

"Yes, actually. Is that so hard to believe?"

"Well, good for you, Caroline," Leo says. I smile at this to reassure Leo that I'm okay, though my mind is already calculating the impact of what Eric just sent me.

"I'm sorry I can't be there this weekend," he adds. He doesn't mention Jenna's funeral. He doesn't have to.

"Thanks," I say, and I watch as he closes the door behind him. I round the corner that demarcates the living area from the "bedroom" of the efficiency apartment. Looking in the brass mirror, one of just two of my collection I kept after Sofia died, I'm happy enough with what I see. Once I'd told Sofia how little I ever thought about my appearance, and she pointed out that only beautiful people have that luxury. I guess she was right.

———

An expensive cab ride later, I'm in front of a swanky high-rise in Midtown. Milo *would* live here. Once I'm in front of his door, I tuck the hem of my black T-shirt into my jeans so it emphasizes my frame, steel myself, and knock.

"Hi," Milo says as he opens the door. He leans forward and brushes my cheek with his lips. There's that warm, woody sage scent again. He's well dressed in a sweater, a blazer, jeans, and a pair of those expensive-looking leather sneakers men his age seem to love.

"Come in," he says, stepping aside to reveal a minimalist bachelor pad that would slide neatly inside the pages of *GQ*. Taking in the modern art on the walls, gas fire flickering in a black marble fireplace, and jazz playing on surround sound, I suddenly feel underdressed. "Thanks for agreeing to a change of plans," I say.

"Of course. Thanks for meeting me here. It's good to know you must think I'm not a psycho, since you're in my apartment," Milo says archly. Then he turns, opens his mouth, and hesitates. "That sounded a lot less creepy in my head." I laugh, and Milo smiles. I can't help but admire the way boyish dimples appear on his chiseled cheeks.

"I got this at a gorgeous little place in Tuscany," Milo says, holding up a bottle of wine with an Italian label. He pours two glasses and motions to a low-slung leather sofa in front of the fire.

"Cheers," I say, and I sit next to him. As our glasses touch, I think about how this could go under normal circumstances. We would banter. Playfully argue, maybe, as we might have matched wits. Over the course of the evening, we would edge closer together on the couch until our limbs touched. I'd enjoy making the first move—Milo seems the type to appreciate that. We'd see each other for late-night dinners and talk about work too much, slowly opening up about our childhoods and taking turns withholding emotional intimacy. We'd learn how the other takes their coffee and whether we actually find them funny. Our best behavior would slowly relax, and we might even have a shot at something real. But none of that is going to happen. I sip the wine.

"This is delicious," I say, surprised to find that I mean it.

"I'm glad you like it," Milo says. I wonder if under different circumstances, I'd ever get tired of that accent. "So tell me." He angles his body toward mine as he sets down his glass. "How does one become a feminist CEO powerhouse?"

"I guess that sort of flattery is meant to be charming?" A charm that no doubt has a high success rate with women.

"Yes, it is, but I do actually want to know. If you're willing to tell me."

"I suppose I can give you the short version," I say, taking my time to decide exactly how to play this.

"Leave nothing out. I want all the details I won't find on your website."

"Are you saying you cyberstalked me?" I raise my eyebrows.

"I'm not *not* admitting to doing that. Does that make me look pathetic?"

"Only a little. It's kind of cute," I say wryly, and Milo shrugs with chagrin. "I just got sick of the tech bro culture in San Francisco. Before I quit, the last straw was this memo that went around saying there aren't more women engineers because we're biologically more 'people oriented.'"

Milo lets out a low whistle.

"I know. Well, it was that and not wanting to go to strip clubs with my coworkers."

"You're joking," Milo says.

"If only I were." I sigh.

"So," I continue after bracing myself with another sip of wine. "I promised myself I would make the world better for women. Which is why I was surprised to learn about Quantum." I can tell the spell of intimacy and anticipation is broken even before I make eye contact with Milo.

"What do you mean?" he asks, clearly taken aback.

"The *Times* investigation. The lawsuit against the company," I say, and I hand him my phone, which is open to the damning document Eric texted me earlier. "The story should be breaking any day now, shouldn't it?"

Milo, perhaps without even realizing it, physically distances himself from me as much as he can without getting up. His shoulders tense as his face struggles to remain impassive.

"How did you—?"

"That's not important," I say, and I take my phone out of his hands, which have gone slack. "It's pretty credible stuff. Well, it must be if these women aren't happy with settling quietly out of court. I'd wondered why you were so keen to partner with us, a no-body startup." I stand up and open my purse. "I mean, the terms you offered us make it seem like you're doing us a favor. But really, it's only a matter of days before you're going to need all the help you can get. Isn't it?" I extract the paper I made sure to bring tonight—the terms sheet Sara had outlined earlier that week that remains unsigned.

"The allegations you're referring to are exactly that. *Allegations*," Milo says, all charm gone. He gets to his feet and, working hard at indifference, takes a sip of what had been get-in-my-pants wine until a few seconds ago. "Scrappy little startups like yours are a dime a dozen, as are feisty thirty-something female CEOs, by the way." He lets emphasis rake over the *female* before CEO. I give a short, harsh laugh at his pathetic attempt to knock me down a peg.

"I guess we'll have to find out which of us is right on that one," I say, reaching for the pen in my pocket, and I start crossing things out and adding zeros on the paper in my hand.

I read over my edits and hand the contract to Milo. "*This* is my offer. I think you'll find it's fair, given your position. I mean, what's one little barely read article compared to a national news story about deeply ingrained corporate misogyny. I *handled* the skeleton in my closet. Not sure Quantum can say the same." I watch as his eyes rapidly scan the terms that will finally put Equilibrium in the black.

"Agree to this, and Quantum will have something to prop up the inevitable press release managing the fallout from this," I say. "We get paid what we're worth to you. It's a win-win. Persuade Sara to see it that way, and she never even needs to know that we were here." I pause. "At your apartment. Alone. At ten P.M." I pause and let the implications do the work for me.

"I'll look for that contract on Monday," I say. He nods. To my surprise, I catch a begrudging expression of respect on Milo's face as we both stand. "Good night, Milo."

As I turn to leave, I consider my gamble. Whether this was the best or worst decision I could have made remains to be seen.

CHAPTER 30

Brooke

Now

Jenna would have approved of the photograph chosen for her funeral. She's beaming in medical school graduation robes, her beauty and potential shining bright enough to break your heart. She also would have been moved by how many people crowded into the little church's pews and the reception hall afterward: family, friends, colleagues, and former patients. Shifting uncomfortably in the itchy black dress, I search the sea of dour faces for Caroline. The service is nearly over, and the crowd is starting to thin. As I cast my eyes around the room, I hope that no one knows exactly who I am to the woman in the mahogany casket wreathed with lilies. I wonder fleetingly if Josh would dare show his face here. My engagement ring isn't on my finger anymore but is instead in its box, stuffed in the back of the bottom drawer of my dresser. The thought of it shoved out of sight like that, like a dirty secret, fills me with sadness, anger, and shame.

I finally spot Caroline at the center of the somber crowd. She's talking to a man I recognize as Bryce's father, Anderson Hostetler, the pharmaceutical mogul who had appeared on the cover of *Time* as the face of a new miracle drug. Wending my way through clusters of mourners, I notice that Bryce is slumped in a chair in a corner. His face is in his hands, his shoulders heaving. When he lifts his head, I can see that his eyes are swollen, but his face is completely dry. He looks, I think, like a caricature of grief. As I draw closer to Caroline, a faint snuffling sound stops me in my tracks.

Turning to my right, I see a door that's a few inches ajar, and I open it. It's just a coatroom. But before I can shut the door again, I spot a small pair of shoes sticking out from around a corner. A very small, very shiny pair of brand-new black shoes: the kind you'd buy a child for his mother's funeral. Hayden is curled into a ball at the back of the closet, his head tucked behind his knees so that all I can see is his neatly combed hair.

"Hey, Hayden," I say as gently as I can, taking a seat on the floor across from him. He lifts his reddened, tear-stained face and blinks rapidly as he looks at me. A clear trail of snot drips from his nose. I reach into my pocket, pull out a tissue, and extend it to him. He takes it so dutifully I feel my throat swell. "Do you remember me?" I ask, thinking of the handful of occasions I'd met him at the park or at brunch with Jenna.

He nods. "You're Mommy's friend." His voice is tiny, and it's all I can do to stop myself from crying. "You have a kitty." I remember how he loved looking at pictures of Piper.

"That's right. You have a really good memory," I say. "Did you come in here because there are a lot of people out there?" I ask. Hayden nods again. "I don't like big crowds, either." He's crumpled the tissue in his little fist, but fresh tears are already starting to pool in the dark eyes that are so like Jenna's.

"Would you like a hug?" I ask. In the split second it takes to wonder if that was the right thing to say or not, Hayden launches himself into my arms, hiccupping sobs shaking his fragile little shoulders. As I hold him, I think of Bryce and what I'd seen on the bank statements. Bryce literally profited from his wife's death, but could he have done this to his own son?

Lost in my own thoughts and the heart-wrenching embrace of a child who loved animals and would never see his mom again, I startle when the door swings open. An elderly woman dressed in a black Chanel twinset stands in the doorframe, the light from the exposed bulb turning her snow-white chignon into a halo. It takes me a few seconds to recognize her—she's not as well known as her husband, but I'd seen her at my mother's charity events over the years.

"There you are, Hayden." She sighs.

"I'm sorry," I stammer, not wanting to cause problems for anyone.

"It's all right, dear," Penny Hostetler says wearily, her eyes on the tearful little boy. "I think it's time I take this one home. He's had . . ."—she searches for the right word—"*enough* for today. Come along now." Hayden walks over to his grandmother. She takes him by the hand and pauses on her way out the door.

"You're Daphne's girl, aren't you?" Her words cast a stone deep into the pit of my stomach. Does she know about Josh?

"Yes," I say weakly. She lifts her chin and fixes me with a piercing gaze. "You know, there's nothing I wouldn't do to protect this family. Nothing." She pauses and looks down at her grandson before leveling her eyes with mine again. "You're better off without that man." With a regal nod, she guides Hayden out of the coatroom.

I slump against the wall and let my legs stretch out in front of me. So everyone knows about Josh and Jenna's affair. Did the detectives share this latest development? All I know for sure is that I need to get out of here out of respect for that heartbroken little boy.

At first, silence greets me when I step back into the reception hall. But then the whispers start, and it's like a seam has been ripped open in the somber atmosphere. I watch as heads turn toward the screen where Jenna's picture had been projected when I walked in. It's obscured by a cluster of people now, so I take a few tentative steps forward. When I can finally make out what everyone is staring at, I freeze. A photo of Bryce and Caroline locked in a close embrace, and it's not a photo from college. Worse, they're in Jenna's backyard, and it looks recent. I scan the crowd desperately for Caroline.

She's been cornered by Anderson Hostetler, who has the look of a powerful man who is struggling to control his temper. His expression is composed, but a vein throbs in his temple, just visible under well-cut gray hair. I wish someone would unplug the projector showing Caroline and Bryce's compromising position for all of Jenna's mourners to see. I feel a twinge of suspicion but swat it away. Things were always complicated between Caroline and Bryce, and this is probably just her way of coping with the insane situation we're in. God knows I'm in no position to judge. "Sofia" must be behind this, but it's not that thought that sends a shiver down my spine. It's that they could be in this room. Now.

Caroline's face is on fire as she turns toward the mourners, who look as if they'd like nothing more than to tar and feather her. Bryce is nowhere to be seen. The crowd parts for her like a black sea, and the whispers simmer back to normal conversation volume in her wake. We need to get out of here. I take careful, quiet steps toward the exit to catch up with her until a strong hand grips my arm.

I wheel around, and my jaw drops as I find the source of the hand. Josh looks like he hasn't slept in days: his eyes are bloodshot, his face covered in uneven stubble, and there's raw desperation in his expression as he jerks his head toward the front door. It occurs to me that the man in front of me is not my sweet, nerdy fiancé who cried during Pixar movies and dreamed of taking our kids to the Galápagos Islands to retrace Darwin's footsteps. This is a man with the nerve to show up at his mistress's funeral. I have no idea what he is capable of. Any thoughts I had of taking Josh back evaporate like water on a scalding surface. I try to wrench my arm from his grasp.

"Brooke, come on," Josh says in a strained whisper. A few heads whip around to look at us. I shake my head vigorously, desperately wishing I could disappear.

"I have to tell you something," he insists, his eyes widening. More heads turn. I wrench my arm out of Josh's grip and walk toward the exit, averting every eye that slings disapproval in our direction. Josh follows me so closely I can smell his stale breath on my shoulder mixed with the cologne I bought for his birthday last year. Outside, the sun beats down on the hoods of the cars that surround the church like a gleaming metal moat. Glancing around quickly, I can't find Caroline.

I wait until the heavy doors close behind us to speak.

"You shouldn't be here," I hiss, not caring that my words send spit straight into Josh's face. The fact that he looks as bad as I've felt since he left me isn't enough to stop my outpouring of rage. If anything, it makes me even angrier.

"I had to come. I had to see you. You said you'd talk to me, but we never—"

"Oh, I'm sorry. Did my failure to follow through on that betray your trust, *Josh*? Did I *let you down*?" He winces. I want to walk away, but I'm paralyzed by roiling contradictory urges to either collapse into him or shove him down the flagstone steps in front of us. "So here I am. What is it? What is so fucking *urgent*?" I glare at him.

"My thing with Jenna. It wasn't all about the sex," Josh says, and I feel my chest start to heave. The word *all* sticks in me, a hot needle slicing deep beneath a fingernail.

"Well, for a while it was, but we were really investigating the lab, Hostetler Pharma." At first these ideas seem so incongruous, so logically absurd, my mind rejects that they're even in the same sentence. "It started because Jenna came to me for help, before everything else happened," Josh rushes on in a manic tone. "She'd stumbled upon something that scared her, something really, *really* bad for the Hostetlers."

Questions swarm on my tongue. "*What?*" It's all I can ask in my confusion.

"Hey, asshole." Caroline's voice booms from a few yards away. She's striding toward us, her face set in a fierce scowl, vicious eyes narrowed at Josh. It's lucky she didn't actually leave. I've never been happier to see her.

"Get away from her," Caroline orders.

"Hold on a second, Caroline," I say without taking my eyes off Josh's face. A few people have started to emerge behind her. Caroline hovers watchfully a few feet from where we're standing, ready to spring into action, if needed. The trickle of people leaving the church has swelled into a black tide.

I lower my voice. "Explain."

Josh takes a step closer to me, furtively checking that we won't be overheard. He opens his mouth, then closes it again as people draw closer to us, many of them throwing filthy looks at Caroline before getting into their cars.

"I can't, not here," Josh says. "Can we talk at home?" The question expels a burst of bitter laughter from my mouth, and it's hard to focus on anything over the howl of sirens down the street. Their wails grow louder, and I can barely make out his next hushed words.

"She was going to expose them. Meet me at home, and I can explain more," he says, and with that, he starts backing away.

"What? How?" I ask as Caroline draws level with us. Josh doesn't say anything but turns and starts to run as a police car screeches to a halt on the pavement in front of us. A uniformed officer springs out and grabs Josh roughly, pushing him against the hood of the car.

"Joshua Green," he says loudly enough for Caroline, the group of onlookers, and me to hear, "I'm arresting you for the murder of Jenna Hostetler-Lee. You have the right to remain silent. Anything you say can and will be—" A piercing ringing sound in my ears drowns out the surreal recitation I'd only ever heard on TV. I'm aware of Caroline's hands pulling me away, of struggling against them as I speak, then scream Josh's name as his body folds into the back of the police car.

"Don't let them see you like this," Caroline whispers in my ear as she steers me away from the scene. "Give me your keys. I'll drive you home, and we will figure out what to do." Her voice is one of forced calm, and she keeps her eyes fixed in front of her so I don't have to look where we're going.

"Brooke Winters?" An authority-heavy voice speaks from behind us. My heart stops dead, and I feel my knees buckle. Caroline's body responds automatically, giving me her strength so I can remain upright.

"Yes?" My voice is barely more than a high-pitched whisper.

"Could you follow us to the station, please?" The officer from the other car is speaking, and I recognize the watery eyes of the man who'd come to our house to ask questions about Jenna's suicide. That day, the last day I had Josh, feels like years ago. It was stupid to think the police would have moved on so quickly without a thorough investigation.

"Brooke has *nothing* to do with this," Caroline says, still holding me tight.

"Caroline, it's fine—" I start.

"Miss Winters is not under arrest," the officer says impatiently. "We just have a few questions for her."

"It's okay, Caroline," I say. Turning to the officer, I square my shoulders. "I have nothing to hide. I'm happy to answer your questions." It takes me a beat to realize that, as far as Jenna is concerned, this is actually true. Or as close to the truth as it gets for me nowadays. The officer hands us his business card with the station address on it, and Caroline insists on driving us both over. I protest at first, but when my hands shake so badly that I can barely fish my keys out of my purse, I have no choice but to let her.

I stay silent as Caroline tries to calm me down on the drive over, to reassure me that everything is going to be okay. Phrases like *Josh would never do anything like this* register vaguely as I watch trees and houses and the outposts of normal lives blur past the car window. Occasionally, I mumble my agreement. I'd perfected the art of fake listening years ago when I learned to tune out my mother's passive-aggressive monologues.

"Hey, did you hear what I said?" Caroline asks firmly. We're stopped at a light and she's turned toward me.

"Yeah," I say as convincingly as I can.

"No, you didn't. You're doing that thing." There's no fooling Caroline. I don't bother to contradict her. "Brooke, this is important. Are you absolutely sure you don't want a lawyer with you? Just in case any of the other stuff comes up?"

"It won't," I say. As soon as the words are out of my mouth, I realize how naive they sound.

"You don't know that. We don't know what the police know, and a lawyer will have to keep what you say confidential," Caroline says.

"I can't afford one," I say, thinking of my checking account, which has been draining at an alarming rate ever since Josh moved out and we stopped sharing expenses along with everything else.

"We both know who can," Caroline says darkly. I can sense the sidelong glance she darts in my direction.

"Absolutely not."

"Okay, what about Mel?" Caroline counters.

"I'm not bothering her with this." Mel is on bed rest at home, and even more than the humiliation of asking my baby sister to clean up my mess, I can't stomach the thought of adding stress to her plate.

"Brooke," Caroline says so forcefully she's almost shouting, and I'm shocked into giving her my full attention by the rare emotion that breaks her voice. "I can't lose you. I won't let you end up like Jenna. Let me help you." For a fleeting moment, I wonder if sudden death would be anything less than what I deserve.

A horn blares behind us, and we jolt in our seats before Caroline makes a left turn.

Reaching for my phone, I close my eyes briefly before I send the text message that I know is going to cost me dearly. The response comes almost immediately, and I reluctantly accept what's going to happen next.

We arrive at the police station, a small flat building with a smattering of cars in the surrounding lot, unsurprising for a Saturday in a sleepy Connecticut town. I grimace at the thought of my fiancé in an interrogation room. *Ex*-fiancé. I ruthlessly slash the mental correction in red pen.

"Ready?" Caroline faces me with determined eyes. I nod.

"My mother just said she's sending Alex, her lawyer," I say, just managing to stop myself from saying *my lawyer*. Caroline can't know about what really happened at Brown. I can't afford to lose another friend, maybe the only one I have left, to my past mistakes. "Apparently, he'll be here in half an hour. Can we wait in the car, though?"

"Of course," Caroline says. A tense silence settles over us, so I decide to bring up the very last thing Caroline wants to discuss.

"Do you want to talk about what happened with Bryce?" I ask, my eyes on a tiny hole in my tights, just above my knee. I can hear her exhale next to me: it's a sound of shame, and I immediately regret saying anything.

"It was just—" Caroline starts and stops. I look up at her, and for once, she seems at a loss for words.

"Hey, it's okay," I say, reaching to cover her hand with mine. "I'm not judging you. I get that you and Bryce have a lot of history." The part of me that would have felt angry or sorry for Jenna died with Josh's confession to their affair. Caroline's face is carefully expressionless, as if she's keeping something—no doubt her complicated feelings about this totally fucked Bryce situation—from me.

"Thanks. I can't really think about that right now," Caroline says, and she turns to me with grateful eyes. "I want to talk to you about Drea and Todd anyway," she adds, life returning to her tone.

I unbuckle my seat belt and turn to fully face her. She fills me in on her trip to see Drea. "Leo and I might just have a few cards left to play with Todd, and even if what he told me about him finding *enlightenment* or whatever is true, I promise it's temporary. It happens with all of his girlfriends—he molds himself into whoever they want him to be. Probably because of all of his mommy issues." She flicks a strand of hair over her shoulder.

"Mommy issues?" I ask.

"Bill was the golden child. Todd was the disappointment. So whenever a woman was nice to him or paid the slightest attention to Todd instead of the great Bill Archer, he was so grateful he would be pretty much whatever she told him to be. I think he gets off on it."

"Gross," I say with a shudder.

"Seriously," Caroline says. "The biggest question now is if Drea actually killed Jenna, because I think we can agree that Josh might be a shit, but not a murderous one." She waits for my reaction, and I nod.

"She could be framing him," I say. Caroline's face doesn't show any sign of surprise. Clearly this thought has already occurred to her.

"Yeah. But *why,* though?" Caroline asks. "I wonder if maybe something happened earlier the night of the accident? And our stalker is picking off everyone who was there the night Sofia died or who was involved in some way?"

With the police station looming in front of us, I remember Drea, the empty husk of a human being I saw at Sofia's funeral. People with nothing left to lose are the most dangerous.

I think of Mel. What would I be capable of if something or

someone took her from me? Caroline might suspect Drea was behind all of this, and while Drea probably does hate us to her core, I
can't shake the image of Bryce's over-the-top display of mourning.
But until I have something solid on Bryce, Caroline will never take
me seriously. Her soft spot for him requires hard evidence.

And that means I need to finish what Josh started.

Minutes unspool in rapid succession, and I lose myself in
thoughts about death and revenge, and about what's really going
on behind the gates of the Archers' Nantucket house and inside the
Hostetler-Lee residence.

When Alex pulls up, Caroline gives me a quick hug before I get
out of the car, and he and I walk into the station together.

CHAPTER 31

Brooke

Now

Alex closes the door to the interview room, and we take our seats opposite Detective Bullock. Give minimal detail, Alex had advised me, and stick to yes-or-no answers whenever possible: remember, you are the grieving friend and betrayed fiancée who wants nothing to do with this. He loves a good narrative, and he knows how to make them work for his clients. Last time, I was the naive girl who was taken advantage of by the much older man who abused his position of power. And as I meet the detective's eye, I realize I'm as ready as I'll ever be to play the new role assigned to me.

"We appreciate your cooperation, Miss Winters," Detective Bullock says. "And I'm sorry we're meeting again under these circumstances." I glance to my left, and I wonder who is watching this interview through the one-way mirror.

"I'm sure you can appreciate how difficult this is for my client," Alex says briskly.

"Of course," Detective Bullock says, adjusting his belt so that he's more comfortable. "Ms. Winters, did you have any suspicions that your fiancé and Jenna Hostetler-Lee were having an affair?"

"I had no idea until Josh admitted to it. That happened the same day I met you," I say.

"Are you sure? Was there anything strange about either Josh or Jenna's behavior toward you in the weeks leading up to her death?"

"No, Josh didn't tell me anything until after Jenna died," I say again, but then something shakes loose in my memory. "Actually," I start, and Alex clicks the gold tip of his pen. This was the agreed signal that I should stop talking or limit the details. I ignore it. "Jenna did pull me aside the night of the gallery opening."

"And when was that?" Detective Bullock asks.

"Um, two weeks ago?" Time is slipping between my fingers. "She said she had something important to tell me."

"Interesting." Detective Bullock makes a note on the pad that lies flat on the table between us. "Do you remember her exact words?" Alex clicks his pen again. I ignore him again.

"Not really—just that she wanted to talk. I assume she wanted to tell me the truth about her and Josh." Her exhausted face surfaces in my mind's eye.

"Were you aware that the two of them were investigating Hostetler Pharma?" Detective Bullock looks up at me from his notes.

"I—what?" To my right, Alex gives a barely perceptible nod of approval. This lie fits the narrative perfectly: distance yourself from further implications, play up the ignorance, add in just the right amount of shock and emotion.

"We have received substantial evidence that this was the case. Email and phone exchanges between Jenna and Josh, recorded conversations that Jenna had obtained of her husband speaking to her father-in-law. We also received evidence that Josh was in Jenna's vicinity at her time of death." My stomach plummets at the detective's slip. *Received.* Not *found.* Not uncovered as part of their investigation. Someone gave the police everything they need to lock up Josh and throw away the key. Someone like "Sofia," punishing me through Josh.

"What do you mean, you *received* the evidence?"

Detective Bullock is cognizant of his mistake too late. "Let's get back to why we're here. Do you know of any motivation, other than wanting to assist Jenna, that Josh would have to investigate Hostetler Pharma?"

"Yes," I say, though my mind is still in a daze. Even a bumbling officer like Bullock was bound to find out anyway, and it would look highly suspicious if I didn't mention it. "Josh's sister has struggled with an addiction to a couple different types of pills for years. They aren't on speaking terms anymore."

"Really?" Detective Bullock takes rapid notes.

"Josh doesn't like to talk about Leah."

"That's very good to know." As the officer says this, he takes on the quality of a well-fed spider who has found a juicy fly tangled and helpless in their web. This self-satisfied manner is getting under my skin, and before I can stop myself, I ask the question that's tugged at me since Josh's arrest.

"But why would Josh want to hurt Jenna?"

"Brooke—" Alex skips the pen clicking and shoots me a warning glance.

"I don't understand why he would go after *her*. She had nothing to do with Hostetler Pharma other than being married to Bryce. It doesn't make any sense." I reflexively curl my lip inward to stop *and Josh would never hurt anyone* from escaping my lips.

Detective Bullock shifts in his chair, weighing how much he wants to tell me. "Jenna was last seen alive on a CCTV camera that picked up her car headed to their family home in the Catskills. She had texted Josh Green the previous evening to meet her there, arranging to meet him for a—" He cuts himself off and does his best to choose more tactful phrasing. "To, um, meet him there the day after the art show you all attended. She stated her intention to end things between them and to stop the investigation into Hostetler Pharma."

My brain comes unstuck, and slowly I start to process this. Unless there's more that Detective Bullock isn't telling me about what my stalker handed the police already, the case against Josh seems circumstantial at best. But then, what did I really know about my ex-fiancé? What does anyone really know about anyone?

Alex takes advantage of my silence. "Do you have any further questions for my client, Detective?"

"Yes. Miss Winters, you should be aware that we have a search warrant for the apartment you shared with Josh Green. I believe officers are there now." I nod my understanding. Alex had warned me to expect they'd begin a search without my consent, because it's only Josh's name on the lease. "Contact me immediately if you think of anything else, even something small, that might help us." He takes a stab at being the macho intrepid detective, and it doesn't exactly work for him.

I follow the two men out of the interview room, and my heart plummets immediately when we reach the main entrance. My mother is there, dressed in spotless tennis whites, her mouth set in a thin line.

"Daphne." Alex extends a hand and shakes hers. My mother says nothing and motions her head pointedly to a far corner of the room.

"Well?" she says, her eyes fixed on Alex.

"Nothing to worry about," he says, and rests a hand on her bony, golden-tanned shoulder. "Brooke did great in there."

"Good," she responds, still not looking at me.

"I'd better go," Alex says with a glance down at his watch.

"Thanks again, you're a lifesaver." My mother favors Alex with a smile, and he walks out the front doors.

"We'll talk in my car," she says in my general direction before turning squeakily on her heel, her pleated athletic skirt flouncing behind her. Despite the circumstances, I suppress a laugh. It's not until we're in her car with the doors locked that she finally looks at me.

"Thanks for sending Alex," I say. It's what she'll need to hear if this conversation stands a chance at a non-disastrous resolution. I watch that chance vanish as I study my mother's face, which wears an expression of thinly veiled rage.

"I suppose I should be thanking *you* for finally getting around to telling me Joshie was *arrested*." Her every word is clipped as if with the tiny razor-sharp scissors she uses on her orchids.

"I'm sorry. It's been a rough few weeks." I look down at my hands and fix my eye on a chipped corner of my nail polish.

"I know, honey." I look up, jarred by the kindness that's softened her voice. "I'm—" She stops talking, apparently at a loss for words, and places a retinol-firmed hand on mine. It rests there uncertainly, like a bird that's alighted on a half-snapped limb of a tree. Just as I'm about to clasp her hand, she withdraws it. My purse pulses, and her next words are drowned by the rush of blood that surges to my ears as I discreetly open the burner in my purse and read the words on the screen.

> You were thinking of taking him back, weren't you? Too bad Joshie is headed to where you'll never see him again. And whose fault is that really, B? xx

CHAPTER 32

Caroline

Now

Eric is waiting outside Thrive when I get back to the city. The police don't want to talk to me. Not yet. But the pictures of Bryce and me displayed at Jenna's funeral are still burned into my mind's eye.

A terrible thought keeps elbowing its way into my head, despite my best efforts to ignore it. With all eyes on Josh, the heat is off me. The police won't be scrambling for suspects. They won't be asking around about what happened at Jenna's funeral. A hot trickle of shame leaks down the back of my neck. Happy your best friend's ex-fiancé was arrested: that really would be a new low. They'll probably let him go though, won't they? I turn my full attention back to my assistant before I can plunge further down that rabbit hole.

Eric has two coffees in his hands. Black for me. Industrial-sized, iced, and with almond milk for him. The sun is setting and the city is abuzz with New Yorkers heading to their Saturday night plans, but we both know we have a long night of work ahead of us.

"Have I mentioned lately that you're my hero?" I say, taking the paper cup from him. His blue eyes glint in the fading sunlight.

"Once or twice," he says. "But we need to talk about Quantum. I have an idea." I nod as I scan my keycard and step inside the elevator. "I think we have an opportunity here, and I just want you to hear me out before you say no."

"Okay," I say cautiously.

"It's a little . . ."—he hesitates—"out of the box, but I think if we really go for it, it could be a game changer." He's speaking fast, his tone electric. Eric gets like this when he's excited about something.

"You're doing that thing," I say, taking another gulp of the coffee that isn't hitting my bloodstream fast enough to match Eric's energy.

"Ugh, I know, I know." He waves away my words with a hand before lowering his voice. "Let's wait till we can talk in private."

The elevator pings our arrival, and we stride on autopilot through the door and across the sprawl of the open floor plan, our footsteps loud on the concrete floor. It's empty on a Saturday night except for a woman wearing cat-ear headphones as she types on her laptop in a corner of the space. We pass the neon signs with sayings like "Thank God It's Monday" and "Rise and Grind" on our way to a conference room. Eric shuts the door and rounds on me, a glint lighting his eyes.

"Okay, so . . ."—Eric takes one of the chairs clustered around the circular table—"we need Quantum, but Quantum also needs us, right?"

"Right," I say. Instinctively I take out my laptop. Eric is already standing again, and he starts pacing.

"There have got to be more companies like them." He gestures with his hands as if pointing to an obvious conclusion, but I can't connect the dots yet.

"More recruiting platforms?" I ask tentatively.

"No," he says dismissively. "More companies with PR crises. Scandals, harassment suits, an executive who's politically incorrect and Twitter-happy. Complaints about unequal pay or a toxic culture.

Think about it." It takes a moment for Eric's point to solidify in my mind. "We see this stuff in the news, like, every other day. We can use that." He looks at me, triumphant, waiting for the brilliance of this plan to catch on.

When I met Eric two years ago, I knew that I might as well cancel the other assistant interviews scheduled for that afternoon. He was nothing like the others, those doe-eyed trust-fund girls desperate to placate their parents with any legitimate internship or job in exchange for a bankrolled apartment in Manhattan. He may have graduated from NYU, but his résumé showed me so much more. He was a scholarship student who'd had half a dozen jobs since he was fourteen—waiting tables, painting houses, working as an assistant to a prominent dean. His 3.8 GPA was impressive, but there was something else that hit home with me more. When he walked into the coffee shop—the only venue I could afford for interviews at the time—I recognized something kindred in him. A drive. A relentlessness in pursuit of whatever he needed to get to where he was going. That day, it happened to be getting Equilibrium out of my brain and into the world.

"So why us?" I'd asked him, a standard interview question with more than its fair share of actual curiosity behind it.

"To be honest with you, equality for women in the workplace is close to my heart because of my mom—I lost her to breast cancer."

My first reaction was shock. Shock that anyone in Eric's suit could transition from professional to deeply personal without some sort of internal alarm going off.

"I'm so sorry," I said, feeling that familiar echo through the empty space my own mother left behind.

"Thank you." He smiled the sad smile then, the kind you put on for other people when death hovers over a conversation, but you want to keep talking. I've worn it many times myself.

"She was an amazing woman. My mom was the first person in her family to go to college, one of, like, three female engineers in her graduating class. We hear phrases like *breaking down barriers*." He made air quotes around the buzzwords, but his face shone with emotion when he talked about his mother in a way that warmed even my skeptical heart. "But she actually *did*, long before it was widely accepted, let alone celebrated, for women to do that in her field. She had more obstacles than she should have, though." He met my eye. "Exactly the paradigm Equilibrium is designed to change."

I offered him the job on the spot. In lieu of the salary he deserved, Eric took a pay cut and accepted a generous equity percentage in Equilibrium, skin in the game, every reason to tell me the whole truth of whatever crisis or opportunity was in front of us. Including, clearly, this latest one.

I blink rapidly as I realize exactly what Eric is suggesting now.

"You mean, scavenge like vultures after sleazy executives?" I say, incredulous that Eric, who so wholeheartedly believed in Equilibrium and everything I want to achieve, would suggest this.

"Well, no, I wouldn't put it that way. But think about it. Wouldn't that be kind of the ultimate revenge?" He leans forward and places both hands on the conference room table. Visceral relish drips from his last word.

"What, so because these companies mistreated people, we should take advantage of them . . . taking advantage?" I ask, my mind spinning.

"Exactly." Eric smiles broadly, pleased I'd finally caught on. He resumes his seat, tents his fingers, and raises his eyebrows, waiting for me to give the green light.

"It's a . . ."—I grasp for the right word that will buy me some time to think—"*strategic* idea." Eric nods vigorously. I consider the implications of this. If we move forward, wouldn't we be profiting from the exact thing we want to prevent? Would this make us any better than the source of the problem? I set these philosophical questions aside in favor of more practical ones.

"And—in this brilliant plan of yours—how are we exactly supposed to find the companies who need our *help*, for lack of a better term?" I ask.

"I don't think the higher-ups at these companies realize how much their underlings talk to each other. Especially after a few margaritas." Eric raises an eyebrow suggestively. "Plus, there are plenty of places we can go digging for this sort of stuff. Glassdoor. Press releases about new diversity programs or initiatives or whatever—those rarely start out of pure altruism."

"I guess you're right about that." I say this slowly, lost in thought. "And wouldn't, theoretically, Equilibrium be in the best position to *help* that type of company?"

"That's what I thought. And our outcome is the same: we're *still* helping people, and we're making sure to do it where the help is needed most. It's a win-win," Eric says eagerly. "Caroline, we are *this* ..."—he indicates the sliver of air that separates his thumb and forefinger—"close to really, *really* getting Equilibrium off the ground. Wouldn't it be nice to get some full-time engineers, work in an actual office, and I don't know, hire some more people so you don't have to do everything yourself?"

"Or another operations slash marketing slash jack-of-all-trades so, I don't know, you could sleep at night?" I ask playfully, but even I can hear the longing that creeps into my voice.

"That was the whole point of the conference, wasn't it? Why not just accelerate things a bit?" He dangles these questions in the air, and I can't deny that the implicit answers are irresistible.

"Yeah," I say. Excitement bubbles in my mind. "Yeah," I repeat, more forcefully and confidently this time.

"Yeah? As in—?" Eric's face lights up.

"As in, let's do it." His smile widens. "We keep doing all of our normal market research and work for existing clients, but you're right, this could be the edge we need."

"Amazing. I've already started a list of potential clients with that extra motivation to partner with us." He pulls out his phone and scrolls rapidly with one finger. "So, we can get cracking right away. We should order dinner. Your usual from Sweetgreen?" He flicks a quick glance at me. "You know you'll forget to eat other-wise." He says this with a beleaguered sigh that makes me smile.

"You're right," I say with a laugh. "Thanks."

"How'd it go with the updated Quantum contract, by the way?" He stops scrolling on his phone and looks up at me.

"Good. Signed. Terms updated." I pull out my own laptop and prepare to get to work. The thrill of possibility still thrums in my mind, and just as I open my inbox, a drop of guilt seeps into the recesses of my thoughts. I ignore it. Now is the time to recognize a good business opportunity. It's savvy, and isn't that what women need to be to get ahead? Savvy, smart, aggressive—words from my own presentation echo in my head. Would a man ever be judged for making a strategic move like this?

No, he would not. And that's what I'm going to tell myself over the mutterings of my conscience. Guilt isn't going to help me. But this next move might.

CHAPTER 33

Sofia

Then

The past few days with Leo end as they always do: in bleary, hung-over silences and poring over his work. The drawing he finished last night is his best yet. *Persephone*—a charcoal rendering of Sofia's sleeping face. Peaceful. Ethereal. Drugged into near oblivion, slipping into the darkness like the visiting goddess of the underworld. An underworld of his making, one that she was just passing through on her way back to Caroline.

He thinks Sofia doesn't know, that she hasn't been able to piece it together yet. But the bruises, the blackouts, the insomnia that bookends their benders clicked in her mind months ago. But she's not worried—Leo would never hurt her, not really. He needs his muse alive.

When Sofia gets back to the dorm, she shuts herself in her room for the sleepless twenty-four hours before her next class. She hears the intermittent voices and footsteps of Brooke, Caroline, Jenna, and Bryce coming and going about their normal days. Smiling to herself, she types furiously on the dinosaur of a laptop she checks out of the library every week. Unlike her classmates' sleek MacBooks, this thing weighs a solid five pounds and exhales a hot stream of exhaustion after a few minutes of running Microsoft Word.

But it doesn't matter. Right now, it's all Sofia needs. Any vessel to get the story she wants to tell out of her head and into her creative writing professor's hands will do to rescue her scholarship status. Then copies of the audio recording sent to the local papers will seal Brooke's fate at Yale and give her a good hard shove out of her privileged world. Brooke and Daphne thought they were untouchable, but soon, Brooke's secrets will be out there for the world to see and relish in judging.

And when she finally races to the library to print the pages, Sofia's heart lifts with hope. With the short story—Brooke's story—safely tucked in her bag, Sofia tidies herself carefully for class. She opts for a healthy and wholesome, rather than her usual grungy but sultry look. This involves a combination of hand-me-downs from Caroline: designer jeans that cost more than Sofia's mom's car payment and a soft hunter-green cable-knit sweater. She surveys the results in the mirror gallery. There, she thinks, is the picture of a successful Ivy League student. Just another part to play.

"You look nice," Brooke calls from the other room. *I know what you did,* she thinks every time she looks into Brooke's eyes. *I know what you think you got away with, and I'm going to expose you.*

"Thanks," Sofia says back. She sounds normal, and Brooke takes this as an invitation.

"Caroline was saying we should all go up to her stepdad's place in Nantucket this weekend," she says, appearing in Sofia's doorframe like an unwelcome salesperson or a pamphlet-bearing Jehovah's Witness.

"Oh, yeah?" Sofia says this casually, as if her heart hadn't just tripped like it missed a step in its excitement.

"Apparently now is the best time to go," Brooke gushes eagerly.

"All the summer tourists are gone. But you'd know better than me—you're from there, right?" When Sofia meets Brooke's eyes, she feels an uninvited flicker of pity. For a second, Sofia wonders if maybe Brooke really *was* just the victim in all of this—she certainly wouldn't be the first impressionable undergrad to have a professor take advantage of them. Maybe she wasn't here to take Caroline from Sofia, but just to start over away from that ice queen of a mother and get over what basically amounted to a messy breakup.

But then Sofia thinks of the other student in Dr. Adams's office, that girl clearly poised to fill Brooke's shoes, and her pity evaporates. Brooke could have stopped that from happening. She had the proof. She decided to walk away, leaving the same trap set and ready to spring on someone else. All she cared about was saving herself. The next girl probably won't slip out of the snare as easily as Brooke did.

"Um, yeah. Sorry, I'm gonna be late for class," Sofia lies. She ignores Brooke's cheerful goodbye and arrives early for her intermediate fiction workshop. Her professor is already seated at the desk in the front of the room.

"Sofia," he begins, taking off the reading glasses he was wearing and perching them on the stack of papers next to his elbow. "I'm glad you're here, actually—I was hoping for a private word. I'm afraid I can't let you pass this class unless—"

"I give you this?" Sofia says, putting on her best roguish grin as she hands him the manuscript that barely had time to cool from the printer. "It's a short story, but I think I can develop it further. Maybe into a novel, even."

"Excellent," he says. "Well—better late than never, at any rate." He gives Sofia an admonishing look, but it's offset by the pleased expression that quickly settles on his face. "I hope you don't mind my saying . . ."—he lowers his voice as more students start to filter into the room—"I'm rooting for you, you know. I had a little chat with your advisor, and she told me a bit about your *situation*." His face is so kind, so well-intentioned, so oblivious of how many times in Sofia's life she'd seen that pitying expression pointed at her.

He doesn't know that look starts to send a spike of shame through a person, along with the bone-deep knowledge that to your benefactor, you are not really a person at all: you are a public service. You're a stroke to their egos that feels so good, they keep coming back for more.

"Thank you," Sofia says, willing herself to see the good in this man.

"I look forward to reading these." Cheerily, he holds up the pages that contain the indictment of Brooke Winters and women like her. He smiles at Sofia, which she takes as her dismissal, and as she's about to take a seat, her phone buzzes.

Caroline's name lights up the screen, and Sofia's breath catches.

> I know things have been weird between us, and I want to fix it. How about we head to Nantucket this weekend?

The professor is starting class, so Sofia types as fast as she can before stowing the phone away.

> Sure, sounds great.

The seminar passes in a blur: they're critiquing one of her classmate's fiction pieces. Sofia carefully puts her two cents in and nods thoughtfully at the appropriate intervals—students who participate don't flunk out of college, after all. But her mind races with thoughts of the Archers' estate, of Caroline, and of how everything seems to be falling into place.

In the days that follow, the prospect of being together with Caroline, of visiting their secret places by the sea, carries Sofia on a strong current of anticipation. Even the fact that "we" includes both Brooke and Leo—Jenna can't make it—doesn't dampen the delicious hum that sizzles under her skin as the weekend grows closer. She goes to her classes, turns in a passable essay on *Paradise Lost,* and receives an approving email from her advisor commending her for "really turning over a new leaf" and "getting back on track."

And all the while, the final part of her plan is snug in the pocket of a coat at the back of her closet. Sofia will play the recording for Caroline this weekend, and then, when the time is right, she'll expose Brooke's scandal.

Brooke and Caroline are on the couch watching a TV show with a laugh track when Sofia gets back to the apartment. They are relaxed, both in loose T-shirts and sweatpants, and they barely acknowledge Sofia. On the screen, a perky actress in a waitress uniform pauses for the laugh track. Sofia tosses her keys on the table, trying to make as much noise as possible. If she and Caroline had still been together, it would be red wine and a black-and-white movie, not this generic trash.

"Hi." Brooke turns her head toward Sofia. "Don't judge me for hate-watching this, okay?" Brooke smiles and reminds Sofia of a puppy desperate for any sort of attention. "We let Leo in, by the way—he's in your room."

"Thanks," Sofia says, and she can see the toe of Leo's leather boot dangling off the edge of her bed. She will have to decide what to do about him, and sooner rather than later.

CHAPTER 34

Brooke

Now

The quickest way to a teacher's heart is usually coffee, or, to be more specific to the Woodlands English department, a dry cappuccino for Akira, an Americano for Antony, and a vanilla latte for Kelly. I balance them carefully in their cardboard carrier as I head into our weekly faculty meeting. My old therapist would say I'm reverting to over-the-top people-pleasing to avoid confronting my own issues. I think of Jenna, murdered; Josh, arrested; and Piper, probably dead in a ditch somewhere; and I realize that on this score, the condescending bastard might have had a point. Going through the motions of my life is all I can do to stop the thoughts that my days are numbered.

"You know Antony was kidding about the hazing, right?" Kelly says as I hand her the coffee. I laugh automatically.

"This is just a little thank-you for all your help last week," I say, and I mean it. Kelly had excellent advice on how to tactfully respond to an overly zealous parent, which is unfamiliar territory for me.

"Don't mention it. But seriously, thank you for this," Kelly says, holding up her latte. "Also, not to be weird, but turn around," she continues, swirling her index finger in a circle. I twist in my seat, and Kelly tugs the zipper of my dress up the three inches it still needs to go.

"Thanks," I say, trying not to think of all the times Josh zipped me up. Images of him standing behind me as I got ready for date night, smiling at his fiancée's reflection in the mirror hanging from the door to our closet. The dress fits more loosely around my frame than it did a month ago. If I'm going to be alone, I guess it's better to be skinny and alone. I can almost see my mother's nod of approval.

"Us girls have got to look out for each other," Kelly says kindly, leaning in closer to me. "Still doing okay in your first few weeks?" Her pretty smile falters and there's a weight to her voice that wasn't there before. I wonder if she's noticed I've stopped wearing my engagement ring, and this is her tentative way of checking in without prying.

"Yeah. Thanks." I force a smile as Akira and Antony join us. The lies are coming so easily to me now. If you play a part long enough, it eventually starts to feel natural. Akira thanks me for her coffee, and the thought of the faith she placed in me fills me with a guilt that almost punctures my veneer of calm.

Antony leans in close to me and starts to say, "Hey, what are you doing after—" But he's interrupted by Dr. Lutz, who had just cleared his throat significantly.

"Good morning, faculty," he says. "Just a few items of business, and I'll let you get back to your classrooms." He consults his notes. "As you are all aware I'm sure, we are fortunate to have Woodlands parents that are as generous as they are philanthropic and well-connected. Thanks to the Delaney family's annual gift to the New York Foundation for the Arts, we will be able to take our students to several exciting events this year, all the better to cultivate a cultured, well-rounded student body."

"Snotty little *patrons of the arts* in the making, more like," Antony mutters under his breath, and I smirk.

"We have chaperones for the Met and the symphony, but we will need a few more for next week's soiree at the ballet." Dr. Lutz gets an inordinate kick out of rhyming those two words. "Any volunteers?" More than anything else, the prospect of an evening outside my apartment shoots my hand into the air.

"Lovely. Thank you, Miss Winters." Dr. Lutz nods at me. To my left, Antony raises his hand. "And Mr. Ramirez. Perfect." He claps his hands together. "I'll have Wendy send you the details."

"Didn't realize you're a fan of the ballet, Antony," I murmur.

"Yeah, well it beats chaperoning the winter formal. Trust me." He shoots me an amused look. "You don't want to witness the mating rituals of teenagers. There are some things you can't *unsee*." I giggle at the thought of my students awkwardly swaying on a dance floor, or, more likely, taking turns looking up from their phones from opposite sides of the room. It's the first time I've genuinely laughed since "Sofia" appeared.

"Fair enough," I say. Dr. Lutz has moved on to other announcements.

I'll see Ezra first thing this morning, and my thoughts slip back to his mother. After Patrick and I started sleeping together, it didn't take long for him to float the idea of leaving his wife. This quickly became our favorite fantasy, one we loved to embellish. Every time our conversation lulled, we would add touches to it, and it became an ever-expanding, detailed canvas.

We would move to Portland or San Francisco. He would teach and write the great American novel, and I would get my PhD. We would cook together as his record player spun in a corner. He'd dip a wooden spoon in a simmering pan of something deliciously spicy and lift it to my mouth, and I would savor it before adding a pinch of salt or a squeeze of lime. We'd fall into an easy rhythm of sharing the newspaper and going for long walks, stopping our seamless, sunlit routine only to have spontaneous sex in our kitchen or in front of our fireplace. It's amazing what you'll believe is possible when you're in love.

The fact that he had a child didn't factor into this delusional daydream. I didn't even know Ezra existed until near the end of our affair. Patrick had stopped seeing me almost entirely. Our messages dried up. At first I started following him not because I thought there was someone else—besides his wife, of course. I was desperate to see his life, the *real* life that he lived out in the open.

I wanted to drink him in as he left the gym in the morning, sweat marking the space between his pectoral muscles. Or to see him as he sipped his afternoon coffee with a colleague at the little place that was too close to campus to ever visit together. I wanted to see the set of his shoulders as he returned home to her.

It was such a beautiful day when I finally saw the three of them together. A picture-perfect image ready for a frame. Fall had just started to cast its rosy glow over the leaves outside the neat brick house where the little family lived. I watched as the whitewashed front door—I still remember the green wreath that hung from it— opened. There was Rebecca, her long auburn hair tumbling over a crisp white shirt thrown over lived-in jeans, emerging hand in hand with their son. His son. And there was the man I loved, practically leaping from the car we'd fucked in half a dozen times. He scooped his son into his arms and planted a kiss on his wife's cheek in a single, easy movement. Because Patrick belonged to this woman and child. Husband. Father. Liar.

———

When I'm alone in my classroom, I set my shoulders back and clear my face of any indication of my emotional state. Today my classes are presenting poetry analysis, and as first period starts, I want to kick myself for putting Hannah and Ezra in the same group. If I had even an inch of brain space to spare, I never would have made that mistake.

After reading the title slide of their PowerPoint presentation, Ezra stands off to the side, his hands shoved deep in his pockets, a bored expression on his face. Hannah offers an insightful interpretation of an Elizabeth Bishop poem. Her face lights up as she dives into the text, and I can't help but beam at her. I make a note on Hannah's rubric to see me after class so I can lend her my copy of *North & South*.

When I look up, a movement in my peripheral vision draws my attention to the back of the classroom. Akira is perched there—she must have come in while I was focused on Hannah. She gives me an encouraging nod as she poises herself to take observation notes. The students at the front of the classroom have finished the bulk of their presentation and are now answering questions from their peers.

"Why would you say this poem is important?" Max, a bespectacled, serious student, asks intently. Hannah opens her mouth to answer the question, but Ezra interrupts her.

"Feminism." The word comes out as a derisive insult, no doubt directed at the *And Yet She Persisted* button pinned on Max's English binder.

"What do you mean by that, Ezra?" I ask.

"Well, a woman wrote it. So it's automatically important, right?" Ezra replies, eliciting badly suppressed laughter from a few of his cronies. Max shifts lower in their seat, fixes their eyes on the desk, and looks as if they would like nothing more than to disappear.

"Work written by women is important," I say carefully, keenly aware of Akira's eyes on me. "But feminism is an *expressed* idea. Where do you see Bishop express feminist ideas in this poem?"

"I just think that just because something *happens* to be written by a woman, we're supposed to think it's amazing, or whatever." He flicks his long hair out of his eyes, unfazed. There's a distinct shift in the room. Teenagers can sense a challenge to a power dynamic better than anyone. I need to walk the fine line between addressing it and not inviting Rebecca's retribution for daring to discipline her son. All with the department head watching my every move.

"In this class, we're going to evaluate the significance of a range of texts based on numerous factors, the writer's identity being one of them." I stand as I say this. Panic starts to bubble in the pit of my stomach. "Let's move on," I say. Out of the corner of my eye, I see Akira lean forward, a slight frown angling her mouth. "Thank you for your presentation and questions. Colin, I think your group is next," I say, and my throat goes dry. As the next group sets up their project, I notice Akira writing rapidly in her notebook. And though the rest of class runs smoothly, the crease between Akira's eyebrows remains in place.

The bell rings twenty minutes later, and before I can approach her, Ezra walks toward me with a determined expression on his face.

"Miss Winters?" he says. I carefully arrange my face before turning toward him, and I wonder if he's gearing up to expand on the display he put on for the class.

"Hey, Ezra," I say as neutrally as I can, unsure of how this conversation is going to go, fully aware that Akira is still watching, able to hear every word in the now-empty classroom.

"Did you get my mom's email?" he asks.

"No, actually," I say, dreading my inbox.

"Oh." He looks disappointed that he will have to explain whatever this is about. "For my college recommendations. Can you, uh, write me a rec letter? My mom was wondering if you could send it to her first? I think she needs it today so she can submit it to my college consultant." Of course Ezra has a college consultant.

"I'll get in touch with your mom after school." It's the best I can manage with any hope of not raising Akira's suspicions beyond the damage that's already been done. Ezra joins his friends who waited for him, hovering at the classroom door like a minor celebrity's entourage.

I know full well that I will not only write the letter but write it glowingly, falsely, and through gritted teeth. Most kids wait until their senior year to ask for rec letters, but obviously, Rebecca wants to capitalize on this situation now.

"Shut the door please, boys," I say. As soon as it closes, it's silent enough for me to hear the tiny disapproving exhale Akira lets out as she gets to her feet.

"So," she begins, advancing on my desk, "let's discuss how that went." She pulls one of the student chairs to sit opposite me. In the seconds her attention is elsewhere, I decide how to play this.

"I was just so taken aback," I say, and there's genuine shock in my voice. Akira nods. She wants to be understanding, and that makes this so much worse.

"I could see that. I noticed his words seemed targeted at Max. What impact do you think that had on the rest of the class?" As she asks this, Akira closes her notebook and presses her hands together, her eyes intent on mine.

"I think Ezra likes to push boundaries," I say, mentally taking the measure of each word that comes out of my mouth. "He can sense the priorities of my class, and he's challenging them. In a way, that's normal." Akira leans back and crosses her arms, considering what I'd just said. I rush to fill the silence. "I'm not saying what he said was right. But I do want to be intentional about not indoctrinating my students into any particular school of thought." I say this so earnestly I almost forget the part of me that wanted to make an example of Ezra then and there.

Akira eyes me thoughtfully. "I can see where you're coming from with that. But I was surprised you let his comments slide." There's disappointment, even warning in her voice. "I need you to bear in mind that your responsibility is to *all* your students. You need to be an ally to kids like Max, too." I think of Max's downcast expression, and I want to go cry in my car.

"Absolutely," I say.

"I have to say, also, I was surprised you agreed to a recommendation based on Ezra's behavior today." Her tone is more skeptical than admonishing. But there's no doubt there's scrutiny where I really don't need it right now.

"Ezra's been very engaged so far this year. To be honest, I was totally blindsided by the attitude he showed today." I repeat the lie my gradebook tells.

Akira raises her eyebrows, then lowers them, seemingly changing her mind about something. "I see. In any case, there are some resources I'd like you to review that should help you better navigate this kind of situation in the future."

"I'd really appreciate that, thank you," I say.

"To be clear, my expectation is that you're able to handle any outbursts like that more directly, with all students in mind. Thanks for talking this through with me," Akira says. Sure my voice will crack if I say another word, I just nod in response, and she leaves the room. Guilt and revulsion of the thought of Rebecca's latest demand rise to a boil inside me, and as I lower my head into my hands, I can't stop the few tears that slip between my interlaced fingers.

"Knock knock," Antony's voice says as the door reopens immediately, and I swipe my fingers under my eyes.

"Hey," I say, and just as I feared, the break in my voice betrays me.

"Hey," he says, lowering his voice with concern. He picks up the container of tissues at the back of the room and hands it to me. "Stressed about Akira observing a class?"

"Yeah. It's just been a long week," I say, grateful to not have to come up with an explanation on my own. I wipe my eyes again and wonder if they've started to swell.

"You know what," Antony says, his demeanor shifting to one of determined optimism, "we're not doing a mentor meeting right now." A lopsided smile shows off his gleaming white teeth and dimples his angular features. "I'm buying you that drink you desperately need. Today. I know just the place."

"You know," I say, thinking of Patrick and his son and the utterly empty apartment waiting for me. "That sounds like an excellent idea."

⸻

After firing off some end-of-day emails, I drive to the bar Antony suggested. "Just the place" turned out to be an unmarked speakeasy-style bar comprised of dim corners, man-bunned bartenders presiding over a complex cocktail menu, and at just five P.M., a mercifully sparse clientele. When my eyes adjust, I can see the edge of Antony's leg and worn brown leather oxford sticking out of a corner booth toward the back.

"Hi," he says with a smile, awkwardly half standing in the confines of the booth. "I wasn't sure what you like, so I ordered these." Antony gestures toward two cocktails: one that looks like an old-fashioned, the other some sort of citrus martini. Did "just colleagues" typically order drinks for other "just colleagues"? "I didn't want to be presumptuous—I've just seen those guys spend twenty minutes making one cocktail." He rolls his eyes playfully at the preening bartenders, one of whom appears to be caramelizing an orange slice with a blowtorch, the other snipping fresh mint leaves with an impossibly small pair of scissors.

"I know the type. Thank you," I say, reaching for the martini.

"Cheers to shitty days." He lifts his glass to mine. I sip, and bright flavors of elderflower, gin, basil, and lime linger on my tongue.

"This is lovely," I say appreciatively.

"It's my favorite cocktail they make here."

"Really? I had you pegged as more of a whiskey guy." The liquor is filling the hollow of my empty stomach, and I welcome the warm rush of it.

"Don't tell anyone this, as it's potentially damaging for my debonair, manly reputation." Antony places his elbows on the table and conspiratorially looks over his shoulder. "But as far as cocktails go, I'm basically Carrie Bradshaw." I almost choke on my drink as I let out a laugh that feels even better than the gin.

"Now that's a name I never thought I'd hear coming out of *your* mouth," I say. Antony shrugs.

"My ex liked the show. Which brings me to . . ." He hesitates. "We're all wondering what happened there." He points to my bare ring finger. I hope the dimmed lighting masks my reddening cheeks and neck. "You don't have to tell me if you don't want to," he adds, holding up his hands. I'm aware of the space that's slowly started to close between us. My knee has grazed his twice already. I'm pretty sure the first time was an accident.

"My fiancé slept with a friend of mine, hence no more." I extend my ringless left hand. "That's the whole sob story." I take a long sip. The glass is already nearly empty.

"That's awful, Brooke. I'm so sorry." His eyes look a few shades darker in here. "And for the record, we all think he's a moron. There's zero chance he was good enough for you anyway."

"We?" I say, my voice rasping with the acidity that's dried out my mouth. I should really drink some water.

"You know what gossips teachers are." I laugh at that, and he joins in as he catches the bartender's eye and signals for two more cocktails.

"All too well. But that's just perfect," I say more lightly than I feel. "Everyone knows my life is a mess, and soon they'll find out what a terrible teacher I am." I rest my hands on the table to stop them from shaking. It doesn't surprise me when Antony covers one of them with his, but the warmth of any human touch is still a shock to my system.

"I'm going to stop you right there. Your ex is an idiot, and for the record, I think you're amazing." Antony's voice is gentle, and the spice on his breath layers seamlessly with my intoxication. We talk for a long time. About teaching. About books. About our families. He tells me about his daughter and we lament our dead-end relationships. As if the scene is playing in the reflection of my drink, I know what is going to happen next.

And as he slides over to my side of the booth, his hand on my waist, I know I'm going to let it.

CHAPTER 35

Caroline

Now

The executives at Wanderly don't look like they're capable of a massive corporate cover-up. A room full of mostly women looks back at me, nodding along as I wrap up my presentation. But then, this group is pretty much the "after" photo of a company post-makeover. I'm not looking at the problem employees: I'm looking at their hastily hired replacements.

"Well," starts Aspen, the newly installed head of human resources. She's a woman in her late thirties with ash-purple hair, and she adjusts the folds of her well-cut suede jacket before continuing. "I think it's safe to say we're all very impressed. We have a press release going live at the end of the month, so this isn't officially *out there* yet, but Wanderly is launching a campaign to promote diversity and inclusion across our global offices." Her tone is friendly: just a few gal pals chatting at happy hour. I already knew everything she just told me, thanks to intel from Eric.

"That's great. There's a lot of room to grow in terms of representation in this industry," I say, and some of the women exchange glances at this. Wanderly's short-term rental site will be lambasted once the trends of discrimination in their booking system become public knowledge. Somehow Eric was able to pick up on whispers that the company's all-male leadership knew that hosts were less likely to rent their vacation homes and condos to people of color and did nothing about it. Investors got wind of this and needed to prepare for the coming shitstorm. Equilibrium would be a nice addition to their sweeping efforts to show that they do in fact care about people who aren't white and/or male.

"Exactly. And we think Equilibrium would be an *amazing* asset to our campaign," Aspen says. She emphasizes *amazing* like every annoying millennial describing an *amazing* matcha latte or an *amazing* indie rock concert.

"I couldn't agree more," I say, and it's true. A partnership with us *would* be a smart move for Wanderly, it *would* genuinely help improve their company, and if it boosted our profits, so much the better.

"Wonderful. You can expect to hear from us very soon," Aspen says, standing and crossing the room to clasp my hand in both of hers. I take my cue and wend my way back to the elevators, saving my triumphant text to Eric until the doors glide shut in front of me.

> All but locked in. Good work finding this one.

I add a few celebratory emojis, and within seconds, Eric responds with a trophy emoji paired with a dollar sign. He's not wrong about the cash. A few more deals like these, and I won't need to rely on Leo's dwindling inheritance. I reach the ground floor and step out into the bustling street. It's just ten blocks back to Thrive, so I pause to dig in my bag for my earbuds.

"Call off your dogs," a sharp voice says from behind me. My spine snaps ramrod straight. I know that voice. Turning, I see Drea leaning against the building I've just exited, a lit cigarette dangling from her lower lip. Even after seeing her at the Nantucket house, I'm still taken aback by her appearance. She looks nothing like the puffy addict I remember. Lean and glowing with health, Drea actually looks younger than she did ten years ago. No doubt the glinting necklaces she's wearing—an eye, an open palm, a crescent moon—all represent some spiritual bullshit.

"Or should I say *dog*?" Drea adds before taking a long, leisurely drag. "Your PI reminds me of an old basset hound. Pathetic, really." She flicks ash in my general direction, and it glows red as it lands in a crack in the sidewalk.

"Haven't you heard those are bad for you?" I counter, lifting my chin at the cigarette. "I'd have thought an enlightened being such as yourself would know that." I take a step toward her but am careful to leave a good buffer of pavement between us. "Or can you break character as long as you're out of Todd's sight?"

Drea lets out a laugh calcified with bitterness. "Sweet, sweet Toddie. He's finding out what it's like to have a woman's approval for the first time in his life. It's kind of cute, really." The suggestive emphasis she laces into her words shoots revulsion through my veins.

"So you're following me now?" I ask over a taxi horn and the screech of tires at the intersection next to us.

"Oh, more like dropping by to tell you the good news. We're just in town so Todd can talk to his Reiki master about performing our wedding ceremony." Drea arches an eyebrow in a gesture that echoes Sofia so exactly, I can only stare at her blankly for a moment. "Don't worry. I'll pass along your congratulations." She tilts her chin mockingly.

"What the actual fuck, Dre?" I spit it out before I can stop myself. There it is—the familiar nickname shimmers darkly between us, the only sign that there was ever a time we didn't despise each other. Her smile widens. Drea knows she's got the upper hand. "I couldn't care less what you and Todd get up to, even if you want to marry the guy," I say, struggling to recover and hoping I sound convincing. "But I wouldn't get too comfortable if I were you. It's only a matter of time before I get proof of what you did to Jenna, to Brooke, and to my family," I say.

Drea takes another drag of her cigarette and eyes me thoughtfully. "Who the fuck is Jenna?" she asks. "You never answered me the other day."

"Don't play dumb," I say. Drea's eyes have a wicked sparkle in them now.

"I'm not playing with you at all, trust me. This isn't a game to me. None of you Yale bitches respected my sister. The shit the three of you let happen to her is disgusting. That's to say nothing of that twisted brother of yours—" Drea's tone is pitch-black and vengeful.

"Did you kill Jenna?" I interrupt, steeling myself for any answer.

"Of course not," she says. Drea's eyes are flinted with gold that gleams like the cigarette embers she sends onto the concrete between us with every lazy flick of her fingers. She regards me with a flat, dispassionate expression that's impossible to read. Far from giving anything away, this just leaves me more confused than ever.

"You need to back off. Stop stalking us," I say. It's all I can manage to stammer as I try to focus on whether I believe Drea or not.

"And why would I do that? After what you and your sick family did to Sofia?" Drea can't have any proof. I'd made sure of that—or at least I thought I had. The only two people who know the whole truth are dead now.

"Your sister died in an accident," I say, my tongue curling in the shape of the familiar lie.

"Who says this is about how Sofia *died*?" Drea asks, and that stops my pulse cold, the emphasis she puts on the last word. She's talking about something that happened when Sofia was still alive, something that I thought no one knew about. I can't show Drea my fear.

"Todd's money has just about dried up," I say. I know enough about the status of the Archer family fortune to do some simple math. The results don't look good for Todd, let alone a psychotic gold digger. "So I'm not sure what you stand to gain there."

Drea scoffs. "You rich people are all the same. You think everyone has a price and that everything is for sale. The only way you can sleep at night is to assume the rest of us can be bought." As she says this, she crushes her cigarette under her heel.

"You honestly expect me to believe this *isn't* about money?" I say.

"Obviously not," Drea retorts, her eyes hardening with hatred. "But money isn't *everything* that matters to me. After what you did to my sister, everything you, Leo, and your little friends did—" Her eyes drift to a point in the distance, and a moment passes that's filled with death and lies and cruel turns of fate. "Let's just say there are a *lot* of ways to pay."

"I'm going to stop you," I say, and I fix Drea with a glare.

"You're going to try." Drea straightens, pops a piece of gum into her mouth, and looks at me, snapping it between her teeth. "That's half the fun." The same unsettling smile I saw at the house coils on her lips as she steps away from me. "And don't worry about Todd," she calls back. "What I have in mind for him is nothing compared to what you did to your dear departed stepdaddy." And with that, she rounds the corner and vanishes from sight.

I don't know how long I've been standing on the street, staring at the spot where Drea disappeared, before I realize I'm shaking. I never even asked her about the threatening texts, but that doesn't matter. It wasn't a confession, but her anger and the lingering threat against Todd are all I need to confirm she's "Sofia," even if she didn't kill Jenna. Now the only question is—how do I get her to stop?

I start walking in no direction in particular, letting the footsteps of the people around me determine where I go. If Sofia did tell her sister what really happened to Bill, there's still no way she has proof. Drea can follow us around, break into Brooke's apartment, and send creepy messages, but that isn't going to scare me into some sort of insane confession. And her feeble attempt to ruin my reputation is no match for Eric and me. And with this determined thought, I nestle my headphones into my ears and send a quick text to Brooke.

Drea followed me to work. Call me.

CHAPTER 36

Sofia

Then

As Caroline promised, they arrive at the Archers' Nantucket estate three days later, and for Sofia, it's better than coming home. Her feet turn instinctively toward Caroline's bedroom when she reaches the top of the familiar sweeping staircase, and Sofia wonders if the tiny scuff mark she left after sliding down the banister is still there. It takes effort to turn toward the opposite end of the long hallway—toward Leo's room. An Archer family portrait hulks behind her from its pride of place on the wall. Sofia can almost feel six pairs of cold blue eyes boring disapprovingly into her back. It's enough to make her rip Leo's clothes off before the door swings all the way shut behind them.

Afterward, they stare up at the high ceiling. It's ribbed with wooden beams that give the impression of being aboard a luxurious ship. Sofia's eyes trace the graceful curves of the wood, one hand stroking Leo's bare chest, the other tucked under the goose down pillow that pokes tiny shafts of feathers into her hand. She pulls one free and sends it floating with an exhale.

"You're sure your dad isn't going to be here this weekend?" Sofia asks as casually as she can. Leo can't know how essential it is that Bill, the one person who knows about her history with Caroline, remains safely ensconced in his Manhattan office. If he saw Sofia with his precious son, there's no telling how he would react.

"Positive," Leo says. He rakes a hand through his tousled golden hair and twists in the crisp white sheets to face her. The Archers probably paid someone to iron them. "Technically, this is still my grandfather's house, and my uncle Todd gets it when he dies, so I think my dad's getting accustomed to not being here much. I'm pretty sure he's in Palm Beach with his new girlfriend." The setting sun illuminates Leo's languid features, and she's momentarily hypnotized by the curve of his lips and the depths of his almond-shaped eyes.

"Have you met her?" Sofia asks, tracing a finger along the smooth ridge of his cheekbone. He laughs and sits up.

"I've met half a dozen of her." He raises a hand and extends one finger. "Bleached blonde." He extends another finger. "Mid-thirties at most, and all dying to be the next Mrs. William Archer III." He waggles the fingers and rolls his eyes. "So have I met this particular bimbo? No. And I don't need to. I call them the Sheris. They all have ditzy names like that." He reaches for his T-shirt and pulls it over his head.

"Oh, yeah?" Curiosity piqued, Sofia rolls onto her side and watches Leo's lean frame against a backdrop of sparkling sea. The windows at the back of his room are open, and the otherworldly glow beyond the glass warms the faded linen chair in the corner and the antique trunk at the foot of the four-poster bed. There's a little balcony beyond the windows, just enough space for an Archer and a lucky guest to gaze at the best East Coast view money can buy.

"And they're all trash: the polar opposite of Mom, which just makes it worse," Leo says. He plays with the latch of one of the windows, and she drinks in the familiar salt-sweet breeze that billows into the room as the wind changes.

"What was she like, your mom?" Sofia asks as she sits up, draws her knees under her chin, and wraps her arms around the Egyptian cotton sheathing her legs.

Leo stays silent for a moment, his eyes fixed on the horizon. "In a way, she was always sort of helpless. Like, she came from *that* generation of wealthy women. Who went straight from boarding school to college for husband-hunting and some bullshit degree they'd never actually use, then marriage. Literally zero time to be independent, you know?"

She doesn't know what he's talking about, but she makes a sound of assent anyway. Women from Diana Archer's walk of life are as foreign to her as the idea of using the word *summer* as a verb. She had only ever known generations of tough, fiercely self-sufficient women who worked like horses until they were dead.

"How did she end up with your dad?" Sofia asks, and she realizes she's holding her breath. Caroline would never talk about her mother, so Sofia gave up asking a long time ago. But, as with just about anything, Leo is much more forthcoming.

"Oh, they grew up together. Their families were close, the Archers and the Montclairs," Leo says, his tone vague. Caroline had never even mentioned her mother's maiden name. "My dad was always kind of in love with her. Everyone wanted it, for them to end up together. And when Caroline's dad left our mom, Bill was her way of finding somewhere safe . . ." Leo trails off. The silence that ensues is a sad one, sad enough to make Sofia's heart ache for him, Caroline, and Diana. Diana couldn't have known just how wrong she was about Bill. Not until it was too late.

"I'm sorry about your mom," Sofia says, and she's gentle in the way he likes as she strokes her long nails down his back.

"Yeah," Leo says. "And the thing is, she was so smart. Could have been a professor or curator or whatever the fuck she wanted to be." Bitterness stiffens his voice like a paper-thin layer of ice over deep, brackish water. "But she didn't think that was even an option, so she stuck with my dad until it killed her."

Leo gets up and crosses the room to stare out the window. Sofia walks over to press her warm skin against him. Nestling her cheek against the nape of his neck, Sofia leans into Leo, and they are still, both gazing at the sun slipping behind the waves on the horizon.

"Let's go to dinner, rally the troops," he says energetically, turning to face her and planting a hard kiss on her mouth. "That new bistro looks fantastic." The restaurants that come and go from this corner of Nantucket are of little concern to people like the Archers as long as there is someone to refill their martinis and tolerate their laundry lists of menu modifications. Sofia had to ask Caroline to explain what *gluten free* meant. To her, it still sounds like a figment of an anorexic housewife's imagination.

"Great," she says with the impish smile she's perfected. Leo's phone goes off, rattling on the surface of the cherrywood dresser. He takes it and stares at the screen, his eyebrows furrowing as he reads the name that appears as it continues to buzz.

"Meet you downstairs in a few? I should probably take this."

"Sure," Sofia says, and she turns to throw on a pair of shorts and a sweater as Leo steps onto the balcony and snaps the door shut behind him. She emerges from the room and has to remind herself that she doesn't have to tiptoe or worry about getting caught anymore. She can hear a shower running from one of the half-dozen bedrooms on the second floor. No doubt Brooke wants to look like preppy perfection tonight.

Caroline had to sneak Sofia in and out of this house so many times that it feels deliciously transgressive as she stands brazenly in the foyer, staring up at the chandelier. She takes her time as she makes her way into the Archer inner sanctum. Her bare feet are soundless on the cold tile that shines underneath sideboards and end tables bearing fresh-cut flowers.

Sofia can see herself, or at least a shadow of herself, in the gleaming floor that transitions smoothly into flawless hardwood as she descends into the sunken sunroom. She reaches for the heavy brass catch of one of the French doors that opens onto the oceanfront terrace and pauses to stroke the gossamer-fine curtains.

The unmistakable sound of the front door unbolting and swinging open snaps her out of her reverie. There are footsteps and a dull thud of luggage hitting the floor, and Sofia slips onto the terrace unseen.

"Bill," a high-pitched breathy voice says over the clack of high heels, "it's *gorgeous.*" A low chuckle of laughter comes in response, and Sofia hears what sounds like an open palm smacking against flesh. The woman lets out a coy shriek and giggles girlishly. Crouching behind a potted boxwood, Sofia narrows her eyes at the scene unfolding in the sunroom.

There looms tall, beefy Bill Archer. He's arm in arm with, undoubtedly, one of his Sheris, a rail-thin woman who would have had Miss America–caliber looks ten years ago. Their voices grow louder as they draw perilously close to where Sofia hides in the deepening shadows behind a screen of dense leaves.

"This place has been in the family for four generations," Bill says. He manages to sound both expansive and dismissive as he talks, as if this monument to the Archer wealth is a mere trifle in their storied legacy. "It's my nice little getaway from the city." Sofia rolls her eyes.

Sheri doesn't need to know that technically the house isn't *his.* His back is turned to Sofia; it's covered in one of those pastel button-down shirts favored by rich men at play. He dwarfs the woman, but Sofia can see one of her hands snake its way around Bill's waist, light glinting off Pepto Bismol–pink nail polish. But then the hand jerks away.

"Who the hell are you?" Bill barks, all traces of the swaggering host gone from his voice. For the first time, an unsteady dip in his tone betrays him. He must have had a few drinks before getting here. Sofia hears something clatter to the floor before Brooke's blond hair swirls into view as she bends to pick it up.

"I'm, um, a friend of Caroline's?" With her startled eyes and innocent face, she looks and sounds like a frightened rabbit at the wrong end of a hunter's shotgun.

"That doesn't give you a right to be in my house." There's a pause, and then the sound of more footsteps approaching. "And what are *you* doing here?" Bill's tone has its familiar bullying quality now.

"I could ask you the same question." Caroline's response is cool, unfazed. "Leo said you were in Palm Beach, so we thought we'd come up for the weekend." There's a moment of tense silence, and Sofia clenches her teeth, hoping the sound of her knee cracking doesn't give her away.

"Would you ladies excuse us? Go ahead and get settled in the master, Kristi. Top of the stairs, first door on your right." Kristi pouts a little as she bends to pick up her luggage.

Turning to Brooke, Bill spits out, "And whoever you are, just give us a sec." His slurred words are calmer, dangerously so. Sofia watches Kristi and Brooke scurry up the stairs.

Caroline and Bill move into the sunroom, closer to Sofia's line of sight, and they glare at each other. Caroline's feet are firmly planted and her arms crossed. Bill paces the room until he hears confirmation of two upstairs doors shutting.

"Now look here, you spoiled little bitch," Bill growls and takes a step toward her, a sausage-thick finger jabbing at Caroline's chest. "I put up with your entitled behavior for your mother's sake, but let—" He opens his mouth to continue, but instead, he stumbles unsteadily into the arm of a leather sofa.

He tries to start over. "Let me make something crystal c-clear." But his speech stops again, and his eyes begin to bulge. One arm has gone slack, and as he struggles to regain his footing, his face suddenly reddens and begins to swell. Caroline doesn't move. She watches as her stepfather opens and closes his mouth, nothing but a guttural moan escaping it. Bill gurgles what might be attempts to beg for help or might simply be the control slipping from his body. He slumps against the couch and begins to slide, inch by inch, to the floor.

Caroline takes a step closer and bends to eye level with him. Several emotions seem to be struggling for center stage on her face: surprise flits behind her eyes at what's unfolding, her darkest wish made real by pure chance, but it's an appraising expression that finally settles on Caroline's aquiline features. It's the face of someone calculating exactly how to turn the circumstances to their advantage.

"I understand what you're saying," she says in an even, clear voice. Bill fully collapses in a heavy sprawl, spittle pooling on one side of his slackened mouth. "And of course I'd never intentionally do anything disrespectful." She steps over his body and looks down her nose at his heaving chest. Even from this distance, Sofia can see bright red spots appear in Bill's eyes as he struggles, and his breath becomes ragged. Frozen to her hiding place, she slowly begins to process what Caroline is doing: watching Bill die from a heart attack and not lifting a finger to stop it.

It's more than that, though. Caroline is enjoying this.

"Mm-hmm. No, I know, we have to do what's best for Leo and for your family," Caroline says as she takes a seat on the far end of the couch and crosses her legs primly. Bill has gone limp, his wide, wild eyes fixed on the floor, his legs splayed in front of him like an abandoned marionette. Caroline tilts her wrist to better consult a slender gold watch, vintage Cartier—it had been her mother's. She waits. Sofia imagines the second hand ticking in its neat infinite circles, oblivious to their deadly task. Sofia's limbs remain locked, her mouth clamped shut, and Caroline's eyes never waver from the watch face as she prattles on to the dying man on the floor.

It might have been three excruciating minutes, maybe twenty, when Caroline bends and places two fingers on Bill's neck. Rising, she allows herself a split-second victorious smile before she resets her features in a mask of shock and horror and begins to say, then shout, then scream, Bill's name.

Kristi is the first to burst into the room where Caroline kneels next to Bill, shaking him and babbling in hysterics. Brooke and Leo follow, and Brooke calls 911 as Leo sinks against a back wall in shock. Sofia watches this scene unfold and knows she has only seconds to decide what to do, and with a long look at Caroline's face, she knows there's only one way back to her now.

She crawls backward along the edge of the terrace away from the house. When her feet meet soft grass, she stoops and runs toward the Archers' private beach and the shadow of the long dock that stretches into waves so hushed it's as if they know what they just witnessed. She ducks into one of Caroline's favorite hiding places—into "nowhere," as she'd said more times than Sofia can count—and catches her breath, eyes locked on the backlit windows. Sofia straightens, then rushes toward the house.

After asking what happened, Sofia tells no one in particular that she was out for a walk on the beach, but only Brooke registers her presence. By the time blue and red lights flash in the windows and uniformed paramedics perform useless CPR on Bill's corpse, it has long been too late. Sudden-onset cardiac arrest—cut, dried, and inked on a legal death certificate. It's half of the truth.

Sofia knows the other half with perfect clarity: Caroline has finally won the soul-crushing battle she's been fighting since her mother married that monster.

CHAPTER 37

Brooke

Now

Antony is sitting up when I step back into his bedroom, having smoothed my hair and rinsed my mouth with mouthwash until my gums burned. He looks good shirtless. Those just-fitted-enough sweaters had told the truth about his physique.

"I've been thinking about doing that since you almost spilled my coffee," he says with a lazy smile, tucking a bare arm behind his head. I laugh, trying not to think about the fact that I was engaged when that happened. Perhaps he realizes the implications of what he just said, because his expression crinkles with worry. "Not that I would have. I mean, I know—" His words tumble out of his mouth, but I smile and hold up a hand.

"It's okay," I say, and I reach for my dress, which lies crumpled on the floor under Antony's shirt.

"Leaving so soon?" he says, even though I think we both know it's better this way.

"Yeah, I should really get home." I glance at the clock next to

Antony's bed—nine P.M.—just enough time to slink back home and recoup for school the next day. I step into my dress and struggle with the zipper.

"Here," Antony says, noticing me fumbling with the back of my dress and motioning me to come closer. His hands are gentle and warm on my back as he zips the dress. I'm embarrassed to realize I've closed my eyes at his touch and am grateful he couldn't see me doing it.

I mutter a thank-you and then realize I should probably address the elephant in the room before slinking away. "Maybe we don't mention this to anyone?"

"I think that's probably for the best, yeah." Antony swings his legs out of bed and approaches me as I'm awkwardly putting on my shoes. "But . . ." He trails off and wraps his arms around me. "What if I want to see you again?" I look up into his eyes, bright under a thick layer of lashes that most women would be happy to swap theirs for. Unease squirms in the pit of my stomach along with the temptation to get back into bed. This is a bad idea.

"We *do* see each other every day, remember?"

"True." Antony pulls me closer. "But I don't think Lutz would approve of this."

He closes the ten or so inches that separate our heights and kisses me, hard. His hand works around my back and up my chest, settling at the nape of my neck in a tangle of hair, which he curls around his fingers. I want to slip off my shoes and push him backward onto the still-warm sheets. But I have to stop. I rest both my hands flat on his chest and edge my foot away from him.

"See you tomorrow," I say.

"Right, and we can pretend this didn't happen." Antony winks. "I don't hate it," he says, easing back into bed and regarding me with a wry smile. I can tell he likes the idea of sneaking around, but the thought makes me want to vomit up those craft cocktails and hide.

"I'll see myself out," I say, and I walk out of the room and down the hall to where my purse is slung over a mid-century modern armchair in his living room.

Eyeing my surroundings, which had been blurry thanks to my focus on getting out of my dress when we came in, I can't help but grin at what a classic bachelor pad this is. It's a stylish one, I'll give him that. A decorative scheme of iron accents and leather, minimal furniture, rubber plants instead of ones that need watering, bookshelves dominated by Hemingway, Vonnegut, and nonfiction titles I don't recognize. The exposed shelves in the kitchen, store-potted succulent plants, and a paltry four bowls, four plates, and four mugs, all in generic white ceramic, which puzzles me for a moment, but I dismiss it.

Most of the pictures on the walls are nature shots, and the idea of Antony ruggedly scaling mountains and kayaking rapids is a bit of a turn-on. There's just one exception. In the center of the cluster of photos is a shot of Antony and his ex: their feet bare on sand, each holding the hand of a small pigtailed child. My eyes linger on his daughter. She has lively brown eyes, soft dark curls, and an adorable toothy smile that scrunches her entire face as she beams for the camera. And she's the spitting image of her mother, the classic beauty Antony had divorced.

I wonder if the photo of the ex should worry me but dismiss the thought before it fully forms in my mind. He and his ex are coparents, nothing more. That's what he'd told me, and isn't that the mark of a good man? One willing to put his child's needs first? I realize I'm lingering and make a beeline for the door.

I hear a heavy automatic lock whir shut behind me. When I'm safely out of sight, I dig in my purse for my phone. Dreading another message from "Sofia," I refresh my emails, but it's Rebecca's name that sends a bolt of anxiety through me.

To: bwinters@woodlandsacademy.org
From: rebecca.adams03@gmail.com
Subject: Ezra's Recommendation

Ms. Winters,

Thank you for agreeing to write Ezra's recommendation letter.
We do need to send it to his college admissions coach tonight.
As I'm sure you can imagine, there could be serious
consequences for missing such an important deadline—please
be more mindful of future requests. Can you send me the letter
ASAP?

Thanks,
Rebecca

Shit. I rub my fingertips against my throbbing temples. Rebecca was careful. No outsider reading her message would suspect
a thing, but her meaning could not be clearer—fail to do my son's
bidding again, and all your dirty laundry lands on Dr. Lutz's desk. I
type a reply.

To: rebecca.adams03@gmail.com
From: bwinters@woodlandsacademy.org
Subject: Ezra's Recommendation

Hi, Rebecca,

I'm so sorry about that! Must have slipped my mind. I'll get
right on that and send the recommendation letter to you shortly.

Best,
Brooke

The false politeness claws at my conscience. As part of my therapy after leaving Brown and Patrick behind, my psychiatrist insisted I delete all communications I'd sent during our affair. Pictures. Text messages. Emails. Pages and pages detailing what a forty-year-old man told a nineteen-year-old girl to do, and to do to him. Closure achieved. Victim mindset avoided. Which means any ammunition I'd once had to fight back, to expose Patrick and tell Rebecca to back off, is long gone.

I think of how easy it would have been to fight fire with fire, to expose Ezra's father for the lying, womanizing, power dynamic abuser he was, how just one of the screenshots I'd had could have ended all of this, and my hands shake with rage as I reach into my purse. Just as I'm about to stick the keys in the ignition, my phone pings Rebecca's reply. It's just one word: *thanks*.

Game, set, and match to Rebecca fucking Adams.

On the drive home, I resolve to use the generic positive recommendation letter from my files, punch it up a bit, and send it to Rebecca. What's one more entitled rich kid at an elite college in the grand scheme of things? As long as Woodlands never gets what Rebecca has on me, this all stays safely tucked away. I wince at the thought of the drunken footage of me showing up on their doorstep, the incident records she must have a copy of—who knows what else this woman scorned squirreled away. I just need to stick this out for a year, and then Ezra won't be my problem anymore. Keep it buried. Keep Rebecca happy. Simple.

———

Longing for a shower, I trudge up the stairs to my empty, darkened apartment, and I freeze. Leaning against the doorframe, his right leg jiggling like it always does when he's nervous, is Josh.

"Hey," he says, shifting to standing upright. "Sorry to just show up like this. Can I come in?" I can hear the keys jangling in his pocket as he says this, and I wonder why he didn't just let himself into the apartment. But then, the sight of a recently released murder suspect just standing in your kitchen in the dark would be enough to scare the living daylights out of anyone. Josh wouldn't do that to me. Not that I know anything about what he would or wouldn't do anymore.

"How long have you been waiting here?" I say, and as I unlock the door, I'm flooded with memories of the two of us standing on this threshold until they're poisoned by thoughts of Jenna. Josh follows me into the hallway and flicks on the lights with an automatic, practiced gesture.

"Not long," he says. I doubt that's the truth.

"I'm glad they let you go," I say. I realize I'm hovering awkwardly, unsure of whether to stand, sit, or get back in my car and drive away. Settling for perching on one of the stools facing the kitchen countertop, I take in Josh's worn expression, rumpled clothes, and the days-old stubble shadowing his face.

"Yeah," he says, taking the stool next to mine. "The evidence they have would never hold up in court, so they really didn't have a choice. Honestly, I think the police are under pressure from the Hostetlers. An overdose in *their* family isn't a good look for the company." He sighs bitterly. "But I think they've accepted it really was suicide. Poor Jenna . . ." Josh trails off with a sad, defeated shrug.

"Yeah, it's awful," I say to fill a silence that presses in from the walls.

"Where's Piper?" Josh asks, searching the floor for the sign of her tail. It's such a natural question, it makes me sick.

"At the vet," I say. It's not a good lie—it doesn't make sense for her to be there at this time of night—but Josh nods absentmindedly anyway. "What did you want to tell me?" I ask. Focus returns to his eyes with alarming speed.

"It's about what we found when we were doing some digging."

This triggers an involuntary angry exhale from me. *Digging.* That's one word for what they were doing. He reaches into his backpack and pulls out his laptop. "Look at this."

"Okay," I say with a note of skepticism that I don't bother to erase from my voice.

"I think Jenna was blackmailing the Archers," he says.

"What?" I say, incredulous. But then I remember the bank statements I'd stashed in my top drawer and the mysterious monthly payments from a nameless bank account.

"Yeah," Josh says, pulling up a spreadsheet peppered with tiny numbers: transaction records, dates, sums of money in the tens of thousands of dollars. It's everything I suspected but didn't want to see clearly on the statements I stole. "At first I thought Hostetler Pharma was paying Jenna off for keeping quiet about all the lawsuits they're facing. And it's some pretty serious shit, like lying to the FDA, covering up how addictive their products are—all kinds of stuff. But then I thought that they would have found a stealthier way to pay her off, and for more money than this."

I pull the laptop closer and read the screen. He's right. The amounts are irregular, and thousands less than a massive pharmaceutical company could probably afford. My brain unsticks and starts to connect the dots.

"Okay, since her in-laws run the company, surely they could have worked something out. Transferred property into Jenna's name, upped Hayden's trust fund, paid off her student loans in a lump sum. With a literal *billion* dollars at their disposal, they would have had more creative, undetectable options," I say, and I feel weeks of suspicion start to activate in my brain. "Whoever was making these transfers must have been limited in how they were going to send the funds. Is this a foreign bank account?" I point to the identical series of numbers associated with every transfer, recognizing the account number I'd seen but careful not to reveal too much of my own snooping.

Josh nods, picking up my train of thought. "I bet you're right about that. And who has things like offshore assets and foreign bank accounts? The superrich with something to hide. A family like the Archers." Josh turns his face away from the computer and toward mine, and it shines with energy and desperation, the kind of look that appears on conspiracy theorists and recent cult converts. His expression pulls me out of the rabbit hole I'd temporarily tripped down. This is crazy.

"But what does Caroline have to hide?" I ask, careful to cover all my bases and reveal nothing. "And why would Jenna know, of all people?"

"Jenna said something to me before she died. The last time we—" He stops abruptly, and the fact of the affair crashes headlong into the conversation. My fingernails dig into the palm of my hand. "The last time we saw each other. She said that no one could know about what we were planning with the Hostetlers, but she went out of her way to single out Caroline and Leo. Doesn't that seem strange?" He has a point, but it's a stretch at best.

"Think, Brooke. Why *them*?" Josh continues. "Why would she make sure the *Archers* didn't know that she was about to invite all kinds of scrutiny into her life? Because she didn't want Caroline and Leo to think someone would stumble upon whatever Jenna had on them and was using for blackmail."

"Jenna did say she wanted to talk to me about something," I say, biting my lip, wondering whether I could trust Josh with what I know. Suspicion I wish wasn't there at all is slithering into my gut.

"When?" Josh snaps.

"The night she went missing, at Leo's show," I say, startled by the intensity of his expression. Josh runs both hands through his hair, his shoulders slumped toward his laptop.

"That's not good," he mumbles.

"Why? What makes you so sure it's the Archers?" I ask, dreading the answer Josh will string together with threads of suspicion and despair.

"I looked into Equilibrium. Have you seen Caroline's client list? Or the companies that tag them on social media? Pretty sure it's enough to pay for more than that crappy studio she lives in. Or a real office space. Or more than just another employee's salary."

I consider this, and Josh uses my silence to press his case.

"Seriously, where is all that revenue going?" He lets that question solidify for a moment. "Are you sure you can't think of anything Jenna might know about Caroline or Leo that they don't want getting out?"

The questions intertwine as I consider my answer. What if Jenna held a piece to all of this that I didn't have? Had she died because she wouldn't give it up?

"Have you told the police this? Shown them this?" I ask, my decade-old instinct to protect my best friend kicking in.

"No," Josh says. And for the first time, I see shame and fear cast shadows across Josh's face. "Jenna didn't exactly know that I have this stuff. And I'm not about to give the police that information. How would that look for me? The police are looking into her finances—if they do their jobs, they're bound to find these records and get to the bottom of it."

"How did *you* get this stuff?"

"I found it at their place in the Catskills. She gave me a key. It's where we did a lot of our research on Bryce's family."

"Okay, let's say *hypothetically* . . ."—I stress the word so Josh doesn't get any ideas—"this is all true. Leo and Caroline were still nowhere near Jenna the night she died." It occurs to me that I'd simply taken Caroline's word for this, as the police's "investigation" pretty much consisted of ticking a box that said "sad, messy life." That was, until "Sofia" stepped in to try to frame Josh.

"I know," Josh says, and there's defeat in his voice. "But I want you to be careful around them, okay?"

"Okay," I say. I look directly in Josh's eyes. I want to tell him that everything is going to be all right. But the thought of his affair with Jenna stops me, and my gaze slips to my shoes.

"So, um, where will you go?" Josh abruptly changes the subject, and at first his question floats in the air, not quite managing to land in my thoughts.

"Go?" I ask.

Josh shifts uncomfortably on the stool. "Well, it's my name on the lease, remember?"

"You're kicking me out?" I blurt, angry and disbelieving. Heat spreads across my chest.

"Look, I crashed with Brian for a while out of respect for you, but now I have to get my life back together," he says with a combination of misery and leaden exhaustion. "The firm fired me. It's not a good look to have a murder suspect working for them."

"They fired you?" I ask, momentarily distracted by the injustice of this.

"Yeah. The Hostetlers have friends everywhere. One word from Bryce's dad about what Jenna and I were up to and—" Josh mimes slicing something from a chopping block.

"I'm sorry," I say automatically. My words cool to ice as they leave my mouth. I don't mean them.

"No, *I* should be sorry." Josh hesitantly places his hand on my arm in a gesture that triggers a muscle memory I wish I didn't have. Bodies, like minds, don't let go easily.

"Don't," I say, yanking my arm away, and my voice is harsher, more forceful than I mean it to be. Grimacing, I feel tears start to prick at the corners of my eyes, and I can't turn my head fast enough to hide them.

"I should have told you about Jenna, about everything. Brooke, I haven't been happy for . . ." He trails off, allowing the silence to fill with memories of us that I thought were good.

"I said *don't*." This time, it's a command. Josh's self-pity is one thing I have absolutely no patience for, and I can tell that what he's about to say is soaked with it. Thinking of the engagement ring I'd hidden away, another question spills out of me before I can stop it. "Why did you propose to me if you were so miserable?"

"I was wrong about what I want out of life, I guess," Josh says, and he doesn't look me in the eye. "I'd told myself for so long it was marriage and kids, but that was just something I wished was true." Disgust curdles somewhere deep in my core as he talks. Josh must see it on my face because he pauses, his words faltering, his face crumpling into a hopeless, weak expression I instantly loathe.

But as it settles onto his face, I feel like I'm seeing him, really seeing him, for the first time. Had I been pretending, just like he was? Had the reality I'd wished for so desperately imploded not because of Josh's lies but because it never really existed in the first place? A long moment crawls through the space between us, and I glare at the stranger sitting across from me, regretting I'd asked the question at all.

Josh opens his mouth to speak but is interrupted by the sound of a knock at the door. As he turns his back to me, for the first time my mind clears enough to think about how royally screwed I am. No home. Next to no money. Were my days numbered, just like Jenna's had been? The front door swings open, and the murmur of a female voice, soft and full of sympathy, purrs from the hallway.

"Oh, hi." Chloe, Josh's ex-colleague, enters the apartment and gawks at me like she might an escaped zoo animal that had wandered into her home. She's carrying a box filled with what looks like the contents of Josh's work desk. A framed photograph of Josh and me sticks out of the jumble. I wonder if she'd be able to stop me from reaching into the box and smashing it over her head.

"Chloe's just helping me move some things," Josh says hurriedly. He even sounds a little guilty. I take in her artfully messy bun, the skintight T-shirt that exposes a half inch of taut skin between the thin cotton and the thick leather belt that cinches her tiny waist. Of course she's "here to help." This must be the next girl, the sexy lawyer who replaced the illicit affair who replaced the sweet teacher who replaced some other girl Josh needed to feed his ego or to fix deep-seated issues that aren't my problem anymore. They're probably already fucking.

A second later, I realize that both Chloe and Josh are staring at me: Chloe with fear expanding her pretty features and Josh with intensifying concern on his face. I realize it's because I'm laughing. Uncontrollable laughter is bubbling from somewhere inside me that just snapped open and has started to swell, refusing to close. The sight of their expressions just makes everything more horribly, completely laughable. Clutching the kitchen counter, I struggle for breath.

"Just let me know when I can come get all of my worldly possessions, will you?" I manage between gasps for air. Josh nods, his mouth slightly open.

"Brooke, are you okay?" he asks. Chloe hovers at the threshold, still clutching the box. I notice a golden tendril has escaped the loose knot at the base of her neck, just as she intended it to, I'm sure.

"Nope. Not even a little bit," I say. My breath is finally starting to slow, the absurdity of the situation at hand beginning to clear and make way for the levee of sadness that's ready to burst. I get to my feet as quickly as I can, and without pausing so much as to get my toothbrush, I head toward the door.

"Good luck with this one, *Chlo*," I call over my shoulder before slamming the door so hard it rattles the frame. It's not until I'm in my car that I realize there's only one place I can go. But as I reach for my cell phone, the burner buzzes in my purse. The dread I expect intensifies as I read the text on the screen.

Poor little Brooke Winters—all alone. You
can't hide from me forever. xx

I feel nothing but a blank, soulless numb. Just like Sofia must
have felt in those last terrible minutes before she died. I need to
talk to Caroline. But first I need to find a place to crash, and the
only option left to me is almost as bad as the scene I just left.

CHAPTER 38

Caroline

Now

I was surprised to get Milo's text message asking me out again, considering that the last time we saw each other I blackmailed him. But after my altercation with Drea, it was a welcome distraction. I survey him over my sake, and anticipation tingles my skin as I watch him get up from our intimate table for two to take a quick call. Milo had chosen the perfect restaurant to celebrate the success of Equilibrium's new, winning strategy: delicious, highly Instagrammable Asian fusion.

With Eric's help, two major accounts are moving forward to contract: a cybersecurity firm whose CFO had a fondness for sending his assistant dick pics and a consulting agency that had covered up a mysterious incident on corporate retreat. Soon I wouldn't need Leo, or anyone else for that matter. Milo respected my unorthodox, ruthless methods, admired them even. Everything I envisioned that night in his apartment didn't feel so absurd after all. I reach for my glass and refill it from the ceramic carafe at the center of the table. The notes of lychee and apple had just settled on my tongue when Milo returns.

"Sorry about that," he says.

"No problem. Remember, you're preaching to the workaholic choir." I raise my glass to him in a toast.

"One of the many things I admire about the amazing Caroline Archer. Which brings me to the other reason I wanted to celebrate tonight."

"Oh?" I ask, savoring the silky heat of the sake slicking my throat. A brilliantly purple orchid drapes over the table, and if I weren't sitting so close to Milo, I'd have a hard time hearing him over the music and voices filling the restaurant.

"Yes." A smile I don't like takes root at the corner of his mouth. "You see, I've had a word with an old friend at Hawthorne and Byers." My eyes narrow. That's the name of one of the clients Eric and I were working on with the help of our new strategy. And as I examine Milo's expression more closely, something about it makes me suppress a shiver.

"He told me that there's been a data breach in their confidential records. Some sensitive information regarding a past, ah, misunderstanding between their CFO and his assistant had been accessed from outside the firm." Milo leans back in his chair nonchalantly, but his steely gaze hardens as he regards me, hungry for my reaction to these words.

"An old friend?" I ask, already suspecting the answer.

"Who would prefer to remain anonymous," Milo says. "Sofia" must be behind this, of course. She's not done raising hell just yet.

Arching his eyebrows a fraction, he continues. "Which I thought was quite the coincidence, but just to be sure, I made discreet inquiries to Equilibrium's other rather recent clientele. And do you know what I found?" In no rush to break the taut, tense silence this question creates, Milo selects a slice of sashimi with his chopsticks and pops it into his mouth.

I will my face to remain blank even as unease coils in my gut.

Milo takes his time chewing and swallowing the fish. This could be a bluff. But maybe I had underestimated him after all. With the killer instinct we have in common, should it come as such a shock if he turned it around on me? I want to kick myself for being so stupid.

Milo leans toward me. "They all reported similar hacks from outside their organizations. Confidential files, data, and financial records corrupted with the same digital footprint. Online bread crumbs, if you will." Milo laughs, and the pleasant masculine sound that had once charmed me is gone. "And the lovely thing about that is, it'll make it so simple for your American authorities to trace the source of these cyberattacks, which are of course felonies." He throws out this last phrase casually before sipping his drink.

"I have no idea what you're talking about," I say, doing my best to match his offhand tone.

"Oh, don't worry, darling. You won't be in the dark for long. We've turned over everything we have to the police, who will have *so* much to discuss with you." He makes the prospect of arrest and interrogation sound like a long-overdue social engagement with an old friend. Nausea floods my throat with saliva. Since when was I so easily fooled? My jaw clenches tight, and Milo gets to his feet.

"I can honestly say it's been a pleasure, Caroline." Milo's eyes travel appreciatively up and down my body, and I want to vomit into his expensive Italian loafers. "Dinner is on me, of course." He throws down a few fifties. No one could possibly have overheard our conversation. Onlookers would assume this is a second date gone wrong and turn their attention back to their sushi and $20 cocktails. "But then, I'm not sure what the etiquette is as far as last meals go," he adds with a smirk. Milo buttons his jacket and bends to press his lips against my cheek. It takes all my willpower not to flinch. The spot burns as I watch him walk out of the restaurant, powerless to do anything but seethe.

I grab for my phone at the bottom of my purse, my fingernails clawing desperately until it's in my hand. This can't be happening. The room is so loud I have to press my phone close enough to my ear to hurt. Eric usually picks up no later than the third ring, so as the dull tone buzzes four, five, and six times, I want to scream in frustration. I leave a voicemail of just a few words that trip over each other.

"It's me. We have a problem. Call me the second you get this."

CHAPTER 39

Brooke

Now

My mother asked mercifully few questions about exactly why I turned up at her house in the middle of the night with nowhere else to go. And as the days passed, she was gone both before I left for work and after I got back to her house. I'm sure the guilt trip is coming soon, fermenting with every twenty-four hours. If passive aggression were a form of combat, Daphne Winters would have a black belt.

As I get ready for this evening's field trip to the ballet, she finally appears at the bathroom door I'd forgotten to close.

"You look nice," she says as she takes in the waves I'd just curled into my hair and the black wrap dress I'd paired with strappy heels.

"Thanks," I say, bracing myself for the sting that usually accompanies her compliments. Our eyes meet in the mirror as I fasten an earring.

"Going somewhere?" she asks.

"Just chaperoning for school," I say, stepping back to assess the outfit as a whole. If Antony weren't going to be there, I probably would have stayed in the slacks and sweater I wore to school that day. The two vodka sodas I'd downed this afternoon as I stared at the ceiling, however, would no doubt still be sloshing in my stomach.

"A school event?" My mother's expression darkens as she crosses her arms.

"Yes," I say, and an automatic defensive note sharpens my tone.

Wordlessly, my mother reaches over my shoulder, opens the medicine cabinet, and extracts a travel-sized bottle of mouthwash.

"Careful, dear." She sets the bottle down on the marble countertop firmly enough to underscore her point. "We wouldn't want anything *else* going wrong, would we?"

As I whip around to retort, my left ankle wobbles, unsteady on its three-inch-high perch. I'm too late: she's already disappeared down the hallway. I cup my hand in front of my mouth and exhale into it. Sure enough, stale vodka wafts sourly back into my nose. I tuck the mouthwash into my purse and flick my eyes back to the mirror. The woman looking back at me looks poised, pretty even, and I brush on shimmery dark eye shadow. This is going to be *fine*.

That thought runs in a loop as I drive scrupulously, not a mile over the speed limit, back to Woodlands. A small crowd consisting of students I don't recognize is grouped around the bus waiting to take us into the city. I spot Antony in their midst. He's chatting with Wendy, the school receptionist, and another chaperone, someone from the math department, I think, and as he locks eyes with me, an admiring smile appears on his lips.

"I think that's everyone," Wendy says briskly, running her finger down the list in her hand.

I smile and help her take attendance as the kids load onto the bus. When I step on, I lean in slightly toward Antony. "Is this seat taken, Mr. Ramirez?" I ask, my voice low. The babble of teenagers masks my flirtatious tone.

Antony's eyes glint up at me, and he gestures to the empty space next to him. "Please be my guest, Miss Winters." He adopts the overly formal tone we've started using to tease each other when we're at work, and I'm grateful the driver dims the lights at that very moment to cover my blush.

"You look fantastic," he murmurs before starting a perfectly audible, appropriate conversation: film adaptations of novels that actually do the original justice. We start with Gregory Peck as Atticus Finch in *To Kill a Mockingbird* and move on to Julie Taymor's *Titus*. Anyone who turned their attention our way would get bored too quickly to notice that Antony's hand had slid under my skirt.

When we reach the theater, I absent-mindedly accept a program from the white-haired man at the door as Antony and I shepherd the students inside. The brightly lit lobby gives way to descending rows of old-fashioned red-velvet-upholstered chairs. I sit at the end of a row next to two sophomore girls who are giggling over their cell phones, two rows in front of Antony. Physical distance was probably a good idea. Reaching into my purse, I silence my cell phone but leave the burner on vibrate.

I look down at the program. The ballet is *A Midsummer Night's Dream,* and it looks like we're catching one of the last performances of the season. I skim over the usual notes about production design and the ensemble. As my eyes scan the bios of various cast members, they snag on a photograph toward the bottom of the page, where the full cast—principals, alternates, and understudies—is listed. Something about the statuesque dark-haired woman looks familiar, and as I find her name, I realize it's Leo's girlfriend, Natalia. I can't tell if she'll be on tonight or not, but my eyes don't stray from the page as the lights dim around me.

Natalia's face is so like Sofia's, not to mention the other headshots surrounding hers. Her black-and-white photograph is so similar to the other graceful ballerinas, I wonder if I'd be able to identify her onstage. But then another thought occurs to me, one that fills me with a biting frost of fear. And as the sound of the orchestra tuning their instruments fills the theater, I can't quite let it go, and I know I have to tell Caroline right away.

I wait until the curtain rises in the fully darkened theater, revealing a woodland set and dancers dressed as fairies springing onto the stage, to duck out into the lobby. It's not far, our seats are toward the back, and I crouch as low as my shoes will allow to slip out the door. Blinking in the bright light of the atrium, I stride in the direction of the restrooms and reach for the burner phone. Latching the stall door behind me, I'm about to start dialing when I hear a woman's voice echo in the tiled space. "Just terrible, isn't it? They work those poor girls to death, then send them straight back to Russia or Slovenia or wherever."

"I know," another voice says. "And it's perfectly normal to starve themselves or just ignore injuries until their bodies just can't take it anymore." The sound of running water punctuates this statement.

"Anyway. We're here for Audrey's fiftieth, remember? Let's just try to enjoy the show and get another strong G&T at intermission," the first voice says pointedly, and the second's reply is muffled by the sound of the door opening and their heels clicking across the floor. Adrenaline kicks in hard as the women leave, jerking me back to my purpose for being out here in the first place. I flip open the burner to fire off a message to Caroline, but several missed text messages from her already light up the screen.

> Equilibrium's been implicated in hacking our clients.

> Call me ASAP

Eric just told me he thinks he's being followed, and someone's trying to incriminate him in some serious shit, and now he isn't picking up his phone. He's not at his apartment.

Where are you?? I need to know you're okay.

I can't call her here, so I text back.

What?? How do you know? And yes, I'm okay. Just at a thing for school. Can't talk right now.

Her response is almost instant.

Got it. I'm waiting to hear from the PI who's been tailing Drea now.

My eyes stop dead in the middle of the text message. PI? Why didn't she tell me about this? Then another question follows the first like a shadow. What else isn't she telling me?

Then going to Leo's to check that he's safe.

I text back.

> Keep me posted.

I'm about to type out my theory and send it to Caroline when the phone vibrates again. This time, it's from a number I don't recognize.

> Enjoy tonight with lover boy. It might just be your last. xx

CHAPTER 40

Sofia

Then

The days following Bill Archer's death were glorious with autumn sunshine and at complete odds with the tension inside the house. Sofia, Leo, and Caroline were back there within a week, awaiting more Archer relatives to descend like hungry vultures for the funeral and, of much more interest, the reading of his will.

Caroline carried the weight of coordinating arrangements with a fervor fueled by his absence. At first it was unnerving to see all that energy set free in Caroline. But by the day of the funeral, Sofia gets a thrill out of the undercurrent in Caroline's gracious words, the look of satisfaction that's barely perceptible in the slight curve of her lips and the brightness of her eyes. But of course Sofia sees it all.

She resolved then and there, watching Caroline accept condolences and direct the caterers, finally in control of her destiny, to never breathe a word of what she saw. With Diana Archer's pearls strung around her throat, Caroline is every inch the woman Sofia loves. And with Bill out of the way, they are one step closer to being together. It was just a matter of waiting for that final secret to seal their fate forever.

Leo stumbles against an end table and sends two glasses crashing onto the floor. The muted conversation isn't enough to mask the sound of their shattering or his gurgle of wild laughter as the overstuffed arm of a sofa stops him from falling over. The memory of his father gripping that same spot as he died resurfaces sickeningly in Sofia's mind as Leo struggles to regain his balance. His tie hangs crookedly from its white collar, which is already splotched with several stains. Caroline extricates herself from a cluster of relatives to grab Leo by the elbow. Her mouth in a thin line, she half steers, half drags him toward the kitchen and out of sight. Sofia follows. Their backs are to her as she approaches the corner where Caroline and Leo whisper-hiss at each other.

"—don't understand why you care, Caroline," Leo slurs.

"Stop telling everyone about Sofia. You're embarrassing yourself," Caroline says in a strained undertone.

"Oh, relax. It's not like I *actually* care about her. Once I finish the next painting, she can go back to waitressing or whatever. Girls like her are a dime a dozen."

"I know—" Caroline starts, but Leo pushes past his sister and stops when he sees Sofia staring at them, her face blank, her heart frozen mid-beat. So that's it. She's nothing to them. Nothing to either of them. Nothing but a means to an end, a muse to a genius, a rebellion to a rebel. Something that, on its own, is completely worthless. Maybe that's less than nothing.

"Sofia," Leo says, stretching out every syllable of her name as his eyes almost manage to focus on her but end up sliding somewhere to the left. Sofia turns on her heel and stalks toward the staircase, pushing roughly through the crowd and past Sheri, or whatever the fuck her name is, who is putting on a show of tears for some thoroughly unconvinced Archer relatives.

Slamming the bedroom door, Sofia swings her battered suitcase onto the bed. She starts peeling off the black Ralph Lauren dress

Leo picked out for the funeral, and there's a tearing sound as she forces the zipper open and pulls the dress over her head. She crushes the fabric into a ball with shaking hands that are white with pressure, as if she could inflict pain on the inanimate dress. Her denim cutoffs and Drea's ancient Rolling Stones T-shirt are crumpled on the floor next to the antique armoire, and Sofia pulls them on with relief before resuming the work of getting the hell out of here.

"Sofia?" It's Caroline's voice on the other side of the door. Sofia doesn't look up, but she can feel her footsteps on the hardwood floor and the weight of her sink onto the bed. "I'm sorry you heard that." Sofia freezes, and for a moment, she can't shift her gaze from the cosmetics case clutched in her hand. It contains another kind of Leo's favorite paints, the ones reserved for Sofia's face and body.

"You knew Leo was using me?" Sofia's words escape on an exhale, barely louder than a whisper.

"Leo's just—" Caroline sighs, apparently at a loss for what Leo "just" is.

"What, Caroline? He's just a sociopath? He's just a monster? He's just as bad as everyone else in this fucked-up family?" Sofia doesn't care if her words carry down the stairs. Let them all hear.

Caroline closes her eyes. When she opens them, she wears an expression that asks *are you done?* She waits, but Sofia is too angry to speak. "He just has a hard time with relationships, especially with women, since our mom died." Caroline's voice is calm, like an adult determined not to lose their cool with a particularly emotional five-year-old. "And it's not like you weren't using *each other.*" Sofia's eyes cut to Caroline's, and she takes in the carved marble-like features: as cold as they are beautiful—beautiful enough to make Sofia's bones ache, cold enough to send a chill through her blood. The silence between them lengthens, then tightens with the pull of what Caroline did and didn't say.

"That's different," Sofia says, and her hands fall limply to her sides. She instantly regrets the knee-jerk need to defend herself.

"Is it?" Callous detachment forms an expression identical to the one Sofia has seen on Leo's face countless times. A flood of memories overwhelms her mind. Caroline's whisper that their world would always be our secret. The last glimpses of Leo's face before the darkness took her. Had Sofia become just like them? A taker. A user. But wasn't that better than being used?

Busying her hands with zippers and shutting the suitcase, Sofia pushes these thoughts out of her head. She knows exactly what she has to do. The Archers have used her for too long, but she still has one card to play. She swings the suitcase hard onto the floor, hoping it scuffs the wood and dents the bed frame. And with all the coolness she can muster, Sofia looks Caroline dead in the eyes.

"I saw you," Sofia says. At first Caroline's face registers no reaction. "The other night. I know what you did. Or at least I know what you *didn't stop*." A crack appears on that Archer porcelain facade, and Sofia struggles to stop a smile from reaching her lips. Caroline blinks rapidly and drops her gaze to the floor. Reaching for the bedpost, she grips it as if it could save her from drowning in invisible waves.

"So here's what's going to happen," Sofia says, stepping around the bed to where Caroline sits. "You're going to wrap up this little charade, and don't worry, I won't get in your way. Then, you're going to tell Leo about us. The truth. Everything is going back to the way it was. At the end of this semester, Brooke is *gone* from our lives. You're going to make her and Leo understand that this is how it is going to be from now on." Sofia extends her index finger and lifts Caroline's chin so she can gaze into her face. Caroline doesn't resist Sofia's touch.

"It's our secrets that bind us forever, you and me. Don't you see that?" Slowly, Caroline nods. Sofia closes the space between them until she can feel Caroline's breath on her face, smell the salinity of the sheen of sweat on her skin. "All we have is each other now." Sofia brushes her lips against Caroline's, picks up her suitcase, and leaves the house without looking back.

CHAPTER 41

Brooke

Now

I stare blankly at the whirl of dancers onstage as manic thoughts race each other through my mind. Would Drea be waiting for me at my mother's house? Or was it Bryce I have to worry about? At intermission, I avoid Antony's eye and go through the motions of ensuring all the students are accounted for. I text my mother to confirm she's home and safe—no answer. And when lights illuminate the vast room once more, I affix a smile on my face and remain mostly silent on the drive back to Woodlands as I frantically check my phone for a response.

I force myself to drive out of the grounds at a normal speed before tearing back to the house. I try calling my mother's cell phone, but there's no answer. Through my panic, another thought occurs to me. Caroline said someone had hacked their way into company files and implicated Equilibrium for it. Does Drea have the technical knowledge to do that? Or, I think as I drive as fast as I dare down the highway, is it more likely that someone else with a motive to see Jenna dead did this? Someone with the resources of the most sophisticated pharmaceutical company in the world at their disposal? Someone exactly like Bryce.

When I finally speed onto the winding gravel drive, nothing looks amiss in the illuminated windows of my mother's house. I rush through the front door, calling for my mother desperately as I sprint into the foyer and fly up the stairs.

"Brooke?" I can just hear her distant voice over the rapid-fire hammering of my heart. Clutching the polished banister, I try to catch my breath as my mother appears on the upstairs landing, clad in a silk robe, her face shiny under a thick layer of face cream.

"It's late," she says in a cold, resigned tone, as if preempting a conversation about what happened in the bathroom earlier. But as her eyes survey my face, something softens in the set of her jaw and the angle of her eyebrows. "Is everything all right?"

"Yes," I gasp. "Sorry. You weren't answering my texts or calls." We stare at each other, the years of unspoken distance and conflict between us sliding back into place.

"I have an important function at the club tomorrow, so my phone has been on 'do not disturb.' Good night," she says, turning away and sweeping back down the hall. Something entirely unexpected rushes through me as I watch her go, and it's not until I've collapsed on my bed that I realize what it is. Genuine relief that she is safe, not just for my conscience, but for her own sake. I don't sleep that night. Caroline has gone radio silent, no response to the text messages I sent her. I check my phone hopelessly after making sure the security system is armed, and I stare for hours at the intricate molding that crowns the ceiling of my childhood bedroom.

It's lucky that I'd scheduled an in-class essay for my students the next day. The three-thirty bell rings, and students filter out of the building with the usual slamming of lockers and thunderous footsteps on the old wood floors. I lose myself in the mountain of essays piled on my desk until a harried-looking Wendy knocks at the classroom door.

"Brooke?" she inquires, and there's a trepidation in her voice I'd never heard there before. Her kind eyes are anxious, and as she steps into my classroom, she fiddles nervously with the chain of the reading glasses draped around her neck.

"Hey, Wendy," I say, looking up from the papers in front of me. Wendy shifts her weight from one foot to the other, hesitating for a few beats.

"Dr. Lutz would like to see you in his office," she finally says.

"Now?" I ask.

"I'm so sorry," she blurts after another moment's pause. She inclines her head conspiratorially and steps away from the open door. "I overheard him talking to Akira, and I just want you to know I don't think it's right." Straightening my shoulders, I feel every step I take down the hall and up the stairs as if it were my path to vacant gallows. It's quiet in the wood-paneled administrative sanctuary tucked away from the hustle and bustle of the school.

Dr. Lutz is seated behind an enormous antique desk, probably donated by a parent looking to ensure their student never found themselves in this room, his hands steepled and his face grim. Degrees in heavy frames glare down at me from the wall behind him, as if daring me to question whatever decision was about to be handed down.

"Please have a seat, Miss Winters. And shut the door."

CHAPTER 42

Caroline

Now

I lose track of the number of times I call and text Eric and Leo in the frantic hours between Milo's departure and the creep of weak sunlight up the walls of my apartment. There was no answer at Eric's place last night. No sign of life from Leo. The text messages I fire off pile into a blue wall on my screen without a single flicker of response. I spend a restless morning at Thrive, willing Eric to appear, before rushing in vain back to his apartment—still no answer, and nothing at Leo's gallery, either. Sick with the knowledge that "Sofia" may have gotten to either of them, I decide I have to get home and call the PI for answers. I'm about to dial his number when Leo's name finally lights up my phone screen.

"Thank god," I say, chaining the last latch behind me after stepping inside my apartment.

"Well, hello to you, too," Leo says.

"Something's wrong." I check every inch of the studio to make sure I'm alone. "Something *bad* is happening," I say as I circle the tiny space.

"What happened?" I can hear Leo's focus snap to attention on the other end of the phone.

"Somehow, I don't know how, Drea figured out how to plant evidence against *Equilibrium* for hacking into our clients' systems and stealing their data. She probably just cozied up to one of Todd's tech-bro friends. Or seduced them. Or something."

"Fuck," Leo says heavily.

"And Eric isn't picking up his phone. Leo, I think she might have gotten to him." My throat tightens painfully at the thought, and I can't get the next words out.

"I'm coming down there. I'm actually in the city right now—" Leo says. A gust of wind and an ambulance siren drown out the end of his sentence. "You shouldn't be alone. Let's get you out of the city, and you can lay low at the Oasis for a few days while all this calms down. I just had a new security system installed. You'll be safer there," he says, and I can hear the sound of a car door slamming. "I'll be there in about half an hour. Lock the door. Don't open it for anyone but me, okay?"

"Okay," I say, wishing I felt more relief. "That's the other thing—I had Drea followed. I'm supposed to meet with the PI tomorrow to find out what she's been up to."

"Tell him to meet you at the Oasis. Or better yet, see if you can get him on the phone now and ask him to email you what he's got. Why wait, right?" There's a pause, a jangle of keys, a sharp exhale. "Promise me you'll stay where you are?"

"I will, and I'll call the PI," I say, struggling to get my breathing under control.

"Good. I'm on my way." Leo hangs up.

Sinking onto the couch, I scroll through my contacts to the private investigator's number. He picks up on the second ring.

"Yeah?" comes the gruff voice on the other end of the phone.

"It's Caroline Archer. I know we had a meeting scheduled for tomorrow, but something's come up, and I was wondering if we could talk now?" I say in a rush. There's a pause, the sound of a file drawer opening.

"Not a problem. I'm actually glad you called," he says. "You were right. I'd definitely want to stay away from Andrea Eliades if I were you. Just give me one second here." My hands are shaking as I wait for him to get his notes.

"The first thing you should know is that it's extremely likely your uncle changed his will to benefit Miss Eliades. He had two meetings with an estate attorney, and Miss Eliades was present for both of them." I dig my nails into my knee and bite down on the inside of my cheek. "I'll also send you the link to a website they seem to have set up." Fingers clatter on a keyboard. "Looks like Thomas Archer intends to bequeath the majority of his estate to a charitable foundation cofounded by Andrea Eliades. So—" He exhales, and I imagine him leaning back in a creaky swivel chair in a dimly lit office. "Unfortunately, there's nothing illegal about any of that. However—" I grip the phone tighter.

"The other thing you should know is that Miss Eliades has been following your assistant, Eric Chapman, for several weeks," he says. "She's been careful. I'll give her that. But she gained access to his apartment today, apparently with a key and no forced entry, but I doubt it was with his consent. I'll send you the photos, and I leave it up to you on whether to turn those over to the authorities."

"Can you send those to me now? I want to get in touch with the police immediately." I'm suddenly dizzy. "I think Eric might be in danger."

"I'll take care of it now. You sit tight." Before I can say anything more, he hangs up.

Gotcha, I think, adrenaline pulsing through me in spikes. But it doesn't last. If Drea broke into Eric's apartment today, there's a high probability he's met the same fate as Jenna. This horrible thought dissolves into corrosive guilt that I tamp down hard in my mind to focus on the tasks at hand. I shove my laptop and some clothes into a bag, mostly to have something to do with my hands. The sound of a fist hammering on my front door makes me jump. I rush to the door and peer through the peephole. My heart stops. I fumble to unlatch the chain as fast as my fingers will go.

"Eric," I say with relief, and I can't stop myself from throwing my arms around him. "I'm so glad you're okay. I was so worried. Someone's been following you, she—" But then, something stops my words and turns the blood in my veins to ice. Something cold, cylindrical, and hard in Eric's hand is pressing into my rib cage. A gun. Eric has a gun.

"Let's go inside, Caroline. We have so much to discuss," Eric says in a low, deadly voice.

CHAPTER 43

Brooke

Now

I perch on the edge of the hard-backed chair opposite Dr. Lutz's desk, and it takes me a second to notice that Akira is also in the room. I steal a glance at her. Akira's expression is grim, her arms crossed tight across her body. I think of how she'd rooted for me, supported me, stuck up for me, and humiliation sends an ugly flush to my cheeks that I wish I could extinguish.

"I think you know why we're here," Dr. Lutz says, and he retrieves a manila folder from the top drawer of his desk. He slaps it heavily, pointedly in front of me, and looks at me over the rims of his glasses.

"I don't—" I stammer, deciding on the spot that playing dumb might be the only way to save any sliver of dignity I have left.

"Woodlands prides itself on being one of the most prestigious independent schools in the country. To maintain the standing we have held for over a century, our faculty must reflect and uphold a sterling reputation." Dr. Lutz flicks open the folder. "The contents of this file are disturbing, to say the least." He pushes it across the desk to me, and as I look down, I find what I've dreaded since my first day here. The worst demons of my past stare back at me in black and white: the evidence of my trespassing at Patrick's house, copies of those last, unanswered text messages and emails I sent to Patrick, photos of me following him home. I will my eyes not to fill with tears, and for once, they obey.

"I don't need to remind you of Rebecca Adams's prominent role in our community, nor the decades of support her family has given to this school. We obviously can't be associated with anyone who's responsible for tearing apart an upstanding family and ruining a man's reputation." Dr. Lutz isn't looking at me but at the space between his folded fingers. "No doubt, she decided to rise above this terrible situation, and someone close to her had no choice but to speak up on her behalf."

"She didn't give you these?" I ask before I can stop myself. Dr. Lutz raises his eyebrows.

"I think it's telling, Miss Winters, that this is your primary concern," he says, surveying me with mounting disapproval.

"None of this should be any of her concern," Akira interjects. "It's an egregious invasion of Brooke's privacy, and absolutely none of this has any bearing on her performance as a teacher here." I don't dare look at her, but the fierceness in her voice is enough to break my heart.

"I respectfully disagree, Dr. Go. You are only privy to this meeting because of departmental protocol—"

"For once, I'm glad to follow this school's draconian policies," Akira cuts across Dr. Lutz. "These *alleged* events took place over ten years ago. They're none of our business." She gestures at the shameful documentation splayed across the desk. I meet Akira's eyes and shoot her a grateful look.

"I think you'll find in Miss Winters's contract that it *is* our business." Dr. Lutz shuffles a stack of papers on his desk officiously. "The document she signed clearly states that any conduct at *any time* that reflects poorly on Woodlands can constitute grounds for dismissal." He's shifted to speaking about me as if I weren't here. Right now, that suits me just fine.

"Oh, I didn't realize that by 'at any time' we mean *a decade ago*." Akira throws up her hands and glares daggers at Dr. Lutz. "And by 'conduct' we mean accusations from an anonymous source. Has Rebecca even been contacted about any of this?"

Dr. Lutz looks affronted. "I'd never dream about dredging up something like this with Mrs. Adams. She's clearly the victim here, but that's not the point." He places both hands on his leather ink blotter, preparing himself for what's coming next. "The point is, Miss Winters, that your employment at Woodlands Academy is terminated immediately." He presses a button on the phone next to him. "Send in Eddie." The school resource officer enters the room, and his six-foot-four presence looms over me in a way that makes me shrink into the chair.

"Eddie, please escort Miss Winters to collect her things and ensure she leaves the school grounds without making a scene." Dr. Lutz keeps up his classist habit of referring to staff without a college degree by just their first names.

"This is wrong, and you know it." Akira says.

"It's all right, Akira." I hear my own voice as if from a far distance. Keeping my eyes on the carpet a few feet in front of me, I follow Eddie's uniformed figure out of the office. We don't pass anyone in the hallway, a tiny mercy. Eddie swings his arms uncomfortably as he waits at the back of what was my classroom.

I carelessly pack the contents of my desk into a cardboard box. My students' faces blur in my mind's eye, and I wonder how fast the rumor mill will regurgitate out a luridly embellished version of the truth. When the drawers are empty, Eddie follows me to the parking lot. He gives me a pitying nod as I get into my car, and just like that, I have nothing left. Except Antony.

I don't really know how I wind up at Antony's house. One moment, I'm dispassionately thinking about how picturesque the pristine green lawns of Woodlands are in the golden glow of the late afternoon sun. The next, I'm hammering on his door. But when it opens, it's not Antony who answers. Instead, a squat Latino man looks at me with a mix of curiosity and impatience.

"Can I help you?" His voice is accented and soft. I blink at him stupidly.

"Uh—is Antony home?" I ask, embarrassed by the wobbling tremor in my voice.

"Antony doesn't live here anymore." The soft voice vanishes with alarming speed. His eyes cool with dislike, his hands go to his hips, and his next words come out in a spit. "That worthless piece of shit can take it up with my sister's lawyers if he wants access to the Airbnb before it sells."

"Airbnb?" I say, and then realization settles in my mind. I'd seen what I'd *wanted* to see at this place, ignoring the lack of decorations, house materials that could accommodate no more than two or three people, the spartan aesthetic I'd wanted so badly to be his but really belonged to no one at all.

"Yeah. I'm helping Mia get it ready for showings tomorrow. I thought he knew he isn't supposed to be here. But then, it's hard to keep track of that guy." This is Mia's brother. He comes back to himself with a shake of his bald head, perhaps realizing he's rambling to a complete stranger. "Anyway, he's not here." He closes the door.

I slink back to my car, and all I can do is stare at nothing for several long moments, dreading my next destination and struggling to process what just happened. My cell phone rings from where it wound up somewhere inside the box in the passenger seat. Digging through papers and folders and other remnants of a life that was mine until an hour ago, I feel my heart lift when I see Antony's name lighting up the screen. No doubt his former brother-in-law called him about the random woman who showed up on his doorstep.

"Brooke, oh thank god. Akira just told me what happened. Are you okay?" Just hearing his voice loosens something in me that had been wound tight since I stepped into Dr. Lutz's office.

"Not really," I say, closing my eyes and pressing my palm to my forehead. "Look, you're going to be hearing some stuff about me—I can explain." My voice is gathering out-of-control momentum. "It was all so long ago and I swear I—"

"Hey." Antony's voice is gentle but firm. "You don't have to explain *anything*. Lutz is an asshole. This isn't your fault."

"Where are you right now?" I open my eyes as if I'd see him standing in front of me. "Can we talk? I'll come to you."

"I wish I could, Brooke." His voice is hesitant now, and something else has mixed into his tone. "Marco just told me you stopped by the townhouse, and I'm sorry I wasn't straightforward about that."

I don't care about the house. I don't care about anything except clinging to the last shred of my reality that wasn't already in tatters. But something in my mind stalls. "Straightforward about what?" I say.

"Look, things with Mia and me . . ." He trails off, and there's silence on the line that I'm willing to fill with just about anything. "They're complicated right now, okay?"

"Okay," I say. I'm not in a position to judge *complicated* right now.

"I want to be with you—I just can't promise you anything," Antony says, and something finally clicks into place.

"You mean—" I bite back the bile that surges as I realize exactly what's happening here. "You're not divorced?"

"I said things are complicated." Antony says this with simplicity in his voice. The irony sinks in slowly at first, then all at once.

"Complicated how, Antony? Complicated as in you're single and separated, or complicated as in your daughter thinks her parents might get back together?" Heat is rising in my body and my voice.

"Don't bring her into this." Antony matches my tone.

"Answer the question, and there's no need to," I say firmly.

"What we have is amazing," Antony says, echoing the words I'd heard so many times before from a different man, a different game of make-believe I let myself play. And for a brief moment, I'm sucked right back in. What we had *was* amazing. It was also a lie. "Can't you just accept me for where I am right now? It's comp—"

"Go figure yourself out, Antony," I say. I hang up, and before I toss my phone back into the box, I block his number.

CHAPTER 44

Caroline

Now

I stagger backward into my apartment, unable to take my eyes off Eric's livid face. The merciless quality in his eyes and the tight aggression in the set of his shoulders fill me with even more fear than the gun he's holding. My thoughts are mired in a molasses of shock and confusion, and as the light catches the barrel of the gun, my body goes stiff. He shuts the door quietly and bolts it.

"Take a seat," he says with chilling normalcy, as if we're here for a drink after a long day at the office. I sit. "Did your date with Milo end badly?" His voice is thick with false sympathy, and he contorts his features into a mock frown. I open my mouth, but nothing comes out. "It's okay. I understand if you're not ready to talk about it. I'd hate to miss out on that British snack, too, whatever his faults." Eric sits across from me, draping one leg leisurely over the other. We're both aware of my cell phone on the table between us, but I don't dare reach for it. I need time to figure out what's happening to me. Time I don't have, but I might as well try to buy some.

"You don't have to do this, Eric," I say, and I watch as his face breaks into an ironic smile.

"Oh, you think so?"

Frantically, I replay every memory I have of him in my mind, as if they could form a map that led to this moment and my being held at gunpoint. What had I missed? I race through everything Eric had ever told me about himself, desperate for something, anything, that could explain what's happening right now. "Anything you want. Money. The company. It's yours. Just don't do this." He lets out a laugh entirely different from the one I'd heard for years. It's cruel, his bleached teeth bared.

"I don't want your Archer blood money," he snarls. "But I can understand why you'd think that. You're used to buying people off, aren't you, Caroline? That is . . ."—Eric leans forward in the chair and gestures with the revolver—"you did that with your dear friend Jenna, didn't you?"

My mind lands on our first meeting—what had I not seen, not understood? We bonded over our mothers; I'd let down my guard the second we talked about how they died. What if Eric knew that would happen? What if he knew exactly the right lie to tell in order to get close to me?

"You—" I start, but there's a knock at the door, and I hear Leo's voice calling my name from the hall.

"Go on, answer the door," Eric says brightly in the tone of a host confirming their final guest had arrived at a dinner party, and he tucks the gun back into the folds of his jacket.

I rise shakily, failing to suppress a flinch as I brush against Eric's shoulder on my way to the door. When I open it, Leo's face relaxes for a millisecond, then tautens with alarm as he looks at me.

"What's wrong?" he asks as he steps into the apartment.

"Join us, Leo," Eric says from behind me. "And don't forget to lock the door, Caroline."

Leo's brow relaxes as he approaches Eric. "Hey, man. Glad to see you're okay." I know the moment Leo sees the gun by how my brother's face blanches.

"I was just having a little chat with your sister, and I was *so* hoping you might stop by. Have a seat," Eric sneers. Leo looks exactly how I feel. Dumbstruck. Terrified. Without a word, he sinks onto the couch next to me.

I search Eric's face, which is still contorted into that terrible mask of contempt, for answers. Why would he do this? What signs did I miss? My memory spits out jumbled scraps of conversation and images of our years of working together. Our first conversation. We talked about our mothers: the loss we had in common. What if his mom didn't die of cancer, like he said?

It's not possible.

But suddenly I realize there is one obvious reason why Eric is doing all of this.

"You're the boy from the accident. Aren't you?" I say, clinging to the tether of my thoughts as reality spins further and further out of my control. Eric is the right age, but he's totally unrecognizable now. A blurred image of the chubby boy struggling out of the car, adjusting his broken glasses, melts into the grown man glaring at me with white-hot hatred in his eyes.

"The other car. Sofia killed your mother." To live with myself, I have never read the news coverage of the accident, letting time instead fill the void and obscure a vague memory of that shadowy figure emerging from the smoke that engulfed the other car, choked by the rain. A little boy, screaming in the dark.

"So you finally figured it out." Eric cocks an eyebrow. "But let me correct you on one thing: *Sofia* did not kill my mother. Or my little sister." Suddenly, what little air was left in the room seems to disappear. "Oh, you didn't know my mom was pregnant when you and Brooke killed her?" Eric leans forward, waiting for an answer. I feel Leo's body slacken next to mine, and it takes everything I have to shake my head.

"Their death might as well have been mine, too, if the next twelve years with my Bible-thumping father were any indication," Eric says. His voice has taken on a dead quality that's somehow even more terrifying than anger, and his eyes are like the windows of an abandoned building. "Turns out you can't pray the gay away, but that didn't stop him from trying," Eric continues. "So many of those 'treatment' centers have been on the news. I think there's even a Nicole Kidman movie about one of them. I won't bore you with the details." He must have been planning this for years. Inventing a persona designed for revenge. He lets out a sigh I've heard dozens of times, and I'm transfixed as my friend transforms again into the man holding the gun.

"Why now?" The question is out of my mouth before I can stop it, and I feel my muscles tense as I wonder if I've put us in even more danger just by asking. Eric rolls his eyes.

"Oh, come on, Caroline. You're smarter than that. You tell me *why now*." He mimics the fear in my voice.

"You—" I start, aware of Leo's unsteady breathing next to me. Eric nods his head a fraction. He actually wants me to continue. "You were just a kid when it happened, and you didn't think anyone would believe you. You need one of us to confess; otherwise there's no evidence to corroborate what you saw."

Eric sits up straighter. "Confess what, Caroline? What did I see?"

I swallow hard, shocked that I'm about to admit what I've hidden for a decade. "That Sofia wasn't actually driving that night."

My stomach heaves sickeningly as I look into Eric's face, a stranger wearing the mask of a friend. "You . . . You needed to get close to one of us to get access, to make it easy for you to threaten us. You picked me."

"Very good," Eric says with a flash of white teeth, his lip curling cruelly. "But you missed just one thing. A confession *would* be nice, but I think we can do better than that. I want whatever Jenna had on you." He points the gun at me. My eyes lock on the black hole at the center of the barrel. "I know Jenna was blackmailing you for at least, what, two years?" He looks at me expectantly. I nod to keep him talking. "Must have been something juicy for you to fork over so much of our profits." He pauses for effect, gesturing with the gun as if it were a cocktail. "You seriously thought I wouldn't notice?" I blink at him, thinking fast.

"You don't have to do this, Eric. If what Milo says is true, I'll be arrested for hacking into our clients' systems. Fraud. Cybercrimes." I'm begging, scrambling for one more scheme to keep the last se-cret safe. "I'll be ruined. I'll go to jail for a very, very long time."

Eric leans back and casts his gaze at the ceiling in a gesture I'd seen so many times it sends frost to my core. He looks as if I'd just raised an interesting idea about Equilibrium's branding that he needs a moment to consider.

"See, I thought about that," Eric says. "But you've wormed your way out of tight corners before, haven't you? I'm looking for some-thing that will really throw away the key, as they say. I think Jenna had exactly what I need. I know you went to Jenna's house to get it back, and I know you got it because you stopped fucking that loser husband of hers. So I'll ask again, where is the evidence, Caroline?"

"It's not here," I say slowly, a fragile plan starting to fuse to-gether in my mind. Leo doesn't know I came out of Jenna's house empty-handed. I have to keep it that way. "It's at the Oasis. I locked it in a safe there after Josh was arrested." Leo is frozen next to me.

"Smart girl," Eric says. "I just need to make sure our other guest of honor makes it. Let's text your bestie." I reach for the phone on the table, trying to disguise a flicker of hope. Brooke might know something was off if I texted her from my cell phone, not the burner.

"Not that one, come on." Eric sounds bored with the proceed-ings. "Get the burner for me." Of course. It would have been easy for Eric to follow my every move, to make a copy of my keys and my key to Brooke's place, to send encrypted messages, all of it. I hand him the burner.

"SOS. New info," Eric whines in a false, high-pitched voice. "Can you come to the Oasis ASAP? Need to see you." He shuts the phone with a satisfied snap. "Let's take a little field trip, shall we?"

CHAPTER 45

Caroline

Then

By the time I realized Sofia had also registered for Art History 100, it was too late to change my schedule. I needed the humanities credit, and sitting in the dark for a few hours a week seemed as painless as it gets at Yale. I was wrong. She knows me better than I know myself, better than Leo knows me, better than my own conscience will admit sometimes. That's how it works with Sofia. Somehow she's always a step ahead, and when you catch on to what she's doing, it's usually too late.

I feel her gaze immediately from across the sunken lecture hall, chilling and heavy as a thick mist rolling over the back of my neck. It's a dare to ignore her, which I try to do as I descend the stairs. There's noise, there must be, of laptops coming out of backpacks, the rustle of students taking their seats, but I can't hear anything but the hard, defiant pulse that's rising from my chest through my throat to my eardrums.

Pulse. *I'm still here. Bill is rotting in the Archer family plot.*

Pulse. *I'm still alive.*

Pulse. *The monster under my bed is dead.*

Pulse. *I* beat *you, motherfucker.*

At Bill's funeral, I savored every inch he sank out of sight, lowered by the dignified, mostly soundless machine at the side of his grave, until he disappeared into the ground beneath my feet. Catholic tradition even let me fill a fist with dirt and tip it over what I hoped was his face under the polished coffin. I was so sure I was free. That his death didn't just mark the end of his miserable life, but the start of mine. The *real* start. But Sofia made one thing clear that day: she's going to take that away from me. At least she's going to try. And I can't let her, not when I've come this far.

It's easier than I thought it would be to meet Sofia's eye, to steel myself. It's harder to ignore the crawling sensation like spider eggs hatching under my skin as I take the seat next to her. See, here's the thing about paying for your freedom with a life. Once you get past the sticker shock of it all, you get used to it. Really, it's amazing what people can get used to, the cuts that callus, the scars that fade. And as this thought settles somewhere between what I know I have to do now and what I know is coming next, the two things I've learned from the now-dead Bill Archer crystallize in my mind.

One: Nothing in this world is free.

Two: Sometimes, the best place to be is nowhere at all.

Something will have to be done about Sofia, and I know Leo will help me.

Our professor appears at the front of the room in a flurry of frizzy silver hair and chunky jewelry. She nods at the TA to dim the lights, and they take their time lowering as I look into Sofia's face. She blinks at me from under those hypnotizing lashes, and I know it's not just her eyes adjusting. A thick sheen coats Sofia's huge hazel eyes, and there's a hope there that used to tear me apart. Even now, it gives a good hard, tug on what I know I have to do to survive. It's the same hope that's lit up her face since we were kids, burning brighter and brighter until it turned the beautiful features I loved into ones that terrify me.

Sofia went through an Emily Dickinson phase in high school that mostly went over my head, but I went with it because I liked that line about hope being the thing with feathers. It perfectly fit the scrappy, gorgeous girl I used to know. But looking at her now, I think hope is the thing that eats you alive until reality is gnawed to the bone and you have nothing left to lose.

I suck in a lungful of air and tilt my head toward hers in the dark.

"Wanna go to a party tonight?" I whisper, and I let my fingers close gently around her wrist.

CHAPTER 46

Brooke

Now

I'm about to put the keys in the ignition when I hear the telltale vibration of the burner. It's Caroline.

> SOS. New info. Can you come to the Oasis ASAP? Need to see you.

Maybe we're about to finally get to the bottom of this thing. I'm done hiding. I respond.

> I'm on my way.

There's just one thing I need to do first.

For the first time in months, my mind is clear. The tires of my car send gravel flying as I speed into my mother's driveway, stopping just inches behind her Mercedes. "Fuck," I mutter to myself.

Delays from her are the last thing I need right now. I race into the house, and I ignore the sound of her voice as I take the stairs two at a time. As soon as I get to my bedroom, I open my laptop and google "Healing House," the couple's retreat Leo said he had attended with Natalia when Jenna went missing.

The first search result leads to a website featuring a modern farmhouse-style building tucked into the mountains, not far from the Oasis, its home page promising love, rejuvenation, and reconnection. Scrolling down to the bottom of the page, my eye catches on a photo of two well-groomed men, arm in arm and smiling knowingly at the camera. Identical wedding rings gleam from their fingers. I find a contact number and start to dial.

"Brooke, are you going to tell me why Linda Peterson called to say you were *escorted from school premises today*?" I look up reluctantly. My mother stands in the doorframe, her face livid.

"I can't right now, Mom. I'm in the middle of something important." I flick my eyes back to the computer screen so I can finish reading the Healing House phone number. I have to chase this lead before I move on to Bryce. A crimson-clawed hand slams my laptop shut with the jangle of Cartier bracelets.

"Talk to me right now, Brooke Eleanor Winters." I look up, and my mother is staring at me, her hands on her hips.

"Fine," I say. Clearly there's no getting out of here without telling her something, which might as well be the truth. "Woodlands found out about what happened with Patrick. His son is—*was*—in my class, and his wife turned over everything she has on me. I'm a disgrace, okay? Is that what you want to hear?" I brace for the explosion. It doesn't come.

Instead, my mother sighs, drums her fingers on my computer twice, and suddenly turns on her heel. "Wait here," she barks before marching from the room. I'm so shocked by this reaction that I obey without a second thought. A minute later, she reappears clutching a thick folder tight against her chest. Setting it down on the desk in front of me, she takes a deep breath before speaking.

"I know I haven't always been the perfect mother to you, Brooke," she starts, her eyes fixed on the desk.

"Mom, I—" I don't have time for a heart-to-heart right now.

"Please, just listen to me." She holds up a hand in a familiar, admonishing gesture, but her tone is gentle, bordering on pleading. "I don't know exactly what went on when you were in—that place. In therapy." She takes a deep breath. "But I kept copies of all the documentation we submitted all those years ago. There was no way—" Her voice breaks, and her gaze lifts to meet mine. "There was no way I was going to let my little girl walk away from that man without a backup plan. To men like *him*." Disgust is soaked into her words, especially the last one. "To men like Patrick Adams, beautiful girls are interchangeable. Replaceable. Usable." I can't tell if she's thinking of me or of my father's long absences that went unquestioned even after he stayed gone. "We can't afford *not* to have a backup plan."

She covers her mouth with one hand to suppress a completely uncharacteristic surge of emotion. I reach for the folder and lift the front cover. It's all here. The compromising pictures of me Patrick had taken, copies of explicit emails he sent, screenshots of text conversations, everything he ever sent me during our affair: undeniable proof that he'd pursued the relationship as much as I had.

"Why didn't you tell me? After all these years?"

"Your therapist said you needed to heal." My mother wrings her hands and blinks rapidly. "I believed them. Sweetheart, I was wrong. I'm so sorry. For everything." The last two words escape between gasps for air. A tear carves a shining track down her powdered cheek. She swipes it away before it reaches the hollow beneath her cheekbone. "You tell those . . ."—she pauses, as if worried we could be overheard—"*assholes* at Woodlands the truth, and you fight back."

Before I can stop myself, I realize I'm standing and that I've thrown my arms around my mother. She's fragile, little more than bones, linen, and cashmere, and unfamiliar in my arms—our physical contact has been limited to air-kisses for as long as I can remember. I feel the weight of the past decade breaking against everything that had happened that day, and for a moment, it feels good just to be still. She breaks away first, gently pressing her index fingers underneath leaking eyes so as not to disturb her makeup. Straightening the periwinkle sweater draped around her shoulders, she regains her perfect composure in a matter of seconds.

"Anyway," she says briskly, "Rebecca Adams isn't the only one with clout in our circle, and goodness knows that Woodlands has its secrets." A small smile appears on her face. "I think they'll soon wish they had left ours undisturbed." The smile widens, this time paired with a steely glint in her eye. "Now if you'll excuse me, I'm going to call in some favors. I'll let you decide what to do with this." She taps the folder with one finger and then turns, her signature poise firmly back in place, and walks out the door.

"Thank you," I say breathlessly, hoping I can convey just how much this means to me in two syllables. My fingers linger on the smooth surface of the folder before they clench into a fist. I snap my plan back into action. First, I try Caroline's burner. It goes straight to voicemail. I dial the number on my laptop screen next. The phone rings twice at Healing House before a placid male voice answers.

"Healing House, how may I assist you on your journey?"

"Hi, I was wondering if I could talk to Avi Rosenstein?" I say, hoping I don't sound as desperate as I feel.

"Speaking," he says.

"I'm a friend of Leo Archer's. I'm not sure if he's mentioned this, but a friend of ours recently died, and I'm compiling a memory book for her memorial service," I lie. "It's helpful to know where her nearest and dearest were when they heard about her passing, just to show how far-flung her circle was. How many lives she impacted. Were Leo and his girlfriend Natalia at Healing House on the twelfth of last month?" It's a flimsy lie, but maybe one sappy enough for a relationship counselor to believe.

"What a beautiful idea," Avi says. "And may I say—I'm sorry for your loss."

"Thank you," I say automatically, and I hold my breath for him to continue.

"Let's see, yes, Leo is actually a friend of mine as well. According to our records—" There's a pause, and I picture Avi clicking through screens or flipping through a calendar. "He was here on the twelfth and thirteenth, and again on the nineteenth. Natalia got here for a workshop on the thirteenth, too." What was the point of a "couple's retreat" if they actually weren't there together on exactly the same dates?

"Are you sure? She definitely wasn't with Leo that first night? Can you say for sure that he never left Healing House?"

"Not for certain, no. We have an open-door policy here." Avi's serene tone is now muddled with confusion. "But surely that doesn't make a difference for what you're working on?"

"No," I say hurriedly. "Not at all. Thank you so much." I hang up and rush back to my car. If I'm right, and I have a sickening suspicion that I am, then Caroline is in terrible danger.

Of course the police didn't check Natalia's alibi. Why would they? As far as they were concerned, she didn't have anything to gain from Jenna's death. Next to nothing to do with Jenna at all. That's where they're wrong. As I gun the engine, my mother's words echo in my head. *Beautiful girls are interchangeable. Usable. Replaceable.* Thinking of the anonymous payments I'd seen on the Hostetler-Lees' bank statements and half-starved ballerinas with nowhere else to turn, I peel onto the highway.

CHAPTER 47

Caroline

Now

It's nearly dark by the time we reach the Oasis. Shadows slip long slender fingers across the lawn and shade the thick pines surrounding the gallery.

"Out," Eric orders from the back seat. "You run, I shoot. You scream for help, I shoot. You get the gist." Leo and I reluctantly slide out of the car and begin the winding walk toward the front door of the barn. Eric keeps pace behind us, and when we're at the front doors, Leo reaches for the keypad. "You enter any kind of code that sends for the police—I shoot," Eric adds, again in that detached tone of complete calm.

Leo and I haven't been able to look at each other, let alone say a single word, since we left the city. And as he types in the keycode and we step into the bright gallery, I start to worry that my plan for stalling won't do anything but give Eric a better place to dispose of our bodies. Sweat has cooled and crusted under my arms and in the small of my back, and I wonder if Eric can pick up on the animal scent of my fear.

"Where is it?" Eric says, the gun trained on me. I open my mouth to speak, unsure of what I can possibly say to buy more time.

"It's in the office. If I get it for you, will you leave us alone?" Leo cuts in, his voice clear. I nod, but perhaps a beat too late. Eric raises his eyebrows at us.

"We'll see now, won't we? I'll also need your security footage, of course. Lead the way." Eric jerks his head, urging us forward. I have no idea what Leo is going to do or how he could possibly get us out of this, but I cling to the hope that he has a plan, since I sure as hell am out of ideas now that we're here. Leo extracts keys from his pocket and unlocks the door to a dark, cramped office. Stacks of half-unpacked boxes line one wall—I almost trip over them as we pile inside—and the opposite wall is dominated by a row of computer monitors. Leo opens a drawer and rummages for a moment before extracting a flash drive.

"Here." Leo holds it out to Eric. "You have your proof. Take it and go."

Eric laughs. "You Archers. If you were half as smart as you think you are, you'd be running the world, not burning through inherited wealth like the entitled brats you actually are. Show me the files." Eric's face is twisted, and his words come out in a low snarl.

"It's what you want, just take it." Leo's gaze is hard, insistent.

"How can you seriously think you still have the upper hand here?" Eric asks sharply. "You show me what's on that file right now, or you're going to have to carry your sister out of this room."

Leo looks over to where I'm standing, wedged between a box and the wall, and I can just make out his expression in the blue light cast by the computer screens. Fear, mixed with remorse. I don't understand. I want to tell him it's all right, that his attempt to trick Eric with fake evidence was a good idea. It was certainly better than anything I could come up with in the past few frenzied hours. Leo inserts the drive into the heavy monitor on the desk and clicks a few keys.

As soon as the screen illuminates, I realize what Leo has done. He hasn't pretended to find a drive that has nothing on it. This contains what I've tried to hide for a decade.

Betrayal seethes through me as the video loads.

When Jenna approached me two years ago, right around when the Hostetlers cut Bryce off, I assume, she made a simple offer: a big slice of Equilibrium's profits or this video goes straight to the police. I don't know how Leo got his hands on it. It would have been hard, but not impossible, to search Jenna's house like I had. But why? Why would Leo turn on me like that?

There's only one reason he would. He knew he might need it, sooner or later, to control me. He learned that from the best: his father. Through tears of anger, I glare across the room at him, and he can't meet my eye.

The video is low-quality, clearly shot from an old cell phone, and the feed spins as Jenna adjusts her camera to zoom in on where I stood, entwined with Bryce, making out in a corner of a crowded room. I remember the chill in the air that night, how we'd all ended up at a house party thrown by a friend of Leo's. It was right after Sofia tried to blackmail me into being with her again. Right after Bryce and Jenna had started dating, just weeks after I watched Bill take his last greedy breaths.

Jenna mutters something that sounds like *whore* and aims the camera at Brooke, who is hovering near us, looking extremely uncomfortable. Jenna had suspected Bryce was cheating on her, and she was right. A few people pass by where she's standing, and the video is obscured for a moment, the camera angle sliding to the floor. Jenna must have been walking out of the room. When the camera refocuses, she's hidden behind what looks like the edge of a doorway, and suddenly coming into view are Brooke and me, supporting an unconscious Sofia.

I tried so hard to forget how Leo had shrugged his shoulders when we found her passed out in one of the bedrooms, unresponsive but still breathing. But even now I don't need the hard evidence in front of my eyes to know exactly what he did to her.

The video is changing again, and I brace myself for the truth Eric is about to see after all this time. He's staring at the screen, transfixed, his hands limp at his sides.

I could get behind him. Just a few careful steps are all it would take. As quietly as I can, I start feeling in the box behind me for something, anything. Ideally something heavy.

At first it looks like Jenna is pointing the camera at nothing but lumps of indecipherable shadow. She must be filming from behind a window. But then an outdoor light switches on, illuminating the cars parked haphazardly in front of the house. One of the boxes next to me is open. I dip my hand inside with my eyes trained on the screen.

Brooke and I stagger from the house with Sofia's arms slung between us, her long legs trying and failing to support the rest of her body. The backs of our heads weave between the cars until we find the Porsche Leo borrowed from Avi. We awkwardly pile Sofia, little more than a jumble of limp semiconscious limbs, into the back seat. I slip into the driver's seat.

"I always knew it was you." Eric says this without taking his eyes from the screen, eyes that now glisten with the tears that fall freely down his face. "Deep down, part of me always knew."

I didn't plan on just letting her die, but what happened next made everything easier in a way. I watch Brooke climb into the passenger seat next to me. The last sound is me honking the horn and calling Jenna's name, impatiently waiting for her to get in the car behind Brooke, before we leave without her.

And now Eric knows—I am responsible for his mother's death.

My fingers close around something hard, smooth on part of its surface, rough on others. A small sculpture, maybe. I tighten my grip. There's only one way out of this. As I start to lift it out of the box, I catch sight of Eric's face and hesitate. His eyes are empty of rage now, and it's easier to let the years fall away and remember the little boy who crawled out of the smoking wreckage. Something else stirs in my memory, something that cracked the night air in half as I shook Brooke awake in the passenger seat. Eric's scream: heartbroken and raw. And I know how that feels. I know exactly what it feels like to have your protector ripped away from you, being left to fend for yourself with your world torn apart. The thought relaxes my hand, and packing tissue rustles loudly. Eric's head snaps in my direction.

"Put it down, Caroline," he says, and with his attention locked on me, Eric doesn't see Natalia's figure appear in the doorway behind him. I do my best to keep my face neutral, hoping she'll spring into action. She's our only hope right now.

In a flash, she bashes him over the head with what looks like a crowbar, and he crumples face down to the floor. Blood pools next to Eric's head, and I stare at him, transfixed. Despite everything, I still see my friend when I look at his limp, most likely dead, figure. I've caused him so much pain, and now he's destined to rot in a corner of Leo's woods. The moment hangs in the air and seems to swell like the expanding dark halo of blood around Eric's face.

"Took you long enough," Leo mutters to Natalia.

"Leo—" I start. The sound of his name sounds hollow: everything I thought I knew about my brother is gone, replaced by what I always, deep down, suspected.

"I handled it, Cee," Leo says, and his features relax. "Well, *we* handled it." Natalia walks over to him, obedient as a well-trained terrier. He sighs, takes Natalia's hand, and blinks at me. "I learned that from you, you know." As he reaches for Eric's gun, I have to grip a box behind me to steady myself.

"From me?" I manage. Something heavy constricts my lungs and starts to squeeze.

"Of course," Leo says as if this is obvious. "You always have a way of getting what you want. With Dad, with Sofia. Oh, yeah, I knew about you two," Leo says in the false offhand tone he uses when he's hiding his pain. I stare at him, and as he opens his mouth to say more, Eric lets out a low groan. Leo and Natalia exchange a look of grim understanding. I cut my eyes to Eric, who's still motionless on the floor, and back to Leo. All at once, I see in terrible clarity what I've done and the monster I've become.

"Look, let's get out of here," Leo continues with inhuman calm. "We need to make a plan, and I can't think straight with him like that." Leo jerks his head toward Eric, but his eyes are on Natalia, so he doesn't see the twitch of Eric's fingers. "And you might want to get rid of that weapon as soon as possible, Talia. My knight in shining armor." Natalia kisses Leo, and neither of them see Eric's eyes flicker open, then close again.

"Where?" she asks, looking down at the crowbar in her hand with mild interest. The shine from Eric's blood catches the light coming from the computer screens.

"I'll show you, don't worry," Leo says reassuringly, and he turns his attention to me. "Just lock the door so we can figure out where we can move him and um—" Leo doesn't have to finish that sentence. Carried away with himself, as always, he thinks Eric is dead. He tosses me the keys to the office before steering Natalia away, no doubt intent on destroying as much evidence as possible before moving on with his plan for Eric. The thought sends ice down my spine.

Alone with Eric's collapsed figure in the shadowy space, I wait for Natalia's and Leo's footsteps to grow fainter on the gallery floor outside. I can feel my heartbeat in my teeth as I approach Eric and place the keys next to his hand. I've made my decision.

Leo will never forgive me. That makes two of us.

"Give me ten minutes," I say. My voice comes out in a barely audible rasp. "Then run."

CHAPTER 48

Brooke

Now

Caroline must have turned off her phone, or maybe she's already lost cell service. My headlights finally skim the long winding drive that threads through the Oasis compound. She once mentioned the property was over twenty acres in size. They could be anywhere in these woods.

The gallery ahead is the only source of light in the pitch-black, the only sounds the distant rush of water and the shrilling of cicadas. It's not until I take my hands off the steering wheel and shut off the engine that I realize how hard I'd been gripping it.

Right away, I can tell something is wrong. A raised voice calls into the darkness, and instinctively, I curl low in the driver's seat as the space fills with the sound of breathing that comes heavier and faster as my ears strain for answers. Someone is running with heavy, staggering steps. They sound too heavy to be Caroline or Drea. Was Bryce sprinting away from his latest victim? The footfalls grow louder and louder as I grab in my purse for my keys and my tiny container of pepper spray, my pathetic line of defense against whatever is hurtling my way. But just as I grit my teeth so hard I can almost feel my entire skull tense, I realize the footsteps have passed my car, thudding away down the road.

I don't stop to think. I throw open the car door and sprint toward the gallery—to where I need to find my friend alive.

As I throw open the gallery door, the bright, custom lighting speckles my vision with black dots as I look desperately for Caroline. My eyes refocus, settling on a door cracked ajar ahead of me, and I walk toward it with mounting unease.

"Caroline," I whisper as I reach the doorway. There's no answer, but a blue-tinted light escapes from under the doorframe. I enter and suppress a scream. A stain of what looks sickeningly like blood covers the floor in a glutinous smear. Is this Caroline's blood? Am I too late? Frantically, I pull out my cell phone. No reception. My eye catches on the row of computer screens to my left.

Most of them display a generic desktop background, but as my gaze trains on one, at first I can't believe what I'm seeing. I step closer to the frozen screen and stare at the front seat of the car. *Caroline* is driving, not Sofia, and I'm looking at where Sofia lies in the back seat. Passed out.

My head starts to pound, as if it's rebelling against the surfacing of what I'd kept buried for so long.

"They sent me to find you, Brooke," an accented female voice says from behind me. In the harsh light of the screens, Natalia's face is gaunt, her ballerina's figure almost skeletal. Shadows pool deep in her hollow cheeks and along the sharp rail of her collarbone. I take a step back. She moves gracefully toward me. "It's okay," she says, her voice sibilant and calm. "Leo and Caroline are upstairs. They will explain."

"You . . . you killed Jenna," I say, and my left hand grips the desk behind me. Natalia's headshot surfaces in my imagination: the striking physical similarity to Sofia finally made it click. Leo had to have used her, just as he used Sofia all those years ago. Natalia smiles, but far from reassuring, her expression is more of a threatening leer. "You killed Jenna. And then you stole this." I jerk my head at the screen.

"We will talk about this, including what happened to your—uh—unfortunate friend," Natalia says, baring a row of crooked teeth. She's inches from me. It's now or death. I thrust the Mace in front of me and press down hard on the plastic trigger. Natalia shrieks in pain, her bony hands scrabbling at her face and eyes, her body collapsing on itself. I struggle out of the room, half tripping over the boxes on the floor, and slam the door behind me. A set of two keys lies next to the door, and I twist the lock shut before shoving them into my pocket.

Panic roils hot in my nerves, but it's kept at bay by something that kicked in not a moment too soon. Maybe it's a survival instinct. Maybe it's the knowledge that Caroline has been alone with Jenna's killer for hours. Whatever drives my swift movements, I cross the room to where an alarm keypad is lodged in a far wall behind Leo's display of miniature drawings. There's a red button that surely can only do one thing, and I reach out to press it.

"Brooke, oh my god. Are you okay?" It's Caroline, appearing from around a corner that leads to stairs and the upper floor of the gallery. I retract my finger, which was inches from the red plastic. Caroline's face is drained of color, and as I throw my arms around her, Natalia's muffled cries stiffen both of our spines.

"It was Natalia," I say, breathless and desperate for Caroline to understand. "She killed Jenna to silence her for Leo. He must have talked her into it somehow." My words spill out in a rush and I push Caroline gently away, my hands resting on her shoulders so I can catch my breath.

Natalia and Leo must have been blackmailing us.

"Sofia" is not one person but two. And there's a murderer behind the closet door.

"I think Jenna has been blackmailing Leo for some reason—she must have known what he was doing to Sofia before she died, the drugging and the assault. Did you see that video? She was drugged out of her mind before we put her in the car. It would prove that that Gawker article was right about *everything*. And Leo couldn't let that happen! We have to get out of here," I say, taking a step back from my friend, preparing to make a run for it. Then I remember what I just saw on the screen. All the lies we told about Sofia. The blame we put on her, when it was really Caroline in the driver's seat, and me along for the ride. Caroline's expression is leaden, and she shows no reaction to what I just said.

And then suddenly I feel like such a fool. It finally clicks.

"You knew," I say.

I take rapid steps away from her and stumble against a glass display case, comprehension unraveling too fast for my brain to process. I point at the locked office door as Natalia pounds against it with surprising force.

"Natalia killed Jenna for Leo, but also *for you*. It wasn't just Leo. You *both* were paying Jenna off to keep your secret, to keep Equilibrium going long enough to fund all of this." I gesture wildly around me at all this indulgence, all this evidence of the Archer wealth and narcissism. My eyes find the row of miniature drawings, all with Sofia in them, still on display so that Leo can use her even after her death, and it makes me so sick I think I might vomit all over the spotless floor.

"Did you pretend to be 'Sofia,' too, just to scare me and get away with this?" My voice shakes.

"No, no, you're twisting this all around. I can explain everything." Caroline is speaking to me as if I were a spooked, gun-shy animal. "It was Eric, my assistant. He was pretending to be 'Sofia.' He's the boy from the accident, remember? He is the one who has been stalking us," Caroline says, holding out both hands, palms toward me like she could physically stop the truth from rearing up between us, ready to bite. And hastily she adds, "He was just here but got away."

I think of the figure who ran past me outside. That must have been Eric.

"You lied to me. All those years ago at the hospital, when you told me what happened, who was driving. It was all to protect *yourself*," I say in an understatement that rips a fresh, bitter wound somewhere deep in my soul.

A current of nausea swirls in my stomach, trapping my next words in my mouth. I never exactly fought for the truth. Does that mean I'm just as bad as she is? Just as guilty? I want to scream at Natalia to shut up. The sound of her trying to escape the locked room is like a thrashing heartbeat keeping this nightmare alive.

"I was protecting you," Caroline says earnestly, but then she registers the disgust on my face. She takes a step back from me. "Like you're innocent in all this?" I think of Alex coaching me through the police interview, my mother's talent for making things go away. Is Caroline right about me? She takes another step that echoes in the high-ceilinged room. "And I don't even blame you." Caroline lets out a long sigh. "You have no idea what Sofia was really like. She was *obsessed* with Leo and me. And obsessed with getting rid of you." Her words pull me toward the easy way out. Forgetting what I saw. Forgetting all of this. Walking away and moving on with my life, just like last time.

"She was delusional, too. She actually thought—"

"You used her," I say. "You and Leo both did. And she kept your secrets." My voice sounds small, but it's getting bigger, filling the space between us. Natalia is eerily quiet now, and the silence lets me finally say what I've been thinking. "And what about Leo? Did you know what your brother was doing to Sofia before we found her that night?" My question crackles at the air, electric, as dangerous as what Caroline won't bring herself to admit. She recoils at my words, but the truth comes into clearer focus with every second.

"Did. You. Know?" I say, and I let each word fall like pieces of a crumbling wall. And for the first time in the ten years I'd known her, tears shine in Caroline's pale eyes. She opens her mouth to speak, then closes it again.

Caroline's problems would have gone away if Sofia didn't wake up after Leo drugged her. As I stare at the woman I thought I knew, her tall, statuesque form starts to shake, her flawless skin blotches red, and one tear, then another, streaks down her face. Right there, in the trembling symmetry of her patrician features, is my answer. She may have never admitted it to anyone, not even herself, but deep down, I think she always saw Leo for exactly who he is. She always knew what he did to Sofia, and who knows how many other women. She was willing to do anything, sacrifice any-one, to protect her brother. And protect herself.

"I'm sorry, Brooke. You have no idea. I was a different person then. I am so, so—"

"She knows too much, Caroline. You know she does." The voice comes from behind me. And as I turn slowly on the spot, Leo ap-pears at the other end of the gallery with a gun in his hand.

"Leo, no," Caroline says. "We can talk about this."

"I think you know that's not true, sister dear." Leo ends this sentence in an offhand singsong voice that makes my skin prickle.

"She knows about Natalia. And she knows about what you did that night," he continues, punctuating every word with steps toward me. Caroline flicks her eyes between the two of us and takes tenta-tive steps to close the distance between her and Leo. Then the sound of Leo's finger cocking the revolver cracks through the gallery, and the three of us go so still, we could be newly installed sculptures.

Caroline suddenly lunges for the gun in Leo's hand. It fires. A bullet pierces one of the tall windows and the taut silence breaks in chaos. Glass shatters in a curtain that covers the floor like deadly snow. Instantly, an ear-splitting alarm reverberates through the space and flickering lights cast brother and sister in sharp relief as they struggle for the gun, each desperate to seize control.

I don't stop to think. I tear through the gallery doors and into the humid night air. My feet are unsteady on the path, blindly sprinting over slippery paving stones and damp grass. I grab for my keys, and the car lights flash fifty yards ahead. Thirty. Twenty. My lungs are raw and airless, my heart sure to explode. There's another gunshot, and Caroline's scream stops my blood cold, but I can't stop running.

I close the final stretch and slam the car door shut, lock it, and turn the key hard in the engine. It won't start. I try again, my every nerve on fire, but still nothing comes. This is what Leo must have been doing while Caroline and I were in the gallery: ensuring I have no escape. A dark figure appears at the edge of the woods.

Leo's silhouette is just visible in the distance, far enough away to barely register in the beam of the headlights. He's walking toward where his prey is cornered, terrified and powerless, in total control. Just like he must have been with Sofia. Just like so many men before him: the kind that everyone fears, everyone knows to avoid, but they remain silent. Just like Caroline and I did. His eyes are livid, his mouth contorted, T-shirt stained with blood. Caroline's blood. There's nowhere to run, but Leo isn't running. He doesn't need to.

"I'm sorry," I whisper, thinking of Sofia as the lights from the gallery seem to flash brighter around me. Desperate tears rush into my eyes, which are still fixed on Leo's looming figure. "I'm sorry for not seeing what they did to you. I'm sorry I couldn't stop them."

But then I realize the lights aren't coming from the gallery. They're blue and red, sharpening by the second, and for the first time I can make out the sound of a swiftly approaching siren. Heavy wheels thunder on the road behind me, and as I dare to turn my head a fraction, I'm blinded by the piercing headlights of police cars hurtling toward me. Turning back to face Leo, I watch him freeze, instantly transformed from the hunter to the hunted. He gives me one last savage look before turning and vanishing into the darkness.

CHAPTER 49

Brooke

Four Months Later

"I just can't believe you got out of there alive," Mel says as she slaps *Vanity Fair* back onto one of my mother's antique end tables. *The Fall of the House of Archer* is printed across the cover, which features a family portrait of Caroline, Leo, and half a dozen Archer relatives, all with black boxes covering their eyes. It's also the name of the true crime podcast Jacqueline Moore, author of this epic takedown piece, launched following Leo's and Natalia's arrests.

I have no idea how to respond to Mel. It's the same thought that had been looping through my head in the weeks that fell on the other side of that night. I couldn't escape it. Not at Caroline's funeral. Not as Jenna's father sobbed into my shoulder, thanking me for bringing his daughter's killer to justice. I was too late to save Sofia, too late to save Jenna, and yet here I am. Alive. Lost in thought, I reach for my tea and stare at the steam curling from the rim of the mug.

"They still haven't caught Eric?" Mel asks, leaning back gingerly in her chair and taking a bite of the enormous cupcake we're sharing. I'd been through all of this with her already, but the postpartum fog makes it hard for Mel to remember the details.

"Nope. He became a completely different person once before, so I wouldn't be surprised if he does it again," I say, staring at the space the photo of Jenna, Caroline, and me once occupied on the piano. My mother had replaced it with one of Phoebe, Mel's baby girl, swaddled in a pink blanket. Life over death. She always had impeccable interior decorating taste.

"And . . . ," Mel says in slow-motion disbelief, "you're not worried about that?"

"Now that he knows what really happened to his mom, I think he's moved on," I say. This isn't strictly true. I'd received what I consider to be certain proof Eric isn't a threat to me anymore. It arrived two weeks ago in the form of a cheery humane society volunteer who said she'd been sent to return a lost cat.

"The nicest guy dropped her off this morning," the woman said brightly as she set the carrier down on the doorstep. "And he said to give you this." She'd handed me an envelope containing a note of just seven words: **May they rest in peace. Forgive me.** Since I'm fairly confident Eric is the reason I'm not dead now, he didn't have to ask for my forgiveness. The gallery alarm I triggered couldn't possibly have summoned the police that fast. Eric must have done that. When he got back into cell phone range, he must have called the police. He *chose* to save me. I wonder where Eric is now, and hope that wherever he is, he's finally found his peace, too. Piper leaps onto the chair next to me, purring and leaving what my mother would consider a problematic amount of hair on the upholstery.

Mel nods thoughtfully. "That Natalia, though." She shivers.

"Sounds like someone's been listening to the podcast," I say, arching an eyebrow at my sister. Jacqueline uncovered more of the details of Natalia's motive for killing Jenna. After Natalia sustained a shoulder injury that meant her ballet career was effectively over, and with it her visa, it was easy for Leo to convince her that he was her only hope. If Jenna exposed the truth about Caroline or kept siphoning off Caroline's Equilibrium profits, there wouldn't be any funding to support the Oasis or the life Leo promised Natalia. Without that, she would be back to Russia with no prospects. Leo always had a gift for manipulating women to get what he wanted, and in a way, Natalia paid the price just as Sofia had before her.

"I cannot believe Natalia pretended to *be* Jenna so convincingly, which is why she showed up on all that CCTV footage. I guess they would look alike from behind the wheel of a car, especially from a distance," Mel says, reaching for her tea.

"I guess that's how she and Leo got away with it for so long," I say. This is another thing Jacqueline figured out. Natalia hid in the trunk of Jenna's car the night of Leo's art show, then drugged her once they got back to the Hostetler-Lee house. It was a well-planned murder, and they must have been watching Jenna and Bryce for weeks, months maybe, before the night at the gallery. They knew Bryce and Hayden would be gone, so Natalia simply put on some of Jenna's clothes, including a pair of oversize sunglasses, and, careful to not leave so much as a stray strand of hair behind, drove away in Jenna's car with her victim unconscious in the back seat.

Once at the Hostetler-Lees' house upstate, Natalia administered the fatal dose of the drugs before hiking to a nearby town. That's where she paid cash for a taxi to take her to meet Leo. A few text messages from Jenna's phone to her most recent contacts, including the ones that implicated Josh, cemented Jenna's "movements" the day Natalia murdered her.

Jacqueline's investigation also proved I was right about Natalia's role in the investigation of Jenna's death. Since there was no known connection between Jenna and Natalia, she had never been considered a suspect in her death. And she had a decent enough alibi: the couple's retreat with Leo, where she was seen just enough to make her cover story plausible.

Between the convincing "suicide" Leo and Natalia staged and Josh as a likely suspect, the police had their focus elsewhere. Leo and Natalia sent the detectives Josh's information to keep the heat off them: it was easy enough to do with Natalia in Jenna's house, where she was able to steal the flash drive. The threatening text I got from Eric probably came after he learned of Josh's arrest, and Eric used it as the perfect opportunity to scare me. The podcast had been thorough, sensitive, and very well done. I don't regret trusting Jacqueline with Sofia's story. Or mine.

"And what happened with Drea?" Mel asks, and I resign myself to opening another can of worms.

"Still married to Todd Archer, apparently," I say.

Mel almost spits out a mouthful of tea. "Wait, seriously? I thought she *despised* the Archers."

"I think she likes controlling what's left of the Archer money more than anything," I say. "Once she legally got her hands on that—no doubt Todd is too smitten to bother with a prenup—she could safely expose Caroline. Jacqueline interviewed Drea off the record and told me that she and Eric were definitely working together in the beginning, but I think he scared Drea in the end. When she confronted Caroline and found out Jenna had been murdered, she wanted out. So—" I decide not to mention Eric's note. I sip my tea. "Are you actually going to remember this time?" I ask, shooting a pointed look at Mel.

"Okay, it's just impossible to keep track of everything!" Mel says. "Especially with Phoebe waking us up every few hours."

"You know Mom would be happy to keep her, right? Like, in-definitely?" I say wryly. My mother is at the park with Phoebe, giving us the space we all need right now.

"Natalia must have really thought Leo was her only way out," Mel says, and there's a note of pity in her voice that strikes a chord of sadness in me.

"Well, she wasn't the first person he fooled," I say. I think of Sofia, Natalia, and Caroline, all taken in by him. All with deadly consequences.

I'll never know for sure if it was an accident, the gunshot that killed Caroline. Just like I'll never know if Sofia would have died anyway from the drugs Leo gave her that night.

The thought of it sends a shudder through my bones.

Mel reaches across the table and gives my hand a squeeze. "Leo's going to jail for the rest of his life. They both are," she says. The last thing I want to do right now is think about Leo, and I hastily grasp for a new subject.

"You really didn't have to help me pack," I say. I eye the suitcases stacked by the door, the remnants of what I hadn't managed to sell or donate: the only scraps of my old life I wanted to take with me.

"Oh god, *anything* to get out of the house." Mel says through a yawn. The doorbell sounds from the foyer.

"I'll get it," I say, grateful for the distraction until I open the door and my jaw drops.

"Um, hi—" I stutter, blinking rapidly and hurriedly closing my mouth. The face looking back at me can't be real. For over ten years, she had existed only on the periphery of my life. "What are you doing here?"

"I won't stay long," Rebecca Adams says, and for a moment, she looks as uncomfortable as I feel, but she recovers fast. "I know I must be the last person you want to see right now." She hitches her purse higher on her shoulder. "But I just came to apologize."

It takes all my self-control to not let my jaw fall open again. "*You* want to apologize to *me*?" I repeat like an idiot.

"It's crazy, I know. I really hated you. I was so angry for such a long time." She looks at me with what starts as a glare, but it softens, and there's a brutal honesty in her tone that I can't help but respect. "But you should know—you weren't the only one."

"The only one of—what?" I ask, my brain still reeling from her presence on my mother's doorstep.

"Patrick had several affairs before we finally got divorced. There were more than a few students over the years." Despite her best efforts at an offhand tone, her words sag under the weight of her pain. "So while I hated what you did, you deserve to know the truth about him. And I know now that you were a victim of his, too." She meets my eye, and I can tell it takes all her strength, plus probably a lot of therapy, to do it.

"I'm so, so sorry, Rebecca," I say, and there's something singularly strange about speaking aloud what has ruled my conscience for so long. "I know it's not even close to—"

"Really, you don't have to." Rebecca waves away the end of my sentence. "I sent some of the, uh, evidence of Patrick's behavior to the university where he works now. Hopefully there will be consequences, but—" She shrugs.

"I'll corroborate that. It can't hurt to have multiple sources, right?" I say.

Rebecca nods, then takes a deep breath before continuing: "I also came here to let you know that I shared Patrick's history with Woodlands to set the record straight, and if the leadership change goes as planned, you should be fully reinstated next semester."

My mother hadn't lied: she knew exactly where to find a mountain of dirt on Woodlands. After a few well-placed phone calls, it came to light that Dr. Lutz had accepted bribes from parents in exchange for his connections at Ivy League admissions offices. After he was fired, Akira stepped in as temporary head of school. She was happy to write me a reference, one that landed me the new job that starts next week. I think she'll understand I can't return to Woodlands, even with the option on the table.

"You really didn't have to do that," I say feebly before clearing my throat. "I mean, I don't deserve that, not from you."

"I know," Rebecca says simply. "I didn't do it for you." Her expression darkens, and I wonder if she's thinking of Ezra, her closure, her ex, or all three. "Here's this, by the way." Rebecca reaches into her purse, extracts a slender folder, and hands it to me. "Someone sent this to me anonymously a few months ago."

I know what it is without opening the folder: it's everything

Eric had managed to find—I still don't know how—and send to Rebecca. He assumed he could keep his own hands clean and that she would leap at the chance to destroy my career. But on this point, Eric was wrong about Rebecca.

"Thanks," I say, wondering if my mother has a paper shredder. Rebecca gives me a curt nod before turning and striding back to her car.

"Who was that?" Mel calls as I close the door behind me.

"Mormons," I say, my head still spinning. But as I watch Rebecca's car drive away, I feel something settle inside me. Something that hasn't been still for a very, very long time. I'll tell Mel everything when I'm ready, and as I cross back into the living room and look at her smiling face, I think that might be soon.

"I should hit the road if I want to beat traffic," I say, scooping up Piper and placing her gently in her carrier.

"Right," Mel says with a sigh and gets to her feet. "Have I mentioned that I strongly protest Colorado on the grounds of excessive distance?"

"Well, there aren't a lot of options for teaching jobs in the middle of the school year. I was lucky to get this long-term sub gig," I say.

"I get why you're leaving. You know that, right?" Mel's eyes are suddenly wreathed with tears. "Just know I'm always here for you for whatever—" I cut off the end of Mel's sentence by pulling her in for a hug, one that lasts long enough to finish it for both of us.

After another minute of goodbyes, I take one more look at my mother's house before loading the last suitcase into the trunk of my car. I think of Josh, Sofia, and Caroline, of all the lies I believed, but mostly of the ones I told myself.

And as I pull out onto the road, I let the rearview mirror swallow them all.

ACKNOWLEDGMENTS

If you open West Elementary School's 2001 yearbook and flip to fourth grade, you'll find a (let's be kind and say *endearing*) photo of me rocking wire-rimmed glasses and a head-to-toe ensemble from an L.L.Bean catalog. You'll also find the word *author* printed under professional aspirations.

So, when I say this is a lifetime dream come true, I have receipts.

First and foremost, thank you, reader, for picking up my first book: I hope you know that means the world to me. I am deeply grateful to you and to the many people who took a messy Google document and crafted it into the novel in your hands right now.

Tess Callero, rock star literary agent *and* Bravo expert (what a combination), had a vision for this book that blew me away from our first meeting. Her expertise transformed *Our Secrets Were Safe* and found it the perfect home. I could not imagine a better champion for my work or a more delightful dining companion to giggle with over truffle pasta in Paris.

Lori Kusatzky, the editor with Shoshanna energy I always dreamed of, has inspired, guided, and pushed me (but in a good way, not like in a Tina Fey's character from *Mean Girls* way) since we started working together. This novel is a sharper, better told story thanks to Lori, and I've learned so much from her. I am very lucky to have her as a creative collaborator.

Thank you to the fantastic teams at Crown and Penguin Random House who invested their time and talent into launching *Our Secrets Were Safe*. I just about fell out of my chair when I read that first email from *the* Amy Einhorn. I am so grateful she believed in this book and welcomed me warmly into the publishing world. Thank you to everyone who had a hand in production, editing, and design, especially Liana Faughnan, Andrea Lau, Nancy Inglis, and Dustin Amick.

Thank you, Andrea Bartz, Amy Tintera, and Avery Bishop, for lending your voices to help spread the word about this debut novel. You have a lifelong fan in me. Readers, you should really check out their stuff.

As it became increasingly clear that my desire to write was more than just a hobby, I was fortunately surrounded by encouraging family and friends. Thank you, Ben, Molli, Andrew, Marielle, Ali, Emily, Annie, and Kicki, for listening to me jabber on about fictional characters and agonize over the process of getting published. It's scary to be creatively vulnerable, to say *I think I can actually do this* out loud, but that was a lot easier thanks to their enthusiasm, patience, and love.

I honestly don't know where I would be in the writing process (or life in general?) without my sister and first draft reader, Emily. This project spanned some of the most difficult times of my life as well as the most joyful, and she was there every step of the way.

And most of all, I want to thank my wonderful husband, Scott.

He shows me every day what it means to pursue your passions with everything you have. Because of his unconditional love, brilliant mind, and puns that are only slightly inferior to mine, we have a life that I never would have imagined possible. Scott, I love you and our family more than words—thank you for being you.

ABOUT THE AUTHOR

VIRGINIA TRENCH studied English at Vanderbilt University before earning an MA in secondary education at the University of Colorado Boulder. When she's not writing, she can be found exploring the Rocky Mountains, struggling on a yoga mat while her cat judges her, or devouring the latest crime novels. She lives in Colorado with her family.